ONE OF THE FAMILY

BOOKS BY JESS RYDER

Lie to Me

The Good Sister

The Ex-Wife

The Dream House

The Girl You Gave Away

The Night Away

The Second Marriage

My Husband's Lover

ONE OF THE FAMILY

JESS RYDER

bookouture

Published by Bookouture in 2025

An imprint of Storyfire Ltd.
Carmelite House
50 Victoria Embankment
London EC4Y 0DZ

www.bookouture.com

The authorised representative in the EEA is Hachette Ireland
8 Castlecourt Centre
Dublin 15 D15 XTP3
Ireland
(email: info@hbgi.ie)

ISBN: 978-1-83790-848-6
eBook ISBN: 978-1-83790-847-9

In memory of my lovely dad

PROLOGUE

Her world was monochrome. The ceiling was black, with dark grey streaks running down the walls. There were white patches where lumps of plaster had fallen off. Everything was covered in a thick layer of soot, and the acrid air was dry to choking. The window had blown out and then been boarded over. A sliver of natural light shone through a gap in the bottom edge of the frame; it was the only way she knew whether it was night or day. The door was locked from the outside. As there was no means of escape, there'd been no need to restrain her. She could bang her fists and scream, but the house was very remote. Nobody would hear her cries for help.

There was no electricity, and the radiator was stone cold. If it wasn't for the luxuriously thick duvet and the blankets she'd found at the top of the wardrobe, she would have already frozen to death. Now it seemed she was going to starve instead. She'd lost all sense of time, but she was sure she hadn't eaten for several days. The room had an en suite bathroom, and the water was still connected, but she wouldn't survive much longer without food. She was sure she must have lost a lot of weight already; her face looked gaunt in the mirror, and she could feel her ribs sticking out. There was a nasty gash on the side of her head from the fall. It wasn't healing properly.

She lay down on the grimy bed, pulling the duvet and blankets over her. Sleeping seemed a good way to conserve energy. She peered into the darkness. Was this how it was going to end? She was only twenty-two years old; she'd been nowhere, done nothing. Would her body be found eventually, or would her family spend the next few decades wondering where she was and what she was doing – hoping against hope that one day she'd get in touch?

If she died here, it would be her own fault. Nobody would come looking for her – she'd told them to leave her alone. They believed she was happily living her new life. They thought she was safe.

PART ONE

ONE

'You *are* coming to my grad ceremony, aren't you?' My daughter Liv was shouting down the phone. She was hundreds of miles away and sounded as if she was speaking from a noisy bar.

'Of course,' I replied eagerly. 'We wouldn't miss it for the world.'

The academic year had ended weeks earlier, but Liv had stayed on, desperately clinging to university life by the tips of her fingernails. After the graduation ceremony there would be no reason to remain. Her friends would disperse, retreating to the comfort of their parental homes while they decided what to do next. The lucky ones would start new careers. I didn't know what Liv was going to do. I'd raised the tricky subject of the future a few times in recent months and had always received a frosty response.

'Is there any chance of getting an extra ticket for Meg?' I asked. 'We'll have to stay overnight, and I don't want to leave her on her own.'

'No probs. It's only two tickets per person, but I can use Jensen's allocation.'

'Are you sure that's okay? There must be somebody he'd like to invite. Grandparents? An aunt or uncle, perhaps?'

'No, there's nobody,' Liv said.

'Really? How awful...'

I knew what it was like when everyone else's parents turned up to support them and yours weren't there. I paused, trying to suppress the memory of my own graduation. My parents had been killed in a car crash only a few months earlier. Everyone in the family had been so consumed with grief that it hadn't occurred to them to attend in their place. I disappeared immediately after the ceremony and didn't have a single photo taken in my cap and gown.

'Don't worry about it, Mum, it's fine,' said Liv, sensing my discomfort. 'I already asked Jensen. He's more than happy for Meg to have the ticket. He loves you guys, you know that.'

'We love him too. He's your best boyfriend yet. I know you've been together for less than a year, but I've a feeling he's The One.'

'Stop it, Mum!'

'Please thank him for us. We'll take you both out to lunch afterwards to celebrate. I can't wait to see you,' I added. 'It's been months.'

Liv had chosen to go to Rutherford University, near Newcastle. It was a long way from where we lived in London, but we were in touch almost every day. Or rather, I was in touch with her. I'd text her from the bus on my way to work, and share silly videos with her in the evenings while I was watching TV. If she wanted to communicate, she usually sent me a voice note. I would have preferred a two-way conversation, but I was grateful to hear her voice and know that she was okay. I'd missed her so much these past three years. Her younger sister, Meg, would be making her university applications in the autumn, and I hoped she'd pick somewhere nearer so that she could live at home. Meg struggled with friendships, and I was worried that she wouldn't cope living in student accommodation.

I couldn't imagine what it would be like to have an empty nest. No queues for the bathroom. No dirty towels left on the bedroom floor. No need to buy vegan cheese and plant-based 'meat'. No restless nights waiting for the girls to come home. Just me and Dom staring at each other across the dining table every evening, wondering what to talk about. I wasn't looking forward to that moment, and that was the sad truth.

We drove up to Newcastle the day before the graduation ceremony, stopping at Leeds on the way to stay with Dom's brother and sister-in-law, who conveniently lived on the outskirts. We had a fun evening, sharing a takeaway and catching up with family news, while the cousins retreated upstairs to play video games.

'Do I have to come?' Meg asked early the following morning, looking up from a mattress on the floor. 'I'm so tired. Can't I just stay here and you collect me on the way back?'

'No,' said Dom. 'Your sister's expecting you.'

'Imagine how upset she'll be if you don't turn up,' I added.

Meg groaned. 'Stop guilt-tripping me, Mum! You know how anxious I feel about going to new places.'

'There's nothing to feel anxious about,' said Dom. 'It's Liv's event, not yours. All you have to do is sit there and clap when she goes up to get her scroll.' He went over to the bedroom window and snapped open the blinds. Light flooded in and Meg buried her face in the pillow as if she'd just been blinded.

'And we're going to support Jensen, too,' I said. 'Poor boy. He hasn't got anyone else.'

Meg seemed unmoved by my entreaties. It was Dom's brother who eventually persuaded her to get out of bed, put on the new dress I'd bought her specially and eat half a bowl of muesli.

The three of us set off much later than planned. I was feeling cross about the delay. It would take us two hours to reach the venue, and we were supposed to be in our seats by eleven at the latest. I'd wanted to see Liv and Jensen before-hand to wish them luck. As Dom drove, I texted apologies, blaming heavy traffic rather than Meg. I didn't want Liv to know that her sister hadn't wanted to come.

Dom put his foot down on the motorway and for once I didn't complain. By some miracle, we found a parking spot and arrived at the Rutherford campus with eight minutes to spare. The ceremony was being held in the theatre. We were in the circle, towards the back.

'Where are they? I can't see them,' I said, scanning the rows of seated students wearing identical caps and gowns.

'Isn't that Liv?' Dom pointed to a girl with red hair tied in a ponytail.

'Oh yes. Why isn't Jensen sitting next to her? They did the same course.'

'They have to sit in alphabetical order. Stop fretting, Rachel.'

It was a warm day and either the building didn't have air con or it wasn't working. Dom tugged irritably at the collar of his shirt while Meg resolutely studied her phone. I sat upright, determined to stay alert through the speeches and the endless parade of young strangers, hoping I would have enough applause left in me for when my daughter and her boyfriend stepped onto the stage.

When Liv shook hands with the vice chancellor, I was filled with immense pride. It was as if I'd earned the degree myself. I clapped extra hard for Jensen too, trying to make up for his parents' absence.

Apart from those two brief moments, the ceremony was

quite a tedious event, followed by a lot of standing around outside in the gruelling heat as we watched Liv and Jensen having their photos taken – posing seriously with their scrolls, or pulling silly faces in group shots, or throwing their caps into the air on cue.

Meg leant against the outside of the building, looking miserable. I felt sorry for her. For all her protests earlier that morning, she adored her big sister, who hadn't given her more than a hello hug.

'This is Liv's last chance to be with her friends,' I said. 'We'll have her all to ourselves soon.'

'I guess...'

'And then you'll be the one off to uni.'

'Maybe,' she murmured. 'I don't even know if I want to go.'

'Of course you want to go. You'll love it.'

'You don't know that, Mum. I might hate it.'

I decided to park the subject for now. 'Go and tell Liv it's time to leave, darling,' I said.

'No way. I'm not your little messenger. Do it yourself.'

'Please... She'll take it from you.'

'She won't.'

I approached Jensen instead. 'Er, I don't want to rush you, but I booked the table for two and I don't want to lose our slot.'

'No worries, Rachel,' he said. 'I'll scoop her up. Everyone's starting to drift off anyway.'

Jensen didn't seem to have any trouble persuading Liv to say goodbye to her friends. We found the restaurant easily, arriving only a few minutes late. We had a round table, so nobody had to sit at the end and feel lonely. Jensen sat on one side of Liv, and I made sure Meg sat on the other. We ordered our food and a bottle of champagne.

'Congratulations!' declared Dom, raising a toast. We all clinked glasses. 'Here's to a successful future for both of you!'

'Thank you.' Liv squeezed Jensen's hand. 'We're looking forward to it.'

'Even though we haven't figured out exactly what we want to do,' said Jensen, kissing her on the cheek. 'As long as we're together, eh, Liv?'

'Absolutely,' she replied. 'That's all that counts.'

I saw Meg's face fall. 'Oh,' she said, turning to her sister. 'I kind of assumed you'd be coming home.'

'Well, I am,' Liv replied. 'In a way. I mean, we're moving down to London. There's no work up here, not the kind of thing we're looking for anyway.'

I wanted to ask what that kind of thing was, but Jensen got in first. 'Yes, we really want to live in the big city,' he said, 'For the work opportunities and the general scene, and to be close to you guys, of course. But rents are insanely expensive. You need a whacking great deposit. Some landlords ask for six months up front. We don't have that kind of cash.'

'But you must have inherited a fortune,' interrupted Meg.

Dom and I froze in horror, but Liv jumped in. 'Meg! You can't say that!'

'It's okay,' said Jensen. 'It's an understandable mistake. I thought my parents were wealthy, too – they certainly behaved as if they were. We lived in a huge house, went on luxury holidays. They sent me to a very expensive boarding school. But when they died, I discovered they were up to their eyes in debt. I had to sell everything to pay their creditors. There was literally nothing left.'

'Nice one, Meg,' said Liv under her breath.

Meg coloured up. 'You told me they were minted! How was I to know?'

'It must have been so difficult for you,' I chipped in hurriedly. 'To have to deal with that at the same time as grieving.'

Jensen nodded. 'It was all a terrible shock. They were rough times. I thought I'd never be happy again, but then...' he reached out and put his arm around Liv's shoulder, 'look who I found. Money doesn't matter as long as we're together. We'll find a way, won't we, Livvy?'

She smiled glowingly as he leant in for a kiss. 'Of course we will. Somehow.'

My heart swelled with love for the two of them. I wanted so much to help. 'Surely the solution's staring us in the face,' I said. 'You can both move in with us.'

'Really? You wouldn't mind?' Jensen's eyes lit up.

'No. We'd love it!'

Liv looked uncomfortable. 'I don't know,' she said. 'We've got a lot of stuff...'

'I think it's an amazing idea,' added Jensen quickly.

I worked the whole thing out in a few seconds. They could have the entire top floor of the house. Liv already had her bedroom in the loft conversion and Dom could move his desk out of the little room next door, which they could use as a sitting room. There was an en suite shower room up there too. It would be like a small flat but without a kitchen – a flatlet, in fact. I'd cook for them every evening, or we could take it in turns, or they could see to themselves. We wouldn't charge them rent or anything, and once they'd found jobs, they could save up for a place of their own. It was a win-win situation. Meg would have her big sister, which she really wanted and needed, and I'd have both my girls under one roof again. Jensen's presence would be a bonus.

Excited by my plan, I detailed the new living arrangements to the others. When I mentioned Dom losing his home office, he kicked me under the table, but I ignored him.

'It's an amazing offer, Rachel,' Jensen said. 'We can't thank you enough.'

Liv smiled tightly. 'Yeah, but we need to talk it over first before deciding. Just the two of us.'

'We *all* need to talk it over,' Dom said pointedly, looking at me.

'Of course,' I said, as our food arrived. 'But I'm sure you'll all agree it's the best idea I've had for years.'

TWO

After lunch, we said goodbye to Liv and Jensen and set off on the long journey home. Meg sat in the back, twisting her body around so that she could put her feet on the seat. She plugged herself into her phone and turned her music up. The only sound we would hear from her for the next five hours would be the bass beat leaking from her headphones. She seemed to find any kind of conversation with us extremely painful, as if it literally hurt her ears. It made me sad to think how much she'd changed from the light-hearted, vivacious teenager she'd been before she joined the sixth form and everything went wrong.

I chatted away about the graduation ceremony, how proud I was of Liv and how lovely it would be to have all of us under the same roof again. Dom didn't respond, just kept his eyes fixed firmly on the road ahead. To be fair, the motorway traffic was hectic, with drivers constantly switching lanes, but we'd been married long enough for me to know that he was sulking. The reason was obvious. I'd invited Liv and Jensen to stay without consulting him first.

I sat in the passenger seat, cross with him for trying to make me feel bad about doing a good thing. As far as I was concerned, there'd been no *need* to consult him. Liv didn't need an invitation to live in her own home. Jensen was her boyfriend – her partner. They'd been living together as students, so it was natural for them to want to carry on in that way. And it wasn't as if Dom didn't like Jensen. The few times they'd met, they'd got on well. So what was the big problem? Was Dom annoyed because I hadn't asked his permission as 'master of the house', or was he just pissed off about losing his home office?

'It makes sense for them to have the whole of the top floor,' I said, voicing the dialogue I was already having with him in my head. 'Young couples need privacy.'

Dom's eyes flicked towards me, then returned to the large truck in front of us, which had suddenly slowed down. He didn't reply.

'And you were working in the dining room before we had the loft done, so all we have to do is move the desk back and—'

He touched the brakes, tutting loudly. I wasn't sure whether it was directed at me or the truck.

'You've been going into work far more often lately anyway,' I carried on, willing him to be reasonable. 'I can't see what the big deal is.'

'I don't want to talk about it now,' he muttered, tilting his head back to indicate that we shouldn't argue in front of Meg. We'd had quite a few rows over the past months, which had upset her. She felt that her world was unstable enough without her parents falling out.

'Fine, we'll discuss it later,' I said, accepting defeat.

I stared glumly at the dull motorway scenery as we sped along, wishing Dom and I didn't rub each other up the wrong way so much. He worked long hours, and as business development director for an international design and engineering company, his job involved a lot of entertaining. When he came home, he just wanted to watch TV or go to sleep. We hardly ever went out or did anything together as a couple. Was it just a phase, or was something more serious going on? Obviously we couldn't talk about *that* either. We spent the rest of the journey in silence, only communicating about toilet stops, refreshments and when to swap over the driving.

We made it back to London just before 10 p.m. Meg, who had fallen asleep, grumpily roused herself and walked up the front path without bothering to put on her shoes. Dom took our overnight bags out of the boot, and I unlocked the door. We were home. But that night, stepping into the hallway didn't fill me with the warm feeling of safety and relaxation I normally had after a holiday, or even just a night away. I felt tense. Something was wrong.

I made Meg a hot chocolate as requested, and she disappeared to her bedroom. Dom switched on the television and pretended to watch a film. I stood in the doorway to the sitting room, arms folded.

'What's the problem?' I asked finally. 'Why are you in such a huff?'

He sighed heavily, irritated that he should have to explain himself. 'I don't want Jensen to come and live here.'

'Why ever not?'

'We hardly know him.'

'He's Liv's boyfriend. They've been together for ages.'

'Yes, but we don't actually know anything about him.'

'That's not true. We know lots of stuff. He's twenty-four, an only child. He had a privileged upbringing, started his degree at Exeter then transferred to Rutherford for his final year—'

'Why did he leave Exeter?'

'Not sure. It was after his parents died, so maybe he needed to take some time out.' I sensed a need in myself to defend him. 'I don't think anything bad happened.'

'No disrespect, but Exeter's a way better university than Rutherford, and it's at the other end of the country. Why didn't he go back to his course and be with his friends?'

'Does it matter? Liv loves him, that's good enough for me.'

'But we don't know him,' he repeated.

'If he's living with us, we'll *get* to know him, won't we?' Dom didn't answer. Resistance was emanating from every pore. It was time to deliver my killer blow. 'If we say no to Jensen, then Liv won't come. Meg will be devastated. She really wants her sister back. So do I. I've missed her so much...' He looked unmoved. 'Please, Dom. Don't spoil this for me,' I added, my voice taking on a pleading tone I hated but couldn't help.

'Okay,' he agreed at last. 'If you think you know what you're doing. But don't come crying to me if it all goes wrong.'

It seemed like an odd thing to say, but I didn't query it. He'd agreed, that was the main thing. He turned his gaze back to the TV screen and I left the room, more troubled than triumphant.

The following morning, Dom rose early. I pretended to be asleep, not wanting to start the day with another row. As soon as he left for the office, I got up. I'd taken an extra day off from the boutique where I worked as a sales assistant, and I wanted to make the most of it.

It was the end of July, and school had broken up for the summer. It was a relief not to have to nag Meg to get out of bed. She showed no sign of making an appearance, so I let her be. Over breakfast, I texted Liv to ask how the rest of the celebrations had gone last night, but she didn't reply. Still asleep, or hung-over, I guessed.

I could have spent the day sunbathing in the garden, or trailing round the shops, but what I really wanted to do was prepare the top floor of the house for Liv and Jensen's arrival. Liv hadn't definitely confirmed that they'd be coming, but I couldn't imagine they would get a better offer.

I gathered together some cleaning materials and went upstairs to make a start. Liv's bedroom was still full of her stuff. It had hardly changed since she'd left for uni, three years ago. Teenage posters were stuck to the baby-pink walls; soft toys she'd had since childhood were lined up on the windowsill. Presumably all this would go when Jensen joined her. I considered stripping everything out and repainting the room a sophisticated adult colour – French grey or duck-egg blue. A new cover on the bed, some matching scatter cushions, new bedside lamps... It would be like one of those room transformations you see on television. I imagined Liv walking in and gasping with delight, throwing her arms around my neck and thanking me for all my efforts.

Then I thought about how Dom would react, and the image instantly vanished. It was probably better for Liv and Jensen to make the room their own, anyway. I abandoned the idea and stuck to cleaning, pulling out the bed and dressing table, hoovering in the corners.

Dom's home office – his old office now – needed completely reorganising. I studied the space, mentally shifting the desk downstairs and bringing up the small sofa bed that was currently in the garden shed, hidden beneath boxes of junk. It wasn't very comfortable to sleep on, but it would be fine for Liv and Jensen to cuddle up on during winter evenings.

Another slight issue was the en suite shower room. With Liv away during term time, Meg had got used to having it to herself. She kept her various lotions and potions there and could shut herself away for hours without being nagged to come out. But as it could only be accessed from the bedroom, Jensen and Liv would need exclusive use of it. It would be hard on Meg, but I hoped she'd feel it was a worthwhile sacrifice for having her sister back home. Whether Dom would enjoy her sharing the family bathroom with us was another matter.

I sat on the bed, suddenly feeling weary. Maybe this wasn't such a good idea. I hadn't thought the logistics through. Having Liv back would be easy. We were used to there being four of us – lots of things came in fours or pairs and the combination of two adults and two children worked well. Now we'd be four adults and one child, I supposed, although at seventeen, Meg was almost a grown-up herself. We'd be five adults, then, living together. Except the balance of power wouldn't be equal. We wouldn't be house sharers, or flatmates. Dom and I would definitely be in charge. And what would Jensen's status be? He wasn't our son. We wouldn't be able to tell him off if he did something we didn't like. Not that it would ever be necessary to tell him off... I was overthinking it.

My mobile rang. It was my kid sister, Karina.

'How did it go?' she asked. My mind went blank. 'The graduation ceremony?'

'Oh, *that*. Fine, thanks.'

'Did you fall asleep?'

'Not at all!'

'So... what's the news? Has Liv found a job yet?'

I explained that she and Jensen wanted to move down to London to look for work and that I'd invited them to come and live with us.

'Wow,' she said, after a beat. 'That's brave.'

'It's what families do,' I retorted. 'I'm trying to help them out. Give them a head start.'

'What does Meg think about it?'

'She's really pleased, I think. She's been hoping Liv would come home.'

'Yes, but she won't want to share her with Jensen. You know how possessive she is. Remember what happened last term when that new girl, Alice, arrived and latched onto Meg's bestie? All hell broke loose.'

'Of course I remember, but it wasn't all Meg's fault. Skyla was as much to blame. She dumped Meg, even though they'd been friends since primary school. It was understandable that Meg got upset.'

Karina laughed grimly. 'She wasn't just upset, Rachel, she went ballistic. All that nasty stuff on social media...'

'Skyla started the online stuff,' I protested. 'I know Meg shouldn't have got involved, but...' I sighed. 'She paid a high price. She was excluded from the friendship group, and her end-of-year grades were terrible.'

'That's what I mean. She's lost all her friends and that's left her very vulnerable.' Karina paused for emphasis. 'She told me weeks ago that she was dreading the summer holidays.'

'Oh dear...' My sister and my younger daughter had always been close. Meg confided in Karina in a way she never would in me. It was great that she had a female role model, but sometimes it made me feel a tiny bit jealous. 'I don't want to upset Meg,' I continued. 'But I can't let her hold us to ransom. This is Liv's home too. She and Jensen are in a serious relationship. They come as a pair.'

'Yes, but having the three of them together? Under one roof? Doesn't sound like a great idea to me.'

'It'll be fine,' I said testily as another call came through. 'Sorry. Got to go. Liv's on the other line.'

'Just think about it before—' Karina added, but I cut her off.

'Liv! Darling! How's things?'

'Good,' she said. 'Can't talk, Jensen's waiting for me. We're going for a picnic with friends. I just wanted to say we've had a chat about moving in. I wasn't sure at first, to be honest—'

'Oh. Why not?'

'Well, you know, I've been away from home for three years, it might be a bit weird... but Jensen has persuaded me it's too good an offer to miss. And he's right, it makes complete sense. We want to go for it.'

'That's fantastic news!'

'It'll only be for a few weeks, a couple of months at the very most,' she carried on. 'Just until we've found jobs and have saved up enough for a rental deposit.'

'You can stay as long as you like, but... yes, I understand. You'd rather have a place of your own.'

'Jensen says thanks, by the way. He thinks you and Dad are amazing. Particularly you,' she laughed. 'We know it was your idea. Are you sure Dad doesn't mind?'

'He's delighted,' I lied, not wanting to put her off. 'We'll all have to make a few adjustments, but it'll be fun.'

'Yeah. I'll have to get rid of some of my things. We've got heaps of stuff, particularly Jensen. We're going to hire a van.'

'When do you think you'll arrive?'

'Next Thursday. Is that okay?'

'Of course.'

'Perfect. Love you, Mum.'

'Love you too,' I replied. 'Can't wait.'

THREE

'There. It's sorted,' Liv said, putting her phone down. 'No going back now.'

'Great!'

Jensen opened the oven door and removed the quiche he'd spent most of the morning making. The pastry case looked over-cooked; the top was crispy brown. He swore under his breath as the hot dish bounced onto the cooling rack.

Liv and Jensen were meeting friends for a farewell picnic in the park. Usually they ran around the supermarket at the last minute, throwing ready-made party food into the trolley, but this time Jensen had insisted they make more of an effort. And he was right, she thought. The gathering today was important; it marked the end of an era. It would never happen again, not in this place, not with these particular people. The occasion merited a home-made quiche at the very least. Not to mention copious quantities of beer and wine.

'I hope we're doing the right thing,' Liv muttered.

He stared at the burnt offering before him. 'You think I should chuck it?'

'No, I meant moving in with my parents.'

'Oh! Of course we're doing the right thing. It's a no-brainer.'

A no-brainer. Was it really *that* straightforward? She'd agreed to it, but she still wasn't convinced. They had debated her mother's offer almost constantly for the last twenty-four hours, listing the pros and cons, assessing it from every possible angle. Jensen had won. Or rather, he'd worn her down with his reasoning.

'Free accommodation, no bills, no council tax, walking distance to a Tube, home-cooked meals, free Wi-Fi and Netflix. What's not to like?'

Liv had sighed. 'Plenty. You don't know my mother.'

'I've only met her a few times, but she's always seemed lovely. Warm, caring, funny...'

'Yes, she's all those things, but she's also a pain in the arse.'

Liv left Jensen to clear up the kitchen and went up to their room to get ready, her mother's thrilled tones on the other end of the phone line echoing in her head. She knew she'd made her very happy, yet it hadn't given her a warm feeling. Quite the opposite, in fact. The prospect of moving back home, even on a temporary basis, worried her sick.

For the last three years she'd lived independently – first with a bunch of strangers in a hall of residence, then in a student flat with two other girls, and for the final year sharing this double bedroom with Jensen. They lived in a large Victorian house with six friends. It was dilapidated in parts, there was mould in the bathroom and the central heating was dodgy, but it was home. During those years she'd formed her own domestic habits, her own routines, her own ideas of the right way to do things. No, that was wrong. She'd discovered that there was no right way, just different ways that were equally valid. Sharing with so many people had taught her to be more tolerant, more open, more easy-going.

Now she was returning to the old structures, the old rules, the old hierarchy. Dad would be okay; he was hardly ever there and would have virtually no impact on their domestic life. Mum was in charge, more by default than design. Liv had a feeling that her parents' marriage, if not rotten, was past its sell-by date. They never went out on date nights and only seemed to communicate about practicalities – whether Dad would be home for supper, who was going to take the car for its service, whose turn it was to put the bins out. Liv had never seen them kiss or hold hands in the street, had never overheard them having sex. She wondered whether they still did it at all, but dismissed the thought immediately as too gross. All she knew was that their relationship was nothing like hers with Jensen, which was passionate and intense. Too intense, sometimes.

How would they manage, all living under the same roof? Her mother talked a good game about giving her and Jensen their own space, but Liv suspected she would struggle to turn it into action. Her motives were benign: she believed that she did everything out of love, that all she ever wanted was to help others, but put simply, she couldn't stop herself interfering in her daughters' lives.

Liv had grown up with it, so for the first eighteen years of her life it had felt normal. She only realised how bad it was when she went to uni. At first her mother called her every day, 'just to say hello', or 'just to see how you are'. If Liv mentioned that she had a cold or period pains or a stomach upset, she would be bombarded with remedies and requests for updates. If she admitted that she was going into town on a Saturday night, she had to send a text to say that she'd got home safely, or her mother would lie awake all night imagining she'd been murdered.

Rachel also liked to engage in daily text exchanges about shows she'd seen on TV, or gossip at work, or issues she was having with Meg. Unfortunately, Meg was getting a double dose of her full-on love, and unlike her big sister, was actively resisting. Liv tried not to get involved. She kept her responses to a minimum, but her mother never took the hint that she was busy or bored or had better things to do with her time.

Unable to persuade her mother to back off, and not wanting to hurt her, Liv had developed coping mechanisms. These days she avoided opening her WhatsApp feed and instantly rejected calls. She sent voice notes to avoid lengthy chats, composed texts at 11 p.m. to say that she'd arrived home safely when in fact she was still in some bar getting wrecked. Or she lied further and said that she was staying in for the whole weekend. It had occurred to her that if she ever *did* get into serious trouble, any police investigation would be severely hampered by her deceits – although she preferred to think of them as 'workarounds', essential for maintaining her sanity.

'You shouldn't be so mean to her,' Jensen would say. 'She misses you, that's all. You're her best friend.'

'Maybe, but she's not mine,' Liv would reply. 'It's bad enough her being my mum.'

'At least you've *got* a mum,' was always the response. Then Liv would feel bad, not for complaining about Rachel per se, but for doing it in front of Jensen. He rarely spoke about his parents, but when he did, it was with great affection. Whether they had always been perfect or had only achieved it in death, Liv didn't know and had no intention of enquiring. Jensen was still raw – you couldn't challenge him about his mum and dad, and you certainly couldn't make jokes anywhere near the subject.

It was a beautiful day for a picnic. She and Jensen put the contents of their fridge into two large bags-for-life and set off to the park to join their friends. They had gathered here countless times over the last three summers – for birthdays, end-of-term celebrations, summer solstice, heatwave hangouts. It was sad to think that she might never come here again. However, a few of their friends were staying on in Newcastle, so maybe they would come back and visit the old haunts – this lovely park,

Kelsey's Bar in the city centre, the café near the Student Union, the chicken shop on the corner of their street.

They laid blankets on the ground in the shade of a large tree and unpacked the feast. Everyone was very impressed that Jensen had made a quiche, although they also teased him for burning it. The alcohol, or maybe just the occasion itself, made Liv feel melancholy. She sat at the edge of the blanket territory, her mouth dry, her head buzzing as if she had an insect in her ear. Everyone else was mingling easily, passing around the food, talking with their mouths full. Bursts of laughter punctured the air. Liv, normally so vivacious, didn't know how to join in.

Verity came over. They'd been friends since Freshers' Week in the first year, living in the same corridor in the halls of residence. She was moving straight on to teacher training and was one of the few staying in Newcastle.

'Here,' she said, refilling Liv's plastic cup with wine. 'Get this down you... Jensen tells me you're moving in with your parents.'

'Yup.'

'Brave.'

'Or stupid.'

'Probably both. I mean, living with the rellies, that's serious. You'll be getting married next.'

'I don't think so. We've been together less than a year.'

'Yeah, but you're made for each other,' Verity replied. 'He's the best boyfriend you've had by miles. And let's be honest, there have been quite a few! I gave up counting.'

'Shh!' giggled Liv. 'We don't talk about that. Jensen doesn't like it. He wants our relationship to be pure.'

'That's unrealistic. Don't tell me he hasn't had girlfriends in the past.' Verity glanced across at Jensen, who was chatting animatedly with a gay couple from the drama department. 'He's an attractive guy... not shy...'

'Of course he's had other women,' Liv replied, 'but we've

never done the dreaded "How many people have you slept with?" routine. Jensen made it clear right from the start. He didn't want to tell me about his former loves, and he didn't want to know about mine. I agreed. What's the point?'

'I suppose so. Once the cat's out of the bag, you can't put it back in.' Verity drained her cup and looked up at the sky for a few moments, thinking. 'I'd still want to know, though. For curiosity's sake. It would be like a scab – I'd keep picking at it.'

Liv laughed. 'It doesn't bother me one bit.' And she wasn't lying. She was glad she and Jensen had got together so soon after his arrival at Rutherford, as she hadn't had to deal with any of his previous conquests. She could pretend they didn't exist. It had been different for him, and she thought he'd taken a very sensible and mature approach to the issue.

She surveyed the scene. There were three men here she'd had brief relationships with during her first and second years, and one with whom she'd had an awkward one-night stand. Jensen had no idea about any of them, and she wasn't going to enlighten him. Not now, not ever.

The past was irrelevant, they had to look to the future. 'London, here we come,' she said, downing her drink.

'Yeah. Exciting!' said Verity.

Liv sighed. 'Honestly, Ver, part of me is dreading it.'

'You'll be fine. If it gets too bad, just come back. You can surf my sofa any time.'

'Thanks.' Liv squeezed her friend's hand.

FOUR

Liv and Jensen arrived just before midnight the following Thursday. They had underestimated how long it would take them to pack, load the van and drive down from Newcastle. They'd stopped on the way for a burger and chips, so didn't want the meal I'd prepared – a home-made lasagne, Liv's favourite.

I was relieved that they'd arrived safely, but exhausted. I'd been at work all day and it was well past my normal bedtime. Dom had spent the evening moaning about their lack of consideration. Nevertheless, he seemed genuinely pleased to see Liv and was at least polite to Jensen, reserving his general grumpiness for me. Meg had already gone to her room, fed up with waiting, saying she would see her sister in the morning instead.

Dom and I helped carry everything upstairs, my husband exchanging horrified glances with me at the sheer quantity of stuff they'd brought with them, most of it belonging to Jensen. This included a piano keyboard and stool, some speakers, an adjustable desk chair, a TV, a free-standing bookcase, a small exercise bike and a shop dummy dressed as a zombie.

'I *did* warn you,' Liv whispered as I heaved a box of redundant kitchen equipment up to the top floor. 'This is everything Jensen owns in the world.'

We left them to settle in and went to bed. Dom fell asleep immediately, on his side with his back turned to me. I lay in the dark, willing myself to drop off but distracted by sounds overhead – footsteps going back and forth, objects being dragged across the floor, muffled conversation. At one point, they even put on some music. It was 2 a.m. Couldn't they wait until the morning to sort everything out? Both Dom and I had to get up for work tomorrow. If Dom had been awake, he would have gone upstairs and told them to stop, but I didn't want to start off on the wrong foot. I just lay there hoping and praying that their staying up until all hours wasn't going to be a regular thing.

After the shaky start, things quickly settled down and we seemed to rub along easily with each other. Dom was enjoying the novelty of going into the office instead of working from home, and the boutique was quiet, leaving me with more energy to look after the house – not to mention our guests. Liv and Jensen made the flatlet their own and Jensen seemed to appreciate my efforts to make him feel welcome and comfortable. Liv spent some of each day applying for jobs, but Jensen was less bothered about finding work. He seemed to think that hundreds of satisfying, well-paid jobs would emerge from their cocoons like brightly coloured butterflies and land on his shoulders.

But he wasn't lazy. If we ran out of milk or bread, he would instantly go and fetch it, bringing back some treat besides – a big bar of chocolate or cakes from the bakery. He was the first to leap up from the dining table, gathering our dirty plates and loading the dishwasher. He insisted on helping with the cleaning, hoovering not just their rooms but the whole house. The only room he wasn't given access to was Meg's, but then she didn't allow anyone into her private space. The same home-made *No Entry* sign had been stuck to the outside of her door since she was fourteen. I used to sneak in when she was at school – airing the room, changing the bed linen, collecting the festering plates and science-experiment mugs, hoovering around the chaos. She knew I did it, and secretly I think she was grateful, but neither of us ever acknowledged that I'd entered forbidden territory.

Jensen was also quick to help with food preparation. He declared that he wanted to cook for the family at least once a week, and proved to be a dab hand at the barbecue. We had some pleasant evenings together in the garden, eating kebabs and veggie burgers, drinking beer and chatting until it got too dark to see each other's faces. Dom seemed to be warming to him. It was only Meg who remained unconvinced.

She was jealous of him, simple as that. Liv was wrapped up in her relationship with Jensen and spent all her time with him. She never invited Meg to go shopping, or for a walk, never even popped into her sister's bedroom for a girlie chat. I tried to encourage Liv to include Meg when she and Jensen went out in the evenings, but she said it would be 'inappropriate'. It was true that Meg was under eighteen and wouldn't be allowed into some venues, and I understood that they needed time to themselves, but it felt harsh to me. Meg had already been excluded from her friendship group and seemed to have nobody to hang out with. She hardly ever left the house.

Liv and Jensen had been living with us for a few weeks. It was a Sunday afternoon in the middle of August. The weather had been very warm for several days and a heatwave had been declared. In spite of this, Dom had gone to the gym, leaving me to clear up after lunch. Meg was hiding in her room with an electric fan on full blast, while Liv and Jensen were in the garden, sunbathing on the patio. They were lying on the same lounger, sharing Jensen's earbuds to listen to music on his phone.

I opened the door of the dishwasher, and a cloud of hot

steam escaped through the open bifold doors. I groaned at the sight of all the crockery that now needed putting away.

'Let me help,' said Jensen, extricating himself.

'I'm okay,' I said, wiping sweat from my forehead. 'Just hot.'

'You've done all the work. It's your turn to relax.' He got off the lounger and stepped into the kitchen.

'Thanks.'

He started removing mugs from the top rack of the dishwasher. He was bare-chested, wearing only a pair of shorts. As he bent down for the plates, I noticed that his back was badly scarred. The skin was raised and puckered in places, with patches of livid red.

'Oh my God,' I said, without thinking. 'Are those burn scars?'

He let go of the plate he was holding, which clattered back onto the rack. He straightened up and turned round, his face suddenly serious.

'Yes,' he said. 'There was a fire at our family home and my parents—'

'Yes, yes, I know, Liv told me,' I cut in. 'I knew you'd lost them in a fire, but I didn't realise you were there at the time. She never said. I'm so sorry, I shouldn't have just blurted it out.'

'It's okay, Rachel, no need to apologise.'

I lowered my eyes. 'I can't imagine how horrific it must have been...'

'Yes... I tried my best to save them, but...' His voice faded away. 'Sorry, I still find it really hard to talk about.'

'Of course you do. I understand. No need to say another word.' I wanted to hug him, but it felt too intimate. 'If there's anything I can do to help...'

'You're already helping,' he replied. 'Being part of a family again... it means a lot to me.' He managed a small smile. 'Sorry, just need a few moments to myself.' He left the kitchen and walked up the stairs. A few seconds later, I heard the sound of their bedroom door shutting.

'Oh dear,' I said, going into the garden. 'I seem to have touched a raw nerve.'

'What do you mean?' Liv asked, removing her earbud. She stared up at me, shielding her eyes from the sun.

'I asked Jensen about the scars on his back. I didn't think, it just came out. Why didn't you tell me he was involved in the fire that killed his mum and dad?'

She sat up. 'He doesn't like talking about it. Not even to me. It brings it all back. He suffers from PTSD, has nightmares sometimes.'

'I'm not surprised, those are major burns. Poor guy. He must have been in excruciating pain. Physically and emotionally.'

'Yeah. And he's full of guilt for not having been able to save his folks,' she said. 'I don't suppose he'll ever truly get over it.'

'Nobody would.'

Liv sighed. 'I'd better go check on him.' She got off the sunlounger and went inside, leaving me alone in the garden.

I was cross with myself. I'd unintentionally upset Jensen and ruined a lovely afternoon. Unable to put things right, I went back to emptying the dishwasher. I was determined to be more sensitive in future and not just say the first thing that came into my head.

About half an hour later, Liv and Jensen left the house. I guessed they were going for a walk, but if so, it must have been a very long one. They didn't return home until after Dom and I had gone to bed.

That night, I listened to the upstairs floorboards creaking, wondering about the fire that had caused Jensen such devastating injuries. How had it started? Why had he not been able to rescue his parents? I was desperate to know more about what had happened, but didn't dare ask for fear of causing him more distress.

FIVE

Over the next weeks, I waited on Liv and Jensen hand and foot. I knew I shouldn't be doing it, but I felt an overwhelming urge to make them happy, especially after Jensen had said how much he loved being part of a family again. I hoped they would stay for as long as possible. Unfortunately, Dom didn't share my enthusiasm.

'You're making them too comfortable,' he said one morning, while he was getting dressed for work. 'We'll never get rid of them at this rate.'

'How can you say that about your own daughter?' I remonstrated from the bed. 'I thought you'd be pleased to have her back.'

Liv did her best to look for work, but most of the time she and Jensen behaved as if they were on holiday. They seemed to have forgotten that they'd graduated and wouldn't be returning to university in September. They woke mid-morning, padded around the house in their pyjamas, ate breakfast at lunchtime and had lunch at teatime. When it was warm, they lounged around in the garden. Otherwise, they lay on the sofa in the sitting room, binge-watching drama series or films on Netflix.

We seemed to be living in different time zones. They often went out just as I was about to serve our evening meal ('No worries, we'll heat it up later!') and came home in the early hours, crashing around the kitchen, talking loudly, listening to yet more music, then going up to their flatlet, showering and having sex – all of which kept us awake.

Dom kept moaning about it. He deliberately made a lot of noise when he got up early to go to work, 'to give them a dose of their own medicine'. Not wanting arguments, I pretended it didn't bother me. In fact, it bothered me a lot, but for different reasons. I desperately wanted Liv and Jensen to behave them- selves so that Dom wouldn't chuck them out, but I didn't want to ask them to change in case they took offence and left of their own accord.

I was strangely obsessed with Jensen and wanted to get to know him better. To me, it felt natural to be interested in other people's lives – their family background, childhood experiences, hope and dreams. And it wasn't as if he was a passing stranger – we were living with him. We had things in common, both having lost our parents in a tragic accident in our early twenties, but I didn't want to blunder in again in case I made things worse. I was tempted to ask Liv for the full story, but I hardly ever saw her on her own. It was as if she and Jensen were superglued together. Had I found the oppor- tunity to ask, she probably would have told me off for being nosy. But it wasn't nosiness. I cared about Jensen, and I wanted to help.

September arrived, and with it the start of the new acad- emic year. Meg was nervous about going back to school. She'd hardly seen anyone over the summer and wasn't sure whether she had any friends left.

'Of course you have friends,' I assured her that morning, as she sat slumped over the table, playing with her breakfast cereal. 'The holiday will have done everyone good. Things will go back to normal. I'm sure Skyla and the others will be really keen to see you.'

'Hmm...' she replied, scooping up a spoonful of milk and slowly dripping it back into the bowl. 'You don't know what they're like.'

'Honestly, don't worry about it,' I said airily, with more conviction than I felt. 'It'll be fine.'

And it *was* fine. She came home from school with a smile on her face. Apparently Skyla and the new girl, Alice, had fallen out over the summer – some boy they'd both had their eye on – and their friendship had cooled. Skyla had welcomed Meg back into the fold with open arms.

'She said she'd missed me and felt bad about how she'd treated me. She wants things to go back to how they were,' Meg told me, eyes shining.

A part of me wondered why Skyla hadn't made any attempt to contact Meg over the holidays, but I said nothing, not wanting to burst her happy bubble.

'She's finally seen Alice for what she is,' Meg rattled on. 'Apparently *she* was the one behind the trolling last term – she's a right bitch. I knew it wasn't Skyla. She just went along with it.'

'I see. Interesting.'

That was not how I remembered it, but I let it pass. When the online bullying had started at Easter, it had come from an unknown sender. It had taken a while for Meg to tell us what was going on, and when we saw the messages, we were appalled that anyone could have been so mean. We told her to block the account, but as soon as she got rid of it, another appeared in its place. We suggested that she came off social media altogether, but apparently this was completely unthinkable.

My suspicions immediately fell on Skyla, so I went to see her mum and asked her to check her daughter's laptop. But Gemma refused to believe that her daughter could be involved in online bullying, and we fell out too. Meg was furious with me for 'wading in', as she called it, and the messages became nastier and more frequent. I had no choice but to contact the head teacher and tell him what I thought was going on. It was only when he contacted Skyla and Alice's parents and threatened expulsion that the truth finally came out. Alice had certainly played a part, but Skyla had been the ringleader; she'd created the fake Instagram accounts and sent most of the vile messages. The girls were made to apologise and were excluded from school for a week, while we were assured that bullying of any kind would not be tolerated and that it would never happen again.

If I'd been Meg, I would have kept my distance from Skyla and her gang this term, finding myself another group of friends to hang out with. But my daughter was vulnerable and too trusting. She believed what she wanted to believe.

'It's your eighteenth coming up soon,' I said, changing the subject. 'Do you know what you want to do to celebrate?'

'Yes, actually.' Her face brightened. 'Skyla says I should have a big party.'

'Does she now?' I bit my tongue again. Meg had always been a shy, introverted girl who spent her childhood hiding behind me at social gatherings, refusing to join in with the games. In contrast, Skyla loved being the centre of attention.

'I'm one of the oldest in the year, so she says I should like, set the level,' Meg continued. 'We were thinking about Snakes. There's a really cool room at the back you can hire out.'

I knew about Snakes, although I'd never ventured inside. It was a relatively new bar on the high street, converted from an old-fashioned hairdressing salon that had lain empty for years. It attracted a young crowd, which often spilled onto the pavement in the evenings. They held open-mic nights for aspiring comedians and there'd been complaints about the loud music.

'But most of your friends will still be under eighteen,' I said. 'They won't get served.'

'Not a problem. They all have fake ID,' she replied nonchalantly.

I frowned. 'That's not the point. As parents, we're responsible. Why don't we just have it at home?'

'If I can't have it at Snakes, I don't want it at all,' Meg said.

Previously I would have reprimanded her for sounding spoilt, but I was so pleased that she wanted a party at all, I let it go.

'Okay, sweetheart. I'll speak to Dad about it.'

Dom didn't get home from work until nearly midnight.

'Where have you been?' I asked as soon as he came into the bedroom.

'Another leaving do,' he replied. 'There was no need to wait up.'

'I've been worried about you all evening. Why didn't you let me know in advance?'

'I did. I mentioned it this morning,' he said.

'No you didn't. And you didn't answer my messages.'

'My phone was on silent. I didn't realise. I was too busy...'

'Having fun?' I finished for him.

'Yes, if you must know. It's certainly not much fun round here lately.'

'What's *that* supposed to mean?'

He sighed wearily. 'I don't want to talk about it now. I'm tired and a bit pissed.' He kicked off his shoes and started to undress. Within seconds of climbing into bed, he'd fallen asleep and was snoring loudly, as he always did after a few beers.

He left for work early the next morning. I had no chance to discuss the party idea with him, so I just made a decision and booked it.

The party room at Snakes was free the night before Meg's birthday. The venue would provide a buffet, and we could put a fixed amount behind the bar, after which everyone would have to pay for their drinks. The maximum number of guests allowed was forty-five, which sounded like plenty to me. I booked it without further thought, paying a hefty deposit.

As I'd hoped, Liv and Jensen were keen to help. I put Liv in charge of decorations, Jensen said he would DJ, and Karina offered to make the birthday cake. My sister was a fantastic amateur baker and had made cakes for the girls for as long as I could remember – unicorns, rainbows, ballet shoes, flower fairies. There was no end to what she could do with icing.

Dom was paying for the party, but that was as far as his involvement went. He was very distracted with his job, working long hours and coming home late at night. To be fair, the rest of us had it covered, but it still irritated me that he was so disengaged.

'We'd better send out proper invites,' I told Meg. 'Otherwise we'll get gatecrashers.'

She looked at me askance. 'It's not a kids' party. You just put the word out and people turn up.'

'But we need to know how many are coming.' I was scared that either we'd be overrun, or nobody would turn up at all.

'It'll be all right,' Meg said. 'I'm back friends with Skyla and she's really popular, so that makes me popular too. That's why it was so bad before when she dumped me. I became a nobody.'

I responded vigorously. 'You're not a nobody, Meg, you're worth far more than Skyla and all her gang put together. You're a lovely person. People will come to the party because they like *you*, not Skyla.'

She shook her head. 'You don't understand how it is, Mum.'

I saw a little-girl-lost look in her eyes, and it made my heart wrench. I wondered whether we were doing the right thing. The party would be very exposing for Meg. Perhaps it was too soon to take the risk. I no longer trusted Skyla – if she really had that much control, she could tell everyone to stay away. But it was too late to cancel now.

Liv received some exciting news. She had an interview for a

place on a graduate training scheme for a well-known chain of department stores. As bad luck would have it, the interview was on the day of Meg's party, and in Birmingham, which was at least a couple of hours away. She wouldn't be able to put up the decorations, and it wasn't at all certain that she would make it back to London in time for the start of the party itself. Meg was really upset.

'I'm so sorry,' Liv said. 'But I can't miss it. It's my first interview, I have to be there.'

'Of course you do, no question,' agreed Dom.

Jensen took a different view. 'I don't know why you're going,' he said. 'We want to work in London, not Birmingham.'

We were all seated around the dining table, eating our evening meal. What had started as a celebration of Liv's success was rapidly descending into conflict.

'You can't afford to be picky,' Dom said. 'You've both been out of work for a while now. Whoever gets a job first takes the lead. The other one has to follow.'

'I want to stay in London,' mumbled Jensen.

Liv groaned irritably. 'Then apply for some jobs!'

'Anyway, back to the party,' I interrupted, sensing the start of an argument. 'Maybe I could leave work early and help.' Beverley, my boss, was notoriously inflexible, but it was worth a try.

'Don't worry, I can put up the decorations,' said Jensen, adding pointedly, 'Seeing as I've got nothing else to do.'

'Well, thank you, that's very kind,' I replied, trying to smooth things over. 'I'll still try to get away early. Karina's dropping the cake off on Friday. Can you bring it with you, Jensen?'

'No problem.'

'Thanks.' I turned to Liv. 'Just get back as fast as you can, please.'

'Of course I will, Mum. You didn't have to say that. It'll be fine.'

SIX

'Shit!' exclaimed Liv, as the information board updated. Her train back to London had been cancelled and the next one was running thirty-eight minutes late.

'It's a fucking nightmare, isn't it?'

She turned to see a young woman standing next to her – petite, blonde, with a gamine haircut and large round glasses. 'Yes,' she agreed. 'Hopeless.'

'I'm supposed to be going to a party tonight.'

'Me too. It's my sister's eighteenth. I can't miss it. She'll never forgive me.'

The woman gave her a closer look. 'You were at the interview, right? For the graduate trainee scheme?'

Liv laughed. 'Yes. How did you know?'

'We were on the same tour of the building.'

'Were we? Sorry. I didn't...'

'You're still wearing your name badge, by the way.'

Liv looked down at her chest. 'Oh yes! Oops.'

'Hello, Olivia Matthews... I'm Sofia.'

'Hi.' Liv fumbled with the safety pin, then tore the badge

from her dress. 'That's better. Sorry I didn't recognise you. It was all a bit overwhelming.'

'There *were* a lot of us,' said Sofia.

'Yes. About fifty altogether. That's a long shortlist.'

'Depends on how many applied in the first place. It was probably in the thousands.'

'Really?' Liv's eyes brightened. 'Do you think so?'

'That's what somebody told me.'

She quickly reframed the experience, which up until that moment had been almost entirely negative. 'Oh well, not too bad then.'

'How did your actual interview go?' asked Sofia.

'Not great.' That was the understatement of the century. Liv, normally so chatty and confident, had instantly become tongue-tied when they'd asked what she – a totally inexperienced twenty-two-year-old – would bring to the company. 'I don't think they liked me,' she admitted. 'I'm not their type.' *Not posh enough*, she added silently.

'Shall we go to the waiting room? It'll probably reek of piss, but it's freezing out here.'

Liv nodded, following Sofia along the crowded platform and entering a large glass box. All the seats were already taken, so they stood in the far corner. The door kept opening and shutting, sending blasts of cold air into the room, but it was warmer than outside.

'Just graduated?' asked Sofia.

'Yes. From Rutherford.'

'Where's that?'

'Newcastle. Sort of. On the outskirts. How about you?'

'Exeter.'

'Really? My boyfriend went there.'

'Then you must know it well.'

'Oh no, I've never been. That was before we met. He did just over a year, then transferred.'

'Why? Did something go wrong?'

Liv lowered her voice. 'He lost both his parents.'

'His parents?' Sofia echoed.

'Yes. They died in a fire.'

There was a long pause. Sofia seemed genuinely moved. 'Oh dear. That's so incredibly sad.'

Liv had a sudden vision of Jensen on the first day they'd met. He'd been put in her tutorial group. His skin was as pale as a ghost's and his eyes were rimmed red, as if he'd been crying for months – which, as it turned out, he had. Her heart had gone out to him immediately. After the tutorial, she'd invited him to go for a coffee, and it had started from there – a tender friendship that had quickly grown into a passionate love affair. She had saved him, which he acknowledged almost every day. Their relationship was a beautiful thing, but it was unbalanced, leaning like a tree that had been battered in a storm. She wished it would stand more upright.

She returned her attention to Sofia, who was studying the information board. 'Maybe you knew him. Jensen Watson?'

'No, sorry... What subject did he do?'

'English lit.'

'You sure? I knew quite a few people from that course. Never met anyone called Jensen.'

'Well, he definitely went there.'

'I'm not saying you're lying, just that it's odd I don't know him.' Sofia's tone changed abruptly. 'Would you believe it? It's saying fifty-two minutes delayed now. It just keeps getting worse.' She started texting on her phone.

'It's such a nuisance,' said Liv. 'I wanted to go home first and change. I've bought a new dress and everything. But Meg will kill me if I don't make it on time.'

'It's not your fault.'

'No, but she's, um...' Liv rootled for the word. 'Hypersensitive. She's had a lot of problems with friends and stuff, and it's made her nervous about people turning up.' She paused, surprised at herself for being so open. She didn't usually confide in strangers. 'I'm amazed she wanted a party at all,' she continued. 'I think it was my mum's idea. She just blunders in, never thinks.'

'I wouldn't worry.' Sofia grinned. 'If there's free booze, they'll all be there like a shot.'

A couple left the waiting room, and Liv and Sofia hurried to their still-warm seats. The surroundings were grim: it was cold and draughty, litter was strewn all over the floor and there was an unpleasant smell coming from the guy sitting opposite.

'So, Olivia—' began Sofia.

'Everyone calls me Liv.'

'Liv. Are you London-based?'

'Just about. At the end of the Central Line. We're living with my parents at the moment.'

'You and Jackson?'

'Jensen,' Liv corrected. 'Yes. Since the end of July. I didn't want to, but he was really keen. It makes sense. We don't have to pay rent, and Mum cooks for us every night. It's only until we can save up for a deposit on a rental. I've been applying for everything, but Jensen is so fussy. If it's not his dream job, he won't even consider it.'

'Sounds like you've got a problem.'

'Potentially, yes.' She sighed. 'I love my parents and all that, and I want to be there for Meg, but it feels like I'm regressing.' She stopped to listen to an announcement, but someone was coughing their guts up so she missed it. 'What about you? Where do you live?'

'West London.'

'What, like in a flat share?'

'No. I live alone.' Sofia paused. 'It's my place. I own it. Outright.'

'Wow... Bank of Mum and Dad?'

'Something like that. Don't hate me.'

'Why would I?' Liv studied Sofia with new eyes – her wrap-around woollen coat and leather boots looked expensive, and her hair had been expertly cut. 'Unfortunately, my dad believes people should stand on their own two feet.'

'Give it another six months and they'll be offering you the earth to leave.'

'I doubt it. If Mum has her way, we'll be living there until we're in our forties.'

'Hah! Oh look, there's been a platform change. We need to move,' said Sofia, rising.

They crossed to the other platform. When the train finally arrived, they rushed to find a free double seat. Sofia went to the bar and came back with two burgers, some chips and four small bottles of wine. She refused to let Liv pay her share.

'If I had a flat in west London, I wouldn't be applying for jobs in Birmingham,' Liv remarked, unwrapping her burger. Hot microwave steam burst forth, scalding her fingers.

'I can always rent it out, or Airbnb it,' Sofia said. 'Anyway, I didn't fancy this one, did you? It seemed so corporate.'

'Yeah. And Jensen would have a fit if I got it.'

'Hmm.' Sofia unscrewed one of the bottles and poured the wine into a plastic cup. 'If I'm honest, I'm not sure I'm ready for a graduate traineeship yet. Too much commitment. I'd like to do some more travelling first. Let the flat out for six months or a year...'

'Well, if you're ever looking for a tenant,' Liv butted in, unable to stop herself, 'I'd love to live out west.'

'Okay! I'll bear it in mind.' Sofia raised her tumbler as if in a toast. 'Good to meet you, Liv. We should stay in touch.'

'Yeah, that'd be great. Shall we share details?'

'Sure. I'll give you a missed call.' Sofia took out her iPhone – the latest version, of course.

Liv checked that Sofia's number was safely stored on her

battered old Android. 'Maybe we'll see each other at the next interview.'

'Yeah, or we could meet up for a drink anyway. Pass on info, compare notes, celebrate, commiserate, whatever. Be a little support group.'

'I'd love that.'

Liv drank her wine and ate her burger, transporting herself to a warm, fuzzy place. The train was crowded and hot, with passengers standing in the aisles, but she and Sofia were so caught up in conversation that the time passed quickly. Sofia asked lots of questions about her family and was very sympathetic about the bullying Meg had suffered. She was more reticent when it came to talking about herself, which Liv put down to modesty and not wanting to rub in her obvious wealth. The two of them had little in common – other than applying for the same kind of jobs – but Liv felt that she'd found a kindred spirit in Sofia. It was funny how you could meet someone for the first time and feel like you already knew them, she thought.

She had almost forgotten about Meg's party, and was a little disappointed when the train pulled into the station and their journey together was over. They went down to the Tube, where they had to take different lines. Sofia spontaneously opened her arms, and Liv went in for a hug.

'So lovely to have met you!' enthused Sofia. 'Keep me up to date with your job searches. Best of luck with the escape plan!'

'Thanks – you too. And yeah, let's meet up for a coffee or a drink. Soon.'

'Absolutely. I'll give you a shout. Girls' support group, yeah? No boys allowed.'

'Sounds good!'

'And don't tell... sorry, what's his name again?'

'Jensen!'

'Yeah.' Sofia's eyes twinkled. 'Don't tell Jensen about meeting me. You know what they're like.' She gave Liv one last sparkling smile and disappeared into the bowels of the Victoria Line.

The human traffic around her was frantic, but Liv stood still for a few moments, feeling as if she'd just been showered with magic dust, letting it settle on her shoulders. Meeting Sofia wasn't a chance encounter with a stranger that she wouldn't be able to remember in a week's time; it was the beginning of something. A friendship, certainly, but perhaps more than that. Fate had pushed them together, she could feel it. Sofia had seemed very open to the idea of Liv flat-sitting while she went travelling. Liv didn't want to be a user, but if Sofia *did* decide to go away for a few months, it could be just what they needed.

She walked onto the platform, exciting possibilities swirling through her head. She had to get away from her mother's constant fussing, particularly around Jensen. He didn't seem to mind, but she found it cringe-making. And she knew it was driving Meg mad, too.

She boarded the train. It was packed, and she was shoved into the corner by the double doors. Meg's party would have already started. She'd have to go straight there, wearing her sweaty interview clothes and with no chance to touch up her make-up. Not that it mattered really. Meg was the star of tonight's show.

She changed at Bank, along with about a thousand other people all wanting to head out of town. Her thoughts returned to Sofia and the founding of the girls' support group. No boys allowed, she'd said. It sounded like she wanted to keep her new friend all to herself.

SEVEN

I worked hard all day at the boutique. A new delivery had come in and I volunteered to price up, hoping it would earn me some brownie points with Beverley so that she would let me leave early. Unfortunately, there was an afternoon rush, so I didn't even dare ask. I carried and fetched clothes for customers to try on, and dealt with one of our notorious regulars who bought expensive dresses, wore them, then brought them back saying she'd changed her mind. I carefully examined the garment, pointed out the wine stain it had mysteriously acquired while hanging in her wardrobe and politely refused to give her a refund. She stormed out in a huff, leaving me feeling frazzled.

I left on the dot of five and ran to the bus stop, hoping that I'd have enough time for a shower before changing into my party clothes.

Meg was in her room – getting ready, no doubt – and Jensen was in the kitchen, making himself a snack.

'How did it go at Snakes?' I asked.

'All good. Room looks amazing, if I say so myself. Music's sorted. Oh, and I gave the cake to the manager, who said she'd put it somewhere safe.'

'Thanks so much, Jensen. What would we have done without you?'

'Nah, it's nothing... happy to help.'

'Any news from Liv?' I'd tried calling her on the way home, but she hadn't answered.

'Yes, her train was cancelled. She's on the next one, but it's running late.'

'How did the interview go?'

'Not great. She got the feeling she wasn't what they were looking for.'

'Oh dear. I hope she's not too down about it.'

'She'll get over it. I didn't want her to take the job anyway,' Jensen said. 'I'm sure Birmingham's got a good vibe, but we need to be close to family. *Your* family, I mean. Obviously I don't have one any more.'

His words touched me. When our parents died in the car crash, Karina and I had had our grandparents to turn to. Not to mention aunts and uncles, cousins and family friends. I couldn't imagine how I would have coped if I'd been entirely alone.

I flew upstairs to have my shower. Dom arrived home in the nick of time and changed into a casual shirt and chinos. Meg emerged from her room looking stunning in her new dress – one of the many she'd bought online and mostly rejected. It was midnight-blue satin with a lacy overlay on the skirt.

'You look beautiful, darling,' I said. 'So grown up.'

'I *am* grown up,' she beamed. 'I'm eighteen tomorrow.'

'I know, I can hardly believe it. No matter what, you'll always be my little girl.' I went to give her a hug.

'Careful, or you'll smudge my make-up!' she cried, backing off.

As both Dom and I wanted to be able to drink, we called a taxi to take us to Snakes. We arrived just before seven o'clock. The function room *did* look amazing. There were purple and silver balloons everywhere, and the *Happy Birthday* bunting

Liv had made in advance was hanging above the buffet table. Jensen had done a fantastic job. There was a small stage, where he'd set up his DJ station, leaving plenty of room for dancing.

A group of girls Meg referred to as the Nerds arrived promptly at 7.30, dressed up and bearing beautifully wrapped gifts. They all made a point of saying hello to me and Dom and thanking us for arranging the party. The Nerds were known for being super clever and hard-working, and they had a ton of A* GCSEs to show for it. I wished Meg had joined their friendship group rather than Skyla's.

Other guests started to dribble in, but by eight o'clock there were only about a dozen of us, and the room felt cavernous. Meg seemed okay, but I was worried. Where was Skyla, her 'best friend'?

Karina and I stood at the bar, drinking Prosecco. 'How's it going with the happy couple?' she asked. 'Have they found a place to rent yet?'

'No,' I replied. 'They've got to find jobs first. And save up for a deposit.'

'Can't you help them with that? Or be their guarantor?'

'Why are you asking?'

'Well...' she leant in, speaking into my ear, 'it's just that Meg's finding it a bit of a strain having Jensen around.'

I frowned. 'What do you mean?'

'She told me she was looking forward to spending some time with Liv, but it hasn't worked out. Jensen's always in the way. Can't he go and stay with someone else?'

'No,' I replied tetchily. 'Liv and Jensen are a couple. If he moves out, Liv will go with him, and Meg will like that even less. Anyway, he's a lovely guy – fits right in.' I glanced in Jensen's direction. He was dancing in front of the DJ station, stabbing the air in time to the music, encouraging everyone to join in.

Karina hesitated before responding. 'Meg told me she finds him creepy,' she said.

My mouth fell open. 'Really?'

'I'm just feeding back.'

'Creepy in what way?'

'Not sure exactly. I don't think he spies on her or anything like that. There's nothing sexual about it. She feels like he's muscling in on the family, pushing her out.'

'He's not doing any such thing. Jensen's a pleasure to have around – unlike Meg sometimes.' Karina inhaled sharply, and I instantly regretted having made the comparison. 'I'm sorry. I shouldn't have said that. I just wish she would talk to me like she talks to you. I'm her mother!'

We were on the brink of straying into an argument, but fortunately Liv arrived. She looked breathless and sweaty and was still wearing her interview suit.

'Sorry I'm late, Mum,' she shouted above the music. 'The train was delayed. I didn't have time to go home and change.'

'You're here, that's the main thing,' I said. 'I gather the inter-view didn't go too well either. Sorry about that, love.'

'It's okay. As soon as I arrived, I realised I wasn't the kind of person they were looking for. But I met this girl who was in my interview group and we travelled back together – it made the time pass so much quicker.'

'I bet.'

'She was quite posh, so I'm sure she'll get through to the next round. I thought she'd be up herself, but she was really cool. We had four of those mini bottles of wine and two cheese-burgers on the train and she insisted on paying for everything.'

'Lucky you. Go and say hello to Meg, she's been waiting for you.'

Liv rushed off to embrace her sister. I stayed by the entrance, checking for gatecrashers. A few more guests wandered in, none of whom I recognised. I was pleased to see that most people had made a real effort with their clothes, hair and make-up. Everyone wanted a selfie with the birthday girl.

Meg seemed to be blossoming in real time – chatting, laughing, even flirting with some of the boys. She looked so happy and confident, although I was sure that inside she was a bundle of nerves. I was very proud of her. Dom, Karina and I stood on the sidelines and watched her go from group to group, tossing her carefully tonged hair over her shoulders, throwing her head back in laughter. But every so often, I caught her glancing hopefully towards the door.

'This party was a great idea,' said Karina. 'It's really given her a boost.'

'Yes. No sign of Skyla yet,' I whispered.

'Good!' she whispered back. 'We can do without her.'

'Yes, but Meg will be upset if she doesn't turn up.'

At around half eight, Skyla waltzed in accompanied by her little gang. I knew them well and had previously thought them lovely girls. They'd come for sleepovers in the past and I'd given them lifts to and from netball matches. I wanted to walk straight over and tell them off for being late, but I couldn't. Meg was clearly delighted – and relieved – that they'd finally arrived.

I watched Skyla survey the crowd, choosing whom to greet first, hugging people like long-lost friends, even though she'd seen them in class earlier in the day. It was all so performative and fake. Anyone looking on would have assumed that *she* was the birthday girl, but Meg didn't seem to mind.

The room filled up and we had just the right number – not too few and not too many. Everyone seemed to be having a great time, and I started to relax. Jensen's choice of music was perfect; the dance floor was throbbing. The buffet had long been demolished and there was literally nothing left to eat. The bar manager informed us that our tab had nearly been used up. Afraid that this might make some people leave, we added a further two hundred pounds. Right at that moment, I didn't care about the cost. I hadn't seen Meg look so happy in years.

The extra money didn't last long. By ten o'clock, the crowd was starting to thin out. I realised our event had only been an amuse-bouche for some. Nicely tanked up, they would probably catch the Tube to cooler parts of London and spend the rest of the night at some club.

'I think we should do the cake now,' I said to Karina. 'Before everyone leaves.'

'Absolutely,' she replied. 'What did you think? One of my best?'

'Sorry, I haven't had a chance to look at it.'

'I went for a jungle theme, to fit the venue. I tell you, it wasn't easy. I'm never making elephants out of icing again!'

'I'm sure it'll be worth it. Your cakes are always spectacular.'

I went over to Jensen and told him it was time. We'd planned this moment in advance. He'd make an announcement, then once everyone had gathered, he'd stop the music and turn off the mirror ball. As we carried the cake in, candles blazing, he would lead the chorus of 'Happy Birthday'.

At first, we couldn't find the cake. Jensen said he'd given it to the manager to look after, but she couldn't remember what she'd done with it. Karina and I went on a hunt, eventually finding it on a table in the lobby between the function room and the kitchen. It was still in its box, surrounded by dirty plates and glasses. Karina wasn't impressed.

The music had stopped. In the room next door, all the guests were assembled and waiting. Some started chanting, 'Cake! Cake! Cake!'

'We need to hurry,' I said.

'I know,' Karina replied, rummaging in her bag. 'I've got to put the candles on first.' She found the packet. 'Get the cake out!'

The tape on the box had already been removed – it looked

as if somebody had already taken a sneaky peek. Eagerly I lifted the lid, gasping as I looked inside.

'Oh my God! Karina!'

She peered over my shoulder and shrieked.

The cake had been vandalised – there was no other word for it. The tiny jungle animals had been squashed and thrown aside. The *Happy Birthday* message had been torn off and the icing smashed. One word was written across the top in thick black marker pen.

LOSER.

EIGHT

'Who did this?' gasped Karina, as we both stared at the ruined birthday cake.

'Skyla, I expect,' I replied. 'Or one of her crew.'

'How *could* they?'

The guests' drunken demands for cake were growing louder.

'What are we going to do? We can't take it in like this.'

'Tell them to wait,' Karina replied. 'I'll rescue it. Somehow.'

'Really? You think you can?'

'I'll try. Give me five minutes.'

'Okay.'

I rushed back to the function room, weaving my way through the throng to the DJ station.

'Jensen! Can you make an announcement? Say the cake's been delayed but is on its way, then start the music again.'

He took his headphones off. 'Is there a problem?'

'Yes, but don't let on. Especially not to Meg.'

'Why? What's wro—'

'No time to explain. Just stop the chanting!'

Jensen got straight onto the microphone and made some

jokey remark, then restarted the music, whacking up the volume. I hurried back to Karina, who had removed the defaced icing and was rearranging the jungle animals in its place.

'Stick the candles into the gaps,' she instructed. 'Once they're lit, it won't look so bad. As soon as Meg's blown them out, I'll whisk it off. We might just get away with it.'

'Whatever happens, she mustn't find out,' I said.

Karina nodded. 'If she asks, we'll say I dropped it.'

We finished the repairs, then I ran back to the room and told Jensen we were ready. He played a recording of 'Happy Birthday' through the speakers, and Karina carried the cake in, keeping it as high as possible so that nobody could see the mess on top. Liv and Dom pushed Meg forward and I told her to blow. As soon as the candles were extinguished, I gave her a huge hug, allowing Karina to run off with the cake.

'I didn't get a chance to look at it properly!' Meg moaned, releasing herself and starting to follow Karina.

I pulled her back. 'To be honest, Karina had a bit of an accident with it,' I said. 'She dropped it on the floor.'

'Oh no, poor Auntie Karina. After all that work!'

'I know, don't say anything, she's upset. It looks a mess, but it'll taste just as good as usual.' I steered her towards the dance floor. 'You go back to your friends. We'll cut the cake up and put it on the buffet table.'

'Thanks, Mum,' she said, embracing me. 'This is the best birthday party ever!'

Whoever had tried to ruin Meg's birthday and humiliate her in front of her friends had failed, but it had been a close-run thing. I presumed it had been Skyla, or one of her nasty crew. I spent the rest of the party studying the girl, looking for telltale signs of guilt, or frustration that her evil plan had been foiled. But she seemed entirely relaxed – dancing and chatting like any other guest. The only thing I noticed was that she didn't go anywhere near the tray of cake. It was interesting, but hardly evidence that she'd committed the crime.

The party was supposed to end at midnight, but in fact we packed up a little earlier, as most of the guests had already moved on. Meg was drunk and unusually affectionate, thanking me profusely as I helped her into the taxi.

'What a banging party,' declared Liv, shuffling onto the back seat of the people-carrier. 'Hah! Beat that, everyone!'

'You did great, Meg,' said Jensen warmly. 'Your friends had a blast.'

I murmured agreement, but inside I was burning with anger. As soon as we arrived home and I had a chance to talk to Dom on his own, I told him what had happened.

'Who was supposed to be looking after the cake?' he asked, taking off his shirt and throwing it into the laundry basket.

I frowned. 'Well, Jensen took it to the venue, but—'

'Jensen! I might have known.'

'What do you mean?'

'He shouldn't have left it unattended.'

'It shouldn't have needed guarding!'

'Kids like playing pranks.'

'It wasn't just a prank, Dom, it was a deliberate attack on Meg.'

'You're making too much of it.'

'I'm not.'

'It was Jensen's fault,' he insisted.

'You can't blame him. He was brilliant. He put up the decorations by himself, and he DJ'd all night without a break. He did more to help with her party than *you*,' I jibed.

Dom rounded on me. 'I paid for it, didn't I?'

'Yes, you paid for it,' I replied through gritted teeth. 'I'm talking about getting actively involved, showing Meg you care.'

'Sorry I was too busy to blow up balloons. Unlike our

daughter's boyfriend, I have a job!' He got into bed, turning his back to me in a huff and pulling the duvet over his head.

I couldn't understand his attitude. Somebody had tried to ruin Meg's special day, but all he wanted to do was criticise Jensen.

It was very late by now. I was exhausted and didn't have the energy for a fight. If we'd had a spare bedroom, I would have gone there to sleep. As it was, I had to lie next to my husband, seething with rage. I was certain the culprit was Skyla. It was tempting to go round to her parents' house and confront her, but I knew she would only deny it. And then Meg would find out and it would just make matters worse.

The following day was Meg's actual birthday, so there were presents to open and more choruses of 'Happy Birthday' to sing. Meg was in a great mood, happier than she'd seemed for a long time. There was no way I was going to spoil it by telling her what had really happened.

'Hey, Meg,' said Jensen, putting his arm around her affectionately. 'Time to get dressed. I'm taking you for a blowout birthday brunch.' He squeezed her and I saw her shoulders stiffen.

'What? Just you and me?' she asked nervously.

'Course not! I'm coming too,' said Liv, laughing. 'But Jensen's paying for it.'

Meg frowned. 'I thought you were skint?'

'I am,' he replied cheerfully. 'But who cares? You're the kid sister I never had. We have to celebrate.'

'Okay. Thanks,' she mumbled, but I could tell she felt uneasy. I thought back to my conversation with Karina at the party, when she'd told me that Meg found Jensen creepy. From what I could see, he was simply being nice to her – although maybe calling her his sister was a bit full-on. I could see how that might have felt intimidating. Meg's recent experience of being bullied had left her distrustful of others, especially when they pretended to be her friends.

I wanted to talk to Liv about what had happened at the party without Meg hearing us, but I didn't get a chance until the following day. Meg was still lazing in bed, Dom had taken the car to be washed and Jensen was gaming upstairs. After breakfast, I asked Liv to come for a short walk with me.

We did a tour of the local park, then sat on a bench near the children's playground.

'I used to bring you and Meg here when you were little,' I said. 'You loved the slide, couldn't get enough of it.'

'I know,' she answered, rolling her eyes. 'You say that every time.'

'It's still true.' I sighed nostalgically. 'Now look at you, two grown-up, beautiful young women. Where did the time go, eh?'

'Please stop getting all sentimental on me, Mum.' She turned to face me. 'Why have you brought me here? What do you want to talk about?'

I gave her the full story about the cake. '"Loser" was written on the top in horrible black marker pen. I can't believe anyone would be so mean.'

'Hmm, *I* can,' Liv replied bitterly. 'You did well to rescue it. Meg didn't have a clue.'

'That's a relief.' I waved to a woman walking her dog, whom I knew from yoga. 'They must have done it earlier on in the party,' I continued. 'Did you see anyone lurking around outside the kitchen? Any of her so-called friends?'

'No, but I was in the main room the whole time. And Jensen was DJing non-stop, so he wouldn't have noticed... Do you have any idea who did it?'

'My gut instinct is telling me it was Skyla,' I said, 'but I've no proof. And I don't want to start an investigation because then Meg will find out.'

'We mustn't let that happen. She's in such a good mood at the moment.'

'I'm glad you agree.' I squeezed her arm.

'Absolutely. Best leave it.'

There was a pause while we watched the children playing for a few moments, resting our thoughts. Toddlers in bright plastic macs and wellies clambered up the climbing frame, pushing each other good-humouredly. Two slightly older kids leapt onto the tiny merry-go-round, shrieking with delight as it spun round. They seemed so happy and carefree, completely unaware that one day somebody might try to hurt them. It made me wish my daughters had never grown up.

'I'm sorry the interview didn't go that well,' I said, resuming the conversation.

'It's probably for the best. Jensen didn't want me to get it. He really put me off. I think that's why I did so badly. I knew there was no point.'

'That was a bit unfair of him,' I conceded. 'Although, to be honest, we'd all much rather you stayed in London.'

'So would I, but it's like Dad said, if it's the only option, you have to take it.'

'I'm sure something better will come along soon.'

'I hope so.' She sighed wearily. 'I really want to move out.'

Her words slapped me around the face. 'Why? There's no rush. I thought we were all getting along.'

'We are. That's the problem. It's too comfortable here. Jensen's not even applying for anything. If he had his way, we'd stay for ever.'

A smile escaped my lips. 'That's nice to hear. I'm glad he likes us... I like him too. Very much.'

'Hmm... You don't really know him.' There was a beat. 'He can be difficult. We've been arguing a lot lately.' She looked down and started picking at the polish on her fingernails.

'Really? I haven't heard any shouting.'

'That's not the way Jensen argues. He's a sulker.'

'Oh... Well, I'm sorry to hear that. What have you been rowing about?'

'You know, nothing and everything. We just keep rubbing each other up the wrong way. It wasn't like that before. I think it's because we haven't got our own place.'

'If there's anything I've done wrong—'

'It's nothing to do with you, Mum!' She sounded irritated. 'I'm just saying, you think the sun shines out of Jensen's bottom, but he's not perfect.'

'Nobody is.'

'He has issues. Big issues. He's quite screwed up, if I'm honest.'

'That's hardly surprising,' I ventured. 'After what he's been through... I remember when I lost my parents, I was all over the place for ages. I felt so lonely – like I didn't belong to anyone. If my boyfriend's family had welcomed me with open arms, I'm sure I would have jumped straight in.'

'Yeah... I suppose I should be more understanding, but sometimes—' She cut off the end of her sentence.

'What is it, love?'

'I feel like he's lying to me.'

I tensed. 'About what?'

'Well... that girl I met at the job interview on Friday – she was at Exeter uni, same as Jensen. She wasn't on his course, but she was friends with people who were, and she said she'd never heard of him. I showed her his photo and she didn't recognise him. Don't you think that's odd?'

'Not necessarily. It's a big university. They probably just went to different parties.'

'That's the thing. They both come from wealthy backgrounds, so you'd think they would have mixed.'

'Have you asked Jensen if he knew her?'

Liv shook her head. 'No. I daren't. He goes weird on me if I ask him why he quit Exeter, like I'm interrogating him. It's a taboo subject, along with most of his past.'

'I expect he had a bad experience and he's not ready to open up to you yet. Give it time.'

She sighed. 'I'm starting to think he didn't even go there.'

'Oh, I'm sure he did,' I said, although a small doubt crept into my mind.

NINE

Hey Meg,

What a sad little party that was. So-ooooo fucking boring. We only came for the free drinks before we went to the real party – the one in Hackney you weren't invited to.

As for that dress you were wearing! Did you look in the mirror before you left the house? Next time, buy a two-man tent and wear that instead. On second thoughts, make it a six-man one, there'll be more chance of it fitting. On third thoughts, just stay at home.

And what was your auntie thinking, making you a kid's birthday cake? With jungle animals on it!!? FFS. Are you eight instead of eighteen? I felt so embarrassed for you. That's why I pulled off the stupid monkeys and elephants and wrote that message instead. So annoying that Mummy managed to cover it up. I guess she didn't want you to know how much we all hate you. Good job I took a pic! Here it is.

LOSER.

Because that's what you are, Meg Matthews. You're one big fat loser.

TEN

Meg was back at school, presumably feeling more confident after the success of her birthday party, although I was a bag of nerves, terrified that she'd find out about the cake. I hated the fact that the person who'd written *LOSER* on it remained unpunished, but I was frightened of my daughter finding out and sinking into another depression, so I kept quiet and did nothing, hoping that would be the end of it.

Nevertheless, I felt weighed down, worried about Meg, concerned about Liv and Jensen's relationship, annoyed that Dom seemed so disengaged from the family – particularly me. Work took up all his time and energy, and he was often home late. I lost count of the number of plates of food he never ate. I spent most evenings on my own, staring at the television. Sometimes Jensen came downstairs and joined me. We drank wine and binge-watched thrillers together, and it was good to have his company. I wished Liv would come down too, but she remained upstairs in the flatlet, filling in application forms for jobs – or so she said.

Things clearly weren't going well between her and Jensen. When they'd arrived, they'd been very loved-up and couldn't leave each other alone. Now they hardly spoke. I understood Liv's frustration. Jensen didn't appear to be making any effort to find employment. As far as I knew, he hadn't had a single interview since coming to London. He insisted there was nothing available in his 'particular line of work', although nobody seemed to know what that line was. He was interested in lots of things – graphic design, animation, film-making, music videos, visual art – but didn't seem to have any of the relevant skills or training. Those areas were highly competitive; it was hard to break in if you didn't have contacts.

'You need some work experience,' I said. 'Why don't you try volunteering, or apply for an internship?'

'I don't see why I should work for nothing. Those schemes just rip graduates off.'

'People are expected to work their way up from the bottom,' I countered. 'You start off making the tea, and eventually you become the boss.'

'I'm not interested in making tea,' he growled. 'I've got loads more to offer than that.'

He never talked about his background, but I started to realise that it must have been very privileged. His boarding school education had rubbed off on him whether he liked it or not. He had never wanted for anything and thought success should come easily. He simply didn't know what it was like to have to graft. I could see how his attitude grated on Dom, who'd taken the first job he could get after leaving school – as an office junior in a small engineering firm. After twenty-five years of hard work, he now held a senior position in a large company that operated all over the world.

The atmosphere at home grew increasingly uncomfortable. My family – and I included Jensen in that – were like individual plates spinning on sticks. I took it upon myself to run between them, constantly trying to keep them all going and stop them crashing to the ground. Everyone else was too wrapped up in their own problems to see that others were wobbling.

November arrived, and with it a bout of cold weather. Our summer clothes hung forgotten in our wardrobes, and jumpers and thick socks were the order of the day. It grew dark earlier, which I hated. Meg hadn't been into school all week, claiming that she had COVID, although she didn't appear to have any symptoms and refused to test for it. She spent hours by herself in her room and ate all her meals there. She claimed it was because she was infectious, but I wondered whether she'd fallen out with Skyla again and was feeling down.

It was Wednesday, my usual day off. I made a point of staying at home, hoping for an opportunity to have a chat with her about what was really going on. The house was quiet. Dom was at work. Liv had gone shopping , and Jensen was out running. He had started the 'Couch to 5K' challenge, much to Dom's irritation. He'd remarked that he'd be better off doing 'Couch to Job Centre'.

I made some soup and sandwiches for lunch and knocked on Meg's bedroom door.

'Can I come in?' I asked. She grunted in assent, and I entered, carrying a tray.

Meg was sitting on the top of her bed, legs outstretched, her back resting against a pile of pillows and cushions. She was still in her pyjamas and dressing gown. Her laptop was on her knees, and she was tapping away. As soon as I approached, she shut the lid firmly.

'How are you feeling?' I asked, putting the tray in front of her.

'Terrible. I've got a fever.'

I laid the back of my hand against her forehead. 'You feel all right to me.'

'I'm not. One minute I'm boiling hot, then I'm shivering.'

'Do you want me to take your temperature?'

'No, don't bother, I'll survive,' she replied with a martyred sigh.

I took a pile of dirty clothes off the chair and sat down. I let her slurp her soup for a while as I tried to find the right opening words.

'How are things with Skyla these days?' I asked eventually.

'Fine.'

'Still besties?'

'I wouldn't go that far. It's not the same as it was, but it's okay.'

'And the new girl who caused all the trouble?'

'You mean Alice?'

'Yes. Are you friends with her?'

Meg frowned. 'Sort of... Not really. I don't like her much.' She put down her soup spoon. 'What's this about?'

'Nothing. I just wanted to check in, make sure you were all right. After what happened last term, with the trolling, you know... If it starts up again, I hope you'll tell us straight away.' She nodded. 'It's important not to keep it to yourself. You mustn't suffer in silence. I know it can be hard to share these things, but you have to remember we all love you very much and we want you to be happy. If you don't want to tell me or Dad, you could tell Liv, or Auntie Karina. Or Jensen—'

'No way would I ever tell Jensen,' she snapped.

'Okay, fine, it's up to you. I'm just saying—'

'Jensen is not part of our family, whatever he thinks.'

'That's true, but he *is* Liv's boyfriend.'

'It's not going to last,' she said. 'I hear them arguing at night. Liv's going to chuck him out, you wait and see. The sooner he goes, the better. He gives me the creeps.'

'I don't want to talk about Liv and Jensen, I want to talk about you,' I replied quickly, determined not to be diverted. 'You never go out with your friends. You spend hours in this room, on that thing.' I pointed at the laptop. 'And now you're not going into school.'

'I've got COVID!' she shouted. 'Do you want me to go in and infect everybody? Do you think that'll make me more popular?'

'Okay, okay, you're ill.' I backed down. 'I don't want to argue with you. I'm just worried, that's all. About your mental health.'

'Worry about your own, Mum.'

'I'm fine.'

There was a long, aching pause. 'Thanks for lunch,' she said, pushing the tray towards me. 'I'm tired now. Need to rest.'

I opened the door and walked out, almost bumping into Jensen, who was standing on the landing in his running gear, his hair wet with sweat.

'Hi!' he said, blushing.

'Hi. How was your run?'

'Good, thanks. I did three K, it was pretty easy. Need a shower now. Then something to eat.' He kicked off his trainers and bolted up to the flatlet.

I stared after him. Had he been eavesdropping? If so, he would have heard Meg saying he was a creep. How awkward... Still, if you listened in on other people's conversations, you were bound to hear something you didn't like. I paused at the foot of the second flight of stairs, wondering whether to go up and say something, but then I heard the shower starting, and went down to the kitchen instead.

I hated there being any kind of tension in the house, but I had to leave them to it. They were grown-ups and would have to sort it out for themselves.

ELEVEN

Liv jumped onto the Tube train and sat down. It was late morning, and the carriage was virtually empty. She was glad to be alone – it didn't happen very often nowadays. Jensen had become a bit of a limpet, hanging around her all day and night. He only went out by himself to go running and had tried to persuade her to join him in that too. Liv had refused, joking that she'd do the Couch and he could do the 5K. But seriously, she badly needed some me-time.

The 'flatlet', as her mother ridiculously insisted on calling it, was driving her mad. True, they had the exclusive use of two rooms, but the smaller was no more than a walk-in cupboard. Dad had previously used it as a home office, although Liv doubted he'd done much work there.

She took out her travel mirror and checked her face for flaws. She applied more concealer beneath her eyes and another layer of mascara, her hand jerking as the train clattered through the tunnels. As far as everyone else at home was concerned, she was going to Westfield shopping centre today to buy a suit to wear at job interviews. The one she already had was a little snug and rode up over her hips.

It was the perfect cover story for spending the day without Jensen. Clothes shopping was the one thing he would happily give a miss. In fact, he'd rather poke needles in his eyes than traipse around a shopping mall. And it wasn't an outright lie. There was a chance that she would have time to go to Westfield later on this afternoon.

The real reason she was on this noisy, rickety train, thundering towards central London, was that she was meeting Sofia for lunch.

Almost a month had gone by since they'd met on the platform at Birmingham New Street station. They'd been good company for each other on the delayed journey and had agreed to stay in touch – not that Liv had expected to hear from her again.

But Sofia had texted her the following day, asking how her sister's party had gone. At the time, Liv had replied that it had been *bussin, thanks*. Then Mum had taken her on that walk and told her about the birthday cake having been vandalised. Liv had immediately messaged Sofia to update her and received several angry emojis in sympathy.

That is so disgusting. Do you know who did it? Tell me and I'll send somebody over to beat them up!

She had briefly wondered whether Sofia had meant it, but then a barrage of laughing emojis arrived, which made it clear that it had been a joke. Contact had continued from there. Sofia was her new careers adviser, sending links to ads for graduate training schemes – *This looks good. Shall we apply?* Or *If I end up working for these losers you have my permission to shoot me!* Followed by an emoji of a smoking gun.

She texted almost every day and sometimes their exchanges went on for ages. Liv found herself opening up, admitting feelings to Sofia that she hardly dared admit to herself. The fact that they were virtual strangers helped – Sofia was like a counsellor or therapist, who listened without judging then made a few perceptive comments, some of which hit home.

'Who are you texting?' Jensen had asked on several occasions, his voice full of suspicion.

'Oh, just a friend,' Liv had replied airily. 'A *girl*friend. No need to worry.'

'Which girlfriend?'

'Nobody you know... Somebody from school.'

She was glad she'd kept her new friendship with Sofia a secret – it made things more exciting, somehow. It had been Sofia's idea, but Liv had been quick to agree to it. She was fed up with sharing absolutely everything with Jensen, as if they were one organism with no separate existence. Had she told him about this lunch, for example, he'd have wanted to come along, and if she had refused, he would have sulked for days. It just wasn't worth it.

Things with Jensen were not good. She was embarrassed that he so obviously wasn't making any effort to find a job. Mum seemed okay with it, presumably because she didn't want her 'lovely young people' to leave, but it was making Dad grumpy and sarcastic. For Liv, getting a job was a top priority, because once they both had regular incomes, they'd be able to rent somewhere and could go back to being independent adults who shopped for their own food and hung up their own washing. They could stop behaving like a couple of overgrown schoolkids who barely knew what day of the week it was.

On the subject of overgrown schoolkids... Liv's thoughts skittered back to her younger sister. She seemed to have returned to her unhealthy habits: shutting herself away in her room for hours; refusing to eat with the family yet mysteriously putting on weight. What was she eating? It wouldn't surprise her if Meg was being bullied by that hideous Skyla girl again. She must have been the one who wrote on the birthday cake. Such a spiteful thing to do. Thankfully Mum had swooped down with her protective shield and the party had been saved. They'd decided to keep it from Meg so as not to hurt her. Yet ever since, she'd been depressed and withdrawn. Perhaps she *did* know after all. Photos of the wrecked cake could well have been anonymously posted on social media.

It was so typical of Meg to keep her problems to herself. The whole family was deceiving each other in various ways. They told themselves it was love that made them lie, but Liv didn't buy it any more. Lying was wrong, whatever way you looked at it.

She got out of the Tube and followed Google directions to the restaurant. As she walked, she admonished herself for not paying more attention to Meg. She knew her sister had hoped they would spend more time together when she came back home, but somehow it just hadn't happened. She'd been too preoccupied with her own issues to sort out Meg's as well. And Meg was not the most scintillating company these days. All she needed to do was finish school, get away from those nasty bitches and – most important of all – leave home. Carve out her own life. Only then could she reinvent herself and become the person she wanted to be. That was what Liv had done, more or less. Except now she was back in the clutches of the family, or in Mum's clutches to be precise, as Dad seemed absent, both in body and spirit.

Her thoughts spun around for a few more moments, then came to rest in the same place. She *had* to move out before her once-beautiful relationship with Jensen was destroyed and her patience with her mother wore so thin it disintegrated altogether, like a piece of old fabric that had been put through the wash too many times.

'There's my friend, over there,' Liv told the FOH manager guarding the entrance to the restaurant. He was armed with a tablet and looked as if his job was to repel customers rather than welcome them. She waved at Sofia, who gestured enthusiastically from the corner of the dining room.

'Ah yes,' he said, reluctantly stepping aside to allow her through. Liv wondered whether she didn't look cool enough or wasn't dressed expensively enough. She'd already checked out the place online and had been shocked by the prices. Thank God Sofia had made it clear that lunch was her treat.

'Sorry, am I late?'

Sofia rose to embrace her, kissing her on both cheeks. 'No, not at all. I was early. Did you find it all right?'

'Yeah, easy.' Liv took off her coat, which was instantly taken by a hovering waiter, and sat down. 'What a great place!'

'It's one of my favourites,' Sofia replied. 'I used to come here with my mother when we came up to town for shopping trips.'

'Why *used* to?'

She looked sad for a moment. 'Oh, I don't know... We don't seem to get the opportunity any more. We're both always so busy.'

'My mum is the last person I'd ever want to go shopping with,' said Liv. 'She's so pushy, I'd only end up buying loads of things I didn't want.'

They spent a few minutes studying the menu, which was all small plates, pretentiously described. There were broths, foams and emulsions and an awful lot of blackening going on. Sofia had tried almost everything before; she knew what was the most delicious and what to avoid, so Liv let her choose for them both. A bottle of crazily expensive wine was added to the order. It would be tricky to explain arriving home from a shopping trip smelling of alcohol, but right at this moment Liv didn't care. She hadn't been spoilt like this for ages.

'So, how's the job hunt going?' Sofia asked.

'Not brilliantly. I've sent off loads of applications, just waiting to hear now. How about you?'

Sofia removed her owl-like glasses and put her elbows on

the table. 'I started a few, then lost interest. I don't know what's wrong with me. Do I really want to be an analyst? I'm not sure. It sounds really tedious.'

'When we met on the train, you said you were thinking of taking some time out to go travelling,' Liv said.

'Hmm... I'm still thinking about it. It's very tempting. To be honest, though, I don't really want to go on my own, you know? Some of the countries I'd like to visit are not great for sole female travellers.'

'True. Haven't you got a friend who'd go with you?'

'Nobody that wouldn't drive me mad after about a week.'

Their first dishes arrived – 'ex-dairy cow with sourdough miso' and seaweed with something fermented. She presumed it was actual seaweed and not shredded cabbage like you got in a Chinese takeaway. Were they supposed to start eating now or wait for the next plates to turn up? She followed Sofia's lead and took a minuscule portion of both dishes.

'So, you're not seeing anyone at the moment?' Liv ventured.

'Fuck no,' replied Sofia, chasing a thread of seaweed around her plate. 'I had a really bad experience with the last guy. Enough to put me off for life.'

'How awful, I'm so sorry to hear that.' Liv found herself leaning forward, eager to hear more. 'What happened?' Sofia looked uncomfortable. 'Sorry, I shouldn't have asked.'

'No, it's okay...' She put down her fork and composed herself. 'We weren't a good match. He was brought up on a council estate or something, know what I mean? Went to a state school. I was very naïve, thought all you had to do was fall in love. I didn't think coming from different backgrounds would matter, but it did.' She sighed. 'Anyway, it turned out he was only interested in me because of my trust fund. He was a total freeloader, latched onto my rich friends, never paid his way. He didn't care about me at all. It hurt me a lot, really knocked my confidence. But fortunately, I saw the light.'

'How did you end it?'

'Well, I knew it wouldn't be easy, that he wouldn't give up without a fight. So...' Sofia paused as two more plates arrived. 'I ghosted him. Changed my mobile number and email address, blocked him on social media and deleted my accounts, stopped going to our favourite haunts, made it very clear to my friends that they had to drop him. I even started using my mum's maiden name so he couldn't track me down.'

Liv's mouth fell open. 'Why did you go that far? Were you scared of him or something?'

Sofia's face darkened. 'Yes. I was terrified.'

'And did it work? The ghosting.'

'Completely. I'm free of him now. He can't hurt me.'

Liv was impressed, but also a little alarmed. There was a bitterness in Sofia's voice. Clearly she was not the kind of woman you'd want as your enemy.

'Anyway, here's to the girls' support group!' Sofia picked up her glass of wine. 'We do what we want, how we want, and we don't let anyone push us around, okay?'

'Sounds good to me.' They clinked glasses.

'Now listen,' Sofia carried on. '*If* I decide to forget the whole work thing and go on a massive world tour, would you flat-sit for me?'

Hope fluttered in Liv's chest. 'Well, er, yes, potentially, I'd love to.'

'I know we've only just met, but I've got a good feeling about you. You're authentic.' Liv laughed self-consciously. 'I wouldn't charge rent. Just council tax, heating and lighting, Wi-Fi and stuff, that's all.'

'That's very generous of you.'

Sofia waved the compliment away. 'You'd be doing me a favour, looking after the place, watering my plants, making sure nothing went wrong. I don't know how long I'd be gone for. Six months? Maybe longer, who knows. I'd keep my room, just in case I needed to come back earlier, but you could have the spare.'

'That would be amazing, Sofia. Of course, we'd be mad keen.'

'*We?*' she echoed. 'Do you mean you and your boyfriend?'

'Well, yes... Is that a problem?'

She pulled a face. 'Kinda. I was thinking of just one person. The bed's only a single, you see, and—'

'We could squeeze up.'

'No, the room's far too small. And couples are problematic – if you split up, who moves out? I'd rather keep it super simple.'

'Right... that's tricky. I suppose *I* could move in and Jensen—'

'I wouldn't want him staying over all the time either,' Sofia interrupted quickly. 'Men are such slobs. My flat is my sanctuary. I think of it as a man-free space, you know?' She registered the disappointed expression on Liv's face. 'Sorry. It sounds like I'm trying to get you and your boyfriend to split up! I'm really not. My bad. Forget I mentioned it, I'll ask another friend. I probably won't even go travelling. It was just a fantasy.' She laughed and returned to her food.

Liv took another sip of wine. 'Well, if you do decide to go, please talk to me about it again. I may well be interested.'

'Really?'

'Yeah... I'm not sure about how things are going to turn out with Jensen. I used to think we were for ever, but it's all a bit up in the air at the moment.' She paused, tempted to share her suspicions that he was lying to her, although she wasn't sure what he was lying about. She had no evidence, no proof. Suspicions was too strong a word; it was more like gentle nudges from her conscience, tripping her up every now and again, whispering to her that just maybe something wasn't quite right. Still, she mustn't be disloyal, it wasn't fair.

'If he gets off his arse and finds a job,' she continued, 'then we can rent somewhere together and get back to our normal life. If not...' She hesitated before completing the sentence. She'd never contemplated splitting up with Jensen until this moment. Was that what she wanted? Was she so desperate to leave the family home that she was prepared to leave her relationship, too?

TWELVE

We were well into the autumn term now. It was the middle of November; before we knew it, it would be Christmas. I hadn't even thought about presents yet. Somehow I just didn't feel in the mood.

The atmosphere in the house was tense. I felt as if we were all tiptoeing around each other. Liv and Jensen spent a lot of time in their flatlet, Dom kept finding reasons – or excuses – to come home late, and I hardly saw Meg.

When I got back from work, she was ensconced in her bedroom and often stayed there until the following morning. She claimed she was studying and that everything was fine, but I didn't believe it. I tried to persuade her to join us for evening meals, but she usually refused. Not wanting her to go hungry, I started leaving plates outside her bedroom door.

One morning, while Dom was away on business, I woke up to discover that somebody had emptied our rubbish bin all over the front garden. There was packaging, vegetable peelings and food remains everywhere, and it stank. Liv blamed local foxes, of which we had many, but I knew they couldn't have opened a large wheelie bin, split open the bags and scattered their contents in deliberate fashion across the path. This was the work of Meg's bullies.

'I haven't got time to clear it up now,' I said, surveying the mess. 'I'll be late for work.'

'Leave it to me, I'll do it,' said Jensen. He was already up and about and had been doing yoga in the conservatory.

'You don't mind?'

'Of course not.' He smiled. 'It's my rubbish too.'

'Thanks, Jensen,' I said. 'There'll be something else next. You wait and see.'

And I was right.

The next attack happened a week later. I'd spent my day off indoors, catching up with housework, baking blueberry muffins and doing a big online food shop. Dom was at work, Meg was at school. For once, Liv and Jensen had ventured out of the house and had gone to an exhibition at Tate Modern. Although usually I hated being alone, I'd enjoyed my day, having ticked off lots of little outstanding jobs and successfully put my worries about the family to the back of my mind.

It was just gone seven, and surprisingly, nobody had come home yet. Neither Liv nor Meg had deigned to let me know whether they wanted a cooked meal, and Dom had texted to say he'd been held up at work and would be an hour late. As I dished up a solitary portion of the vegetarian tagine I'd cooked, my good mood evaporated.

I'd already cleared up the kitchen and was watching television when I heard the front door opening. I shouted out a greeting from the sitting room. When Dom walked in, his face was like thunder.

'Have you seen it?' he asked.

'Seen what?' I sat up straight. 'What's wrong?'

'The car's been keyed. Deliberately.'

'Seriously? Oh God!' I stood up and followed him back

outside. He was right. There was a deep wavy scratch running the full length of the car.

'It wasn't like that this morning,' he said.

'Are you sure? You were rushing for the train, remember?'

'I wouldn't have missed this. Did you take the car out today?'

'No. Didn't need to.'

He seemed annoyed with me. 'So you have no idea when it was done. Or who did it.'

'No more than you do,' I bristled. 'But whoever it was, they wouldn't have dared do it in broad daylight. It must have happened last night.' I traced the line of the scratch with my finger, feeling the hatred that must have gone into making it. 'First the birthday cake, then the rubbish, now this.'

'You think it's all coming from the same person?'

'It can't be a coincidence. Somebody's out to get Meg.'

'But why scratch the family car?'

'I don't know. Maybe they want to get at us, too.'

He bit down on his lip. 'It's starting to feel that way.'

'We're going to have to be vigilant,' I said. 'Work together – you, me, Liv. And Jensen. Most of all, we've got to protect Meg. Whatever happens, she mustn't find out.'

Meg came back later that evening, saying she'd been on a theatre trip with school. Liv and Jensen didn't get home until after we'd gone to bed. I took the car to the body shop the following day to have the scratch filled in and repainted. I told Meg it had gone in for a service, but she seemed spectacularly uninterested.

As soon as we had the chance, we told Liv and Jensen what had happened but asked them not to mention it to Meg.

'We don't know for sure whether it was targeted against us,' Dom said. 'It could have been totally random – kids on a dare.'

'No, it was Skyla,' I said. 'It has to be.'

'Really?' Liv looked doubtful. 'I'm surprised she'd go this far.'

I couldn't get the incident out of my head. I was convinced that Skyla – or possibly that new girl, Alice, or the two of them working together – was behind all the aggression. But how would I ever catch her – stay up all night, on guard?

I might as well have done, because over the next few days, I hardly slept. I lay in bed with my eyes wide open, listening out for suspicious sounds in the street, every so often rising and rushing to the window, peering through the shutter slats, staring into the blackness, convinced there was a malevolent figure lurking in the garden.

'You look exhausted, Mum,' said Liv one morning over breakfast.

'Do I?' I yawned. 'I'm not surprised – not sleeping too well at the moment. I feel like we're being attacked on all sides.'

'You could go to the police, I guess.' She put some bread in the toaster.

'What for?'

'Harassment? Criminal damage?'

'I'm not sure it would count. Anyway, I don't know where or when the keying was done, let alone who did it. I need concrete proof.'

'There's something else.' Liv leant against the kitchen counter. 'The trolling has started up again. Meg is getting DMs from a new fake account.'

'I knew something was wrong,' I replied. 'Why didn't she tell me?'

She shrugged her shoulders. 'Too embarrassed, I guess. Or she's scared you'll go up to the school again.'

'What are the messages about?'

'It's brutal stuff, Mum. The first one slagged off the party, said people only came for the free booze. They admitted to writing on the cake and sent her a photo.'

A shiver ran through me. 'Oh no! That's terrible. Poor Meg, I was hoping she wouldn't find out.'

'Don't let on that you know. Meg made me promise not to tell you.'

'That bloody Skyla. She's got to be behind it.'

'Yeah, she's the obvious candidate, but we can't go round making accusations,' Liv warned me. 'We need proof.'

'If we could find out who's sending the messages, it would be a good start. How can we do that?'

'It's really difficult,' she replied. 'They're using fake accounts, which are virtually impossible to trace.'

'Couldn't you try?'

'Me?' She screwed up her face. 'I'm no expert, Mum.'

'Could Jensen do it?'

'Maybe, but we'll need Meg's permission and I'm not sure she'll want to give it. She's scared.'

'We've got to do *something*,' I said. 'Talk to her for me, Livvy. Please. And ask Jensen if he—'

She raised her hand to stop me. 'Yeah, yeah, I'll try. Only things between us aren't great at the moment.' Tears filled her eyes. 'I'm not sure what to do about it.'

'I'm really sorry to hear that, darling.' I went to hug her, but she batted me away. 'Meg told me that she'd heard you arguing. I was hoping it was just a tiff.'

'It's definitely more than a tiff.'

'Okay... So what's the problem? Talk to me, Liv. Let me help.'

'I'm not sure you can.' She drew in a breath. 'I'm working so hard making these applications, but Jensen's not even trying. He's not interested in getting a place with me any more, keeps saying it's too expensive and we'll never get somewhere as nice as this. Which is true, but it's not the point. Why doesn't he want to be with me?'

'He *does*! He's just thinking about the cost.'

'He's very insecure. Obviously it's connected to losing his parents, but... I think it's more complicated than that.'

'How do you mean?'

'I don't know. I've tried to get him to tell me the full story, but he finds it too painful to talk about. He says if I love him, I should let him be. And I *do* love him. He loves me too, but he can be so intense. It's like there's only one person in this relationship. Him.' She wiped a tear from her cheek with the back of her hand. 'Sorry. You've got enough to worry about with Meg without me making it worse.'

'Don't be silly. I'm here for both of you. You're my girls. You'll always come first.'

She forced a smile. 'Thanks... I don't understand, everything was working fine between us when we were at uni. We were together the whole time, and we got on so well. If we had our own space, I'm sure everything would go back to how it was, but we need jobs so we can earn money—'

'Sounds like you need some proper time to yourselves,' I cut in, my brain whirring into action. 'I've an idea. Dad and I could go away for the weekend, and maybe Meg could go and stay with Auntie Karina. We'd leave you in peace. You could have the run of the place, talk everything through without worrying about anyone overhearing or interrupting.'

'Really?' Her eyes shone with gratitude. 'That would be amazing!'

'I'd love a weekend by the sea,' I replied, warming to my theme. 'I'll see what I can sort out. In the meantime, if you could persuade Meg to let Jensen into her social media accounts, that would be really helpful.'

'Of course, Mum,' she answered, visibly cheered. 'I'll do what I can.'

That evening, I scoured the internet looking for accommodation and found something perfect. Dom was out, entertaining business clients from Dubai. Again. When he arrived home, slightly drunk and dishevelled, looking as if he'd been dancing or in a minor fight, I was already in bed. I'd been reading in order to stay awake.

I put my book down and explained the situation as best I could. 'I've found a lovely Airbnb right on the Suffolk coast. We could drive up on Friday evening, stay two nights.'

'Sounds good, but I'm knackered,' he said. 'I'd rather stay at home this weekend and relax.'

'Please. The break will do us good.'

He slumped onto the bed and started undressing. 'Do we *have* to?'

'No, but I want to. We need some time together, too,' I argued. 'Just the two of us. We've hardly seen each other these past couple of months.'

He couldn't dispute that, but he was still reluctant. 'What about Meg? Won't she be in the way too?'

'She can go to Karina's. I've already asked, and Karina says it's fine. In fact, she'd love to have her. They can have a girlie weekend together.'

He took off his socks and threw them in the general direction of the laundry basket. 'She's eighteen. She should be having girlie weekends with her friends, not hanging out with her aunt.'

'She'll have a lovely time. And hopefully she'll open up to Karina about these disgusting messages she's been getting.'

'I've had enough of all this drama,' Dom moaned, putting on his pyjamas. 'I thought once the girls were grown up we'd be free.' He got into bed. 'Now I have to leave my own house just so that Liv can have a heart-to-heart with her boyfriend! It's ridiculous.'

'Every couple needs privacy to talk through issues.'

'What sort of issues?'

'Nothing serious.'

'What issues?' he repeated.

'Well, Jensen's a bit secretive,' I answered cautiously. 'He needs to confide in Liv more. It's like he doesn't trust her, and that makes her feel like she can't trust him.' Dom frowned, not liking what he was hearing. 'They need to work through it, that's all. He's a lovely guy. They make a great couple. I'm sure there's nothing to worry about—'

'You *would* say that,' he interrupted.

I turned my head. 'What do you mean?'

'Come on, I'm not stupid. I know why you've got such a soft spot for him.'

There was a beat. I felt as if he'd grabbed my heart and was squeezing it tightly. 'I don't know what you're talking about,' I lied, hoping he would take the hint and back off.

'Yes you do, Rachel.'

'Well... it's true that we have a connection,' I blustered. 'We both lost our parents at around the same age in tragic circumstances. It was devastating for me, even with my sister and grandparents to support me. But Jensen literally has no one. I can't help but sympathise.'

'That's not what I meant.' He paused to look into my eyes. My heart jittered in anticipation of what he was going to say. That huge, sad, heavy thing that we kept locked away and couldn't bear to talk about.

'You see Jensen as the son you always wanted but never had,' he said gently.

'We *did* have a son,' I snapped. 'Don't ever say that. He existed. He had a name.'

'Yes, but we never got to know him, did we? Never got to look after him or see him grow up.'

'Peter has nothing to do with this.'

'Are you sure?' Dom pressed.

'Absolutely.'

'Okay, okay... I'm sorry I mentioned it.'

'Can we go to sleep now, please? I'm worn out.'

I turned off the lights. Dom fell asleep within minutes, but I lay awake, emotion churning through my body. My husband had seen right through me. I *did* think of Jensen as a surrogate son. I couldn't help it.

We lost Peter a long time ago, and he'd only lived for a few hours. But he still came into my mind every day, often at strange, unexpected moments. Whenever I saw Liv and Meg together, I was aware of the four-year gap between them, that space where he should have been, growing into a beautiful young man with his whole life ahead of him. He would have just turned twenty. He would have had brown curly hair like Dom's and blue eyes like mine. He would have had Liv's steely intelligence, and a touch of Meg's creative dreaminess. He would have been the best of all of us, and we would have adored him.

I'd always wanted 'one of each', a boy and a girl. When I was pregnant with Peter, I asked Dom what sex he wanted the baby to be, as if it were in my gift. 'I don't care, as long as they're healthy,' he replied. I nodded in agreement, knowing that was the right answer and feeling guilty for my secret preference. When Peter was taken from us, I wondered whether it was because I'd jinxed it in some way. Wanting a boy too much.

THIRTEEN

Hey Meg,

Yes, it was me. I trashed your garden. Did you see it, or did Mummy clear it up before you got the chance? Aww, she tries so hard to protect you, but she fails every time.

I'm a bit like Banksy. My artwork contains a message. I think it's obvious, but seeing as how you're so fucking stupid, let me spell it out. What I'm saying, Meg, is that YOU are rubbish. You're even more rubbishy than all the shit in those wheelie bins. In fact, you're so rubbish, your mum should put you in a black bin liner and ask the council to take you to the dump. You're not even worth recycling. You're useless.

And I keyed Daddy's car the other night. That was so fun. I don't suppose they told you about that either. They always keep you in the dark. Do you know why? Because they know how weak you are, and how easily you could think your life wasn't worth living – which, let's face it, it isn't. Everyone knows that.

Don't forget, you can always KYS.

FOURTEEN

Jensen agreed to try to track down the online troll, as long as Meg was okay with giving him her passwords. Liv asked her, reporting back that she wasn't okay with it. Not at all.

'Why not?' I asked. 'We're only trying to help.'

'She says she knows who it is anyway.'

'Meaning Skyla?'

Liv shrugged. 'She wouldn't say. If Meg doesn't want to confront her, that's her choice. Maybe it's better to ignore it.'

'You can't ignore having your car scratched and rubbish being dumped in your garden,' I huffed. 'They're waging a campaign of abuse, and they need to be stopped before anything worse happens.'

'Okay, but how?'

'Can't you just break into her Insta without her knowing?' I asked quietly. 'Maybe her passwords are written down somewhere.'

'Mum...' Liv said in a reproving tone. 'We can't do that.'

'Can't we? Why not? It's in a good cause. We're doing it to help Meg. It's important.'

'Yes, you're right,' Liv agreed. 'Actually, I think her passcodes are saved on her laptop. The problem is, she never leaves her room.'

'Apart from this weekend,' I said triumphantly. 'I'll make sure she doesn't take her laptop to Karina's.'

'Hmm... she'll want it for gaming.'

'Surely she can have a break from it for a couple of nights.'

Liv cast her eyes to the ceiling. 'I thought this weekend was supposed to be about me and Jensen sorting our shit out, not hacking into Meg's computer.' She caught my disappointed expression. 'All right, we'll have a go while you're away.'

'Thanks, darling,' I said. 'It means a lot.'

On Friday, I went to work as usual, having already packed a bag for our two nights away. Dom decided to work from home so that we could set off soon after I returned. I felt excited all day and found it difficult to concentrate. As soon as the shop closed, I ran to the bus stop and hurried back. When I arrived, Meg was standing in the hallway, ready to leave.

'Don't take your laptop,' I said, eyeing the case. 'You won't need it. You'll be too busy to do any gaming. And you could do with a break from the screen, anyway. It's not good for your eyesight.'

She looked anxious, as if the laptop were a comfort blanket that she needed to wrap around her body.

'Karina will think it rude if you've got your head buried in that thing all the time,' I pressed. 'She's really excited about you coming, and wants to spend as much time with you as possible.' I was laying it on a bit thick, but I was desperate for her to leave the laptop behind.

'Okay, I suppose you're right... it *would* do me good.'

I tried not to look too pleased. 'Good call. We'll drop you off at Karina's on the way,' I told her. 'Save you catching the bus.'

'Thanks.' She threw me a gentle smile. 'I hope you and Dad have a nice weekend too,' she added. 'You deserve it.'

Liv and Jensen stood in the doorway waving us off, as if the house was theirs and we'd just been visiting. Jensen had his arm around Liv, and she was snuggling into him. They looked so good together, the perfect young couple. I really hoped they would sort things out between them while we were away.

We delivered Meg to Karina's flat, refused the offer of a cup of tea and got onto the A12 heading for the east coast. The Friday-evening traffic was horrendous, red tail lights snaking ahead as far as the eye could see. We would be very late arriving at the Airbnb, but that was okay. The key was in a security box, so we could check ourselves in when we liked. I'd even found a pub that we could stop at for something to eat on the way.

As we crawled our way to Suffolk, I imagined a totally successful weekend ahead. Liv and Jensen's relationship would get back on track, and they would manage to unmask the bully. Meg would have a fantastic time with her favourite aunt, who would make her feel wanted and special. Meanwhile, Dom and I would reconnect – relaxing in our cosy cottage, sampling the local gastro pubs, taking long walks on the beach... Maybe we'd even have sex.

I glanced across at Dom, who was looking forward, eyes fixed on the busy road. We hadn't made love for about two months, not that I was particularly worried. It just hadn't happened. Dom had always been too tired, and to be fair, I hadn't felt the inclination either. A weekend away was just what we needed to reignite the passion between us. In fact, everyone in the family was going to benefit from a couple of nights apart from each other.

By the time we arrived in Southwold, it was nearly eleven o'clock. Our Airbnb was in the middle of a row of cottages that sat right on the seafront. It was dark, and there was a stiff wind blowing off the cold North Sea. I punched in the code for the key safe and let us in.

The front door opened directly on to the living room, where there were two comfy-looking sofas draped in woven throws,

and a small dining table. Everything had been beautifully deco-
rated in seaside-chic style – soft shades of blue and driftwood
grey with mustard-yellow accents.

Dom stood in the middle of the room, holding our overnight
cases and yawning, while I walked around exclaiming at the
gorgeous wooden shutters and artfully distressed furniture, the
carefully chosen cushions and clever banquette seating in the
breakfast area.

'Oh, look!' I said, pointing at the fireplace. 'There's a log
burner. We can make a fire.'

'Not tonight,' Dom replied. 'I want to go to bed.'

'Ooh, now you're talking!' He shook his head emphatically
at me, so I quickly backtracked. 'It's okay, I was joking. I'm tired
too.'

I found the staircase hiding behind what looked like a
cupboard door. 'The bedroom and bathroom must be up here,' I
said, turning on the light switch. I ran up the narrow stairs,
eager to see where we would be sleeping.

The bedroom looked just as gorgeous as it had in the
photographs – off-white decor with dusky-pink notes. Everything was designed to make the most of the sea view. Double
doors led to a narrow balcony, where there were a couple of
bistro-style chairs.

'Isn't it stunning?' I enthused as Dom brought the bags up.

'Yeah, very nice,' he admitted.

'Obviously it's pitch black out there now, but in the morning, the view is going to be amazing.' I sighed dreamily. 'The
weather forecast is good, too. Lots of sunshine and a gentle
breeze. Perfect.'

Dom went to use the bathroom. I took a couple of photos
and quickly WhatsApped them to Liv and Meg, with a short
message – *We've arrived!! The cottage is FAB-U-LOUS. More
pics tomorrow.* I added, *Missing you like mad!* then deleted it,
because at that moment I wasn't missing them, and I wanted to

be honest. I was glad to be alone with Dom, even though he was being grumpy. I typed a long row of kisses instead and pressed send. Meg immediately gave it a heart, but Liv didn't respond. She often ignored my messages, so that didn't worry me. I assumed she had better things to do than stare at her phone.

I didn't sleep very well, even though the mattress was comfortable and the sheets were crisp and clean. Daylight crept into the room. I was desperate to look at the view, but Dom was still fast asleep and I knew he would be cross if I woke him up with a blast of sunshine.

I got out of bed and went down to the galley kitchen to make myself a cup of tea. Taking my mug into the living room, which was chilly and a little gloomy, I unfastened the shutters and pushed them back against the wall, gasping as sea and sky filled my vision. The tide was high, almost covering the beach. Gulls circled overhead. A small fishing boat bobbed in the water and the grey shape of a tanker was visible on the horizon. I stood at the window, cradling my mug, marvelling at it all. A couple of people passed by, walking their dogs. They made me feel impatient to be outside.

I made a cup of tea and some buttered toast for Dom and took them up on a tray. His eyes were open, but he wasn't really awake.

'You're perky,' he said, as if it was a criticism. 'What time is it?'

'Just before eight.'

He sat up with a groan. 'Too early.'

'Yes, but we mustn't waste the day.' I put the tray on his lap. 'It's looking gorgeous out there. I was thinking,' I went on, opening the shutters. 'We could go for a long walk this morning, to the end of the promenade, then cutting across the creek to the fish sheds. Apparently they sell oysters...'

I stopped short of reminding him that they were supposed to be an aphrodisiac. My jokey reference to sex last night hadn't gone down well and I didn't want to make the same mistake again. But for some reason, the idea of making love kept entering my head. The conditions were perfect, and we had total privacy. Sadly, it seemed to be the last thing on Dom's mind.

I left him to drink his tea and eat his toast while I had a shower. Then, while he was taking his turn in the bathroom, I messaged the girls again on our group chat. *Morning, my lovelies! How are you? All good here. What are your plans for today?* Neither of them responded this time. I pushed aside my disappointment, telling myself it was far too early for them.

We dressed and left the cottage in search of a mug of coffee to accompany us on our walk, finding a quirky café just around the corner. Dom was in a better mood than the previous evening, but he was unusually quiet. The more he retreated into himself, the more I bounced around, blathering away about this and that and sometimes nothing at all. I was making conversation, which I didn't normally have to do with him. It bothered me that he was making so little effort, but I tried not to show it.

We walked the length of the promenade, stopping every now and then to sip our drinks and look out at the great expanse of water.

'It's so awe-inspiring,' I said.

'And bloody freezing.'

'I'd love to live by the sea...'

'No, you wouldn't. You'd miss London too much.'

'I suppose so. And I'd miss the girls... I wonder how they're getting on.' I took out my phone to see if either of them had responded to my morning greeting. There was a thumbs-up from Meg, but still nothing from Liv. I started tapping a brief follow-up message.

'Stop it!' said Dom suddenly. 'You've only been away from them for a few hours. For God's sake, give them a break.'

'I just want to know how they are, that's all.'

'They're fine. Leave them alone. Isn't that what this weekend is supposed to be about? Giving the girls some space?'

'Well, yes... in a way.' I paused. 'But it's also about us.'

'Us? That makes a change,' he scoffed. 'I thought you'd forgotten all about *us*.' He put a sarcastic emphasis on the final word.

'What are you talking about?' I retorted. 'I give you bags of attention, always have. I organised this weekend, didn't I?'

'You're more interested in Liv and Jensen's relationship than your own marriage,' he continued bitterly.

'Of course I'm interested in our marriage, but we don't have any problems. Our marriage is fine. Isn't it?' I left a gap for him to agree, but he didn't fill it. 'At least I thought it was...' Still no response. 'Okay. Maybe it isn't fine. Maybe it's up shit creek, maybe it's hit the rocks, or whatever nautical metaphor you want to apply, seeing as we're at the seaside—'

'Rachel—'

'Sorry if I'm being thick here, but I don't know what you mean!'

'Please stop talking,' he said quietly. 'You're giving me a headache.'

'And you're making me upset,' I bit back. 'I'm worried enough about Meg and Liv, and now you're making me worry about us too. It's not fair. This is supposed to be a romantic weekend!'

'Please, for once in your life, stop trying to orchestrate everything. You can't just decide it's going to be a romantic weekend and – boom! It has to happen in an organic way. It has to evolve.'

'I know that, I'm not stupid,' I said. 'I'm trying my best to be cheerful and affectionate, but it's like trying to hug a stone. You're giving me nothing back, apart from a load of criticism.'

'I can't do this,' he said, swigging back the last of his coffee. 'You enjoy your walk, I'm going back to the cottage.'

'No, Dom – please don't!'

But his back was already turned and he strode off, crushing the paper cup in his clenched fist and tossing it into a bin. As I watched him go, I felt as if *I'd* been crushed too.

I sat down on the nearest bench. I was upset, but I didn't want to cry, not in public. Why had he attacked me like that? He'd seemed so angry. All I'd ever tried to do was look after the people I loved – including him. I didn't understand how he could see that as a failing. I concluded that he was jealous because recently I'd given the girls more attention than I'd given him. But their need had seemed greater than his.

I took out my phone. Still nothing from Liv. Her lack of response was starting to worry me. I decided to give her a call. I put the handset to my ear and stared out to sea while I waited for her to pick up. It rang and rang, eventually cutting me off.

I was at a loss as to what to do next. I no longer wanted to walk to the fish sheds, and there would be no point eating oysters – not by myself. Not that I had any desire to have sex with Dom now. At that moment, all I wanted to do was go straight home. But it was out of the question. We'd promised Liv and Jensen some private time together.

The tide was starting to go out. I walked along the beach for a while, slowly making my way back to the holiday cottage.

Dom was sitting outside on the veranda, staring miserably at the sea.

'Hi,' I said.

'Hi,' he replied without looking at me.

'Was that just a stupid spat, or is there something more serious going on?'

He shook his head. 'It was my fault. I'm sorry.' He heaved a sigh. 'You're a great mum, and wife. We don't deserve you.'

'Well, I don't know about that,' I said, sitting next to him and squeezing his hand.

He squeezed back. 'It was a great idea, coming away, but there's no point if you won't leave the girls alone.'

'Okay. I won't contact either of them for the rest of the weekend.' Dom looked at me sceptically. 'Promise!' I said.

FIFTEEN

Liv lay in bed, feeling that annoying combination of hunger and laziness. It was late morning, way beyond breakfast time. Jensen was still fast asleep, eyelids fluttering, mouth half open. He had stretched out, hemming her in against the wall. If she moved, she might disturb him. She didn't want his Saturday to start yet. Once he was up and about, he would be demanding all her attention, and it would be impossible to think clearly.

For the first time since they'd moved in, they had the whole house to themselves. It had been her mother's idea – of course – to give them space in which to 'sort things out', which was code for making up and falling in love again. Mum wanted everyone around her to be happy – it was virtually an order. Liv had felt under pressure to oblige ever since she was a little girl. *Are you having fun, Livvy?* The answer always had to be yes. If Mum returned home on Sunday to discover they'd split up, she would be bitterly disappointed. But Liv couldn't stay in a relationship that wasn't working simply to please her mother.

Her passion for Jensen had been cooling for weeks – day by day, degree by degree – so gradually that he hadn't noticed. Even she hadn't noticed it at first, putting her reluctance to have sex down to external forces, such as her parents sleeping on the floor below, or feeling stressed about job applications. When they'd been living together in Newcastle, they'd made love almost every day, but now it was the exception rather than the rule. With no excuses for refusing him, this weekend was a test of her true desire.

They'd made love last night – after consuming nearly two bottles of red from her father's wine club collection. The alcohol had helped. Liv had done her utmost to remain in the moment, but her mind had kept wandering into dangerous territory in which she was single and living in Sofia's apartment.

She was thinking about it now. It was her secret obsession. She'd visited Sofia just once, last week, on her way back from a meeting with a recruitment agency, and had been shocked by how cool the location was – just off the Portobello Road, in the heart of Notting Hill. The apartment was on the second floor of a double-fronted Georgian house. Sofia had served Earl Grey tea in proper china cups and melt-in-the-mouth macarons from her local patisserie.

She'd announced that she was almost definitely going travelling in the new year and would love it if Liv could look after the place in her absence. She'd shown her the bedroom where she would stay. It was extremely small, with a narrow single bed more suitable for a child than an adult. Everything was white – walls, flooring, furry rug, bed and bedding, fitted wardrobe, window blinds.

'It's my safe space,' she explained. 'This is where I come when everything gets too much.'

Liv couldn't imagine what troubles Sofia could possibly need to escape from – she seemed to have everything – but she had said that it looked very peaceful, like sleeping inside a cloud.

Sofia had kept the door to her own bedroom closed, but gave Liv a tour of the rest of the apartment, where there was a lot more colour and character. Dark blues and dead, flat greys mixed with coral-pink accents and sudden bursts of tangerine. Abstract art, all originals, graced the walls. The bathrooms were sumptuous, and the kitchen was so pristine and perfect it looked like a feature in a luxury style magazine.

'And this belongs entirely to you?' Liv had marvelled.

'Yup,' Sofia had answered casually, as if it were no big deal to be in her early twenties and own an apartment in one of the most expensive parts of London. 'Do you like it?'

'Oh my God, I love it.' Liv had felt overwhelmed. 'And you'd really let me stay here when you go away?'

'Yes!' Sofia had smiled. 'But only if you don't bring that rubbish boyfriend with you.'

Liv desperately wanted to live in the apartment, but she wasn't sure she was prepared to pay the price that Sofia was demanding. It was a dilemma that sat heavily on her chest. She slightly regretted having confided so fully in Sofia about her troubled relationship. They'd had dozens of long text exchanges and secret phone conversations mainly held while Jensen was out running, or downstairs hoovering – 'sucking up the dust and sucking up to your mum', as Sofia had quipped. Her new friend, who seemed to have rapidly become her best friend, was not backward in coming forward with her opinions.

'Jensen's a user,' she pronounced. 'He's not in love with you, he's in love with your family, or rather your mother, which – no disrespect – is gross.'

She had sent Liv links to various blog posts with apocalyptic titles such as 'When It's Over It's Over', 'How to Leave a Toxic Relationship' and 'Telling Him Your Love is Dead'. Liv had read them in the toilet, skimming through the advice and wondering just how much of it really applied. Jensen wasn't a bad person. Up until they moved in, they'd had a great relationship. She still loved him. True, it had been hard to locate that love recently, but she felt it was there, an underwatered plant that had been left in the dark, wilting but still alive. All it needed was the right kind of care and it would flourish again. But did she *want* it to flourish? If she asked Sofia for her opinion, she'd tell her to kill it off.

'What are you thinking about?' Jensen asked. He'd woken without her noticing and was gazing intently into her eyes.

She started guiltily. 'Oh, nothing.'

'I've been watching you. You've been miles away.'

'Have I? Sorry.'

'Your head is full of secret thoughts,' he said, stroking her arm. 'I can always tell. What are they? What's going on? Talk to me, Liv.'

She hesitated before replying. Maybe this was the right moment. He'd asked, so she might as well tell him.

'Okay then.' She sat up, drawing her knees to her chest and hugging them close. 'This isn't working.'

He looked confused. 'What isn't?'

'Us. Living here. We need to move out. As soon as possible. Or...' She ground to a halt, not wanting to say the words out loud.

'How can we move out?' he said, putting his arms behind his head and staring up at the ceiling. 'It's impossible. We can't afford it.'

'I know that, but we have to find a way. Get work in a call centre, or a bar. Borrow money. Something. I can't go on like this.'

'You're talking crap,' he replied scathingly. 'We have a really good deal here. Your mum is amazing, she looks after us so well and—'

'Can't you see? That's the problem!' Liv retorted. 'I'm not a child. I don't want to be looked after by my mother.'

'At least you've got one,' he said bitterly. 'I *have* to look after myself, I've no choice. You're lucky to have parents, and a comfortable home, with free food and everything on tap, but you take it for granted. It's pathetic. You think you're badly off, but your problems are nothing compared to what I've been through.'

She sighed. 'Here we go again...'

'Oh, sorry if I'm boring you with my loss.'

'Look, I know it was really bad, but you can't keep using it every time we have a row, like it's a Get Out of Jail Free card. I'm not talking about the past, Jensen, I'm talking about now, you and me.'

'We're good,' he insisted, sitting up. 'Everything's fine.'

'It's not fine.'

He attempted a cheeky grin. 'Okay, we haven't had much sex recently, but that's easily fixed. It's what this weekend's all about, eh? Reconnecting.'

'It's not just the sex,' she muttered. 'It's more fundamental than that. We need our own place.'

'We really don't, Liv. It'll be shit, we'll be ripped off by some evil landlord and there'll be no money left for fun stuff. Forget about renting, make the most of the situation we've got here.'

'It's not about the money – it's about being independent.'

'Who cares about that? Come on, we're supposed to be having a romantic weekend, just the two of us.' He started to paw her, hoping perhaps to distract her with another bout of lovemaking.

'Please. Leave me alone.' It was impossible to have this kind of conversation naked. She got out of bed and slipped on her dressing gown. 'Everything's not fine for me,' she said. 'I've had enough. I knew it was a bad idea coming here and I've been proved right. It's spoilt everything, it's spoilt *us*. If you refuse to find somewhere with me, I'll have to look on my own.'

He frowned at her disbelievingly. 'Who's going to rent to you? You don't have a job any more than I do.'

'No, but I could probably stay with someone until—'

'Like who?'

'It doesn't matter,' she said, annoyed with herself for letting on that she had another option – potentially, anyway.

'Yes it does. Who would you stay with? Give me a name.'

'Nobody. Forget it.' She sat down in the corner chair, as far away from him as possible. His temper was rising, she could feel the heat from across the room.

'You've met someone else, haven't you?' he said. 'I've seen you texting away when you think I'm not looking. Going off on your own, pretending to go shopping and coming back empty-handed, smelling like a brewery. Who is it? Is it someone I know? Where did you meet him?'

'There's nobody else,' Liv insisted.

'I don't believe you. You're lying to me.' He reached for her phone, which was lying next to him on the bedside table.

'Hey! What are you doing?'

He picked it up and made several unsuccessful attempts to get in. 'You've changed your PIN.'

'So?' She'd done it a few days ago, anxious that he might read her moany exchanges with Sofia.

'Why?'

'Just good practice, that's all. For security.'

'What's the new one?'

She demurred. 'It's private.'

'Not from me, it's not. What is it?'

'I'm not telling you.'

'Why not?'

'Because it's my phone and I didn't say you could look at it.'

'Let me guess. Your birthday?' He punched in the digits, but it didn't work. 'My birthday then.' He tried again. 'No? Okay... Let's try Meg's. What is it now? October something...'

'Give it back,' she demanded, rising and walking over.

He jumped out of bed and opened the window. 'If you don't tell me your PIN, I'll throw it out.'

'Stop being such a dick! Give it back right now, or...' She

hesitated, trying to think of a threat she was prepared to carry through.

He tossed the handset in her direction, and it fell at her feet. 'Have it. I don't want to read your smutty little messages anyway. If you're cheating on me, just tell me straight.'

She snatched it up. 'Of course I'm not cheating on you.'

'Then what's going on?'

'Nothing. Honestly. I'm sorry if you've smelt alcohol on my breath. I was feeling really stressed about the job situation and went into a bar by myself, had a couple of glasses of wine to calm my nerves.'

'Really? You're sure? You weren't with anyone?'

'No,' she lied.

'Promise?'

'Promise. I'd never do something like that.'

'So everything's cool between us?' he persisted. 'You swear?'

There was a beat. She retied the belt of her silky dressing gown, pulling it more tightly across her body. 'There's nobody else,' she said after a thoughtful pause. 'But that doesn't mean everything's perfect.'

'It's perfect for me.'

'But not for me. You have to respect that, Jensen. If one person is unhappy in a relationship, that means there's a problem.'

She looked around. This had been her teenage bedroom, where she'd done her schoolwork, experimented with clothes and make-up, dreamt about boys she fancied, or careers she might follow... It had been a springboard for so many of her plans, a gateway to the future. Now it felt like a prison.

'I'm sorry,' she went on. 'I know you love living here, and that it's really cheap, and that we'll struggle to get anywhere a tenth as nice, but I don't want to be here. I want to be free, grown up. It's non-negotiable, Jensen. We have to move out.'

'No way. Not doing it.' He set his jaw determinedly.

There was a long silence. She didn't know how the conversation had ended up here – it hadn't been planned – but if felt like they'd reached the point of no return. Suddenly she knew what she wanted to say.

She drew in a breath. 'In that case, I'm sorry, and I'm really sad about this, but... you give me no choice. It's over between us.'

'No it's not,' he snapped dismissively. 'Don't be so fucking stupid. We love each other. How can it be over?'

'Because I've just said it is.'

'And I've just said it's not!'

What was wrong with him? He didn't seem to get it. She tried again. 'I don't want to be in a relationship with you any more, Jensen. And I don't want to live here either. I'm moving out whether you like it or not. Which means you'll have to leave too.'

'No it doesn't.'

He was testing her patience. 'Of course it does. Think about it. You can't carry on living here once we've split up.'

'Yes I can,' he insisted. 'This is my home. I'm one of the family now.'

'Not really. Not once you stop being my boyfriend.'

'Don't even think about splitting up with me. I won't allow it. We're solid as a rock, together for ever, come what may.' He inhaled deeply, gathering himself. 'Now shut up, Liv, and come back to bed.'

'What?! Are you fucking crazy? You think I'm going to have sex with you when I've just told you it's over?'

'It's not over,' he repeated.

She felt breathless. What part of it didn't he understand? He was acting as if he were in charge, as if he could force her to stay. His eyes were glittering manically. For the first time in their relationship, she felt frightened of him.

'I'm going out,' she said, picking up yesterday's clothes off the floor and starting to get dressed. 'I don't want you here when I get back.'

He walked towards her, grabbing her by the shoulders, slamming her against the wardrobe door. 'You're not going anywhere,' he growled. 'And neither am I.'

SIXTEEN

The atmosphere between me and Dom completely changed after the row. It was as if a storm had broken and cleared the air. We both felt lighter and freer. I kept my phone in my bag and didn't take it out once all afternoon, not even to check the time.

After lunch in a café – a very pricey crab sandwich with red cabbage coleslaw – we walked around the town with its pastel-painted cottages and elegant Victorian houses. We went to the end of the pier, visiting the tiny museum, browsing in gift shops, buying fudge, then returned to the cottage for a rest. Dom dozed off upstairs while I flicked through the books that had been left for us on the coffee table.

That evening, we found a quirky gastro pub. There were no oysters on the menu, but we drank enough alcohol – a pint of the local beer followed by a bottle of good wine – to loosen our inhibitions and increase our attraction for each other. After dinner, we took the long way back to the cottage, via the prome-nade and the seemingly endless row of beach huts, several of them shut up for the winter. We walked hand in hand, leaning into each other, more out of affection than drunkenness, although we were quite pissed. We paused to look back at the view of the town. It looked so cosy, picture-book perfect. The pier was illuminated, and a bright beam of light was coming from the inland lighthouse.

Dom took me in his arms and kissed me hard. It made me feel like a teenager, unafraid to snog in public.

'Easy, tiger,' I joked. 'Let's wait until we get back.'

The heating had already come on when we arrived at the cottage. We didn't bother with the log burner, but went straight upstairs, falling onto the bed, wrapped in each other's arms. I'd imagined Dom ripping my clothes off and was prepared for riotous passion, but he was in no hurry. Our lovemaking was slow, tender and beautiful. We made up for two months of abstinence in one night. When we finally let each other go, drowsy and exhausted, I felt we were at peace, even though I'd barely realised that we'd been at war.

We both slept well and woke late. Morning sunlight seeped between the shutter slats, gently rousing us. Unfortunately, we had to be out of the cottage by 10 a.m., which meant we had to rush breakfast. I wasn't ready to leave yet, so we put our bags in the car and then went for another walk, taking the route that we had started on the day before. This time we made it all the way to the harbour, wandering around the boatyards and finally stopping off at the fish sheds for utterly delicious fish and chips.

I'd kept my promise. I hadn't contacted the girls, and – a little surprisingly – they hadn't been in touch either. For most of the weekend, I'd felt fine about it, but now the trip was almost at an end, I started to think about them again. I wondered whether Liv and Jensen had settled their differences, and whether they'd had any luck identifying Meg's troll. I hoped Meg had had a fun time with Karina and that she'd feel strong enough to go to school on Monday. I kept my thoughts to myself, however, not wanting to break the romantic spell with Dom.

We set off in the middle of the afternoon, our stomachs heavy with overeating. The journey back felt quicker, although the traffic was just as bad. Our conversation flowed more easily. I felt good and was eager to see my girls.

We stopped off at Karina's flat to pick Meg up. She greeted us with a smiling face, waving beautifully manicured fingernails before our eyes.

'Karina took me for a pamper day,' she explained. 'I had a manicure, pedicure and hot stone massage. It was incredible. So-ooo relaxing!'

'Wow, that was very generous,' I remarked, mouthing a thank you to Karina.

'Think of it as an extra birthday present,' she said.

'I'm glad I didn't take the laptop, Mum,' Meg said in the car on the way home. 'It did me good to have a break from gaming.'

'For sure,' I replied. 'You probably noticed that I had a bit of a digital detox too. From Saturday lunchtime I didn't use my phone once.'

'Yeah, I was waiting for pics, but none came. I thought maybe you'd run out of battery and forgotten your charger.'

'No, Mum resisted the temptation,' said Dom. 'She did really well.'

We were home. Dom drew the car onto the driveway and we bowled out. I rushed inside, eager to see Liv and Jensen, but the house was cold and quiet. I sensed they weren't in, but I called out for them just in case. Predictably, there was no answer.

Meg was also disappointed not to see her sister. 'Why did they have to go out?' she moaned.

'They've probably gone for a walk, or to see a film, or shopping, or...' I ran out of possibilities. 'Anyway, I'm sure they'll be home soon.'

'I'll message her, tell her to get her arse back here fast,' said Meg, going upstairs to her room.

Dom brought our bags in. I unpacked in our bedroom, then brought the washing downstairs. The kitchen was horribly untidy – crumbs on the chopping board, stains on the worktop, dirty mugs and dishes next to the sink. They hadn't even bothered to put the dishwasher on. I was surprised, because although Liv was messy, Jensen was usually very good at clearing up. I made a mental note to have a word with Liv about it later.

Although we'd eaten a good lunch, Dom and I were hungry. Meg claimed she was too full of cake to want anything else, so I cooked a cheese omelette, which we ate in front of Sunday-evening television. I tried to concentrate on the drama, but my mind kept wandering. I couldn't understand why Liv and Jensen hadn't come home. Liv hadn't replied to her sister's message either, which was odd.

'It's no good,' I said to Dom once the ten o'clock news came on. 'I *have* to call her.'

He laid a restraining hand on my arm. 'No you don't. Leave her alone.'

'But what if something's gone wrong?'

'Nothing's gone wrong. They're out. Having a life,' he said. 'They're in their twenties. You can't treat them like teenagers.'

'I know.' I turned away. 'I just have this strange feeling...' I got up from the sofa and headed out of the room.

'Where are you going?'

'I just want to check the flatlet, in case Liv left a note.'

'Why would she leave a note?' he called after me as I climbed the stairs.

I had hardly ventured up to the top floor since Liv and Jensen had moved in, trying to give them a sense of privacy and ownership of their space. I was shocked when I saw how chaotic it was. Drawers and cupboards were open, their contents lying all over the floor. Jensen's desk chair had been turned over. His zombie shop dummy was lying on its side, one arm wrenched off. Books and ornaments had been swept from the shelves. A broken vase – still full of flowers – was lying in a wet patch on the carpet. Had there been a fight?

I shut the door and went back down again, feeling extremely worried.

'Well? Any note?' asked Dom as I came back into the sitting room.

'No, but it's like a bomb's hit it up there.' I went to my handbag and pulled out my mobile. 'Sorry, I know I promised I wouldn't, but the weekend's virtually over and I need to talk to Liv.'

'Why?'

'Because something's wrong, Dom. I feel it in my gut.'

I tried her number, but she didn't pick up. Next I tried calling Jensen, but there was no reply from him either. By now it was late, and we all wanted to go to bed. Dom and I had work in the morning, and Meg had school. I knew I wouldn't be able to sleep until I knew that Liv was okay.

I stayed up for as long as I could manage. Dom had already gone upstairs, saying I was mad. It was threatening to spoil the lovely weekend we'd had. Finally I succumbed to tiredness and followed him to bed. We turned the lights out, but I couldn't drop off. Anxiety was coursing through my veins, though I couldn't understand why. Liv and Jensen had stayed out late many times before and it hadn't bothered me one bit. Eventually I fell into a light, troubled sleep, waking up every half an hour or so to listen for evidence that they'd returned home. But the house was eerily silent.

At around two in the morning, I heard the front door opening and closing.

'They're back!' I hissed, nudging Dom awake.

'Good,' he groaned, turning over.

I got out of bed, put on my dressing gown and left the room, finding Meg on the landing, fully clothed.

'What are you doing, still up?' I asked.

'Waiting for Liv, of course.'

We went downstairs. The hallway was empty, but a light was on in the kitchen. We followed it.

Jensen was at the sink, bending forward, splashing his face under the tap.

'Hi,' I said quietly, not wanting to make him jump.

He turned round, drops of water running down his cheeks. His hair was tangled, his T-shirt and jeans were dirty and there was mud on his trainers.

'Rachel!' He looked startled. 'You too, Meg. Sorry. Did I wake you?'

'I wasn't asleep,' she replied tersely.

I looked around. 'Where's Liv?'

He dried his face with the hand towel. 'She's, um... gone to stay with a friend.'

'What?'

'Yeah. Didn't she let you know?'

I shook my head. 'We haven't heard from her all weekend. She's not answered any of our messages or picked up any of our calls.'

'No? Guess she didn't feel like talking. She, um... needed to get away.'

'From what?'

'You know... the situation.'

I instantly thought of the state of their bedroom. The clothes strewn across the floor, the overturned furniture, the broken vase. It made me feel uneasy.

'I went to see if you were in your room,' I told him. 'It's a real mess up there. To be honest, it looked like there'd been a fight.'

'Nah, that's just me being untidy.'

I looked at him disbelievingly. 'What happened, Jensen?'

'Nothing.'

'No way would Liv just leave for no reason,' said Meg.

'We had a slight row, that's all… Not even a row, more of a deep chat. Liv got a bit upset. Decided she'd had enough – said she was leaving. I tried to get her to stay. I offered to go instead, but she insisted. I suppose it made sense. I don't know anyone in London.'

'What had she had enough of?' I asked. 'The relationship?'

He laughed. 'No! Of arguing. We haven't split up or anything. She's just taking some time out. She'll be back in a few days.'

'I see…' He was behaving like it was no big deal, but I still sensed something was wrong. 'And who's this friend she's gone to stay with?'

'Dunno. She wouldn't tell me. A school friend?'

I tried to think of who that might be. Three years ago, Liv's friends had scattered to different universities all over the country, and I wasn't sure which, if any of them, had come back. Her best friend had gone to Australia. I couldn't think of anyone else she would turn to at short notice. Apart from Karina, and she definitely hadn't gone there.

'When did she leave?' I asked.

'Not sure. She waited until I'd fallen asleep, so around midnight on Saturday, I guess.'

'That was late.'

'Yeah, I know,' he agreed, rubbing his eyes tiredly.

'Has she been in touch with you since?'

'No. But that doesn't surprise me. She told me not to contact her. I'm trying to respect that.'

I felt hurt. It was understandable that Liv might not want to speak to Jensen, but why was she giving me the silent treatment?

'So,' said Meg, 'what's with all the mud?'

He looked down at his clothes and blushed. 'I needed to clear my head, so I went for a walk in Epping Forest.'

'Till two o'clock in the morning?'

'Yeah! I had no idea it was so massive. Got totally lost... it was dark, I fell over a couple of times. Ended up walking most of the way back.' He let out a loud yawn. 'Sorry. I'm knackered. Need to sleep.' He shuffled past me and started climbing the stairs.

'As soon as you hear from Liv, let me know, okay?' I called after him.

'Sure.' He glanced back at me. 'Don't worry about her. She's fine.' He went up to their room, shutting the door behind him.

But I *was* worried about her. She and Jensen must have had a serious row for her to walk out in the middle of the night. I had a feeling he wasn't telling us the whole truth. I grabbed my phone and tried calling her again, but as before, it went straight to voicemail. Frustrated, I sent her a text.

Just spoken to Jensen. Sorry the weekend didn't go too well. Where are you? If you don't want to speak now, that's okay. Just let me know you're all right. Love you xxx

I sat up for the rest of the night, waiting, but she didn't reply.

SEVENTEEN

I slept – or attempted to sleep – with my phone next to my bed, so that I wouldn't miss any messages or calls from Liv. It pinged all night with various irrelevant notifications, but there wasn't a peep from my daughter. In the small hours, Dom told me to 'turn the bloody thing off'.

'I'm sure she's okay,' he reassured me. 'She's probably sound asleep right now. Unlike us.' I suspected he was right, but I couldn't bear the thought of not being instantly available if she needed me. I turned down the volume and put the phone under my pillow instead, hoping I would feel any vibrations if she got in touch. Sadly, she didn't.

Morning dawned. I got up early and went down to the kitchen. While I was making myself a cup of tea, I tried to picture Liv. Where was she now and how was she feeling? Who was she with?

As I sat in the conservatory, watching a squirrel run along the top of the garden fence, I realised that I knew very little about the people she might confide in, or turn to in times of trouble. When she was a baby, I was her whole life. She wouldn't have survived without me. But as she'd grown, and become more independent, I'd been pushed further and further to the edge of her circle. She was still at the centre of *my* life, though, and her lack of contact was hurting me.

'There you are! Where's my tea?' said Dom, entering the conservatory in his dressing gown. 'I've been waiting ages.'

'Sorry,' I replied. 'I thought it was too early. I've been awake since five.'

He flicked the kettle back on and put a tea bag in a mug. 'Has she been in touch?'

I checked my phone again, just in case. 'No, not a word. She hasn't read any of my messages either. There are no blue ticks against any of them, which is odd.'

'She probably switched off so Jensen couldn't call her. I'm sure there's nothing to worry about.' Dom added a spot of milk and picked up his mug. 'Right. I need to get ready for work. I'm going to be back late tonight, sorry.'

I groaned. 'But I need you here.'

'Sorry. Got some big clients flying in. I have to take them to dinner. Can't be helped. Any news, just message me.' He disappeared upstairs to get dressed.

I went to wake Meg. She was buried under her duvet, full of sleep.

'Time to get up,' I said breezily. 'Shall I open the curtains?' She swore in response. I drew them back all the same, letting light into the room. While I waited for her to emerge, I looked around at the mess. Her laptop was sitting on her desk, its lid closed. I remembered that Jensen had promised to try and hack into Meg's social media accounts to discover who was sending her the bullying messages. In all the kerfuffle last night, I'd forgotten to ask him if he'd had any success.

'Come on, sweetie,' I said, gently prodding the mound on her bed.

She poked her head out, like an animal creeping out of its den. 'Is Liv back?' she asked in a fuzzy voice.

'Not yet. Have you heard from her?'

'No.' She sat up. Her hair was tousled and her skin was blotchy. 'I've sent her loads of messages, but she hasn't even read them.'

'Same here.'

'Jensen was weird last night, don't you think?'

'Weird? In what way?'

'He was wired. His eyes were all starey, like he'd taken something. And what was he doing walking in Epping Forest until gone midnight? Nobody does that.'

'I know what you mean,' I replied, having had the same thoughts myself. 'But it's easy to get lost if you don't know the area.'

'Do you think Liv's all right, Mum?'

'Of course!' I tried to sound reassuring as I picked up her dirty clothes and cradled them in my arms. 'She and Jensen just had a little falling-out, that's all. I expect she'll come home today and all will be forgiven.'

'Hmm... You don't want them to split up, do you?'

'I want what's right for them,' I said guardedly.

'You love Jensen. You think he's rizz.'

'I don't even know what that means.'

'You know. Prince Charming.' She rubbed her fingers together. 'And he's minted.'

'He's not,' I insisted. 'His parents were well-off, but they only left debts.'

'Why isn't he in touch with the rest of his family? It's a bit sus.'

'Please talk properly, Meg.'

She sighed and cast her eyes to the ceiling. 'He's got you totally under his spell.'

'No, he hasn't. That's a silly thing to say. Come on, we don't have time for this. I've got to get to work, and *you*' – I tugged at the duvet – 'need to get up and go to school.'

· · ·

It was Monday, and the boutique was very quiet. I would rather have been busy, as it would have distracted me from the endless thoughts that jostled for attention in my head. Despite dismissing Meg's fears, I was a little worried. Where was Liv? Why wasn't she answering my messages? We weren't supposed to use our phones at work, but I couldn't stop myself from checking mine whenever there were no customers.

'Rachel! What's wrong with you today?' Beverley asked when she caught me out for the third or fourth time. 'We don't do mobiles here. You're like a teenager, can't keep off the thing.'

'Sorry,' I said, putting it away. 'I'm waiting to hear from my daughter, that's all.'

'Oh. Is everything okay?'

'Yes! At least, I think so... *hope* so. She had a row with her boyfriend and walked out on him...' I stopped, seeing her irritated expression. 'Sorry, you don't need to know that.'

'This is not Primark,' she clipped. 'We pride ourselves on giving our customers individual full attention.'

'Yes. And I always do,' I replied curtly.

'There are lots of women who would kill to have this job,' Beverley said, like she really believed it.

I couldn't wait for the day to end. The bus ride home seemed interminable. As soon as I got home, I rushed upstairs to the flatlet and knocked on the door.

'Liv? Are you there?'

Jensen opened it. I looked over his shoulder, hoping to see my daughter sitting on the bed, smiling sheepishly, but the room looked strangely bare. Jensen had cleared up the mess and hoovered the carpet.

'No, she hasn't come back,' he said, answering the question before I'd asked it. 'I haven't heard from her either. Have you?'

'Not a word... I hope she's all right.'

'Why wouldn't she be?' He patted my arm consolingly. 'Don't worry about her, Rachel. She'll come home when she's ready. We just have to be patient.'

'I know, but I'm not very good at it.' I made to go. 'Oh, by the way, did you, er... you know...' I dropped my voice. 'Did you manage to break into Meg's laptop?'

He gasped. 'Sorry! It completely went out of my head.'

'Never mind,' I said, disappointed.

'I'll try as soon as I get the chance.'

'Thanks. Right, better get on.' I turned to descend the stairs.

He called after me. 'Do you want some help with the evening meal?'

'That's kind of you, but no, I'll be fine. Dinner in about an hour, okay?'

'Great. If you need me for anything, just shout.'

I left Jensen and went to see if Meg was in her room. She was sitting in front of her computer, gaming away, her face lit by the yellowish glow of the screen.

'Have you heard from Liv?' I asked.

She slipped off her headphones. 'Nope.'

'Nor have I... or Jensen. I'm sure she'll get in touch soon,' I added, trying to inject some confidence into my voice. 'How was school?'

'Don't want to talk about it.' She turned back to the laptop.

There was no point pressuring Meg into talking, so I went to the kitchen and started preparing the evening meal. But my heart wasn't in it. With Liv absent and Dom out entertaining clients, Meg, Jensen and I were going to make a strange trio at the dinner table.

About ten minutes later, my phone bleeped. I put down the vegetable peeler and picked it up. At last! Liv had sent me a text. Relief rushed through me as I read her message.

Hi, Mum. Sorry about not being in touch. Forgot to take my charger and my phone died. Doh! Don't worry about me. I'm fine. Staying with a friend. I don't want to talk to ANYONE right now, so please don't call. I need some space. Xx

I ran up the stairs. 'I've just had a text from Liv!' I cried.

Meg opened her bedroom door. 'Is she all right?'

'I think so.'

'What does she say?'

I handed her the phone so she could read the message herself.

'Why doesn't she want to talk to us?' she asked.

'I don't know... maybe she doesn't feel up to it. The main thing is, she's safe.'

Jensen came out of his room too and joined us on the landing. 'Can I read it?' Meg stuck the phone under his nose. 'See?' he said. 'I told you there was nothing to worry about. It's all going to be fine. She'll be home tomorrow.'

'Hmm... she doesn't say that,' I ventured. 'In fact, it sounds like she might be staying with her friend for a while.'

Meg and Jensen went back to their respective rooms. I went back downstairs, feeling relieved, but also troubled. She hadn't explained anything. I sent her a text.

Hi, Liv. Thanks for your message. I'm glad you're okay – tbh, I WAS starting to worry. Who are you staying with? And what's happening with you and Jensen? Have you split up? Do you want us to ask him to leave? Please come home soon. Love, Mum xxx

I tried to return to the cooking, but I couldn't concentrate. I checked my mobile every few minutes. My ears were on stalks, waiting for the sound of the ringtone or the ping of an incoming text, but there was no response from her at all. Not that evening, or the following day.

By Thursday, I was feeling frustrated. I still didn't know who she was staying with and was worried that she might be feeling depressed. I didn't want to judge, I just wanted to help. But she seemed to have her phone turned permanently off. I respected her right to privacy, but it left us with an awkward situation at home. If Liv and Jensen's relationship was over, he needed to find somewhere else to live.

Surprisingly, he didn't appear to share our concerns. 'I've got a plan,' he told me. 'Liv's been nagging me for ages about finding work. I was holding out for the perfect job, but I can't wait any longer. Anything will do. I want to show her I'm serious about us getting a place together.'

The following day he went for a walk along the high street and came back with a zero-hours contract working as a potboy in our local pub, the George. He immediately started working twelve-hour shifts, starting at noon and ending at midnight, although he rarely got back before 2 a.m.

Dom could no longer complain that Jensen was lazing around, but he still wasn't happy. 'He can't stay here,' he said that evening while we were sitting in front of the TV. 'It makes no sense. Liv's given him the heave-ho—'

'We don't know that for sure.'

'Come on, it's obvious! It's over, dead in the water. He needs to leave so she can come back home.'

'She hasn't actually said that,' I replied carefully. 'She hasn't said *anything*. It's really tricky...'

'He can't live here if she's living somewhere else. If you won't tell him to go, I will.'

'No, no, leave it with me,' I replied, dreading how I was going to broach such a sensitive subject.

Now that Jensen was working shifts, we hardly saw each other. He was still asleep when I left the house for work and came back long after I'd gone to bed. The following Wednesday – my day off – was my first chance for a chat.

'How's the job going?' I asked when he finally emerged for breakfast at just gone eleven.

'Really well, thanks,' he said. 'I've never done bar work

before. It's tough. But I'm taking every shift they offer me so I can save up. Liv's going to be so proud of me.'

I winced inwardly. 'Have you told her about the job?'

'No. I want it to be a surprise. For when she comes home.'

'Has she said anything about that?'

'No,' he sighed. 'We're still on a break. No contact allowed – no calls, texts, emails, nothing.'

'Hmm... It's turning into quite a long break, isn't it?' He shrugged. 'Don't you think, given she hasn't been in touch, that it might actually be over?'

'No.' His face had an innocent expression. I couldn't tell whether it was genuine.

'The thing is,' I resumed, 'we want Liv to come home as soon as possible. She belongs with her family, you know? But if *you're* living here—'

He cut in. 'You've got it wrong. This isn't about me and Liv. We're fine. It's about living with you guys. Whatever happens, she's not coming home. Ever. She hates it here.'

It was as if he'd punched me in the gut. '*Hates* it? What do you mean?'

'She never wanted to move in in the first place. I persuaded her. She feels like she's regressing, becoming a child again. She can't stand the way you baby her. That's what the row was about. She wanted to leave. I wanted to stay.'

'I see...' I sank into my own thoughts for a few moments. Did Liv really think I babied her? I knew she got irritated with me sometimes, but I'd always believed that deep down, she'd enjoyed being made a fuss of.

'Sorry,' he said. 'But it's the truth. That's why Liv doesn't want to talk to you. She wants to break free. I think she's wrong. She doesn't know how lucky she is. You're amazing parents.'

I felt utterly wrong-footed, didn't know what to say. 'This is so difficult,' I began. 'We've loved having you around these past few months, you've been a joy, so helpful and...' I swallowed.

'But if Liv doesn't want to live here any more, then you can't either. Regardless of whether the two of you are still together. It doesn't work.'

He turned to me, tears welling in his eyes. 'You mean you want me to move out?'

'Well, yes.'

'But I've got nowhere else to go, no family to turn to. I'm on my own. And I've only just started this job...'

'We're not going to throw you out onto the street. You can stay here until you find somewhere else.' I didn't know whether Dom would agree, but what else could I say? Jensen was virtually in tears. I felt so sorry for him.

'Okay,' he mumbled. 'I'll start looking.'

'Thanks. I really appreciate it.'

'I just need to save some dosh. If Liv gets a job too, that'll be easier. Much cheaper if we're living together.'

I thought he was deluded about Liv, but I didn't want to crush him any more than I had already. 'Yes,' I said. 'I think it's for the best.'

EIGHTEEN

Hey Meg,

I heard your sad news. Big Sis has run away and left you all on your own with Mummy and Daddy. Aww, poor you... You must miss her so much.

She's not missing YOU, though. You were the main reason she left. She can't stand the sight of you. Or your smell. You stink! That's why she never asked you to go out with her. It was just too embarrassing being seen with such a fat, smelly, ugly person.

And you're so fucking boring, too. You literally have nothing interesting to say about anything. It's like, OMG, Megan Matthews is coming this way, yawn, yawn... Pretend you haven't seen her.

That's why you have no friends. No real friends. Nobody you can trust.

Mummy and Daddy don't like you much either. Liv is their favourite. They'd much rather you left, and she came back.

I'm going to be paying you another visit very soon. Does that scare you? Hope so. It's gonna be massive. The whole street's going to know just how I feel about you.

And this time, do as you're told.

NINETEEN

The next morning, Dom came downstairs carrying a small suitcase.

'What's that for?' I asked.

He gave me a weary look. 'I'm going to Dubai today, aren't I?'

'Dubai? But you can't!'

'I *have* to go. It's work.'

I felt panic rising within me. 'But what about Liv? We haven't heard from her in over a week. We don't know where she is or who she's staying with.'

'I'm sure she's fine.'

'How can you say that? We don't know what's going on. What if she's having a breakdown? What if she calls us in the middle of the night and asks us to come and pick her up?'

He sighed. 'Please stop catastrophising. It doesn't help anyone, least of all you.'

'You never said you were going to Dubai,' I added after a beat.

'I *did*, Rachel.'

'No you didn't. I would have remembered.'

'I told you about ten days ago. You were obviously too worried about Liv to take it on board.'

'Hmm...' I didn't believe him. 'How long for?'

'A week.'

'A whole week?'

'Yes, a whole week. I'll be back next Friday. Unless the negotiations get stuck, in which case they'll make me stay another day at least.'

'I wish you didn't have to go. It feels like the whole family's under attack – first it was the birthday cake, then the rubbish all over the garden, then the car was keyed. Meg's shutting herself in her room again, Liv's run away... I need you here.'

'I'm sorry. It can't be helped.'

'Sometimes I feel like I'm a single parent.'

'I can't have this conversation now. Got to get to the airport. All being well, I'll see you next Friday.' He nodded upwards in the direction of the flatlet. 'With a bit of luck, our house guest will have moved out by then.'

'I doubt it,' I whispered. 'He needs to find somewhere to go first.'

'Is he actually looking?'

'I don't know. I *think* so. We've got to give him time, Dom.'

'I suppose so.'

Once Dom had left, I put the breakfast things away, then went back upstairs to get ready for work. My spirits were low, and I didn't feel like making any effort with clothes or make-up. Unfortunately, I was expected to look at least as smart as our smartest customer.

We were busy at the boutique, mainly with women looking for clothes for Christmas parties. The window had been dressed in sparkly tops and velvet trousers, and this week's colour theme was red, green and black. I couldn't even *think* about Christmas yet. I had no idea who might be with us or how we were going to celebrate. Everyday life seemed difficult enough. I felt as if I was holding the entire weight of the family in my hands. I was desperate to put it down, even if just for one day, but there was nobody to pass it on to.

Fortunately, I was distracted by my customers. I spent the morning enthusing about sequinned jumpers and silky skirts, then made a lunchtime escape to a nearby café. I only had half an hour in which to grab a toastie and a coffee. As soon as I sat down, I took out my phone and switched it back on, hoping that Liv had been in touch. She hadn't. I opened WhatsApp and typed her yet another message.

Hi. What is going on, Liv? We miss you so much. I thought you should know that we've asked Jensen to move out. Is that okay with you? If you don't want him to go, let me know. Are you in London? It would be good to meet. Or at least call me. I need to hear your voice. Love you, Mum xx

I ate my sandwich and drank my coffee while staring constantly at the screen, hoping Liv would come back online. But the ticks against my message remained stubbornly grey. My lunch break sped by, and before I knew it, I had to go back to the boutique and turn my phone off – Beverley's rules. The afternoon was just as busy as the morning, and I didn't even stop for a cup of tea. We had a lot of tried-on clothes that needed returning to their rightful places on the rails, so I didn't leave work until after six. I turned my phone on as soon as I sat down on the bus, but Liv hadn't been online.

I came home to an empty house. Dom would have landed in Dubai by now and Jensen was working his shift at the pub, but I had no idea where Meg was. It was dark and cold. I turned on all the lights downstairs and boosted the central heating. I tried calling Meg, but like her sister, she didn't pick up. I sent her a grumpy text.

Where are you? Are you coming back for dinner or not?

Surprise, surprise, she didn't respond either. I poured myself a glass of red wine and sat in the sitting room, feeling resentful. Home-made tuna pasta bake was on the menu for tonight, but I couldn't be bothered to cook, especially as I would probably be the only person eating it. I waited for twenty minutes, then went and made myself a cheese omelette.

At around 9 p.m., I heard noises coming from the hallway. Leaping up from the sofa, I hurried into the hallway to see Meg trying to creep up the stairs.

'Where have you been?'

'Out.'

I sighed irritably. 'Yes, I gathered that. Why didn't you answer my messages?'

'My phone ran out of juice.'

'Really? Show me.'

'Get lost, Mum!' she retorted. 'I can go out for the evening if I like. I'm not a kid any more.'

'We've already spoken about this. It's important to check in so that I know you're safe.'

She pouted. '*Liv* doesn't check in.'

'That's different. She's a grown-up.'

'So am I. I'm eighteen now, remember?'

'Yes, but...' I was about to say 'she doesn't live at home any more', but stopped myself. 'I'm not talking about Liv, I'm talking about you.'

'Why doesn't she call?' Meg replied, sidestepping the argument. 'Something weird is going on. She hasn't posted anything on her socials, you know. Not one thing.'

'Really?' Liv had refused to give me her Instagram handle. I'd spent ages trying to find her account only to conclude that she must have blocked me. When I'd challenged her, she'd said it wasn't 'appropriate' for mums to be followers.

'How often does she usually post?' I asked.

'Sometimes once a week. Other times, every day. Depends if she's got something exciting to talk about.'

'Hmm... that does sound a bit worrying.'

'I don't like it.'

'Nor do I, love, but what can we do?'

'Call the police?'

Her words stopped me in my tracks. I'd had an urge to call them several times over the past week but had always talked myself back from the brink. Liv's behaviour was odd, but there was no evidence that she had come to any harm.

'They wouldn't take us seriously,' I said. 'I mean, it's not like she's missing.'

Meg frowned. 'But we don't know where she is, do we? Nobody does. So she *is* missing.'

'Not really, not if it's her choice. I know it's worrying, but people have a right to cut themselves off from family and friends. Sometimes they have very good reasons – if they've been abused, for example. Not that Liv has been,' I added hastily. 'It's just an example. We may find it hurtful, but she doesn't *have* to tell us where she's living, or post on Insta, or answer our calls, or—'

'Maybe she *can't*,' Meg said ominously.

'What do you mean?'

'We don't know for sure that she sent that message. Somebody else could have been using her phone, pretending that she's alive when in fact—'

'Whoa! Slow down, Meg!'

'We don't know what really happened that weekend we were away,' she persisted. 'We've only got Jensen's word for it.'

'They had a row,' I said. 'She wanted to move out, he didn't. So she left. Now she's trying to work out what she wants to do next. I don't think it's any more complicated than that.'

'Hmm...' She sounded unconvinced. 'I hope she's okay, that's all.' She went into her room and shut the door. I heard the bolt move across.

I went downstairs and tried to distract myself by watching the late news. I'd thrown up my hands in horror at Meg's suggestion that Liv was in some kind of danger, but such a scenario had also occurred to me over the past few days, in the dead of night when I hadn't been able to sleep. I'd dismissed it as a lurid fantasy, but now it returned to me again. A picture of the flatlet flashed through my mind – the upturned furniture, the smashed vase... Jensen had claimed that it was untidiness, but they'd clearly had a fight. And his account of getting lost in the forest hadn't completely rung true either. My pulse started to race. Maybe I should follow my own advice, I thought, and stop overdramatising.

I checked my phone one last time before going to bed. Talk of the devil... Liv had put a thumbs-up against my message. I was hugely relieved to get a response, such as it was, but disappointed that she could only manage an emoji. Seeing that she was online, I quickly typed, *Hi! Lovely to hear from you. What are you giving the thumbs-up to? Not sure! Xx*

The answer came immediately. *Let Jensen stay.*

I was very surprised. Neither Dom nor Meg would be happy about that, I thought. I composed a careful reply.

Can we talk about this, Liv? On the phone, or face to face? Maybe we could meet up. Just tell me when and where and I'll be there.

She typed back, *I don't want to talk. Or meet up. Leave me alone.*

I hesitated before writing my reply. But what the hell, I thought? We couldn't keep pussyfooting around.

What's going on? You're making us worry, Liv. Why won't you just call me? Are you in trouble? I need to see you or at least hear your voice so I know you're okay. If you don't want to talk to me, call Meg or Dad or even Auntie Karina. I just need to know you're safe then I'll leave you alone. Promise! Love you lots xx

The two ticks turned blue, then she went offline.

TWENTY

Wednesday, my day off, couldn't come soon enough. I'd heard nothing more from Liv and it was making it difficult to sleep. I would have liked a lie-in, but I wanted to make sure Meg went into school, so I got up and knocked on her bedroom door.

'Time to get up, sweetie,' I called. She opened up straight away, already dressed. 'Oh, there you are! Shall I make some porridge?'

'No thanks,' she replied. 'I've got to be in early.'

'What for?'

She coloured up. 'Interview with the head.'

'Oh. What about?'

'My attendance.'

'But I thought you'd been going in?' She looked down, shaking her head. 'I see...' I sighed. 'Do you want me to come with you?'

'No. It's not required now I'm eighteen.'

'I know, but I can support you.'

'I don't need supporting. What I need is for you to butt out.'

'Okay, okay!' I held up my hands in surrender.

'I can handle it!' She pushed past me and marched down the stairs.

'Don't go without breakfast!' I said, following her.

'No time.'

'Take something with you. The bananas are ripe—'

'I'm not hungry.' She put on her coat and pushed her feet into her heavy boots.

'Just tell him the truth,' I said. 'You've been suffering from anxiety and—'

'I know what to say.' She opened the front door and walked out.

'Meg?' I called after her, but she didn't look back. 'Good luck!' I added lamely, too quiet for her to hear.

I had a shower and got dressed, then had some toast and coffee. We were running low on quite a few essential items, so I decided – reluctantly – to do a supermarket run. I made a list, found some plastic bags, picked up my keys and left the house.

The car was parked on the drive. I unlocked it and opened the boot to put the bags in. That was when I saw it.

Somebody had graffitied the front bay window. Three giant letters were spray-painted on the glass.

KYS.

My heart leapt into my mouth and I let out a scream. Slamming the boot shut, I rested on it to catch my breath. The ruined cake, the scratch on the car and the rubbish in the garden had been bad enough, but this was in a different league. I stared at the three letters, sprayed in blood red. What did they even mean? It was macabre. Vicious. Cowardly, too, as I assumed it had been done overnight, under cover of darkness. The graffiti would have been there as the sun came up, waiting for Meg to see it when she left the house to go to school. Thankfully she'd refused to turn round when I'd called after her. I felt sick at the thought that she could so easily have spotted it. But at least now I had a chance to clean it off before she came home.

I ran into the house and went straight upstairs to find Jensen. He was asleep, and it took several knocks on his bedroom door to rouse him. I told him what had happened.

'What does KYS stand for?' I asked him.

He screwed up his face. 'Kill Your Self. It's a troll thing. On social media.'

My mouth fell open. 'Oh my God. That's... that's... unspeakable.'

'Yeah. Pretty hardcore.'

'It's not even proper English. Yourself is one word, not two.'

'I don't think anyone cares much about that,' he muttered.

I blew out my cheeks. 'I'm really shocked that Skyla could do such a thing.'

'Do we know for sure it was her?'

'It has to be. She was behind last term's bullying, it can't be anyone else.'

'Makes sense, but without proof...'

'Well, we've got to find some. Please can you try and get into Meg's laptop? She's gone to school, won't be back for ages.' I looked at him appealingly.

'Of course,' he said. 'My shift starts at twelve, but I should have enough time.'

'Great. Thanks. Now I've got to find out how to clean off the paint.'

According to Google, my best option was nail varnish remover. I found a small bottle and a bag of cotton wool balls and went outside with a stepladder. The remover worked, but I soon ran out of it, and I had to rub so hard that the cotton wool balls disintegrated. I would have to go to the shops and buy some more.

I heard a voice behind me. 'What the...'

It was Meg. I spun round to face her, almost falling off the stepladder. A guilty look spread across my face. I almost felt as if I'd sprayed the offensive message myself.

'Hi! Wasn't expecting you back... um... so...' I faltered.

'Did that say KYS?'

'Yes... I'm so sorry.' I climbed off the ladder. 'I was trying to get rid of it before—'

'When did it happen?'

'Last night, I think. While we were all asleep.'

She nodded slowly. 'Hmm... I missed it this morning.'

'Look, I'm sorry, but I think we need to get the police involved, Meg. She's gone too far this time—'

'It wasn't Skyla,' she interrupted. 'She wouldn't go out in the middle of the night – she'd be too scared. It was somebody much closer to home.'

'Who?'

'Jensen.'

'Jensen?! Why on earth would you say that?'

'He hates me,' she carried on. 'He can't bear it that Liv and I are close. He doesn't have any sibs, you see. He's dead jealous. Liv told me. She said we had to dial down the sister vibe in front of him.'

'Really? She actually said that?'

'Yes! And it was straight after he moved in that the trolling started again. Only it wasn't the same as before, it was slightly different. The messages are more creepy – they sound like they come from an older person.'

I started to feel weak at the knees. Surely Jensen wouldn't get involved in something so petty and spiteful? He'd done everything possible to be liked by us. And he'd been lovely towards Meg – DJing at her party, offering to help with her homework... I couldn't believe it. I didn't *want* to believe it.

'He told me he wrecked my birthday cake,' Meg continued. 'And did the littering. And scratched the car. He was pissed off because you tried to keep it from me. And last week he sent me a message saying he was going to do something worse. This!' She pointed at the graffiti. 'KYS. He's used it before.'

'Jensen *admitted* it?' I whispered, gasping for breath.

'Of course not. The accounts are fake, they change all the time so you can't trace them. But I know it's him. It's obvious. He moves in and all this shit happens. Like, duh.'

'Meg, darling,' I said. 'You can't just go round accusing people.'

'You accused Skyla,' she reminded me.

'Yes, but only because I knew for certain she was behind the last lot. Jensen is Liv's boyfriend...'

I stopped, suddenly remembering that he was in Meg's room, trying to break into her Instagram account.

'Let's talk about it later,' I said hurriedly. 'I need to buy some more nail varnish remover. Do you want to come with me? We could go for a coffee, chat this over, decide what you want to do.'

'No thanks,' she said, walking past me into the house.

I stared after her, helpless to stop the inevitable blow-up that was about to take place, then followed her in, desperately trying to think of a way to smooth things over. I would take the blame, of course. I had asked Jensen to hack into her laptop, after all.

Raised voices were coming from her room. I ran up the stairs. Her door was wide open. Jensen was seated at the desk, in front of her laptop, and Meg was standing over him.

'Get out!' she screamed.

'Okay, okay,' he said.

'It's my fault...' I began, but it was as if she couldn't hear me. She went to push Jensen off the chair, but he moved back and stood up. 'Meg, please, Jensen was only doing what I asked him to.'

'Your mum's right,' Jensen said. 'I was trying to help, that's all.'

'No you weren't. You were trying to cover your tracks. I know it's you!'

'What do you mean?'

'Why don't *you* Kill *Your* Self?'

'Meg—'

'Get out of my room. Now!'

'Yeah, of course. Sorry. I'll leave you to it.' He grimaced at me as he passed, and I mouthed a 'sorry'.

'Listen, Meg. I know you're upset,' I said, shutting the door behind him. 'So am I. This is utterly disgusting behaviour. But as far as I can see, Jensen has nothing to do with any of it.'

'You don't actually know that, do you?' She left a beat. '*Do you?*'

'No, but—'

'You believe him over me, your own daughter?'

'No. I didn't say that. I just don't think we should start making hasty judgements.'

'I mean, like, why is he even still living with us?'

'He's agreed to leave as soon as he can find somewhere to go.' She snorted. 'He has no family, Meg. We can't just chuck him out.'

'Even though he wants me to kill myself?!'

'He doesn't...' I took a deep breath. 'I'm sure this is all Skyla's doing. Her and that girl Alice.'

'It's Jensen! He's got rid of Liv and now he wants to get rid of me, too.'

'Look, darling, I understand. You've been traumatised. I want to find out who did this just as much as you do, but we have to calm down.'

She crossed her arms defiantly. 'One of us has to go. It's him or me, Mum. You choose.'

I left her and went downstairs. Jensen was in the kitchen, making coffee. 'That was awkward,' he said as I came in.

'I'm so sorry.'

'No need to apologise,' he said smoothly. 'It's understandable. Bad timing, too. I wouldn't like it if someone tried to break into *my* accounts. Still, Meg really lost it. I thought she was going to kill me.'

'I should never have asked you to do it. I've made things worse.'

He poured the coffee into two mugs and handed me one. 'Here.'

I laughed weakly. 'Thanks. What I really need is a gin and tonic.'

'It's a bit early for that.' He gulped some coffee, then glanced at the clock on the oven. 'Sorry, I've got to go. I'm going to be late for my shift.'

'Oh dear, I didn't mean to keep you.'

He put down his half-empty mug. 'Look, I'd love to help you get rid of the graffiti, but—'

'Don't worry. I can do it.'

Jensen left shortly afterwards. I popped to the chemist for some more remover, then resumed the task. The acetone gave me a headache. Or maybe I was simply feeling stressed. Some of the paint had strayed onto the UPVC frames and was being very stubborn. I had to use a razor blade to remove the last spots and streaks.

By the time I'd finished, it was growing dark. I was exhausted, and my fingers were numb with cold. I also felt hungry – with all the mayhem, I'd forgotten to eat lunch. Tidying everything away, I went back indoors. I put the kettle on and was wondering whether I should check on Meg when I heard a strange noise coming from the hallway.

I walked out of the kitchen. Meg was thumping a large suitcase down the last couple of stairs. She had a rucksack on her back, and her laptop case was wedged under one arm.

'What's going on?' I asked, although it was obvious.

'You refused to choose between us, so I chose for you,' she said.

'You don't have to do this.'

'I do.'

'Where are you going?'

'To live with Auntie Karina.'

I inhaled sharply. 'Does she know about this?'

'Duh… I called her. She's totally cool with it.'

'Well I'm not,' I bristled. 'She should have spoken to me first.'

'I'm eighteen, Mum. You can't control me any more. I can live where I like.'

'Meg, please don't do this. Let's talk it through.'

'I told you to get rid of Jensen and you refused.'

'I didn't actually refuse, I just wanted—'

'Yeah, whatever.' She glanced at her phone. 'My Uber's here.' She opened the front door.

I tried to stand in her way. 'But how will you get to school?' Karina lived in Hackney. It wasn't far away in miles, but the public transport links were terrible.

'Karina says she'll give me lifts.'

'Best of luck with that in the rush hour.'

'Stop trying to think for everyone, Mum. It's not your problem any more. *I'm* not your problem.'

'Of course you're my problem.' I checked myself. 'I don't mean it that way. You're not a problem, you're my daughter and I love you. But I'm worried—'

'Jensen's the one you want to worry about,' she said, carrying her luggage over the threshold.

'Please don't go, Meg. We can work this out.'

She waved at the taxi that had just drawn up outside. 'Be careful, Mum. He's evil.'

TWENTY-ONE

Hey Meg,

What's going on? You're still alive! You were supposed to KYS. Accept the truth. There's no place for you in this beautiful world. Did Mummy clean my message off for you? Did she scrub away until her fingers bled? You know why she did that? Not because she loves you. Because she didn't like her windows getting all messy. She cares more about her fucking windows than she does about you.

I hear you've left home and are staying with your auntie. Does she make you cocoa and tuck you up in bed at night? Does she read you bedtime stories about fat ugly girls without any friends?

How do Mummy and Daddy feel about you going? Shall I tell you? They LOVE it. The moment you left they cracked open the champagne and jumped around the house. Yayy!!! Miserable old Meg has gone! With her shapeless clothes and her greasy hair and her dull skin and her zero sense of humour.

But there's no point in running away. It doesn't matter where you are, I can still get inside your head.

TWENTY-TWO

I took the next couple of days off, telling Beverley that I'd come down with a bug. Meg's departure had really upset me. I was also worried about Liv. She'd gone off the radar again, even though I'd begged her to call me.

It was a relief not to be at the boutique, smiling at customers and putting up with their petty-minded attitudes. Dom's flight was due to land at midday, and I wanted to talk to him as soon as he arrived home. He'd been so busy we hadn't had a chance to speak properly. It was always difficult to talk to him when he was on these trips. He was usually in meetings all day and entertaining clients all evening, and I wasn't allowed to interrupt – not unless it was a dire emergency.

We had so much to discuss, such as what we were going to do about these attacks, and how we could help Meg cope. I'd already looked at the possibility of getting her some therapy – we'd have to pay for it, but it would be worth the cost. I didn't know what we were supposed to do about Jensen now that Liv had said he could stay. Dom would have a fit if he knew, and I'd have no chance of getting Meg back. I decided not to mention it to anyone. It would only complicate an already difficult situation. Jensen needed to go as soon as possible. For everyone's sake.

In the morning I tidied up and hoovered, then after lunch I changed out of my slumpy clothes and put on some make-up. All was quiet upstairs. Jensen hadn't surfaced for either breakfast or lunch. I guessed he wasn't working until the evening and was spending the day catching up on sleep. I was relieved, as it would give me and Dom the opportunity to talk openly without fear of being overheard.

'God, I'm knackered,' Dom said as soon as he walked in. He dumped his suitcase at the bottom of the stairs. I stood smiling in the kitchen doorway, waiting to welcome him into my arms, but he muttered something about needing a pee and rushed to the cloakroom instead.

Shrugging, I went back into the kitchen and put the kettle on for a cup of tea, taking his favourite mug out of the cupboard and setting it down on the counter.

'Sorry about that,' he said, entering. 'Are there any biscuits? I'm starving.'

I reached for the biscuit tin. 'You're not going to do any work today, are you?'

'I'll have to check my emails, but otherwise, no. Why?'

'Because we need to talk about Meg.'

He hesitated. 'Actually, I need to talk to you about something.'

'Okay, but this is urgent. She's left home and gone to stay with Karina.'

'What? Are you kidding?'

We took our mugs and a plate of chocolate digestives into the conservatory. The weather outside was cold, but sunlight was streaming into the room, making it feel hot and airless. We sat down and I told him the whole story.

'It's on a way more serious scale this time,' I said. 'It feels like the whole family is being attacked.'

Dom nodded. 'These are hate crimes. We should call the police.'

'Meg doesn't want us to. She's too frightened.'

'We ought to speak to Skyla's parents, at least.'

'She doesn't think it's Skyla.'

'No? Then who the hell is it?'

'She's convinced that it's Jensen.'

His eyes widened. 'Jensen?'

'Yes.'

'How come?'

'Apparently the nasty DMs started again shortly after he moved in. She won't show them to me, but she insists they're different to before, more like a grown-up speaking. And whoever it is knows personal information about her.'

'Shit...' He puffed out his cheeks. 'Do you think she could be right?'

'Possibly, but it seems very unlikely.' I sighed. 'I don't know, Dom... I'm really confused. I don't know what to think any more.'

'Either way, we need to show Meg that we support her. Which means, guilty or not guilty, Jensen needs to leave. Soon as.'

'Yes, you're right,' I agreed reluctantly.

'He's a grown man – he's not our responsibility. We've got enough to worry about with the girls.' He put his mug down. 'Sorry, but I've got some follow-up emails to attend to. I'll be in my "office",' he added with edge, standing up and walking into the dining room.

It was nearly four in the afternoon, and Jensen, by the sound of it, had finally woken up. I could hear the dull bass of his music thumping through the ceiling.

I climbed the stairs to the top floor and knocked on the door of the flatlet.

'Come in!' he shouted. As soon as I entered, he killed the sound. 'Sorry. Was I blasting the place out?'

'A bit,' I admitted. 'It's fine with me, but Dom's home and he's trying to work.'

'Shit. I didn't realise he was back. And I assumed you were at the boutique today. Sorry, Rachel, I genuinely thought I had the house to myself.'

Silence fell between us. It seemed to go on for ever.

'What are you going to do about the graffiti?' he asked. 'Report it to the police?'

'Maybe. Not sure.'

'I swear I had nothing to do with any of this. You can search my phone and laptop if you like. I've never bullied anyone, online or in real life. It's obscene.'

'I don't think you did it, but it's making things very awkward for us. Meg needs our help and it's difficult if you're here. I'm really sorry, Jensen, but you need to move out as soon as possible.'

'Oh...' His eyes moistened and he looked away. 'I'm trying to find somewhere,' he said, 'but it's really difficult. Landlords won't accept people on zero-hours contracts. I can't afford to get a place on my own and I don't want to live with strangers. I'm stuck.'

'Maybe you could go back to Newcastle?'

He shook his head. 'I need to be here for Liv.'

'But Jensen... it's over, isn't it?'

He stiffened. 'Not officially. There's still hope.'

'Really? She hasn't been in touch with you once since she walked out. Isn't that, like, a sign?'

'Not necessarily.'

'Look, your relationship with Liv is your own business. I don't want to intrude. I'm sure somebody will let you sofa-surf until you find somewhere better.'

He looked as if he were about to burst into tears. I couldn't bear it. I turned and made for the door.

'Happy fucking Christmas,' he muttered to himself as I left the room.

Feeling awful, I went downstairs. Having said I didn't want to intrude, I was suddenly filled with an overwhelming urge to call Liv and tell her to stop mucking about. Jensen needed to be put out of his misery. I took out my phone and opened Whats-App. To my complete amazement, she'd sent me a video message half an hour ago. At last! All my worries about her immediately went out of the window. I plonked myself down on the sofa and pressed play.

There she was, large as life. She'd had a haircut and was wearing a bright pink dress with a sparkly thread. It strobed every time she moved. I had seen her wearing it many times; it was one of her favourites. The colour clashed with her auburn hair – but in a good way, making her look arty and unconventional.

She was in a bar, sitting at a table with a large glass of white wine in front of her, peering into the camera lens as she spoke.

Hi there, just to say everything's fine. I'm doing okay. I'm out for the evening with a few of the girls. Just wanted to say love you, love you, love you. Byeee!

I played it again, bathing in the sight of her, only realising in that moment how desperate I'd been to see proof that she was okay.

I homed in on the frozen frame, trying to work out where she was. The bar looked familiar. I recognised the distressed leather seating, the rusted beaten-metal cladding on the walls, the industrial-chic light fittings and exposed ducting. Liv had taken us there last year, when we came to pick her up at the end of term. I did a quick search for interior images of bars in Newcastle and immediately came up with a name – Kelsey's. Yes, that was it.

At last we knew where she was, and that she was okay. More than okay, it seemed.

I ran into the dining room. 'Guess what?' I cried. 'She's sent us a video! She's in Newcastle.' Dom swivelled round in his chair, and I thrust the phone in front of his face.

'She sounds pissed,' he said, unimpressed. 'Is that the best she can manage?'

'Come on, it's great news.'

'I told you she was okay.' He made to go back to the computer.

'Yes, but we didn't know for sure.' I felt heady with relief. 'I must forward this to Meg. She'll be so pleased. She was panicking because Liv hadn't posted on social media.'

Dom started tapping away on his keyboard.

'By the way,' I continued, 'you said there was something you wanted to talk to me about.'

He froze for a moment. 'Not now,' he said softly 'Another time.'

'You sure? We don't often get the chance to have a good chat.'

'No, really. I'm busy,' he replied, still looking at the screen. 'It'll keep.'

TWENTY-THREE

Dom and I were alone for dinner on Friday evening. I cooked lamb shanks with couscous and lit some candles. Although we still had problems, I felt that we'd made a tiny bit of progress towards solving them. Jensen had agreed to leave as soon as possible, and Liv had sent us the video. I was still worried about Meg, but there was nothing I could do about that for now.

Dom was in a strange mood. Either he'd run out of things to say, or he didn't want to say them. He played with his food and kept topping up his glass without asking me if I wanted more wine.

'What's wrong?' I asked. 'Are you cross with me?'

He looked up, as if surprised to find me sitting opposite him. 'No, not at all,' he replied. 'I'm just tired. It's the travelling, you know...'

I sensed there was more to it than that, but I couldn't make him talk. After dinner, he got up from the table and announced that he was going out for a walk.

'Really?' I said, following him into the hallway. 'You never go for walks. And it's a terrible night. That wind is icy.'

'I've got a headache,' he replied, putting on his jacket.

'Take some painkillers then.'

'I need some fresh air, okay?' I saw him slip his mobile into his pocket and wondered who he was going to call at this time of night.

Blaming his headache on too much red wine, I went back to the dining room and started clearing up. I loaded the dishwasher, then watched a bit of television, but I couldn't concentrate on the programme because Dom hadn't come home. He'd been out for well over an hour. I tried calling his mobile, but he didn't pick up.

I finally heard him arrive back at about 11 p.m. I'd already gone to bed and was trying to read my book.

'What happened?' I asked as soon as he walked into the bedroom.

'Sorry.' He gave me a sheepish smile. 'I popped into the George for a pee and bumped into some guys from the golf club. They were just getting another round in...'

'Did you see Jensen?'

'No.'

'I thought we were going to spend the evening together,' I said ruefully.

'One thing led to another. You know how it is with that lot.'

'I put a lot of effort into that meal. You hardly said a word and then you left me with all the clearing-up. What happened to the headache?'

He started getting undressed. 'Better, thanks. A cold blast through the earholes did the trick.'

'I just don't understand why you were out for so long.'

'For God's sake, Rachel. Leave me be. I'm knackered.'

I put my book down and burrowed beneath the duvet, annoyance coursing through my veins. Dom got into bed next to me a few minutes later and turned out the light. I lay in the darkness, still fuming, unable to relax, my thoughts flitting uselessly from Meg to Liv to Dom to Jensen and back again.

Dom seemed to have no trouble falling asleep, and began snoring so loudly I wanted to put a pillow over his face.

Sick of lying awake staring at the ceiling, I finally got up and went downstairs. The central heating had gone off hours ago and the sitting room was freezing cold. I lay on the sofa, covered myself with a blanket and switched on the TV. I didn't care what I watched; the more boring the better. I didn't remember dropping off, but I must have managed it somehow because when Dom found me in the morning, I was fast asleep in front of a Saturday-morning cookery show.

'Here you are,' he said, putting a cup of tea on the side table.

I opened my eyes. 'What time is it?' I swung my legs round and budged up, expecting him to sit next to me, but he chose an armchair on the other side of the room.

'Just after seven.' He paused. 'I had a bad night too.'

'You could have fooled me. You were snoring for England.'

'I've been awake since five.'

'Worrying about the girls?'

'Yes, sort of... but mainly about something else.'

There was a long pause. The expression on his face was hard to read. He looked like he might burst into tears.

'What is it, Dom?' I picked up my mug and gripped it tightly. 'You're looking really tense. Spit it out, for God's sake.'

He dragged his fingers through his hair. 'I feel terrible. The timing couldn't be worse. It's way too much. I can't do this to you.'

'Can't do what?' I took a sip of my tea and waited for an explanation. 'You're making me nervous. What's wrong?' I asked finally. 'Did it all go pear-shaped in Dubai? Have you lost your job?'

He inhaled, then paused. A feeling of dread came over me as I waited for the truth to fall like an axe on my head. 'I wasn't in Dubai,' he said.

'What do you mean?'

There was a beat. 'I lied to you.'

My blood froze. 'Why lie about that? I don't get it.'

He looked away from me as tears started to roll down his cheeks. 'I'm sorry, Rachel.'

'For God's sake, tell me. If you haven't been in Dubai, where *have* you been?'

'Menorca.'

My mouth dropped open. 'Menorca? What, for work?'

'No. On holiday.'

I let out a laugh. 'On holiday? What do you mean? You went on holiday on your own? I know it's been difficult here, but—'

'No, no, you misunderstand.' He shook his head. 'I was with someone else... A woman. Not just any woman. Someone I've been seeing for a while.'

I heard the words, but I couldn't put them together. 'Sorry? What did you just say?'

'I've been having a relationship... an affair, I suppose you'd call it... for about a year now. She's a sales agent, we met at a conference.'

His words fell right through me. 'How could you? How *could* you?'

'I thought it was just a fling at first,' he went on, 'but it turns out it's serious. For both of us. This week was make or break. Either we were going to leave our partners or split up.'

'And?' I waited. But he didn't have to say any more, the answer was obvious. 'You're such a coward,' I said. 'Running away just when we need you the most.'

'You don't need me, Rachel,' he said sourly. 'You've never needed me.'

'That's not true! You're my husband, we're a team.'

'Not really. You've taken the lead for years.'

'Only because you held back.'

'Anyway, the girls are grown up now. Our job is done.'

'It's not done. It's very far from done.'

'This isn't about the girls,' he insisted. 'It's about us. Aren't you even jealous that I've met someone else?'

Jealous? Of course I was. But mostly I was angry – angrier than I could remember being in my life. I stood up and grabbed the nearest hard object – it happened to be a vase that we'd been given as a wedding present – and threw it at his head. He ducked, and luckily for both of us, it missed him.

'What the fuck, Rachel?' he shouted.

He stormed out of the living room and stamped upstairs, as if he were the aggrieved party. I stayed where I was, surrounded by shards of glass. My body was shaking with anger and shock; I could hardly breathe. I sank to my knees, doubled up in agony. The pain was emotional, but I felt as if I'd been punched in the stomach.

Why hadn't I seen it coming? Looking back, the signs were there – the downturn in our sex life, the evenings out 'entertaining clients', the nights away 'negotiating important deals', the lack of interest in the family. I'd put his physical and mental absences down to the demands of his job and the stress of everyday life. I hadn't for one second suspected him of cheating.

How could he have done this to me? I was his wife. We'd been married for twenty-three years; we had two beautiful daughters.

I pulled myself up, surprised when my knees almost gave way. I hung onto the arm of a chair and slowly got to my feet. I didn't want him to see me like this – humiliated and defeated. What the hell was he doing upstairs? Sulking in our bedroom, waiting for me to come up and apologise for not having been a good enough wife?

He'd behaved as if his affair was my fault – I'd given too much attention to our children and not enough to him. I hadn't involved him, apparently, preferring to be the hero of the family, solving everyone's problems. It was so far from the truth

I almost laughed. This past year, I'd looked to Dom for help and support time and time again, but he'd always been busy, too wrapped up in his career. Or so I'd thought. Now I realised he'd been wrapped in another woman's arms instead.

I went back over our awful, strangely brief conversation. He'd said the affair had started as a casual fling then turned into something serious – as if it had happened by accident, like he'd stepped into the road and been hit by a car. How many other flings had there been? I wondered. Encounters that had barely left a scratch. It made me sick that I could even be thinking such thoughts. My husband was suddenly a stranger to me. I no longer recognised him as the man I'd married all those years ago.

I went upstairs and found him in our bedroom. A suitcase – one of the enormous ones we used to take on family holidays – was lying open on the bed, and he was neatly folding in his shirts.

'You're leaving?' I said.

'I told you.'

'Right now?'

'Yes. I'm not staying to be attacked again.'

'Where are you going? To this woman's place?' He shook his head. 'Of course,' I continued. 'She's married too. How awkward.'

He started taking trousers off their hangers, pressing the legs neatly together before placing them in the case. 'There's no need to be sarcastic,' he muttered.

'I'm sorry, how am I supposed to behave?'

'I can't deal with this,' he said. 'Just let me leave... We'll talk later, when you've calmed down.'

My hackles instantly rose. 'When I've calmed down?! How dare you say that!'

'There's no point screaming.'

'How did you think I was going to react?'

He paused the folding and looked up at me. 'Not with violence.'

'I was angry.'

'I thought you were going to kill me.'

'Come on, the vase didn't touch you.'

'Yes it did. Look!' He pointed to his left cheek. A piece of glass had nicked his skin. It wasn't even properly bleeding. 'You're pathetic,' I said. 'If you're going to use that as an excuse for running away—'

'I'm not running away. I'm leaving to be with Charlotte.'

Charlotte. So she had a name. Suddenly it all felt real.

'Dom, please,' I said, changing tone. 'We can't end twenty-three years with one short row. This is a huge decision you're making. You're not giving me any time. We need to talk everything through, get it all out there, look at options, go to couples' counselling, give ourselves a chance.'

'Charlotte and I have been thinking about nothing else for months,' he replied coldly. 'We know it's hard, and that it's going to hurt other people, but that's just how it is. We love each other and we want to be together.'

'You sound like a couple of teenagers,' I said, losing my patience again. 'We're married. We're a family!'

He went to his underwear drawer and took out several pairs of socks that only yesterday I'd washed and dried and carefully put into matching pairs.

'Things haven't been right for a long time – you must know that.'

'We've had a lot on our plate,' I answered, trying to stay steady. 'Some major challenges to deal with – Meg's bullying, her eighteenth, Liv and Jensen moving in.'

'Liv needs to sort her own shit out.'

'You can talk,' I retorted. 'You've got more shit than the rest of us put together.'

He made a small noise in his throat. 'We should stop talking, we're only going to say stuff we regret.'

'I'm not going to regret it. There's plenty more I want to say.'

'Not now.' He shut the lid of the suitcase decisively. 'That's most of it. I'll come back for the rest.'

'If I haven't already taken it to the charity shop.'

'Stop it, Rachel. I know you're upset and bitter, but it's not helping. You can have the car, by the way.'

'Huh. Thanks a lot.'

'I'll give you a call in a few days, okay?'

'Whatever.'

He pulled the suitcase off the bed, briefly glancing around the room, saying goodbye to his old life. I followed him downstairs. He left his luggage in the hallway and ordered a taxi.

'It's five minutes away,' he told me, as if I cared. I wasn't going to spend the time persuading him to stay. I'd had enough now and needed him to leave me in peace.

While he waited, he went around the house collecting personal items and putting them into a plastic carrier bag: his TV glasses, a book he'd been reading, his slippers, a woollen scarf and hat that he wore on our weekend walks around the park – things I barely noticed normally, but which now I would miss. My husband was leaving me. For another woman, who until an hour ago I'd had no idea existed. Everything was moving too fast; I couldn't keep up with it.

The taxi beeped its horn to signal it was outside. Dom opened the door and picked up his luggage. Suddenly remembering his waterproof jacket, he took it off the hook and slung it over his arm.

'I'm sorry,' he said as he stepped onto the driveway. 'But I know I'm doing the right thing. For both of us. For everyone.'

Sanctimonious bastard, I thought, but I didn't reply.

TWENTY-FOUR

I should have collapsed the moment the taxi drove away, but I just closed the front door and went to fetch the dustpan and brush. My brain had gone numb; it was like none of it was really registering. As I knelt down to sweep up the shards of glass, I cut my hand quite badly. Wincing with pain, I rushed to the sink and held it under running water, watching the diluted blood trickle onto my wrist. Then I found a plaster and wound it round my finger. It was as if I was watching someone else going through the motions. Nothing seemed to connect.

What was I going to say to my girls? I still thought of them as girls, even though they were now both officially grown up. Meg was in a bad way as it was; her parents splitting up wasn't going to help. It could send her over the edge. Not that Dom cared now he had *Charlotte*.

As for Liv... I didn't know how she would take the news. I realised that I wanted – even expected – them both to be on my side. Mother and daughters united against the cheating father – that was how it played out in the movies. But real life was different. My relationship with them was push-me-pull-you – close, but complicated. They could be very critical. They might blame me for not giving Dom enough attention, for 'letting him stray'. I would find that hard, I thought.

But I had to tell them. I called Liv first. The phone rang for a few seconds, then cut out. I wasn't able to leave a message either. Reluctantly, I composed a WhatsApp.

Hi, darling, is everything okay? I know you want to be left alone, but I really need to talk to you. I have some difficult family news, and I want to tell you in person, not in a text. Please, please get in touch as soon as you can. It's urgent. Love you xxxx

I pressed send. Surely this time she'll respond immediately, I thought.

I went back to bed and lay there for hours trying to process what had just happened, replaying the scene with Dom over and over in my head. I still couldn't believe he'd been having an affair for a whole year, or that he'd walked out on me. It felt as if someone or something was leaning heavily on my chest, making it impossible to take deep enough breaths. I'd had no idea that emotional pain could feel so physical, so draining.

I kept my mobile close by, waiting for Liv to ring. I knew she'd read my message because the two ticks against it had turned blue. Every time I heard a buzz or a ping, I leapt to the home screen, but they were just irrelevant notifications. I started to feel aggrieved. I'd made it clear that it was important. Why hadn't she called?

As the day wore on, I felt increasingly lost and desolate, finally realising that what I needed more than anything else was a hug from someone who loved me. The only people I could think of were Karina and Meg. I got up and had a shower, in an attempt to make myself feel human again. I had no appetite, but forced down a sandwich and a cup of tea before setting out for Karina's flat. As I drove through the traffic, my eyes kept blurring with tears. At one point I had to pull over and have a good sob before I could continue.

'Rachel! My God, you look terrible,' Karina said when she opened the door to me. 'What's happened?'

'Is Meg in?' I whispered.

'Yes. She's in her room, gaming as usual. What's wrong?' I paused, terrified of uttering the words out loud. 'Is it Liv?' she pressed. 'Have you heard from her?'

'Sort of. She sent me a video.'

'At last. How is she?'

'Fine, I think. In Newcastle. It's not that.'

'Then what is it? For God's sake, tell me!'

'It's Dom,' I said. 'He's left me.'

Her mouth fell open. '*Left* you?'

'Yes. For some woman called Charlotte.'

'Jesus... Come in, come in, take your coat off.' She steered me into the sitting room and pushed me onto the sofa. 'I'll make some coffee.' She went over to the kitchen area and started busying herself with the Nespresso machine. 'What a shit. I can't believe it! How could he?'

'It's been going on for a year,' I told her, laying my coat on the arm of the sofa. 'I thought he was in Dubai this week, but it turns out he was in Menorca with her, deciding who to choose. Me or her. She won.'

'Oh Rachel, I'm so sorry... As if you haven't got enough going on right now.'

'I've lost everyone,' I said, starting to cry again. 'Liv, Meg, now Dom. It's like nobody wants to be with me.'

'That's not true. Meg and Liv have their own problems – they're nothing to do with you, not really. This is different,' Karina insisted. 'Dom should be utterly ashamed of himself.'

'He told me he's in love with her.'

'That's pathetic.'

'Says he's doing the right thing. For him, obviously. Doesn't seem to give a shit about the rest of us.'

She pressed the start button and turned to face me. 'How did you find out?'

'He told me. He tried to do it yesterday afternoon, when he came home, but there was all the other shit going on with Meg, and in the end, he lost his nerve. I knew something was up, but I never guessed... Anyway, he finally came out with it this morning.'

'Just like that?'

'Yup. We had a terrible row. I threw a vase at him.'

'Good for you.'

'Then he packed a suitcase and left.'

'Jesus, Rach. Why didn't you come round straight away?'

I screwed up my face. 'I don't know. I felt ashamed, I guess. Like I was somehow to blame... you know, for not being enough. Or for giving too much attention to the girls.'

'This is not your fault, okay? You've been a fantastic wife. You've done more than your fair share of looking after everyone. He's just a selfish git. Probably having a midlife crisis, God help us. How old is this woman – what did you say her name was?'

'Charlotte. I don't know. Younger than me, I expect. He met her at a sales conference. She's married too.'

'Really? Then she's as bad as him.'

'I'm incredibly angry,' I continued. 'And upset. I've been crying my eyes out. But if he doesn't love me any more, what can I do? I'm not going to beg him to come back. Even if I wanted him, my pride wouldn't let me.'

'Well, you know my feelings about men,' said Karina, bringing over two mugs of coffee and sitting next to me. 'In general, I think women are better off without them.'

'They're not all bad... You've had some awful experiences.'

'Being single is fine, that's what I'm trying to say. I know you're hurting right at this minute, but you *will* get over it.'

I drank my coffee. 'Thanks, sis,' I said. 'Right. I've got to tell Meg now.'

Karina twisted her mouth. 'Are you sure? She's very fragile at the moment.'

'She has to know.'

I went to her room and told her. As I'd expected, she was very upset by the news, although she didn't seem surprised.

'Dad's been in a weird mood for months,' she said. 'Even when he was at home, it was like he wasn't really there.'

'You noticed that too?'

'Defo! It was obvious he didn't want to be with us. But I had no idea he was shagging someone else.' She pulled a disgusted face.

Her clumsy choice of words hurt. 'No, nor did I,' I said.

'I can hardly believe it.'

'I know, it's hard to get your head around. But that's how it is. He's left and I'm on my own. I'm hoping Liv will come home now... And you. At times like this, we need to stick together, yeah?'

'Hmm... Is *he* still there?'

'Jensen?'

'Yes, Jensen! I'm not setting foot in that house until he's gone. I already told you that.'

'I know, and I'm working on it. But things have changed. Dad's left and I need you to—'

'As soon as he's gone, I'll come home, okay? Not one second before.'

'Please, Meg.'

'No way.'

'Okay,' I said. 'Okay. I get it, I understand. He's due to leave very soon, in the next couple of days.'

'Whatever. Just let me know.' She swung back to the screen.

I hesitated before carrying on. 'The thing is, he's denying everything.'

'Well, he would.'

'And I think he could be telling the truth. There's no hard evidence pointing to him.'

'We don't need hard evidence. It's got to be him, Mum. The DMs mention personal stuff only he could know.'

'Well, if you're that certain, we should go to the police and ask them to investigate.'

She flashed her eyes. 'No! No way.'

'Why not?'

'Because he'll find another way to get to me! Things will get worse. You don't understand, do you? He hurt Liv and now he wants to hurt me.'

'Liv's fine. She sent that video, remember? She's in Newcastle.'

'I don't believe it! It's him, *him*! He's playing with us, Mum. You need to be careful. You're going to be on your own with him now. You'd better get rid of him before it's too late.'

My head was rocking; I didn't know what to think any more. I left the room and went back to talk to Karina, who had started making the evening meal.

'How did she take it?' she asked.

'Badly. She didn't say as much, but I got the feeling she thinks it's all my fault.'

'I'm sure she doesn't.'

'She's refusing to come home until Jensen leaves.'

'Oh. I thought he'd already gone.'

'Not yet.' I sighed. 'He keeps saying he hasn't found anywhere yet. He hasn't got any family.'

'Everyone has family. Of some sort. He must have an aunt or a cousin...'

'He says not.'

'That's very strange.'

'I know, but what am I supposed to do? It's nearly Christmas, Karina. I can't just throw him onto the streets.'

She looked me straight in the eye. 'If you want the girls to come back, you'll *have* to.'

'I know... it just seems unfair. Remember how it was for us when Mum and Dad died? Our world fell apart.'

'Yes, and I'm sure you've enjoyed having a boy to look after. You know, given that you never got the chance...'

'It's got nothing to do with Peter,' I muttered.

'Hasn't it? Don't you think that might have blinded you a bit?'

'No.'

'Okay, fair enough. All I'm saying is, you have to be firm with Jensen, put your foot down. There's something about him...' She searched for the right phrase. 'I can't explain, he just seems false to me. Like it's all an act. He knows you feel sympathy for him and he's taking advantage. It's like he's got his claws into you and won't let go.'

I let her words sink in. 'Do *you* think he's behind the online bullying, and the graffiti and stuff?'

'I don't know. Possibly. The thing is, Rachel, now that Dom has gone, and it's just the two of you in the house... you're vulnerable.'

'I'm going to tell him tonight,' I said, putting my jacket back on. 'I'll give him an ultimatum. He has to leave by tomorrow.'

'Good.' Karina smiled. 'I'm so sorry about Dom. Don't be on your own at a time like this. Eat with us. Stay the night if you like.'

'I'd rather go home, thanks.'

'Okay. But if you need us, just shout. And good luck with Jensen. I'm sure Meg and Liv will come straight back as soon as they know he's gone.'

I drove home fighting back the tears that threatened to blur my vision. The house was empty. Jensen must have gone to work. If he was on a late shift, he wouldn't be back until the early hours of the morning. I didn't want to wait up all night. I had to tell him now, before I lost my nerve.

I checked my phone again – still no reply from Liv.

I didn't bother to take off my shoes or jacket, just turned round and left the house. The George was on the high street, about fifteen minutes' walk away, just beyond the Tube station. It was properly dark now, and there was a sharp chill in the air. Christmas trees twinkled in bay windows, but I felt untouched by their jollity. The city foxes were out in force, cutting between driveways like they owned the place, nosing around wheelie bins and builders' skips. One stood in my path, staring up at me with bright yellow eyes. I stopped and waited for him to move, but there were several seconds of stalemate before he finally slouched off, unfussed and unhurried.

I crossed over at the traffic lights. It was raining now, and I didn't have an umbrella. The George was in front of me. It was a boozer's pub, not the kind of place where I would normally venture on my own. The cheap beer made it popular with sixth-formers from the local secondary school, particularly on exam results day or at the end of the academic year.

I walked up the steps and entered through the glass double doors. The place was packed, predominantly with groups of older men, but there were also some couples and even a few families who'd come for their Saturday tea. I wandered around looking for Jensen, but he wasn't there. Guessing he was either in the kitchen or on a break, I went up to the bar and waited patiently to be served.

'Yes? What can I get you?' asked the young barwoman when it was my turn.

'A small Pinot Grigio, please,' I said. 'No, actually, make it a large one.' I needed Dutch courage to do this.

She poured out the measure and put my glass on the counter. 'Anything to eat?'

'No thanks.'

'Card or cash?'

I took out my card and pressed it against the reader. 'I don't suppose you know when Jensen will be taking his break, do you?' I asked, as it bleeped acceptance. 'Only I'd like to have a quick word with him if possible.'

She frowned at me. 'Who did you say?'

'Jensen Watson. He collects glasses and stuff.'

'Sorry. Don't know who you mean.'

'*Jensen Watson,*' I repeated loudly, as if she were deaf.

'Nobody by that name works here,' she said.

'He does, he does.' I sighed irritably. 'I know for a fact that he's on shift tonight.'

'And I know for a fact that he isn't,' she retorted.

'Sorry. This doesn't make any sense.'

She went to serve the next customer, but I called after her. 'Can I speak to the manager, please?'

'*I'm* the manager,' she replied, turning back.

'Jensen definitely works here,' I insisted. 'He started about two weeks ago.'

She looked me up and down. 'Are you his mum?'

I shook my head. 'No, no. He's my daughter's boyfriend. He lives with us.'

'There's no Jensen here,' she said. 'Sorry, love, but it sounds like he's been lying to you.'

PART TWO

<h1 style="text-align:center">TWENTY-FIVE</h1>

I read Rachel's message again, clenching my jaw with irritation, biting down on my lip until I taste blood.

I have some difficult family news, and I want to tell you in person, not in a text.

What difficult family news? What on earth is she talking about? Sounds like this is just another ruse to get Liv to go home or at least pick up the phone. The woman sounds desperate, like she's losing the plot. Makes me really mad. Why won't she back off and leave Liv alone? It's only been fourteen days since she last saw her. Jesus! That's nothing! Growing up, sometimes I didn't see my parents for weeks. They didn't text or call me every fucking day – they had their own lives to live. Careers to follow. Friends to hang out with.

More to the point, I don't see them at all now. Ever. So, Rachel – quit whining.

The texts I sent would have been enough to keep most normal mothers at bay, but not Helicopter Mum of the Year. Make that the Decade. The Century. Sending the video was a risk, but I got away with it. Funny how people see what they want to see, believe what they want to believe. She didn't suspect a thing. I thought the video would give me breathing space, but no, now she wants more. The stupid woman won't be satisfied unless she gets a face-to-face. Preferably an in-person meeting, a video call at a pinch. Neither of which, I'm afraid, is possible.

I so don't need this complication. I've got enough to deal with. There's so much to do, and I'm on a deadline. Time is ticking.

I return to Liv's phone. Such a pity I read the message. That was a mistake. Rachel has hope now. She's waiting for the call. And when it doesn't come, she'll worry, telling herself that it's not like Liv to ignore her when there's something really important at stake. She'll make excuses for her, but deep down, she won't fully believe them. She'll sense that all is not well, which is exactly what I don't want.

Got to be careful here, got to be smart. I need to quash those creeping doubts before they take root. If I don't give Rachel *something* to cling to, there's a chance she'll go to the police and report Liv missing. Not that I think they'll be interested. Not yet, anyway. It's too early and there's not enough evidence. Young people leave home every day, especially in London. Nobody's going to bat an eyelid at a girl having a row with her boyfriend and going to stay with some unspecified friend in Newcastle. It's understandable that she needs space to think things through. She doesn't want said boyfriend – who I happen to know can be rather intense – to find out where she's living, in case he pays her a visit. That's a solid scenario. Even so, I could do without the police sniffing around.

It's all about timing, creating a believable narrative, keeping Liv 'alive and well' for as long as possible. To help with this, I've played some games on her phone and liked a few posts on Insta. Haven't dared post, though. That felt too risky.

The police will get involved eventually, of course, I'm not stupid. When the weeks and months go by and still Liv hasn't been in touch. When her birthday passes, when Mother's Day comes and goes. Does Liv usually send a Mother's Day card? I've no idea. It doesn't matter – I can't keep this up for much longer. By the time Mother's Day arrives, I'll be long gone.

I've always known that at some point I will have to step back and let events take their natural course. But it can't happen yet. I'm still working on parts of my plan. Liv is just one cog in the machine. An important cog, but just a cog. I'm still refining the details, making sure everything fits neatly into place. There can be no loopholes, no discrepancies. It has to be perfect, or it won't work.

I go back to Liv's phone, with its turquoise plastic cover wearing at the edges. It smells faintly of her perfume. I stare at the image on her home screen: two radiant, smiling faces pressed cheek to cheek. 'Look how happy we are!' they tell the camera. 'So very much in love!'

Horrible, violent memories instantly lurch into my brain, making me retch. I can't look at that photo. I want to change it. Now. But I can't afford myself that luxury. Everything has to appear normal. There must be no deviations, no thoughtless clues left behind.

TWENTY-SIX

I knocked back the wine in one gulp and slammed the glass down on the bar. Then I turned on my heel and left the pub, my head reeling with the implications of what I'd just discovered. Jensen didn't work at the George. It sounded like he had never worked there. Yet he'd left the house to do his 'shift' almost every day for the last two weeks, dressed all in black. He'd regaled me with stories about the regulars, spoken about how the manager liked him and wanted to train him to do proper bar work. But he'd made it all up. Deceived us.

As I walked home in the darkness, I tried to work out what was going on in his head. Had it not occurred to him that it would be incredibly easy to uncover his lie? True, Dom and I rarely drank in the George, but it was our nearest pub and popular with Meg's crowd. What really bothered me was where he had been going instead. And what he had been doing for twelve hours a day, often not returning until well after midnight.

I unlocked the front door and stepped into the hallway. The house was dark and cold. Jensen would be back later, and I would have to spend the night alone with him in the house. I felt scared. If he'd lied about his non-existent job, he could easily have lied about other things...

I went around turning on all the lights, claiming the space as my own. I entered Meg's room and stared at her empty bed, the walls stripped bare of her posters; even the dream catcher she hung from the light fitting had gone. Guilt washed over me. I'd dismissed her claims that Jensen was behind the trolling, believed him over my own daughter.

I climbed to the top floor and entered the flatlet. I didn't know what I was looking for exactly – evidence of his wrongdoing, I guess. I blamed him for everything now – the ruined birthday cake, the rubbish in the garden, the scratched car, the graffiti. The more I thought about it, the easier I found it to associate him with every incident. He'd been present every time. He was also savvy with technology and probably knew how to create fake Instagram accounts.

But although he had definitely had the opportunity to commit these crimes, I couldn't think of a motive. He loved living here and had done everything he could to ingratiate himself with our family. His desire to stay with us for as long as possible had been a big part of the argument with Liv. Why would he risk that by attacking Meg? It didn't make sense. I could understand – almost – why he would pretend to have a job. He knew Dom had been unhappy about him freeloading, and also that Liv had wanted him to earn some money to put towards a deposit on a flat rental. But why hadn't he found a *real* job? There were so many vacancies, particularly in hospitality. I realised I didn't know the guy at all.

I stared at the room, looking for clues. His laptop was lying on the bed – that was where people kept their secrets these days and seemed the obvious place to start. I sat down, flipped open the lid and switched it on. After a few seconds, a photo of Jensen flanked by a couple of about my age filled the screen. His parents, no doubt. I studied their smiling faces, noting the enthusiastic way he had his arms around their shoulders, drawing them close. It was a simple portrayal of family happiness.

Emotion choked in my throat as I remembered that Jensen's parents were dead and that he was alone in the world. I didn't know the full details of what had happened, but I knew he'd tried to save his mum and dad and had failed. It must have been a deeply traumatic experience, enough to put any young person off balance, maybe even make them do stupid things. Feeling suddenly uncomfortable, I shut the lid and put the laptop back just as I'd found it.

I opened the wardrobe next, still not sure what I was looking for. Most of the clothes hanging there belonged to Liv rather than Jensen. I distracted myself for a few moments flicking through her dresses, most of which were familiar to me. I found the one she'd worn to her graduation ceremony – it was bottle green with a fitted waist and cap sleeves and had a vintage look about it. I remembered how beautiful she'd looked that day, the colour contrasting with her almost golden hair. I pictured the five of us sitting around the restaurant table, congratulating Liv and Jensen on their achievements, toasting the future. Even Meg was full of smiles.

Then I saw it – the dress she had worn in the video she'd sent me only a few days ago. It was there right in front of me, hanging in all its pink, floaty sparkliness. I took it out and spun it around; put my nose to the flimsy cloth and smelt the lingering notes of Liv's Good Girl perfume. How was this possible? Did she have two identical dresses?

The Newcastle bar, the shorter hair, the drunken, carefree tone of Liv's voice... it was blindingly obvious now. I sat on the bed and took out my phone, trembling as I played the video yet again, this time watching it with new eyes.

This was an old video, made months ago, when she was still at university. If I had to guess, I would say she'd originally sent it to Jensen. *Love you, love you, love you.* That wasn't the way she usually spoke to me.

What if someone else had her phone and had used it to trick us? And what if that someone was Jensen?

My heart pounded as I scanned my memory for details of the last time I'd seen Liv in person. It had been that Friday, two weeks ago, when we were about to leave for Southwold. She'd said goodbye and wished us a good trip. I'd tried to contact her on Saturday, but she hadn't responded. Dom had been angry with me for pestering, and I'd had to promise to leave her alone for the rest of the weekend. How I regretted that promise now.

We'd returned home early Sunday evening. Neither Jensen nor Liv had been there. We assumed they'd gone out for a drink or to watch a film and didn't think much of it. Then Jensen came back on his own. It was late, and he seemed in a bad way. He admitted that he and Liv had had a terrible row on Saturday. She'd walked out, and he'd spent Sunday getting lost in Epping Forest, arriving home in the middle of the night covered in mud. At least that was what he'd told us.

At the time, there'd been no reason not to believe him. I knew Liv could be volatile – her emotions continuously bubbled just beneath the surface, while Meg buried hers deep. As a teenager, she had stormed out of the house during arguments several times, although she had always come crawling back eventually and, as far as I could remember, had never stayed out all night.

As I went back over Jensen's account of the weekend, little things that had nagged at me before suddenly seemed like gaping holes. I had never really understood why Liv had been the one to leave, when this was her childhood home. She wasn't a wimp – she could stand up for herself. Maybe she'd told Jensen to get out, but he'd refused to go. But if that had been the case, it was strange that she'd left in the middle of the night – like many young women, she was nervous about being outside in the dark by herself, especially with nowhere to go. But maybe that wasn't what had happened at all.

My gaze drifted back to the pink dress, which in my panic I'd dropped to the floor. It lay splayed out on the carpet, like a dead body. How had I been so stupid as to not realise what had been going on? Perhaps Liv had finished with him, and he'd refused to accept it. Had he hurt her? Had he *killed* her? Had he buried her body deep in Epping Forest?

I gasped for breath. I couldn't believe I was entertaining such absurd and terrifying thoughts. Jensen was a great guy, warm and friendly; he'd been nothing but kind and generous towards me. I'd welcomed him into our home, encouraged him to feel like he was one of the family. And I'd been certain that he loved Liv. She was everything to him.

But I also knew that sometimes love made people do unspeakable things. Women were attacked and even murdered every week by their husbands or boyfriends – ex-partners who wouldn't take no for an answer, or who refused to accept that the relationship was over. Could Liv be such a victim? It seemed utterly unthinkable, and yet here I was thinking it. Suddenly I felt horribly sick. I ran into the bathroom and threw up into the toilet.

If Jensen had Liv's phone, it would be hidden somewhere, possibly in the flatlet. I tried calling her number, more in hope than expectation as it seemed unlikely that he would have left the phone switched on. I strained my ears for the familiar ringtone but was met with insolent silence. Of course he wouldn't have made that basic a mistake. I would have to conduct a thorough search of the place.

I dug into pockets and felt inside shoes. I opened drawers and cabinets, looking inside, behind, on top, underneath. I got down on my stomach and peered under the bed. I went into Dom's old office and searched behind the bookshelves, rummaged through a box of stationery items and another of random computer leads. I tried the bathroom cabinet, checking behind bottles of shampoo and mouthwash, moisturiser and massage oil. The phone wasn't anywhere.

Perhaps he'd hidden it in the loft, I thought, although there'd been very little space left following the conversion. I opened the tiny door and crawled into the dark, narrow passage, feeling my way past boxes of family memorabilia. I delved into the boxes, but her phone wasn't there.

Feeling despondent, I reversed back into the bedroom, almost bumping my head on the sloping ceiling as I stood up. My jeans were covered in dust and my hands were filthy. I had to get out of here before Jensen came home.

He would be back later, wearing his blacks, pointing to the beer stains on his shirt, talking about the punters and his colleagues. It was all manufactured to deceive me. But I wasn't going to betray the fact that I was on to him. Nor did I want to call the police. Not yet. I didn't have enough evidence against Jensen, or proof that Liv had come to harm. There was a chance that she was still alive, and that he was holding her somewhere against her will. If the police brought him in for questioning now, he would only lie or say 'no comment', and we might never find out what had happened to her.

Next time he left for work, I would follow him. Maybe he would lead me to her. It was a long shot, but worth a try.

TWENTY-SEVEN

That night, I lay in bed wide awake with fear. As there was no lock on my door, I'd barricaded myself in with furniture, jamming a chair under the handle. There was no logical reason why Jensen would want to come into my room, but I felt safer knowing he couldn't.

At about 2 a.m., I heard the squeak of the front door opening and shutting. He was back. I listened hard, trying to decipher the noises. He stayed downstairs for a while, boiling the kettle for a tea or coffee, taking something from the fridge. About ten minutes later, he climbed the stairs. I felt so tense I could hardly breathe.

The floorboards creaked as he walked around the flatlet, but after a few minutes, all noises stopped. I imagined him switching off the lights and getting into bed. How could his conscience allow him to sleep? I wondered. I tried to settle my mind and think of other things, but it was impossible.

Jensen slept in on Sunday morning. He was tucked away up there, but his presence was a toxic fog permeating through the house. It filled my lungs, choking me. I wanted to be as far away from him as possible, but at the same time I didn't want him to be alone in the house any more. Once a welcome guest, now he was an intruder. In an hour or so's time he might get up and come downstairs for a bite to eat before leaving for his non-existent shift at the pub. I wouldn't be able to face him. I needed to stay out of his way until then.

Apart from a brief foray to the kitchen for tea and toast at seven o'clock, I remained in my room all morning. I tried not to make any noise. If he heard me and knocked on the door, I would pretend I was ill, but with luck, he'd assume I'd gone out.

I already had a plan in place. When he left the house, I would follow him. I'd never done such a thing before, didn't have a clue how it worked. When people were trailed in detective dramas, there was a whole team on the job, in cars and on foot, taking it in turns to get close, communicating with each other all the time. In contrast, I was on my own, and what was more, Jensen knew me. How would I even attempt it? Skulking in doorways or crouching behind parked cars was not my style. I decided I would hide in plain sight, walking behind him at a distance. If he turned round and saw me, I would pretend I was on my way to the shops. 'Oh, it's you, Jensen!' I'd say. 'I didn't realise.' In my head, it sounded feasible.

I started to hear noises from upstairs just after 11 a.m. – footsteps going back and forth overhead, the shower on full blast, music that sounded so upbeat and smug I wanted to march up the stairs and smash his face in. Part of me longed to confront him – to beat the truth out of him if I had to – but another, more intelligent part of me knew that would be a stupid thing to do. I couldn't let him know I suspected anything was wrong. So I just listened and tried to stay calm.

At a quarter to twelve, Jensen descended the stairs. I lay on the bed, holding my breath. He went into the kitchen for a while, presumably for a late breakfast – helping himself to coffee, eating food I'd bought – then returned to the hallway. I guessed he'd put his boots on because he started to clump around on the tiled floor. I pictured him slipping on his jacket and tying a scarf around his neck. I was fully dressed myself, ready to spring into action the moment he left the house.

As soon as I heard the front door click shut, I leapt up and went to the bedroom window. I watched him walk up the road, then hurtled down the stairs, threw on my coat, picked up my bag and let myself out.

He was already halfway up the hill. I walked as quickly as I dared, my gaze a laser beam on his back. At the top, he turned left, disappearing from sight. I accelerated my pace, hoping to reach the corner before he made another turn, although I had a pretty good idea where he was heading. Our nearest Underground station was at the end of the next street. My heart sank. If he took the Tube, it would be extremely difficult to follow him without being spotted, but I had to try.

I needed to get closer, but not too close. I quickened my step, my heart pounding, a painful stitch developing in my side. The wide street was lined with trees, but they were winter-bare and gave me no cover.

As I'd predicted, he went into the Tube station. I followed cautiously. It was the middle of the day, off-peak, and the station was quiet. I glanced up at the board. The next eastbound train left in three minutes, the westbound in four. Jensen had already gone through the ticket barrier and was heading down to the platforms. There were no crowds to lose myself in, so I had no choice but to do the same. I stepped onto the escalator. He was no more than a few dozen steps ahead. His head was down, suggesting that he was absorbed in his phone and completely unaware that I was behind him.

Keep it that way, I thought.

At the bottom of the escalator, he went in the direction of

the westbound platform. The train was due in a couple of minutes. I had to make sure I was on it, but I didn't dare walk onto the platform in case Jensen spotted me. Nor did I want to leap into the same carriage as him. Peeping around the corner, I saw that he'd gone to the far end, aiming for the rear of the train. Good. All I had to do was stay where I was and climb aboard at the very last second, just before the doors closed. But how would I be able to see where he got off?

A sharp wind blew through the tunnel, heralding the arrival of the train. It thundered in and came to a standstill. The doors whooshed open and he got on. I waited for as long as I could, then sprang onto the platform and threw myself inside.

I was too excited to sit down, although there were plenty of empty seats. I stood by the double doors, at the ready. I had no idea where I was going, or whether I would be able to continue following Jensen. Every time the train stopped, I poked my head out to see whether he was getting off, but he remained on board.

We'd reached the City, where the platforms were far more crowded. Every time the train stopped, more people got on and off. I saw a sea of bobbing heads, several of which could have belonged to Jensen. We arrived at Bank, where a number of Tube lines converged. I peered out again, more in hope than expectation, and there he was – stepping onto the platform. I was so surprised that I nearly forgot to leave the train myself. I jumped off and pursued him, weaving through the throng, training my eyes on his dark hair and buff-coloured jacket as he shuffled onto a downward escalator. From there, he took a travelator, walking in that slow, meandering way everyone does while studying their phone. He appeared to be heading for the Northern Line. I tucked in behind the other passengers, keeping him in my sights.

He went and stood on the southbound platform. He was going to the other side of the river. But where exactly? London

Bridge? Borough Market? I had to get closer, or I would lose him.

The train thundered in and Jensen climbed aboard. I was about to make a dash for the carriage further along when a family trundling a load of suitcases walked right across my path. I darted around them, but I was too late. The doors shut in front of me and the train set off, disappearing into the tunnel.

I cursed loudly. I'd got so far, only to be thwarted at the last moment by a bunch of tourists. There was no point my catching the next train – I had no idea where Jensen would get off. I could be wandering around south London all day looking for him. Feeling desperate and defeated, I retraced my steps and went home.

I climbed the stairs to the top floor and entered the flatlet. I needed to look for clues as to where Jensen might have gone. I realised that I knew very little about him. Every time I'd tried to find out more about his past and the tragedy that had befallen his family, I'd been shut out. Liv had warned me that conversation about the fire might trigger a bad reaction, so for once I'd done as I was told and avoided the subject.

His laptop was still on the bed. I opened it up and stared blankly at the desktop image – Jensen and his parents, arms around each other, smiling to camera. The picture had been taken in front of a large double-fronted country house, built in brick and covered with ivy. The windows were generous, and there was a grand entrance with steps and a stone porch, above which was chiselled a name. I could only see part of it, the rest obscured by Jensen's father's head. The word began with 'Briar'. Briar what? I wondered.

My brain went into overdrive as I tried to remember the few details Liv had divulged last year, when she'd first got together with Jensen. She'd told me he'd been brought up in a mansion with a swimming pool and tennis courts and enormous grounds. But what was its full name and where was it situated? I couldn't remember. All I knew was that there had been a terrible fire, and the place had burnt to a shell.

Surely a disaster like that would have made the local news. I shut Jensen's laptop and went back downstairs, switching on the family computer in the dining room. I typed various keywords into the search engine, including Jensen's family name, *fire*, *briar* and anything else I could think of, praying for the whole story to appear instantly on screen. No such luck. I tried again and again, using different combinations of keywords, first with Sussex, then Surrey, Suffolk, Essex, Norfolk...

I found a surprising number of reports of house fires, but nothing seemed to fit. It seemed that local papers were reluctant to name victims, and the locations given were a little vague, perhaps deliberately. I floundered around for what felt like hours, making guesses and assumptions, going down blind alleys, thinking I'd found the correct report only to later realise that it came from the United States or Australia. Without the heating on, the house grew cold, but I barely felt it. I forgot to eat or drink, my full attention focused on my fruitless search.

I knew I had to take a different approach. Think more laterally. I dismissed keywords associated with fire and Jensen's name and concentrated on the word *briar*. At first it was just as hopeless, but then I played around with the word, adding different suffixes – Briarwood, Briardene, Briarhill – and eventually found an article in an online newspaper that made my heart race. It was dated seven years earlier and was about a summer fete that had been held in the gardens of a large country house called Briarfields, situated just outside Carlington, a small village in the Surrey Hills.

I read feverishly through the piece, looking for evidence that I'd found the right place, but the discussion was all about pony rides, the WI cake stall and a display by the local gymnastics club. The only name mentioned was some minor TV celebrity who lived nearby and who had drawn the raffle.

I peered at a grainy photo featuring the winners of the fruit and vegetable competition. They were all elderly, apart from a teenage girl who looked as if she might have won a sulking contest. A woman was standing next to her, shaking the hand of one of the successful growers. Could that possibly be Jensen's mother? I compared it with the photo I'd taken of the picture on Jensen's desktop. Yes, it was her, I was sure of it. She had the same smart, expensive haircut, the same open expression, the same confident smile.

I searched for the fire again, this time with the name of the house and village, and within seconds it popped up before me.

Two fatalities after fire tears through Grade II listed country house near Carlington

Surrey Fire and Rescue Service were called to a blaze at Briarfields, near Carlington, at 11.55 p.m. on 24 December. Eight fire engines, around sixty firefighters, two water pumps and an aerial ladder were employed. Firefighters said the blaze was extinguished by 6.15 a.m. Four fire engines remained on site, working to secure the building and dampen hotspots.

A man and a woman, as yet unnamed, were trapped on the upper floor of the house by smoke. Despite efforts to save them, they died at the scene and their bodies were later recovered by firefighters. A third person was taken to a nearby hospital by ambulance, suffering from smoke inhalation and burns. There were no other casualties.

The cause of the fire is as yet unknown.

I'd found it.

The fire had taken place nearly two years ago. The damage

must have been repaired by now, the house sold to pay off Jensen's parents' debts. New owners would be living there. Hopefully they could give me some information about the family and what had happened that night. If not, I would go into the village and ask around.

TWENTY-EIGHT

I got up at six the next morning and crept around the kitchen, making sure I didn't disturb Jensen. I forced myself to have some breakfast before I left. It would take me a couple of hours to drive to Carlington, crossing the Thames at Dartford and taking the M25, then the M23. I hated driving in heavy traffic, but there was no other option. According to Google Maps, the house was twenty minutes' drive from the nearest railway station. As a Londoner who complained if I had to wait more than a few minutes for the Tube, the remoteness of the place astounded me. Why would anyone choose to live so far from amenities?

I sat in the car letting the engine run to clear the windscreen before I set off. There was a damp chill in the air. It was still dark, the sky illuminated at the edges by an industrial glow – purple streaked with rusty orange.

The roads were already congested. Factories and office blocks lined the highway, black boxes piled up all higgledy-piggledy. Everything looked unreal, as if I was driving through a comic book landscape. It was hard to concentrate and I kept finding myself in the wrong lane. Trucks and pantechnicons thundered past me on both sides, trapping me in the middle, refusing to let me tuck in. I gripped the wheel tightly, my eyes flicking between the road in front of me and the rear and wing mirrors. My hunched shoulders burnt with pain, but I couldn't relax them.

I have no idea how I made it onto the M25, or picked up the M23, or how I managed to navigate to the correct turn-off. The time slipped by without my knowing, as if I'd been hypnotised, guided in a trance. Without the sat nav, I think I would have driven straight past the exit.

As soon as I left the motorway, I entered an utterly different landscape. I drove along country lanes, through one-street villages, past lush green fields and thick grass verges, plunging myself deeper and deeper into the Surrey Hills. After about ten minutes, I reached the outskirts of Carlington.

It was a neat, well-cared-for place. You could almost smell the privilege seeping through the brickwork of the large houses that lined the main street. In the centre of the village was a small green with a horse trough and a shelter. On one side was an attractive stone church with a tall spire, and on the other a gorgeous-looking pub covered in ivy. There was no supermarket, just a short row of small shops – bistro, café, hairdresser, newsagent and traditional butcher. It was perfect – too perfect, perhaps – and reminded me of an illustration on an old-fashioned jigsaw puzzle.

I checked the time – half past eight. All was quiet. The shops were closed and the only people about were mums taking their children to school. I slowed down as I approached St Mary's Church of England Primary. Jensen must have gone there, I thought. I tried to imagine him growing up in these idyllic and protected surroundings, where you never saw a homeless person on the street, or witnessed a nasty argument on the bus, or had your phone snatched by somebody whizzing past on an electric scooter. Jensen had always seemed so down-to-earth and streetwise. I couldn't quite bring the picture into being.

The sat nav took me through the village and a mile later told me to turn down a narrow unsignposted lane. It was lined with thick hedgerows and trees, the top branches of which grew over the road to form a dark green tunnel. The narrow lane led to an even narrower track, marked *Private*. Taking no notice, I carried on. The ground was muddy and full of potholes. The hedgerows hadn't been trimmed, and thorny branches stuck out, scratching the sides of the car. Straggly, unkempt grass grew down the centre, brushing the undercarriage as I drove. Nobody had ventured this far for a long time, I thought, starting to lose confidence in my theory.

After almost half a mile, I rounded a bend and the track abruptly came to an end, opening out to face a gravel driveway pitted with weeds. Briarfields loomed over me – the charred shell of what would have once been a beautiful old country house, its red bricks blackened with smoke, its windows blown, its roof smashed to pieces, its burnt rafters sticking out like the ribs of a whale.

I stopped the car and got out, shivering as I reached for my coat. The grand entrance I remembered from the photo on Jensen's desktop had been boarded up, as had all of the ground-floor windows. *Danger! Keep out!* had been sprayed in red paint in several places. I walked around, hoping to find a way in, but the place was secure.

To one side of the house there was a modern single-storey building – a gym, perhaps, or some kind of studio. Its roof had also gone and its glass doors had exploded. I edged forward and looked through a tiny gap between the boards, which had warped in the rain. Inside was a mass of indistinguishable black rubble.

Next to the annexe was a large garage, similarly destroyed. A melted object that might once have been a quad bike lay in front of it. I walked around to the back of the house, where there was a wide stepped terrace. The decking was slippery with moss. Six wooden chairs were arranged around a long table, their seat cushions wet and dotted with mould. Beyond the terrace was the swimming pool. Nobody had drained it. Its plastic cover had broken free, and it was full of dead leaves and rotting vegetation. There was no obvious way into the building, no prised-open door, no hole to crawl through. The only sounds I could hear were the rustling of trees and the creaking of rafters in the wind.

Jensen obviously hadn't been here since the fire. Nobody had, other than to board it up. The place was secure from squatters, but it had been left to rot. Perhaps the insurance company had failed to pay out, or maybe Jensen had been so traumatised that he hadn't been able to face returning. I remembered him saying that his parents had left large debts he'd had to settle, and that he'd inherited nothing. But surely this land was very valuable. It was a large plot in one of the richest parts of the country. Why hadn't he sold it?

I drew my coat across my chest, shuddering with cold. The house was giving me the creeps. I didn't want to stay here a moment longer. I rushed back to the car, drove round in a large circle then took the track back to the road.

I wanted life. People. More than anything, I wanted to see my daughter.

My nerves were so rattled I could hardly drive. I was scared that if I went straight back onto the motorway in this state I would have an accident. I decided to return to Carlington and have a coffee at the café I'd spotted earlier. It was after 9 a.m., so I hoped it would be open by now. I might even meet a local who'd known Jensen's family and liked to gossip.

I crawled into the village, parking in one of the spaces outside the row of shops. The café was indeed open. Four young mums were seated around a large table, fresh from the school drop-off, drinking lattes and nibbling cinnamon buns as they chatted. An older man was reading the paper over a mug of tea. I took a seat by the window, removed my woolly hat and unzipped my coat.

'Hi there. What can I get you?' I looked up at the waitress. 'Something to drink? Breakfast?' She pointed at the menu on the table. 'Everything's locally sourced.'

'A coffee would be lovely, thanks.'

'Latte? Cappuccino, flat white, Americano?' She waited patiently for my response.

'Oh, um... flat white. And maybe a croissant?'

'Sure.'

'Excuse me... are you local?'

She nodded. 'Yup. Born and bred. My grandparents were from around here too.'

'Good. So you must have known the Watsons.'

'The Watsons?' She put her head on one side. 'Don't think so. Sorry, that surname doesn't ring a bell. Do they live in Carlington itself or outside?'

'Just outside. They owned Briarfields, the big house that burnt down two years ago.' I lowered my voice. 'They died in the fire.'

'Oh, you mean Claire and James Ambersley. Yes, that was a terrible tragedy, totally shocking. They were such a lovely couple, too, gave so much back to the community.'

'Ambersley?' I repeated. 'No, no, you're mistaken. Their surname was Watson. I know that because I know their son. He lives with us. In fact, he's my daughter's—'

'Their *son*?' she repeated, frowning.

'Yes, Jensen Watson. You must know him. Twenty-four, tall, dark... He was there when the fire broke out. He tried to save them – nearly died in the process. It was in the papers, he was taken to hospital...' I tailed off as I caught the strange expression developing on her face. 'What is it?'

'I've lived here all my life,' she said, slowly and deliberately. 'I wasn't close friends with the family, but they were well known locally. I went to the funeral, the whole village turned out for it. And I can tell you with utter certainty that Claire and James Ambersley didn't have a son.'

TWENTY-NINE

Hey Meg,

Seems like everyone's forgotten about poor little you and your evil troll. They think that now you're staying with your auntie, you're safe. That it's all over. The cake, the rubbish, the graffiti...

I haven't forgotten you, though. I've still got you firmly in my sights.

But first I wanted to say that I feel your pain. All this fuss about Liv, it must be so annoying. Once more she's grabbing all the attention, pushing you into the background. Nobody cares any more about how you much you're suffering. How you can't bear the idea of sleeping without the light on, how you're terrified of walking through the estate at night. And it gets dark so early these days...

But don't worry, girl. Help is at hand. I'm going to do something to make everyone sit up and take notice of you again. Mummy and Daddy will come running and you'll be the star of the show. They'll forget all about your missing sister for a few minutes.

Or I suppose you could do something... You know what I'm talking about.

Just a thought.

THIRTY

I pressed the buzzer for Karina's flat and waited impatiently for her to answer. I'd driven back from Carlington with my brain on fire and my stomach contorted with anxiety. I was desperate for her to be in.

'Rachel? What are you doing here?' She sounded surprised to see me, and not particularly pleased. Karina took working from home seriously and didn't like to be interrupted during office hours.

I spoke into the camera. 'Sorry. Please can I come in? I need to see you, it's important.'

There was a brief pause, then she sighed and said, 'Okay.' The front door released, and I ran inside, taking the lift to the tenth floor.

Karina was standing in the open doorway, wearing a smart work shirt and a pair of scruffy jogging bottoms. 'What's wrong?' she asked as I approached. 'Only I've got a Zoom meeting soon, so I can't—'

'It's Jensen,' I said, almost pushing past her and walking into the living room.

'What about him?' She shut the door and followed me. 'Rachel?'

I paced about. 'He's been lying to us – about his identity, his parents, his past, his job, everything. I'm scared, Karina. I'm really scared!'

'Hey, hey, slow down!' She took hold of me. 'You're not making any sense. Take your coat off. Sit... I'll get you a drink.' She moved to the kitchen area and ran the tap. Like a glass of water was going to help.

I sat on the very edge of the sofa. A hoodie of Meg's was lying over the arm. I grabbed it and held it to my chest like a comfort blanket. 'Where is she? Meg, I mean.'

'At school, of course.'

'That's good... She's safe.' I gripped the hoodie tighter. 'She said there was something odd about Jensen, but I wouldn't listen, couldn't see it. I took his side over the graffiti. Now I'm sure he did it. He probably did everything – ruined your lovely cake, scratched the car... What if he's done other, even more terrible things? What if...' I couldn't say the rest out loud, but it had been all I'd been thinking of for the past two hours. 'How am I going to tell Meg?'

Karina put the glass on a side table. 'Tell her what?'

'That her sister's been kidnapped. Or worse!'

'Please, Rach, roll it back. I can't understand a word you're saying. Start at the beginning. What's been going on? And take it slowly, please.'

I sipped my water and told her what had happened over the last few days – discovering that Jensen didn't work at the George, following him on the Tube, driving to Briarfields and talking to the waitress in the café. I stumbled over my words as I tried to put my discoveries in the correct order. Karina's eyes grew wider and wider as she absorbed the full extent of Jensen's deception.

'This is really strange,' she said when I'd finished. 'Why did he pretend the Ambersleys were his parents? To get attention? To make people feel sorry for him, or think he's a hero, or what?'

'I don't know,' I replied. 'I've been racking my brains trying to work it out. I know from the photo on his desktop that he had *some* kind of relationship with Claire and James Ambersley, and he was definitely involved in a fire – I've seen the scars on his back. But the newspaper reports don't mention him by name and the waitress had never heard of anyone called Jensen Watson.'

'Okay...' Karina said, trying to be the calm one. 'I can see it looks bad, but we mustn't jump the gun here. Just because he lied about his job and his family, it doesn't automatically follow that he's harmed Liv.'

'I'm wondering whether she found out somehow and confronted him,' I said. It was just one of the many scenarios I'd imagined during the drive back from Carlington. 'Liv hates liars. I expect they had a terrible row.'

'Yes, possibly.' Karina didn't look convinced.

'I've never understood why she was the one that left. It's her home. She should have chucked *him* out.'

'Well... it was complicated.'

'What do you mean?' I asked. She looked away shiftily. I sensed she knew something I didn't. 'What is it?'

It took her a moment to reply. 'Liv didn't like being back at home. She said it was like being a child again. She begged Jensen to agree to move out, but he loved being part of a family and refused to budge.'

'She told you all this?'

'More or less.'

'Before she moved out?' Karina nodded. 'But she never said anything about it to me.'

'No, because she didn't want to hurt you. She loves you, Rachel, but...' Her eyes lowered. 'You know how it is. You've always had a tricky relationship with her.'

'No I haven't.'

'Well, she's had a tricky relationship with you, let's put it that way.'

I flinched. 'I don't know what you mean.'

'She finds you... overbearing... No, that's not quite right. Overinvolved. You hover above her the whole time – you won't leave her alone. All the way through uni, you contacted her every single day—'

'She was away from home – I didn't want her to feel lonely.'

'You were the one who was lonely, not Liv.' Karina walked to the window and looked out at the grey cityscape stretching before us.

'You don't understand,' I protested. 'You don't have children of your own, you don't know what it's like. Being an aunt is not the same.'

'Don't start on this again,' groaned Karina. 'You've always been jealous of my relationship with Liv and Meg.'

'It doesn't matter any more,' I replied, trying to sound brave. 'Liv can confide in who she wants. I just need to know she's safe.'

Karina's eyes flicked to the time on the cooker. 'What makes you think she's not?'

'Several things. I received this video of Liv in a bar in Newcastle, a bit pissed, sending me her love. She's got different hair and she's wearing a dress that's hanging in her wardrobe at home.'

'So, it's an old video. And probably not originally meant for you.'

'Exactly. Somebody's trying to pull the wool over my eyes, make me think she's in Newcastle, having a good time.'

Karina frowned. 'I suppose she could have sent it herself.'

'Yes, but why would she?'

'To stop you pestering her for a video call?'

'You can have another dig, but I don't buy it. I've begged

and begged Liv to pick up the phone and talk to me, but she refuses. Now I know why. Because she can't. Because he won't let her! Because she's...' My breath hitched in my throat. 'Oh God, Karina, what has he done with her? What have *I* done, letting him into my family? You were all right and I was wrong. I've been such an idiot. Harbouring a murderer in my house!'

Karina sat down next to me, took my hands and held them tightly. 'Enough! You've got to stop thinking like this. You're getting way ahead of yourself. It's all conjecture, there's no evidence that Liv's been harmed. Think about it. If Jensen *had* hurt her, he wouldn't have hung around waiting to be caught. He'd have run away, left the country. We don't know what happened on the day she left.'

'It was something bad, that's for sure. Something really, really bad. I know it, I can feel it!'

'Calm down, for God's sake.' Karina released my hands and stood up. 'Let me try calling her.'

I held my breath as she dialled Liv's number. The ringing pierced the silence as we waited for her to pick up. As usual, it went to voicemail, with no opportunity to leave a message.

'See?' I said. 'She never answers.'

'I'll send her a voice note.' Karina cleared her throat and spoke into the microphone. 'Hi, darling, Auntie K here. Hope everything's okay. We're all really worried because Mum sent you that urgent message and you haven't called her. She's really upset. Please give her, or me, or Meg, or your dad, a quick ring, just so we know you're all right. It doesn't need to be a deep chat – we just need to hear your voice. Otherwise we might have to report you as a missing person. Love you lots. Talk soon, byeee!'

'You made me out to be a right panicker,' I said grumpily.

'So? You want her to call, don't you?'

'Yes, but she won't. I know she won't.' I stood up. 'Thanks for trying. If she hasn't called either of us by tomorrow morning,

I'll go to the police. They need to bring Jensen in for questioning, find out who he really is, check his phone and computer. And they need to trace Liv's phone calls, access her emails, see if she's been using her bank card.' My voice started to choke up. 'I expect we'll have to give them a sample of her DNA, too. You know, in case—'

'Let's not go there until we have to.' She paused. 'Have you told Dom yet?'

'Dom?' I stepped away. 'No. Why would I? He's left the family – he couldn't care less.'

'That's not true. Liv's his daughter too.'

'He'll go mad. He never liked Jensen. He'll blame me for everything.'

'He needs to know. Think about it, Rachel.' She walked me to the front door. 'As soon as I hear from Liv, I'll call you, okay?'

'I don't want to go home,' I said. 'Not with him there. He scares me.'

'Try to avoid him. If you see him, don't let on that you know about the lies. I'm pretty sure Liv is absolutely fine, but if ...' she swallowed hard, 'if it turns out that he *has* harmed her, we don't want to warn him in advance, do we? He might run off, or panic, and that would make the police's job much harder.'

I shuddered. 'Yes, you're right.'

'Once we know Liv's okay, you can chuck him out on his arse, but until then, keep him close.' She smiled apologetically. 'I'm really sorry, my meeting's about to start. We'll speak later. Stay positive. Everything's going to be all right.'

The lights in the house were on, even though it was only mid-afternoon. As I pulled onto the driveway, I could see Jensen in the front room, sprawled on the sofa, scoffing a bag of crisps. Coloured lights from the TV screen flickered across his face. When I slammed the car door, he looked up and waved at me through the window. I forced a smile and waved back.

'Hi there!' I shouted cheerily as I entered the house.

'Hi, Rachel!'

I took off my coat and hung it on the hook, setting my face in a mask before I opened the door to the sitting room. 'Not working today?' I asked innocently.

'No, I decided to take some time off. I've been working non-stop for days. I'm knackered.'

'They work you hard at the George,' I said, studying his face for any twitch of guilt.

'Tell me about it.' He looked me up and down, registering my casual clothes and lack of make-up. 'Day off for you too?'

'Yes,' I said, suddenly remembering that I'd forgotten to call in sick earlier. 'I went to see Karina.'

'Oh, right. Is Meg still staying with her?'

'Yes. It seems to be working out quite well. She's going to school regularly, doing her homework...'

'Great. When kids lose their way, sometimes all it takes is one adult to get them back on track. Doesn't have to be a parent, or a teacher. It can be anyone.' There was a tenderness in his voice, and I wondered whether he was remembering Claire and James Ambersley – not his actual parents, but people who had perhaps had a parental influence on him. I wanted to ask him about it, but I didn't dare. Karina had warned me not to tip him off by asking too many questions. We were already uncomfortably close to the subject.

His gaze rested on my face, noting my pale skin and red-rimmed eyes, no doubt. 'Everything okay?'

'Yes, fine... well, not really, but... you know.'

'Yeah, a lot going on.'

'You're telling me.'

'I don't mean to, er, intrude, but is everything okay with you and Dom? Only I heard shouting on Saturday morning.'

'Did you? Sorry. It was just a tiff.' I put my plastered finger behind my back.

'It sounded like more than that.'

'Honestly, we're fine.' I was sure he knew more than he was letting on, but I didn't want him to realise how vulnerable I was.

'Oh good,' he continued, his gaze piercing me. 'It's just that I haven't seen him since, and I was wondering if something bad had happened. Like he'd walked out or something.'

'No, no, nothing like that. He's had to go back to Dubai, that's all,' I lied hurriedly. 'He'll be home in a couple of days.'

'He shouldn't leave you on your own.'

'It's okay, I'm used to it.'

'Even so... Fancy doing something together later? Seeing as how we've both got the day off. We could see what's on at the cinema, or go for a walk.'

The idea made me squirm inside. 'No thanks. It's very kind

of you, but I just don't feel up to it at the moment. I think I've got the flu coming.'

'Really? Is that why you look as if you've been crying?'

'My eyes are watering, that's all.'

He stood up and went towards the door. 'Let me make you a Lemsip.'

'No, I can do it. Please, don't fuss. I just need to rest.'

I tried to move past him, but he was standing in my way, half smiling. There was a very long pause. I felt goosebumps rising on my arms.

'You can tell me anything, you know,' he said. 'Liv may have walked out, but I'm still your friend.'

'There's nothing to tell. Sorry, I need to lie down.'

He didn't move. 'Has Dom left you?'

'No. I told you, he's gone away on business,' I blustered.

'That's not true, is it, Rachel?' I looked away. 'It's okay. I understand, I know what it's like to be rejected. It's tough to take. I hope you don't mind my saying, but you're a lovely person, you don't deserve to be treated like this. Dom's an idiot – he'll regret it for sure.'

'I really don't want to talk about it,' I muttered.

'You're embarrassed, I get that. But don't hide in shame, it's not your fault. You need support from your family right now. Liv and Meg should come home straight away.'

'Yeah, well... I expect they will.'

'I hope so. I presume you've told Liv?'

'Not as such. I want to speak to her in person.'

'Of course. Makes sense. Not the sort of thing you want to do in a text.' He sighed. 'Well, hopefully she'll get in touch soon.'

'Yes. Now I really need to go to my room.'

'You've always got me, you know,' he said, stepping aside to let me pass. 'Whenever you need a shoulder to cry on, I'm here for you.'

'Thanks.' I almost ran up the stairs.

'Oh, by the way, Rachel,' he called after me. 'I'm going out this evening to see some friends, so I won't need any supper.'

'Okay.' I thanked God that I was going to be spared from sharing a meal with him. We'd already had far too much interaction for my liking.

I shut myself in my bedroom and had a text exchange with Karina.

Jensen's at home. Acting a bit creepy. Kept asking about Dom.

Try to keep away from him as much as possible.

I told him I had the flu, but I don't think he believed me.

Good idea. Stay in your room! Have you heard from Liv?

No, not yet. I'm getting really worried now.

I'm sure she'll get in touch as soon as she can. Try not to worry. Xx

I lay on my bed waiting for Jensen to leave the house. I'd told Karina that I'd wait until tomorrow morning before contacting the police, but after that strange encounter downstairs, I decided it couldn't wait.

Exactly how do you report somebody missing? I didn't have a clue. I did what I seem to do every time I have a question about anything these days – googled it. It was obvious that there was no point in dialling 999. Liv's disappearance wouldn't be considered an emergency, although it felt like one to me.

According to AI, there were various options available – I could call 101 and speak to someone, go in person to our local police station, or report it online. Allegedly, each method was treated with the same seriousness and within the same time frame. In which case, there seemed no reason not to go down the online route.

Finally, at about 7 p.m., I heard Jensen leaving the house. I ran downstairs, fired up the computer in the dining room and started filling in a form. It seemed a strange way to report somebody missing – as unemotional as if I were completing a job application or customer survey. The initial questions were very hard to answer.

Are they in immediate danger or likely to come to immediate harm? Yes/No? There was no option to explain the nuances of the situation, so I had to put *No*.

Are you looking for someone you've lost touch with? I felt I *had* lost touch with Liv, because I didn't believe that the message we'd received had actually come from her, so I put *Yes*. The response was instant.

Someone you have lost touch with is not classed as a missing person.

I could go no further.

Determined not to give up, I went back and put *No* instead, which was obviously the correct answer, because it took me to the form proper. Giving Liv's personal details was easy, but I stumbled over stuff about her mobile phone. Did I think she had it with her? Well, yes and no. What were her social media accounts? I didn't know because she'd never let me follow her or be her friend.

The form went on to ask more detailed questions about the last time anyone had seen Liv, what I'd done so far to look for her and why I was concerned. *What kind of danger, if any, do you think the person might be in?* I started to tell the story of the past few months, but it sounded like a simple family falling-out, a load of fuss about nothing. It wasn't as if Liv hadn't been in contact since she'd left home. I'd received a message early on and had had some text exchanges with her. Although the video was old, one could argue that she'd sent it herself to make me believe she was in Newcastle.

Then came the questions that I couldn't answer. I didn't know what had happened immediately before she went missing, or what she'd been planning to do, or what kind of mood she'd been in or what she'd been thinking, or whether she'd been suitably dressed for the weather. Had she been having any issues in her relationships with friends, family, partners or other people in her life? Well, according to Karina, yes, she had, but could I say with any honesty that she'd been a victim of domestic abuse? No. Jensen himself had told us that he and Liv had had a bad row, and that was what had prompted her to leave. I'd seen the mess in the flatlet. He'd had plenty of time to clear it up before we came home but hadn't bothered. Was that because he'd had nothing to hide, or was it a double bluff?

I went to the next question. Was there anyone else I thought the police should talk to? Close friends, colleagues? Liv had always had lots of friends, but nobody she was really close to. Her bestie was in the Australian outback, and I didn't know who her uni mates were. She had no job, so there were no colleagues to ask. The closest person to her was Jensen, and he was my prime suspect. I wanted the police to arrest him, not come round for a cosy chat.

I got to the end of the form, where they asked me to upload a recent photo. I scrolled through my phone gallery and found the pictures I'd taken at Liv's graduation ceremony, just a few months ago. To outsiders, we'd seemed like the perfect happy family, celebrating our daughter's achievement, but now that I knew the truth, our smiles looked fake. At that time, Dom was having an affair with another woman, Meg was still being bullied, Liv was unsure about her future and possibly her relationship with Jensen. She wanted to break free from the family – specifically me. In just a few months, I'd lost them all and been left with a stranger whom I could no longer trust.

Tears welled in my eyes. The screen blurred and I had to look away. I went to the kitchen and poured myself a glass of cold wine, hoping it would calm me, but it didn't work. I had hardly eaten all day, and the alcohol made me feel light-headed and sick. I grabbed a biscuit from the tin and tried to settle my stomach, but the damage had already been done. What the hell? I thought, topping up my glass.

I took the wine back to the desk to finish the job. I cropped a photo of Liv wearing her graduation cap and gown, uploaded it and pressed submit. The form generated a reference number, and I was assured that the police would aim to respond within the hour.

I messaged Karina and she immediately sent a brief reply. *Well done. Have you told Dom yet?*

No, I had not told Dom. Since he'd walked out on me, I'd tried to banish all thoughts of him from my mind. I'd told myself it was because the situation with Liv was more important, but the truth was, I was in denial. He'd gone away so often for work – or so I'd thought – it had been easy to pretend that his absence was normal, maybe even that he'd return at the end of his trip. Of course, I wasn't so stupid that I believed it, but I couldn't face dealing with the new reality of my life.

Karina was right, though. Dom needed to know what was happening. The police would probably want to speak to him, and he would be angry with me if it came as a shock. I picked up my mobile and called his number. The call was refused after a couple of rings. I slammed the phone down. Okay, I thought, if you don't want to talk to me, that's your lookout.

I received an email from the police just over an hour later.

We've considered all the information you've given us, and it's our assessment that according to our criteria, we cannot consider Olivia Matthews a missing person.

I wasn't surprised. Liv's life didn't fall neatly into boxes – the situation was complex and messy. The police acted on evidence, and although the circumstances were odd, I could see how they didn't seem suspicious enough.

Right at that moment, I felt I didn't need evidence. I was tugged by an umbilical cord that had never been cut. I *knew* that my daughter was in danger. But I wasn't going to waste any more time asking others for help. I would find her myself.

THIRTY-TWO

This is getting very difficult. Rachel has put Karina on the case now. She's making vague threats, talking about getting the police involved, putting poor Liv under pressure to pick up the phone and reassure them that she's safe. Which of course she isn't. Far from it, in fact.

Another one of those horrible images jumps into my brain. I see her lying on the floor, head covered in blood. I remind myself that I didn't want to do it – it was never part of the plan – but she gave me no choice. It doesn't help, though.

Still, not going to think about that. What's done is done, it is what it is, as they say. Can't change it now. Just got to move with the mess, even though as messes go it's pretty fucking massive...

Back to this annoying message from Auntie Karina. It can't be ignored. Liv has to respond. Otherwise the police will be contacting her mobile network and tracing her whereabouts – correction, *my* whereabouts – via GPS tracking, mast pinging, something called stingrays and cell analysis. I know. I've looked it all up. It's been a risk using her phone, but I've had to keep various functions active to give the impression that everything's fine and there's nothing to worry about. But it's getting increasingly difficult to maintain. Now I either have to come up with some magic trick to make Rachel think she's talking to Liv, or I have to destroy this phone and get the hell out of here. And I don't want to leave just yet.

Things to do...

I return to Liv's tatty old mobile. It's unfortunate that normally mother and daughter are in touch all the time. Or rather, Rachel is in touch with Liv all the time. Scrolling back through their WhatsApp chat, I see that she does the vast majority of the heavy lifting. When Liv was at uni, she contacted her every day. And I mean, like every single day. Pointless rubbish and so many irritating questions!

How are you doing? How's the course going? How are you getting on with your new flatmates? Are you eating properly? Are you getting enough sleep? What do you want for your birthday? How's the cold? Why didn't you reply to my question? Has the landlord fixed the shower yet? What are you up to this weekend? When do you think you might be able to pop home?

Liv's responses amuse me. They're so short, you'd think she was paying to use WhatsApp by the word.

Fine. Good. Great. Of course. Yes. Don't know. Better. Been busy. No. Nothing much. Soon.

Sometimes she fobs Rachel off with an emoji – a smile or a thumbs-up, never a heart. Maybe she fears that it might be interpreted as a stamp of approval, signalling that she's perfectly happy to be bombarded with relentless Mum spam. Or maybe she can't bring herself to say she loves her mother. Ouch! That must hurt.

Hmm... Now I think of it, I did 'heart' one of the messages she sent recently. That was a slip. Hopefully nobody will look that closely. Rachel certainly didn't comment on it. She was probably thrilled.

Poor old Rachel. She never takes the hint, just carries on scattering hearts across the ether like digital confetti. Red, pink, purple, blue, green, orange, yellow – she has no idea what the different colours are supposed to mean. She pins them to Liv's brief replies, or lines them up in rows, or makes them explode like popcorn. Sometimes she intersperses the hearts with random 'fun' items, such as a cocktail glass or a flamenco dancer, a birthday cake (really?) or balloons. Then there are the giant pulsating hearts that are so full of love they could punch through the screen and knock you out.

Liv resolutely ignores her attempts to get the emoji party going. And to be honest, I don't blame her. I carry on scrolling back through their chat, boring myself to death, hoping that inspiration will suddenly strike. And it does.

I realise that Liv sends a lot of voice notes. I totally get why she does it. They satisfy her mother's desire for human contact while avoiding the tedium of live interaction. I play a few of them, listening to her hurried tone, the background noises that betray she's combining this chore with something more important – washing up, walking down the street, queuing at the supermarket till. They are rarely more than twenty seconds long. Reassuring yet deflecting.

This is exactly what I need.

I do a quick google and discover that it's frighteningly easy to fake somebody's voice. You don't have to be an AI nerd – anyone can do it. I watch a YouTube vid. It seems that all I have to do is download an app – there are several good ones on the market, but one is particularly recommended – feed it with some voice samples, write a script, make a few personalising tweaks, and there you go, job done. According to this guy from Texas, if you do it properly, it's very hard to detect. He doesn't seem bothered by the fact that it must be illegal.

The idea takes hold. I really like it. It'll take time to perfect, but if it gets Rachel off my back, it'll be worth both the effort and the cost. I'll create a lovely voice note from Liv, apologising for making everyone worry unnecessarily, begging for understanding and sympathy, promising to come home as soon as she feels able, maybe adding a touch of guilt-tripping... The phrases are already forming in my head. *Sorry, but I'm not in a great place right now. Can't face anyone. Please don't make me call.*

I've nothing else to do, so I spend hours writing the script, trying to get every aspect right, like I'm working on some new Netflix drama. For a start, where is it set? As far as Rachel is concerned, Liv is back in Newcastle, staying with uni friends. I think about creating a believable soundscape for the background.

Rustle of trees. Footsteps walking along the pavement. Traffic noises in the distance. People passing, mumbling in Geordie accents.

Too much? Too contrived? Would it be better – not to mention easier – to set this in an indoor environment? In a kitchen, perhaps. Liv often sends voice notes against the noise of domestic appliances.

A washing machine spinning. The thrum of an old fridge freezer. A kettle boils. We hear water being poured into a mug.

Now it sounds like an investigative journalist interviewing illegal immigrants in a dodgy HMO. This is a voice note, not a podcast.

I let out a frustrated sigh. This isn't as easy as the guy on YouTube made out.

Over the next day, I spend yet more hours learning how to master this 'amazing' free voice-cloning app. I upload samples taken from voice notes on Liv's phone and run some tests: Liv reciting 'Baa Baa Black Sheep' and reading a paragraph from an article from the *Guardian* online. The results are pretty rubbish. It sort of sounds like her, but there's no music in the voice, no space for taking a breath, no physicality in the expression. I think I'm going to have to pay for the pro version with extra features. Or splash out on something more sophisticated altogether.

I start googling other applications, and a warning message pops into my feed.

Voice cloning without consent is a violation of privacy. All individuals have a right to control how their likeness, including their voice, is used by third parties. Unauthorised use of a cloned voice for commercial purposes, practical jokes or to harm someone's reputation can be grounds for a legal claim.

There's no mention of voice cloning for *criminal* purposes, but I guess that goes without saying. Why should I worry? I've already gone so far beyond violations of privacy it would be foolish to get squeamish about breaking the law now.

Back to the script. Let's keep it simple. I want Rachel to have no problem picturing her daughter as she listens. There should be no audio distractions, nothing that sounds inauthentic or incongruous. I'm going to place Liv in her new bedroom, somewhere in Newcastle. On the outskirts, not the city centre. She's lying on top of her duvet, legs outstretched, head leaning against an upright pillow, her battered old phone with the worn blue cover in hand, clearing her throat as she prepares to speak. It's the afternoon. Quiet. Maybe a few birds are tweeting in the garden, or am I drifting back towards radio drama?

I tut to myself. Get the words sorted first and worry about the sound effects later, eh? I'm only looking for about twenty seconds of guff; the shorter I make it, the less there'll be to scrutinise. The subtext is easy – 'if you don't leave me alone, I'm going to kill myself', basically. It's the actual text that's the problem. It's got to sound natural and unscripted. Except there has to be a script, otherwise AI can't do its job.

I delete everything I've written before and try again. An hour later, I'm pretty satisfied with the result. Now I just have to feed the lines into the app and wait for Liv's voice to pop out at the other end. I guess?

I feel a lot calmer, now. Back in control.

Just got to keep Rachel and the rest of the family fooled until Christmas Eve. That's when the shit really hits the fan. It's only ten days away – not too long to wait.

I've got this.

THIRTY-THREE

'Is that you, Rachel? What's happening? Are you coming in to work today or what?'

It was Beverley, calling me at five past seven, wrenching me out of a strange but instantly forgotten dream. It had been another bad night. I'd woken at three, my thoughts so urgent I'd been unable to go back to sleep until six.

'Um, no, sorry, I can't,' I replied, groggy with tiredness.

'Why not? Are you ill?'

I reached over with my free hand and switched on the bedside light, flinching at the sudden brightness. 'No. There's been other stuff going on, family problems.'

'I'm sorry to hear that,' she clipped, not sounding sorry at all. 'But I have a business to run, I need reliable staff, not people who only turn up when they feel like it.'

'That's not fair—'

'You left me stranded. Nobody else would come in at short notice and I was completely on my own. You know how busy it is, everyone wants their outfits for Christmas. If you won't come in today, I'll have to start thinking about hiring a replacement.

God knows how at this time of year...' she muttered, almost to herself.

'Please don't sack me,' I said. 'I need this job.'

'And I need people I can trust. If you want something more casual, you'd better look for something else.'

I knew Beverley meant what she said, but I also knew that I couldn't go back to work until I'd found Liv. I had to appeal to my boss's compassionate side – surely it existed, tucked away somewhere beneath her expensive Italian blouses and tailored woollen suits. Beverley was a force of nature. I remembered that she'd started the boutique after her husband ran off with a younger woman, believing that success was the best revenge.

'Look, I'm really, really sorry,' I repeated. 'It's just that things have been incredibly difficult recently. We've had a lot of problems with our younger daughter, and now our older one has left home and is refusing to talk to us, and...' I left a dramatic pause, 'my husband walked out on me at the weekend. It was a total shock – I wasn't expecting it.'

I heard Beverley gasp. 'Oh no! You poor girl! Why didn't you tell me immediately?'

'I don't know. I was embarrassed, I suppose.'

'Embarrassed? He's the one who should be embarrassed. I suppose there's somebody else involved?'

'Yes, a woman he met at a conference.'

'Of course. They never leave unless there's someone to go to. They need a woman to massage their ego, cook their meals, pick up their socks... Have you seen a solicitor yet?'

'No, I've been too upset.'

'You must, Rachel, you must!' she said firmly. 'You need to take advice and act on it fast. He'll have emptied your joint bank account before you know it and you won't be able to pay your bills. I've been there, believe me.'

Had Dom done that? I hadn't checked. The idea hadn't even occurred to me.

'Yes, you're right,' I replied. 'I need to see someone today. So is it okay if I don't come in until next week? Or I can work the weekend, if you like...' Nobody wanted to work weekends just before Christmas, so I was confident this might swing me back in her favour.

'Yes, of course. Don't worry, I'll try to swap things around,' she conceded. 'But get a grip, Rachel. If you don't, you'll go under. Do you understand? We can't let these men defeat us.'

I ended the call promising that I'd take Dom to the cleaner's. In many ways, Beverley was right, I *did* need to wise up, but at that moment I couldn't have cared less if he'd made me penniless. I had no intention of trying to talk to a solicitor today. My mind was fixed on far more important things.

Karina contacted me next to see how I'd got on with the police. I told her that my attempt to report Liv missing had come to nothing. She replied to say that she was disappointed but not surprised, and asked me what I planned to do now. I texted back two simple words.

Find Liv.

Be careful, she wrote back. *Don't put yourself in danger.* I knew I was placing myself in the way of the enemy, but it felt like I didn't have much choice.

Last time I'd tried to follow Jensen, I'd only got as far as the southbound Northern Line before I'd lost him. Today I was determined to do better. I decided not to hide in my room this time, but to behave as normal. I had a shower, got dressed and went downstairs, making myself scrambled eggs on toast. I was too wound up to eat, but I forced a few forkfuls down. After breakfast, I pottered around the kitchen, waiting for him to emerge. I had some questions I wanted to ask him. Although I already knew that he'd been lying to me from the start, I wanted to hear the lies again and look for tells I'd missed before – a twitch of the eyes, a blush in his cheeks, a smear of sweat above his top lip.

He came downstairs at around 11 a.m. He'd clearly had a shower too, because his curly dark hair was wet. As usual, he was wearing his barman's blacks.

'Morning!' I said, with as much cheer as I could muster.

'Hi, Rachel,' he replied, reaching for cereal. 'How are you? Sorry I haven't seen you since Saturday. I've been thinking about you a lot. Are you okay?' His eyes searched mine. 'It's all a bit much, isn't it? First Liv walks out, then Meg, now Dom.'

'He hasn't walked out,' I insisted. 'He's in Dubai.'

'Fair enough,' he replied, clearly not believing me. 'Well, either way, we're the last men standing. Well, man and woman. Last people, I should say.' He smiled awkwardly as he poured milk over his Weetabix.

He was toying with me, deliberately making me feel uncomfortable. I almost told him to get out of the house that instant, but I'd promised myself to play it cool.

'I wish Liv would come home,' he continued. 'It's December now. She can't possibly stay away for Christmas.'

My hackles rose, but I quickly changed the subject. 'So what are you up to today, Jensen? Another shift at the George?'

There was a pause. 'I think this milk might be off,' he said, holding up the plastic bottle and sniffing the rim.

'Oh dear. I'll have to pick some fresh up.' He didn't answer my question, and I didn't need to ask again. His lie was in the silence. I made an excuse to leave the kitchen and went up to my bedroom, where I stood by the door listening to the sounds below as Jensen finished breakfast and prepared to leave the house.

I followed him as before, wearing trainers instead of winter boots as they made less noise on the ground. I made it to the Tube station without him turning round. We had a few minutes to wait for the westbound train. Jensen walked to the far end of the platform while I skulked at the entrance, jumping aboard at the last second, just as I'd done before.

We eventually arrived at Bank. I left it until the last moment before I got out. Jensen was way ahead of me, heading in the direction of the Northern Line. I hurried along, peering over the heads of other passengers to keep my gaze firmly fixed on his green woolly hat. I *had* to catch the same train as him this time, I couldn't fail.

The area dividing the north- and southbound platforms was vast. I lingered there for as long as I could, waiting for the next southbound train to thunder in. As soon as it did, I sidled onto the platform, trying to hide myself in the throng of passengers waiting to board. I couldn't see where Jensen was, but assumed he was in another carriage. The train set off. I remained standing, gripping the pole, my heart pounding in my chest.

The first stop was London Bridge. Several people were waiting by the double doors to board. I tried to peep out, but was shoved in the back by someone wanting to get off. I made an involuntary landing on the platform and looked around for Jensen. He'd got off too and was heading towards the exit. Feeling at last that luck was on my side, I quickly followed, darting between passengers, my eyes once again locked on the dancing bobble of his hat.

He went through the ticket barrier, then stopped to look at his phone, turning around as he tried to get a better signal. I froze, hoping he wouldn't glance up and see me. After a few seconds, he put the phone back in his pocket and carried on, disappearing round the corner in the direction of the mainline trains. I passed through the barrier, then tucked in behind a small group. My mind started to race. Which train was he going to catch? Would I be able to get on it too without him spotting me?

The thoroughfare was rammed. Hundreds of people were walking in both directions, some running, others walking purposefully, a few just sauntering along. I was constantly having to change pace. And I'd lost sight of the bobble hat. Had

Jensen gone into Marks & Spencer without my noticing? Or slipped into the public toilets? Or was he by the ticket machines? I couldn't see him. Damn.

I was trying to decide what to do when he suddenly jumped out at me from behind a pillar.

'Rachel!'

I halted. 'Jensen! Hi. It's you. What a surprise.'

He grimaced. 'Cut the crap. I know you've been following me.'

'I haven't.'

'You have. What the fuck are you playing at?'

'What the fuck are *you* playing at?' I retorted, throwing his own words back at him.

We stood before each other defiantly, each claiming the higher ground. People weaved around us, tutting as they grazed our shoulders, trailing the wheels of their suitcases across our toes.

'I can explain,' he said finally.

'Good. Go on then.'

'Not here. Let's find somewhere quieter.'

We left the station, and after walking in fuming silence down a side road for a couple of hundred metres, I agreed to enter a tiny café. Jensen went to the counter and ordered two coffees while I parked myself at a table. I was furious with myself for having been caught; I'd handed him the right to be indignant when he was the one in the wrong. In the meantime, my brain was practising somersaults as it tried to decide on the best tactics for extracting the truth.

He took off his hat and put it on the table, shook out his hair and sat back. 'Okay,' he said. 'Ask your questions.'

'Where's Liv?'

He frowned. 'In Newcastle. Staying with friends. Sorry, I don't know any more than you do.'

I wanted to punch him in the face, but I had to control

myself. 'Okay... let's start at the beginning. Do you work at the George?'

'You already know the answer to that. How did you find out?'

'I went in there hoping to see you, but the manager said you'd never set foot in the place.'

'That's not quite true. I had a day's trial. With the other manager. It didn't work out.'

'Why didn't you tell us?'

'I was embarrassed. I knew Dom would have a go at me, and I didn't want you to think I was useless. I thought that if Liv found out I had a job, she might come home. Turns out that was a waste of time.'

'Where have you been going every day?' I asked. 'Roaming the streets? Some evenings you don't come back until after midnight.'

'I've been volunteering at Sunshine and Showers,' he said. 'It's a homeless shelter. I work in the kitchen, loading and unloading the dishwashers mostly. Some nights I go around with the rough-sleeping teams, offering help. It's tough out there, especially in the freezing cold.'

I studied his face. His eyes were open and his jaw was relaxed. Could he be telling the truth?

'I'll take you to meet my boss now, if you like. She'll vouch for me.'

I was confused. 'But why not just get a job? And why come all the way into central London? There must be homeless shelters closer to home.'

He pushed his hair off his face. 'Dunno. I was out this way and saw an advert asking for volunteers. It felt like a good thing to do. I've not been thinking straight these past couple of weeks.'

Conflicting thoughts were playing pinball in my head. I didn't know what to believe. 'The job isn't the only thing you've lied about, is it?' I continued, feeling my way carefully.

He frowned. 'What do you mean?'

'Tell me about Claire and James Ambersley.'

'Oh...' His face clouded over. 'You already know what happened. They were killed in a fire.'

'Yes, but they weren't your parents, were they?'

Silence fell. 'How did you find that out? Have you been checking up on me?'

'Sort of. When I found out you'd lied about the job, I started to think nothing was true. I went to Carlington, talked to some people who knew the family. They'd never heard of you.'

He shifted in his seat. I could see that he was having trouble speaking. 'James and Claire were as good as parents to me, better in fact,' he said, keeping his head down. 'Being a parent has very little to do with blood. Virtually nothing. I've never met my birth parents. I was taken away from my mother soon after I was born. I don't even know my birth father's name. They didn't give a shit about me. I grew up in care.'

There was genuine emotion in his voice. This I *did* believe. 'So what happened?' I pressed. 'Did the Ambersleys adopt you?' He shook his head. 'They fostered you, then?'

'Sort of. There was nothing official.'

'They obviously gave you a good life, a great education—'

'I don't want to talk about it,' he snapped. 'It's too painful – brings it all back. I can't go there.' He stood up. 'I'll have a panic attack. Sorry, I need some fresh air.'

'Don't go. Please, stay and talk to me. Be honest with me, tell me everything. I want to understand!'

'No. I can't. Not here, not now. I need to get to the shelter.'

'We can sort this out, but you need to tell me the truth.'

He picked up his hat. 'Sorry, Rachel. I shouldn't have lied to you. I'm really, really sorry. I'll move out today. I should have left earlier, but I simply didn't have anywhere to go. You've been wonderful to me, and I've abused your trust. I feel very bad about that. I understand why you're worried about Liv, and

I can guess what you're thinking, but I promise you, on my life, I haven't hurt her. I want her to come back just as much as you do.' He walked towards the door and left the café without looking back once.

I could hardly breathe. What had just happened? Was Jensen a vulnerable young man who'd had a troubled upbringing, who'd made some mistakes but was good at heart? Or was he a consummate liar?

THIRTY-FOUR

I went straight round to Karina's flat. Fortunately she was working from home again.

'Well? What did the police say?' she asked as soon as she opened the door. 'Are they investigating?'

I shook my head. 'They said she didn't count as a missing person.'

'Shit...' She ushered me inside.

'But I followed Jensen this morning.'

'Rachel—'

'I know, I know, but I had to do *something*. Anyway, it didn't work out. He caught me at London Bridge.'

'London Bridge? What was he doing there?'

'Volunteering at a homeless shelter, apparently. We went for coffee. He admitted lying about his parents, said he'd been brought up in care. The Ambersleys took him in, treated him like their son. He swore he hadn't harmed Liv and had no idea where she was.'

'Did you believe him?'

I shrugged. 'To be honest, Karina, I don't know. I think some of what he told me was definitely true, but...'

'But what?'

'I'm not sure what to think any more. He could just be messing with my head. And the big problem is, if he *has* got Liv or done something horrible to her, now he knows I suspect him. He was very apologetic about not moving out, promised he'd do it today. Is that a sign of guilt or innocence? I don't know.'

'Nor do I,' Karina replied. 'I'm sorry, Rachel. Let's just hope he's telling the truth. Maybe we're reading too much into everything.'

'In what way?'

'You know... putting it all on Jensen's shoulders because we can't face the truth.'

'Which is what?'

'That this is more about Liv's relationship with her family than it is about her and Jensen. She's broken free and doesn't want to have anything more to do with us.'

'Or rather with me,' I muttered.

'No, I didn't say that. But... you are very much the centre of the family. If Liv wants to cut off from you, she has to cut off from all of us.'

'Oh, you're making me feel so much better,' I snapped. 'Does everything have to be my fault? What about Dom?'

'This is not about blaming, it's about understanding the situation. And not panicking.'

'Okay... I suppose you're right.' Her analysis made a kind of sense, but I still felt something was wrong.

'You've been through so much these past few weeks. What with Meg, and now Dom, too... I'm not surprised your head is reeling.'

'Yeah, that's true,' I agreed. 'I can't keep up with myself. But now Jensen is leaving, Meg can come home. In fact, as soon as she gets in, she can pack a bag and come back with me.'

Karina pursed her lips. 'Hmm... maybe. I've loved having her here, and I think, on the whole, it's worked out. But as for whether she's ready to go back to you... that's another matter. You'll have to talk to her.'

'There's nothing to talk *about*. There's no reason for her to stay.' Karina's face clouded over. 'Unless you're saying she doesn't want to have any more to do with me either.'

'That's absolutely not what I'm saying,' Karina protested. I sensed a row coming on, but before I could respond, I heard my mobile bleep.

Every other thought immediately evaporated. Diving into my bag, I took out my phone.

'It's Liv! She's sent me a WhatsApp.' I swiped into the feed. 'No! It's a voice note!'

'Oh, thank God, thank God,' said Karina. 'See? I told you not to panic. She's fine!'

'Let's listen to it first,' I replied. My heart pounded in my chest as I pressed the play button. Her voice rang out loud and clear.

'Hi, Mum. Sorry it's taken me a while to call back. I got your messages. I didn't mean to worry you or anyone else in the family. There's absolutely no need to call the police. I'm okay. But I still don't want to talk to anyone right now or meet up. Please understand. I will be in touch again when I feel up to it. Love you all.'

A tight knot in my stomach I hadn't even known was there suddenly undid itself. All the fears I'd just been expressing to Karina instantly disappeared. I was hungry to hear her voice again, replaying the message several times.

'That's such a relief, I can't tell you,' I said, almost crying with joy.

Karina's reaction was more controlled. 'Of course it's lovely to hear her voice, but it's a shame we can't have a proper conversation with her. Why is she holding back?'

'She probably doesn't want us asking awkward questions or making her justify herself.'

'I suppose so...'

'It doesn't matter. The main thing is she responded. It's what we've been desperately waiting for.'

Karina frowned. 'Her voice is a bit strained, don't you think?'

'I know what you mean, but I think it's tiredness.'

I quickly texted a reply. *So happy to know that you're alive and well. I won't bother you any more. You know where I am if you need me. Lots of love xxx*

I drove home with a light heart, feeling as if a huge weight had been lifted from my shoulders. Liv had unwittingly put me through hell, and it shouldn't have taken the threat of calling the police to get her to record that voice note, but I didn't care any more. I forgave her for being so elusive, and for sending the old video and trying to make us believe she'd gone back to Newcastle. I wished she'd tell me where she *actually* was, but I resolved to be patient and let her be. She hadn't been kidnapped – or worse – by Jensen and was physically safe. It seemed that Jensen had been telling the truth about that after all. Now I just needed him to go, so that I could bring Meg home. Once he'd moved out, I'd tell Liv. Then maybe she'd come home too.

As soon as I entered the house, I knew that someone had been here while I was out. The day's post – a handful of Christmas cards and some junk mail – was sitting on the hall table in a neat pile, and there was a dirty mug next to the kitchen sink.

Guessing it had been Jensen, I went straight up to the flatlet. The room had been tidied. I opened the wardrobe and saw that most of the hangers were empty. He'd taken his clothes and laptop but left all the larger items, including the keyboard, exercise bike and zombie shop dummy. He hadn't left his door key, so presumably he planned to come back for them later.

It was a great relief that he'd finally gone. Even though I'd enjoyed the earlier part of the summer, looking after him and Liv, pretending I had a grown-up son, the relationship had turned sour. He had lied to us and abused our trust. I tried not to worry about where he'd gone and where he would sleep tonight, telling myself that he was not my responsibility any more. He'd *never* been my responsibility. That chapter was closed. I had more important things to deal with. Like what the hell I was going to do about my wrecked marriage and my troubled daughters.

I rang Meg straight away to tell her that it was safe to come home. Of course she didn't pick up. I called Karina instead and asked her to pass on the message.

'Tell her I'll come and collect her tomorrow morning,' I said.

There was a long pause. 'I already spoke to her about it,' Karina replied. 'She wants to stay here for now. I'm sorry, Rachel. Just give her time. Let it be her own decision, eh?'

That night, I lay in bed listening to the silence, feeling the emptiness all around me and wondering how and why I'd ended up alone. Christmas was thundering towards me like a red and green juggernaut. What was it going to be like this year without Dom? Until a few days ago, such a prospect would have seemed unimaginable. Now there was even a chance that I would have to spend it completely on my own, without my girls. They had always loved Christmas – the food, the parties, the present-giving, the silly family rituals. We'd never spent it apart from each other before. Sad, self-pitying thoughts started to crowd in. I pushed them away, reminding myself that there was a week to go – still time for them to come home.

I needed to focus on the positive. All in all, it had been a good day. Liv had sent me the voice note. She was safe. I switched the bedside light back on and played it several times, as if it were a soothing lullaby. Eventually it did the trick, because I fell asleep and didn't wake up until gone eight the following morning. I got up and rushed into work. I didn't feel like going, but I'd promised Beverley.

The boutique was heaving with customers looking for party dresses and gift ideas from the accessories bar. There was tinsel everywhere and a large wreath on the door. Festive hits blared through the speakers. Every so often a song reminded me of the early days with Dom, before we were married, or when the girls were tiny and still believed in Santa Claus. I started crying and had to take time out in the loos.

'How did you get on with the solicitor?' Beverley asked at the first opportunity. It was lunchtime and there was a bit of a lull.

I'd almost forgotten that I'd promised her I would take legal advice. 'I was too upset to organise it,' I said, which was partly true. 'Everyone's shutting down for Christmas now. I'll never get an appointment. I think I'll just have to leave it until the new year.'

'Well, make sure you do it as soon as you can,' Beverley replied, refilling the display of leather gloves. 'Is your house in joint names?'

'Yes.'

'Good. Then he can't force you to sell.'

I was taken aback. 'He hasn't said anything about selling.'

'Oh, he will. You wait,' she said knowledgeably. 'Remind me, how old are your girls?'

'Twenty-two and eighteen.'

'Hmm... Still in full-time education?'

'Liv graduated this summer just gone, but Meg's in the sixth form. I want her to go to university, but I'm not sure she will.'

'Make her go,' Beverley urged. 'That way the courts will allow you to stay in the house until she finishes.'

The idea of making Meg do anything she didn't want to do was laughable, while the prospect of asking a court to decide whether our 'for ever home' should be sold sent my head spinning.

'I'll take advice, I promise,' I said.

By the end of the day, my feet were aching with tiredness and I felt ready to drop. I took the bus home as usual. Christmas lights twinkled down the length of the high street and there were decorations in all the shop windows. Many of my neighbours had covered their house fronts with flashing illuminations, their gardens populated by sparkly reindeers and eerie Santa inflatables. In contrast, our house looked dark and unwelcoming. As I turned the key in the door, I made a promise to myself to put our decorations up. Just in case there was something to celebrate after all.

I made some beans on toast. It wasn't much of an evening meal, but I didn't have the motivation to cook properly. Taking my plate over to the desk in the corner of the dining room, I switched on the computer. It was time to check my financial situation.

Even before we married, Dom and I had pooled our resources and opened a joint bank account. Our salaries had gone into it, and all our expenses had gone out of it. We had a joint credit card, too. I no longer had an account in my own name, not even for savings – it hadn't been worth the bother. Dom had always earned a lot more than me – his salary covered the mortgage, food, utilities, and so on, while my wages paid for extras like birthday presents and holidays. We didn't explicitly divide things in that way, but it was how I thought of it. Dom did essentials and I did treats.

My heart was in my mouth as I punched in the security code to get into my online banking. I clicked on recent transactions. Dom's November salary had gone into the account at the end of the month, as normal. However, two days ago he'd transferred two thousand pounds to an account I didn't recognise. Some of our direct debits – the mortgage, utilities, council tax, credit card – hadn't gone out yet. I checked the balance and did a quick calculation. There was enough to cover them, but there wouldn't be much left.

Beverley had been right. Dom hadn't completely drained our bank account, but he'd withdrawn a substantial sum. If he arranged for his December salary to be paid elsewhere, I would be in difficulty by the end of the year. All thoughts of quitting my job instantly evaporated. I had to talk to him and check that he wasn't going to leave me in the lurch. Not feeling up to a call, I sent him a WhatsApp asking him to come over 'to discuss the financial situation'. I could see that he'd read it, but he didn't respond. The non-communication bug was catching, it seemed.

After a wretched night, I was up early. I was feeling increasingly furious with Dom but was determined not to buckle under the strain. I had to make some Christmas preparations, even if they were tentative and on a smaller scale than usual. The normal large turkey would not be appropriate, nor would there be any point in making dozens of sausage rolls, but I should get a tree at the very least.

I drove to the local park. An open-air pop-up was selling trees, donating some of the proceeds to charity. The best ones had already gone, and those remaining were straggly and misshapen. It felt like a metaphor for this year's Christmas. I made my choice and paid up. The guy put the tree through the bagging machine and offered to carry it to the car.

I drove home with the topmost branches scratching my left ear, thinking about Christmases past. Dom had always bought the Christmas tree – his one contribution to the festivities – and had also always complained about the exorbitant price. 'Get an artificial one,' I used to say, 'you'll soon make your money back,' but he'd scorned such an idea.

'Real trees are what make it smell like Christmas,' he'd say.

I held the piney aroma in my nose for a few seconds, then let it go, along with the memory. I had to get hold of my emotions, or I would never complete the task today. I wanted Meg to come home to a jolly, beautiful house, not to a mother lying in a pool of tears.

It took all my strength to heave the tree inside. I cleared a space in the bay window, which was where we always put the tree. As children, Liv and Meg had loved walking around the local streets, counting the trees in the windows. It had seemed churlish to put ours out of sight. If Liv decided to come home, she would see the tree and immediately know she was welcome.

I had a terrible struggle putting the bloody thing into the stand, then screwing the bolts to secure it in place. It was really a two-person job. The tree looked wonky and forlorn, but hopefully I could disguise its shape with lots of fairy lights and baubles.

I fetched a small set of steps and went upstairs to Meg's bedroom. When we'd had the loft conversion done, we'd had to find somewhere else to keep the Christmas decorations. Meg's room had lots of fitted wardrobes, so they had become their new home. I climbed onto the steps and opened the top cupboard. There were the familiar cardboard boxes, looking rather battered and tatty, held together with brown sticky tape. I hauled the first one down and put it on the floor, then reached for another. It had been pushed to the back, and I couldn't quite reach it. I stretched and strained into the darkness of the cupboard, cursing that I wasn't tall enough. My fingers closed around a cylindrical object. Intrigued, I pulled it towards me and took it out.

It was a can of red spray paint.

THIRTY-FIVE

Judging by Rachel's reply, the fake voice note worked. I seem to have got away with it. I expect she's disappointed that Liv doesn't want to talk to her, but at least she's not going to the police. Not yet anyway. The time will come, but by then I will be long, long gone and I'll have covered all my tracks.

Poor Rachel. She's putting on a brave face but she must feel absolutely awful. I sense that she's holding out for her own Christmas miracle – Liv standing on the doorstep wearing a Santa hat, arms full of presents, eyes shining with happy tears. I can picture it now.

'Happy Christmas, Mom! I'm home!' Just like in the movies.

Unfortunately, that's not going to happen. I've another kind of drama planned for 24 December. Different genre altogether. Definitely not a family feature, although family is what it's all about. More of a revenge tragedy.

Not long to go now. I'm almost ready. Bring it on.

THIRTY-SIX

I knew instantly what I was looking at. I'd spent hours scrubbing at graffiti of the same colour on the front of the house.

The can was covered in red fingerprints. They had to be Meg's, no one else's. My heart sank to the depths of my stomach as I absorbed the implications of what I'd found. I went back over the events of the last few months – the vandalised birthday cake, the scratched car, the rubbish in the garden... And what about the nasty DMs on Insta? Had Meg written those to herself?

I didn't want to believe it, but I knew it was true. Although I'd been hurt when Meg had chosen to go and stay with my sister, I'd also been let off the hook. I'd told myself the bullying was Karina's problem now – that she could sort it. I'd turned all my attention to Liv, but it had been my younger daughter who had needed me, and I had failed her.

I popped the can into a bag and drove round to Karina's flat.

'Rachel! Are you okay?' she said, peering into the entryphone.

'I need to speak to Meg. Is she in?'

'Yes. Come on up.' The door opened with a buzz, and I stepped inside.

As I emerged from the lift, I saw Karina leaning against the open doorway of her flat wearing soft grey jogging bottoms and a matching top.

'She's in her bedroom, gaming, I expect,' she said. 'What's wrong? Has something happened?'

'Yes,' I said, taking out the spray can. 'I found this. It was hidden in her room behind some boxes of Christmas decorations.' Karina stared at it, not comprehending. 'She did the graffiti.'

'No... she wouldn't.'

'In fact I think she did all of it. The cake, the rubbish, the car... and the messages too.'

'Oh God... Poor thing. What are you going to do?'

'Talk to her about it, of course.'

Karina put her hand on my arm as I went to knock on Meg's door. 'Be gentle with her, Rachel.'

'Don't worry, I will.'

I knocked quietly. Meg didn't answer, so I pushed the door open and went inside. The room was dark, her laptop turned off. I could just about see her head poking out of the duvet, her brown curls spread across the pillow.

'Meg? Are you awake?'

She turned onto her back with a groan. 'Mum? Is that you?'

'Yes. Can I let the light in, please?' She grunted, which I took as a yes. I picked my way through the trail of clothes and damp towels and pulled up the blackout blind. Soft winter sunshine entered the room. 'There. That's better.'

I sat on the edge of the bed, resisting the temptation to comment on the chaos around me. She shuffled onto her elbows and looked at me bleary-eyed. 'Why are you here?'

'I found this.' I put the can down next to her. She gasped,

her eyes widening with fear. 'I'm not here to judge. I just need to know what's been going on.'

'I'm sorry,' she kept saying, over and over again. 'I'm so, so sorry.'

I drew her towards me. She nestled in the crook of my arm and I let her sob for a while.

'Why did you do it, Meg?' I asked once she'd calmed down a little. I had a pretty good idea, but I wanted her to tell me herself.

'I wanted Jensen to go,' she replied. 'I didn't like him – he gave me the creeps. He wasn't genuine. I thought he was wrong for Liv.'

'Hmm... weren't you just jealous?'

She heaved her shoulders up and down. 'I suppose so. Liv was all over him, so were you. It was vomit-making. And I was right,' she said with a spark of her old defiance. 'Karina told me he lied about working at the George.'

'But he didn't write "Loser" on your birthday cake,' I said. 'That was you, right?'

She lowered her head in shame. 'Yes.'

'That really surprises me. I thought you enjoyed your party. You seemed to be having a great time. And Auntie Karina went to such a lot of trouble.'

'I'm sorry,' she said. 'I don't know why I did it. I saw the cake, and instead of making me feel loved and wanted, it made me feel bad, like I didn't deserve it.'

'Of course you deserved it!'

'You didn't say anything about it, it was like it didn't matter.'

'No, no,' I insisted. 'We assumed it was Skyla. Karina and I covered it up because we didn't want your friends to know. It would have spoilt everything.'

'I just thought you didn't care.'

'Of course we cared, silly. We were all really worried about it. I nearly went to the police.'

'But you never mentioned any of it to me. Even when I scratched your car, you said nothing.'

I sighed. 'I didn't tell you because I didn't want you to be upset. I was trying to protect you.'

'It didn't feel that way. It was like none of it was happening. Or it was so minor it wasn't worth thinking about. You were way more bothered with Liv's job applications, and feeling sorry for Jensen.'

'That's not true.'

'The more you didn't react, the more I felt I had to do worse and worse things.'

'Yes, I understand now. Sort of.' I let out a breath. 'And what about the online bullying? Did you make the fake accounts and send yourself the horrible messages?'

'Not all of them. Only the ones this term. The stuff last year was all Skyla and Alice, I swear.'

I hadn't been able to understand why they'd started it up again after they'd got into so much trouble, but now it made sense.

'Was that why you didn't want me to tell the head this time around?'

'Yes.'

'I thought it was because you didn't want me to get involved.'

'No.' Meg almost smiled through her tears. 'Actually, I kind of liked it last time. It was scary, but on the other hand, it felt good to have someone stand up for me.'

'You felt seen. And loved.'

'Exactly. But then Liv and Jensen turned up and it was like I was invisible again.'

'Honestly, Meg, that's not the case. We've misunderstood each other. Oh God. Come here, give me a hug.'

'I'm sorry, Mum.'

'You're the one you've hurt the most,' I replied. 'Listen. Jensen has gone. It's time to come home. For Christmas.'

She screwed up her nose. 'What's the point? Dad won't be there, nor will Liv. It'll be sad, just the two of us.'

'We'll invite Karina.'

'I'd rather stay here.'

'Please don't make me leave here without you. I can't go back to an empty house.' I was aware that I was begging, but I couldn't stop myself.

'All right,' she said finally. 'To be fair, I've missed my room.' She thumped the mattress. 'This bed is like sleeping on concrete. And I miss your cooking. Karina makes great cakes, but her veggie spag bol is nowhere as good as yours.'

I laughed. 'Then you'd better get up and start packing,' I said.

I drove her home. We brought the boxes of decorations down from her room and spent the next hour arranging the lights and hanging baubles. Meg put the angel on the top of the tree – she'd made her at primary school out of an empty toilet roll and a paper doily. Her wings were torn and crumpled and her felt-pen rosy cheeks had faded, but we would never replace her. She was as much part of our Christmas tradition as real trees and Thorntons chocolates. I reminded myself to put a large box on the shopping list.

'Looks good, eh?' I said, putting my arm around her. 'I know it won't be the same this year, but we'll do our best to have a good time. Karina says she'll come on Christmas Eve and stay for a few days.'

'Will Dad come?' she asked in a small voice.

'I doubt it. He'll be spending Christmas with his new girl-friend, I expect.'

'What about Liv?'

'I don't know. She didn't say anything in her voice note about coming, but I have a feeling she's going to turn up at the last minute and surprise us.' I attempted a laugh, but Meg didn't join in. She could tell that it was wishful thinking. Neither of us said another word on the subject.

Meg went upstairs to put her stuff away and reacclimatise herself to her room. I poured myself a glass of wine and sat down, staring at the Christmas tree until the coloured lights became a blur. It was wonderful to have my younger daughter back, but I felt greedy for both my girls. I knew I was supposed to leave Liv alone, but I couldn't resist sending her a picture of the tree in all its glory. Recalling the Mariah Carey hit, I added a brief text accompanied by musical emojis and a flurry of hearts.

All I want for Christmas is YOU!

THIRTY-SEVEN

I continued with the last-minute Christmas preparations, buying all the things we usually bought, like port (although Dom was the only one who drank it) and a chocolate log (Liv's favourite) and a box of twelve crackers when six would have been more than enough. I made sausage rolls and mince pies, a lasagne for Christmas Eve, paid a fortune for a wreath to put on the front door. I went to the gift shop and stocked up on scented candles – red, green and white, classic, tapered and ribbed. I even bought one in the shape of a Christmas tree. I tried so hard to make it special, even though there would only be three of us this year – me, Meg and Karina. I wanted Meg to feel that she was worth making a fuss for.

Our household had been torn apart, but I was determined to put as much of it back together as I could. As Jensen hadn't been in touch about collecting the rest of his stuff, Meg and I carried it all downstairs and put it in the garage. We reinstated the office in the box room and brought up the computer. I made up the bed, while Meg dusted and hoovered. I couldn't remember her ever doing housework before – she seemed to quite enjoy it. It felt good to be doing something practical together.

'There!' I said when we'd finished. 'It's Liv's bedroom again. All ready and waiting for her.'

'Do you think she'll come?' Meg asked.

'I honestly don't know.' Liv had replied to my last message with a party hat emoji but no words. It had felt like a positive sign, but I was clutching at straws. 'I hope so,' I said, putting my arm across her shoulders and giving her what I hoped was a reassuring hug.

Dom finally got in touch the day before Christmas Eve. I was at work, on my lunch break. 'Sorry, I've been up to my eyes,' he said, calling me from what sounded like a supermarket. Since when had he gone food shopping? 'I'm off for the holiday now. Is it okay if I pop over this evening after dinner?' He sounded so casual, as if he were a mate from the golf club rather than my husband of twenty-three years.

'Yes, okay,' I said. Meg was meeting up with some friends for a drink, so it was good timing. I couldn't guarantee that I'd be able to keep my temper, and the last thing I wanted was her witnessing a screaming match.

I changed and refreshed my make-up before he arrived. Not because I wanted to tempt him back, but so that I didn't look like a woman whose life had fallen apart. I sat in the sitting room anxiously picking at my fingernails, waiting for the sound of his key turning in the lock. He was twenty minutes late and he rang the doorbell. I almost didn't answer.

'Forgot your key?' I asked, opening the door after the second ring.

'No. It didn't seem appropriate, you know, letting myself in.'

'You never let inappropriateness stop you before,' I poked. 'Come in, you're letting all the warm air out.'

I pointed at the large suitcase he'd brought with him. 'Has she chucked you out already?'

'What? No, not at all. It's empty. I've come to collect the rest of my stuff.'

'Too late. I took it all to the dump.'

'What?! Rachel—'

'Calm down. Of course I didn't. Tempting as it was.'

He sighed, as if he were summoning all his patience. 'I don't want to make this more unpleasant than it has to be. I won't be long, then I'll be out of your hair.'

'Good. Be as quick as you can.' He took off his coat and scarf and hung them on their usual hook. I followed him upstairs and stood in the doorway of our bedroom, watching him pack, making it as awkward for him as I possibly could.

'How are you?' he enquired, in an annoying 'how are you *really*' kind of tone.

'Oh, full of joy and goodwill to all men,' I replied sarcastically. 'How do you think I am?'

'Sorry... I know it's been tough. Any news from Liv?'

'Yes. Finally. She sent one of her voice notes saying she's okay but not up to a chat.'

'Oh well, that's something, I suppose... Does she know about us?'

'No. I want to tell her in person. Haven't had a chance yet.' I gave him an arch look. 'Maybe you should do it. You initiated it, after all.'

He ignored the jibe. 'And how's Meg?'

'Doing okay. Considering. She's back home.' I told him that she'd confessed to the bullying. 'It was her all along,' I said. 'The vile messages. Even all that horrible graffiti.'

He looked astonished. 'But why on earth...?'

'To get attention, basically. Although she hated the real bullying last term, she'd appreciated the fact that we stood up for her and sorted it out. Or *I* did. And she was dead jealous of

Jensen, of course. When he and Liv moved in, she felt sidelined.'

Dom held up a hanger draped with work ties. 'Is he still living here?'

I shook my head. 'No, he moved out a few days ago.' I told him about the lying.

'I knew there was something off about him,' he said. 'He took us for a ride. And Liv. Perhaps she'll come back now. Have you told her that he's gone?'

'Not yet.'

'Why not?'

Because she doesn't want to talk to me. Or anyone, for that matter.'

'We should have chucked him out the day after she left,' he huffed. 'It was your fault – you were too soft on him. I expect Liv had already told him your parents had died at a similar age. And that we'd lost a son. He preyed on your weakness.'

'Don't criticise me, Dom,' I replied, with as even a tone as I could manage. 'You've no right. Especially not after what you've done.' He lowered his eyes and there were a few moments of silence while he continued packing. 'I imagine you're spending Christmas with Charlotte.'

'Oh, yes... I'd, er, like to pop in on Christmas Day, if that's okay.' More 'popping', I thought, but I just nodded. 'To see Meg. I've bought her a new phone.'

'Did that come out of the money you withdrew from our account, or did you put it on our joint credit card? Because if it's on the credit card, I'm not sure we're going to be able to pay it off next month.'

He held up his hands in surrender. 'Okay, Rachel, I get it, you hate my guts. I suppose I shouldn't have taken that money out without telling you first. But the thing is, Charlotte and I have taken on a new place, and you know what it's like, you have to pay a huge deposit and rent in advance. I'm strapped.'

He added a few more items to the case, then sat down wearily on the bed. I hung back, feeling the chasm between us. I knew him so well and could tell that he was preparing to deliver the killer blow. I readied myself for it. 'The thing is, I need to sell the house. We're paying stupid sums in rent, so we need to buy as soon as possible.'

'Good God, Dom, you only walked out ten days ago. Isn't this a bit sudden? You're moving way too fast.'

'Not really,' he replied. 'Charlotte and I have been talking about it for months.'

'It's still raw to me. Anyway, the house is jointly owned, so you can't force me to sell. We have to mutually agree. I know, I've looked it all up.'

'I won't be able to afford the mortgage,' Dom said. 'If we default on the payments, we'll lose the place anyway. It makes sense to sell.'

'This isn't one of your business deals,' I cried, 'this is our home! The girls have lived here their whole lives.'

He seemed unmoved. 'We have to get real. Our marriage is over. Liv has already moved on, and Meg will be off to university next year. You'll be rattling around here on your own, getting depressed, worrying about money—'

'While you're having a lovely time with Charlotte,' I finished for him.

'I'm not going to apologise for finally finding someone who makes me happy,' he retorted.

I felt my insides caving in on themselves, but I tried not to let him see my pain. Instead, I channelled Beverley, remembering the advice she'd given me. 'No court will force someone to sell if there's a child still in full-time education,' I said. 'Especially not if they've got mental health issues. Meg's been through a lot. We're making progress, but she's still vulnerable. She'd be utterly destabilised if we had to move.'

He nodded. 'I get what you're saying. Let's not argue about

it now. We'll sort Meg out, but the sale has to happen, Rachel. We'll split the proceeds fifty-fifty. You can buy yourself a nice flat or a cottage on the coast. You've often said you'd like to live by the sea.'

'Yes, but not on my own with my knitting and a load of bloody cats. Stop being so patronising and just go, please.'

He stood up immediately – couldn't wait to leave. 'I'm offering you a fresh start.'

But I didn't want a fresh start. I wanted everything to be back to how it was.

'Are you going to keep having your salary paid into the joint account?' I asked, as he zipped up the suitcase and stood it on the floor.

'Um, actually, I've changed it for December onwards.'

I gasped. 'But you can't!'

'I'll put an amount in every month to cover my share of the mortgage, but the rest of the bills you'll have to manage yourself.' He picked up the case and took it downstairs.

'You know I won't be able to afford it, Dom,' I said, pursuing him.

'Sell, then.' He put his coat back on and wound a scarf around his neck. I wanted to strangle him with it. 'Tell Meg I'll come over on Christmas morning at about eleven. If you don't want me in the house, we'll go for a walk or something.'

He opened the door and peered into the darkness. 'Hmm,' he said. 'Looks like they've gone.'

I followed his gaze. 'Who? What do you mean? Who was there?'

'When I arrived, there was somebody standing on the other side of the road, outside number thirty-two. They looked like they were watching the house. I thought maybe they were a porch pirate.'

'A porch pirate?' I repeated.

'Yes, you know, people who steal parcels from people's

porches. There's a lot of it going on, especially at this time of year. You weren't expecting any parcels, were you?'

'No. Was the person you saw a man or a woman?'

'Couldn't tell. They were wearing all black – hat, coat, scarf over their face. Anyway, looks like they've gone now. Hopefully not with everyone's Christmas presents!' And with that pathetic attempt at a joke, he left, walking up the hill in the direction of the Tube.

I stood in the open doorway, staring into the shadows – the dark shapes of cars, wheelie bins, shrubs and trees illuminated by the twinkle of Christmas lights in my neighbours' houses. Had Dom seen a porch pirate, or had it been someone else watching us, debating whether to ring the bell?

'Liv?' I called out. 'Liv? Are you there?'

There was a sudden movement in the bushes in the front garden of the house opposite. I caught my breath and waited, hoping that she might suddenly appear like a Christmas angel. But there was nothing there. Not even a fox.

THIRTY-EIGHT

As soon as the front door opens, I crouch down behind a wheelie bin and hold my breath. I can hear Rachel and Dom, but they're talking too quietly for me to make out any words. Their tone sounds as frosty as the ground beneath me. It's fucking freezing out here.

I wait for the sound of the door closing, then peer round just in time to see Dom trundling the large suitcase he brought with him back up the road. He walks more slowly than when he arrived, suggesting that he came to collect stuff rather than drop it off. I hesitate before moving, wondering whether he's going to turn round and cast a regretful look at all he's left behind, but he doesn't.

I stand up and release the tension in my knees. By my calculations, Rachel is on her own. I saw Meg leave the house a while earlier, wearing a thick pale coat, looking like a giant snowman. I have no idea how long she's going to be out, but it's still only mid-evening and nearly Christmas. Party time! Surely she's not so lame that she's going to come home before 10 p.m. I hadn't intended to hang around here for long, but Dom turned up and thwarted me. At least he only stayed for half an hour.

My fingers have gone numb with cold, even though I'm wearing gloves. My toes feel like stones in my boots. I can't last like this much longer. Tomorrow night I'll wrap up more warmly. Maybe even bring a hot drink.

I watch the house, trying to chart Rachel's movements. She comes into the sitting room and closes the curtains. Then the hallway light goes out. A few moments later the chandelier goes on in the front bedroom and she reappears, approaching the bay window and stopping to look at the street below. I instantly freeze, like a kid playing musical statues – my head slightly tilted, one arm lifted. It's important not to move. The eye easily picks it up.

Has she spotted me? I don't think so. This front garden is particularly gloomy. Whoever lives here doesn't celebrate Christmas.

My nose starts to itch. Why is she still staring into the darkness? It's almost as if she's looking for me, as if she senses I'm here. *Don't scratch, don't move.* I'm too far away to make out her expression, but there's something about her weak posture and the pitying angle of her head that tells me she's sad. Unsurprisingly. Was that a tear she just wiped away with the edge of her sleeve?

Poor Rachel. She must be missing Liv so much, praying for a miracle. Maybe she's imagining that she'll turn up tomorrow, taking the last Tube before the network shuts down for the holidays. Or that she'll appear like magic on Christmas morning, Santa's best present ever.

I do have compassion for her. She's tried really hard to be patient and accept Liv's pleas to be left alone, although she hasn't entirely managed it. These past few days I've turned the phone on in neutral, generalised locations and given her messages or an emoji or two. It keeps up the illusion, stops her from calling the police.

Only one more day to go.

Rachel closes the shutters one by one, gradually reducing my view of her until the window becomes a blank wall. The internal music starts again, and I unfreeze and shake out my limbs. Stomp the ground, bang my gloves together. The game's over. I need to do what I have to do now and then get the hell out of here.

I try to work out exactly where Rachel is. Has she gone to bed? No, too early. Perhaps she's gone downstairs to watch TV. Or to the back of the house to finish the washing-up. I should be safe. All I have to do is turn the key in the door to make sure it still works. I've been plagued by the idea that she might have changed the locks, in which case I'm fucked. It's an unreasonable fear, I know that. She hasn't had time. And why would she do it anyway, when she desperately wants her to daughter to come home? I'm just anxious about it, that's all. I can't afford any slip-ups. This is my one chance. It's tomorrow night or forget it.

Everything has to be replicated. The same day, the same method. Will it be the same outcome? I don't know. That's not in my power.

I look around to make sure nobody's walking down the street or putting their bins out, then cross the road. I tiptoe up the path and stand in front of the door. Removing my gloves, I stuff them in my pockets. The porch light is off, so it's hard to see the lock. Holding my breath, I locate the hole with my fingers and carefully push the key in. It fits. I turn it, ever so slowly, waiting for it to catch. Suddenly it releases, and the door starts to open inwards, as if pushed by an invisible hand. I grab the handle and pull it back, shutting it with a loud click. Too loud! Fuck. Did she hear it?

I quickly take out the key, then turn and run away, back up the hill towards the Tube station. I'm sweating now, my heart beating out of my jacket. Has she come to the door? Is she standing on the driveway, looking after me? I don't dare turn to find out. I keep going, head down, slowing my pace to a brisk walk.

This is going to be harder than I thought.

THIRTY-NINE

Karina came over on Christmas Eve. She brought three bottles of Prosecco, luxury chocolates, a tin of her famous salted caramel brownies and lots of presents, which she stashed under the tree. Meg took her bag up to the top bedroom while I fixed us each a gin and tonic.

'How is she doing?' Karina asked me quietly. She'd been deeply shocked by Meg's confession.

'Very well, all things considered,' I replied. 'We're much closer now. I feel as if we've got our relationship back. She's agreed to having some counselling, too.'

'That's good. When does that start?'

'I haven't organised it yet, but it'll be in the new year. If I can afford it.' I passed over her drink. 'We've just got to get through these next few days.'

We clinked glasses. 'We'll do our best to give her a good Christmas,' Karina said, 'but it won't be easy.' She sipped thoughtfully. 'No word from Liv, I suppose.'

I shook my head. 'I keep wondering where she is, what she's doing, who she's with. She's never not spent Christmas with us. It feels wrong.'

'And what about Dom?'

'He can go stuff himself.'

She laughed. 'I'll drink to that.'

Meg came downstairs. 'What's funny?'

'Oh, nothing. Just getting into the Christmas spirit.'

'Steady on, Mum.' She smiled. 'The evening has only just started.'

The lasagne was already in the oven, browning nicely. I finished making a salad while Meg and Karina laid the table. They used the red linen tablecloth that always came out at this time of the year, the best cutlery and glasses. Karina showed Meg how to fold the napkins into swans and made a beautiful arrangement of assorted candles in the centre of the table. Once they were all lit, they turned the dining room into a magical Christmassy space.

Karina uncorked the first bottle of Prosecco, and I brought out the lasagne. We sat down in a triangle shape. I reached out on either side and took their hands.

'Thank you for being here,' I said. 'I love you both so much. What would I do without you?'

'Eat all the lasagne,' said Meg, and we all laughed. 'Dish up, Mum, it's getting cold.'

After dinner, we cuddled up on the sofa and spent the rest of the evening devouring chocolates and watching two Christmas romcoms, one straight after the other. They were exactly the kind of films that Dom was snobby about. He would have refused to have them on. Watching them with Meg and Karina made me feel like a teenager again. We polished off another bottle of Prosecco and were all feeling pissed, but in a nice, cosy way.

Midnight came and went without our realising it. Suddenly the second film was over and it was Christmas Day.

'Time for bed, everyone,' Karina said, extricating herself

from the tangle of arms and legs. We stood up and yawned. The room had gone cold.

'Happy Christmas, my lovelies!' I said. 'Come on, group hug!'

We were mid-embrace when my mobile rang. My heart leapt.

'Probably Dad,' said Meg.

'I doubt it.' I ran into the kitchen and extracted my phone from the charger. Liv's name flashed onto the screen. 'It's Liv!' I shouted as I swiped into the call. Meg and Karina came to join me, excitement on their faces. 'Liv!' I cried. 'Happy Christmas!'

'Happy Christmas!' the others echoed.

We waited for her to answer. 'Liv? Darling! Are you there?'

'She must have lost signal,' said Karina. 'Hold on, she'll try again.'

We huddled around the phone, willing it to ring, but nothing happened. 'I'll try calling her instead,' I said, now desperate to hear the sound of her voice. The phone connected, but after a few rings it cut off. I tried again, but this time my call was immediately rejected.

'Let me try,' said Meg. She fetched her mobile and rang Liv instead, but the same thing happened. Liv seemed to have had second thoughts about talking to us.

We'd been doing so well until that point, but in an instant, all our efforts to be jolly crumbled.

'Oh, what a shame,' I said, now feeling desolate when only a few moments earlier I'd been fine – superficially, at least.

Meg looked close to tears. 'I don't get it,' she said. 'Why's she doing this to me? It's not fair. *I've* done nothing wrong!'

'Of course you haven't, Meg,' Karina soothed. 'Nobody's done anything wrong.'

'At least she's taken the first step,' I said.

Karina nodded enthusiastically. 'Exactly. It's a really positive sign. I expect she'll call tomorrow. But now we need to sleep.' She took Meg's arm and coaxed her upstairs. I stayed behind to lock up and turn out the lights, then followed them. We wished each other happy Christmas again, although with less conviction this time, then retired to our rooms.

I fell asleep quickly and was soon caught up in a deep, elaborate dream. Liv and Meg were in it, and so was Dom, which was annoying, but I couldn't get rid of him. We were at a party, or perhaps on holiday, abroad. I didn't recognise the place, but I liked it. The plot was fast and confusing. I tried to keep pace with it, but the dream seemed to be running away from me. And there were some strange noises that I couldn't identify – three high-pitched bleeps followed by a pause, the same rhythm repeating over and over again. I couldn't make it stop. It sounded like a warning, but as I wasn't feeling in the least bit troubled, I ignored it. I was enjoying the atmosphere of the dream and didn't want it to come to an end.

It was the sound of my own coughing that woke me. My throat was incredibly dry. I switched on the bedside lamp, but it didn't seem to be working. Had there been a power cut?

I could still hear the bleeping. It wasn't part of my dream at all. It was a smoke alarm, and it was coming from downstairs. What had happened? I leapt out of bed and felt my way towards the door, opening it and stepping onto the landing. Smoke suddenly whooshed up the stairs, engulfing me, filling my lungs. I couldn't see properly, but I knew from the intense heat that the ground floor was on fire. Flames were licking the banisters. There was no way I could get out.

'Meg!' I shouted into the darkness. 'Karina! The house is on fire! Don't come out! Stay in your rooms!'

I ran back into my own room and slammed the door shut, but the air was already thick with acrid smoke. It was making my chest hurt and I couldn't breathe properly. I banged on the wall of Meg's room, screaming her name, then called up to Karina through the ceiling, but there was no response from her either. Surely the alarm had woken them too. Had they already escaped, or were they trapped upstairs like me? Karina was on the top floor. How on earth would she get out?

My lungs were hurting. I badly needed some fresh air. I got down on my hands and knees and crawled blindly to the window. Pulling myself up to the sill, I felt for the latch, but couldn't open it. The damn thing was locked! I cursed Dom and his obsession with security. Where did he keep the bloody keys? If I didn't open the window within the next few seconds, I was going to pass out.

I crawled back through the dense, foul-smelling smoke and managed to open the drawer of the bedside cabinet on Dom's side. I rummaged around, then grabbed what felt like a small key. Fighting the pain in my chest, I went back to the window, hauled myself to my feet again and found the keyhole. Miraculously, the key turned. Squeezing the latch, I pushed the window open, leaning out as far as I could. I took a large gulp of oxygen, but the smoke billowed out from behind me, wrapping me in its embrace, making me cough even more.

The house was burning. More plumes of asphyxiating smoke were rushing up from the ground floor, obscuring my vision, filling my lungs again. It was so thick I couldn't see the houses opposite, or the driveway below, or even my own hand. I waved and screamed for help. Voices started shouting at me, but I couldn't see who they belonged to.

'Hang out of the window!'

'Don't jump! Wait for the fire brigade!'

'They're on their way!'

'There are two more of us!' I cried. 'In the back bedroom and on the top floor!'

I could hear sirens in the distance. That must be the fire brigade. Would they make it in time? I leant out of the window as far as I could, but my grip on the frame was weakening. I was frightened of falling head-first onto the hard ground below.

My lungs were so painful it was like they were going to burst. The fire below was getting closer by the second. How long would it be before the flames got past the bedroom door?

The sirens were growing louder. Help was nearly here, but my body was shutting down. I couldn't see, couldn't breathe. I felt as if I were drowning. I tried to call out to Meg and Karina, but I simply didn't have enough breath.

The fire engines arrived, blue lights flashing in the darkness. There was a lot of noise and commotion as the firefighters dismounted, but I couldn't make out what was going on. Could they see me? Did they know I was here? I made a supreme effort to cry for help, but no noise would come out of my mouth.

'She's up there, hanging out of the window!' a voice cried.

'Two more round the back,' yelled another.

An officer shouted up from below. 'I'm going to put a ladder against the wall so you can climb down. When I say go, I want you to sit on the windowsill, then turn round and reach out for the ladder. Put one foot on the nearest rung, then the other. Can you do that for me?'

'I'll try,' I said weakly.

'Good. Don't worry, we'll guide you down.'

Normally I would never have the guts to launch myself out of an upstairs window, but strangely, I didn't feel afraid. There was no choice. Either I had to risk falling or burn to death. I did as he instructed. The air was so thick I couldn't see the rungs and had to feel my way down.

'That's it, you're doing brilliantly,' he said. 'Only a few more steps to go.'

As soon as I reached the ground, my legs collapsed under me. The fire officer scooped me up and carried me to safety.

'My daughter and sister,' I gasped, 'They're still inside.'

'Yes, we know. We're on it,' he said, handing me over to two paramedics.

I remember being taken into the ambulance and an oxygen

mask being put over my face, but I must have passed out soon afterwards, because the next thing I knew I was in hospital. My skin and hair were blackened, and I couldn't stop coughing, but I was alive.

'Where's my daughter?' I rasped. My throat was incredibly sore. 'And my sister? Were they rescued? Are they here?'

'Yes,' the nurse said. 'Your sister's absolutely fine. I'm afraid your daughter is suffering from smoke inhalation but it's all under control. I'm sure she'll make a complete recovery – we just need to keep an eye on her for now.'

'Can I see her?'

'Soon. First you need to rest.'

I let out a deep sigh of relief. Meg and Karina were both safe; that was all that mattered. I had no idea whether the house was still standing, but at that moment, I didn't care. Material possessions meant nothing. I lay in my cubicle in A&E, trying to rest, but my mind was whizzing round and round. What had caused the fire to start? Faulty Christmas tree lights? A pan left to burn on the stove? I hoped to God it hadn't been my fault.

My instinct was to call Dom. I looked around for my phone, then remembered that I'd left it in the kitchen to charge overnight. In fact, I had nothing on me – no handbag, no credit card, no cash, no coat or shoes... How would I get home, and did I even have a home to go to?

The porters were wearing tinsel scarves and Santa hats. Paper chains decked the corridors. With a sickening thump in my chest, I remembered what day it was. The enormity of my predicament hit me. I turned my face to the pillow, black tears running down my cheeks.

'Hey, Rachel.' I lifted my head to see Karina standing next to the bed. She was still wearing her Christmas pyjamas. 'They told me you were here. How are you?'

I coughed on cue. 'Alive. Just about. I thought I was going to die.'

'Me too,' she replied. 'Thank God you had decent fire doors.'

'Yes. Stupidly, I opened mine.'

'I threw my bedding out of the window and jumped onto the roof of the conservatory.'

'Wasn't it on fire?'

'Not then, but the windows exploded soon after, so I was lucky I got out when I could.'

'Meg's got smoke inhalation,' I said. 'So have I, apparently.'

'Yes, they told me. They've already admitted her, so we can't see her until visiting time tomorrow. But I had a word with the doctor. She's going to be okay.'

'Thank God. If I'd lost her...' I couldn't finish the thought. 'What am I going to do, Karina? We've lost everything.'

'Let Dom deal with the insurance company,' she replied crisply. 'It's his house too. I'll call him, let him know.'

'Thanks.'

'It probably won't be safe for you to go back yet. You and Meg can stay with me for as long as you need.'

'Thanks. I still don't know how it started. I've been racking my brains...'

'Don't even think about it, just rest.' She squeezed my hand. 'Now I'd better go back to my trolley, or they'll think I've done a bunk.'

FORTY

Karina and I were discharged after breakfast due to a shortage of beds, but Meg was kept in for observation. Back at Karina's flat, I stood under the shower, scrubbing the soot from my skin, rinsing my hair over and over again. The water ran black, reminding me of how close I'd come to death. I stepped out of the cubicle and wrapped a towel around my shivering body.

We'd been assured that Meg was going to be fine, but I was still worried sick about her. What if the smoke inhalation had caused permanent damage to her lungs? I felt guilty for not having tried to rescue her, even though Karina kept telling me I'd done the right thing by staying in my room. Had I opened Meg's door, or tried to help her down the stairs, the smoke would have overcome us both. Rather than saving her, I could have caused her death. In fact, we all could have died. That didn't make me feel lucky to be alive – it terrified me.

Karina had kindly laid some of her clothes out on the bed for me. I chose a pair of pale pink jogging bottoms and a matching sweatshirt. They weren't my style, and the pants only just fitted, but I was grateful to have something to wear. I didn't know if any of my possessions had survived the blaze. Everything in my wardrobe was bound to be smoke- or water-damaged, probably both.

I wasn't too upset about losing my clothes – they were easily replaceable. It was more personal stuff that I mourned: old photos and family memorabilia, splodgy paintings the girls had done at nursery, Mother's Day cards, school reports and certificates, tacky holiday souvenirs from my own childhood, my mum's jewellery, ornaments that had belonged to my grandparents. There was a chance that the boxes in the loft might have been saved. I wouldn't know until I got back to the house and checked.

But it was unlikely that the furniture downstairs would be salvageable. The lounge and dining room would have to be refurbished; we'd need a new kitchen, maybe even a new conservatory. What if the insurance company wouldn't pay up? It felt overwhelming just thinking about it.

The situation was distressing yet in other ways liberating. Just a few days ago, I'd been adamant that I wouldn't sell the house. I'd refused to give up everything I'd worked so hard for during those twenty-three years of marriage. But now that everything had gone up – literally – in smoke, I had no choice but to start again from scratch.

I stood before the mirror in my pink leisure combo, looking pale and tired, hardly recognising myself. In that moment, I knew that I would never go back home. My old life was over, burnt to the ground. I'd find temporary accommodation for me and Meg, and as soon as the house was repaired, it could go on the market. At least there'd be no arguing over the contents. Half the proceeds should be enough to buy me a decent flat or a little house further away from the Tube station. Dom would get what he wanted, but I no longer cared.

I padded into the living room to find Karina. She was in the kitchen area, trying to cut slices of bread from a loaf that was still half frozen.

'I'm afraid I'm very low on supplies,' she said. 'I ran everything down because I was coming to yours for the week. It might have to be beans on toast for Christmas lunch.'

'Fine. I don't care what I eat.' I sat down on the sofa. The shower had worn me out. I was still wheezing, and my airways were very sore. 'What happens now?' I asked. 'Do the police investigate?'

'Only if there are suspicious circumstances.'

'Oh. And do they know yet what started it?'

Karina pulled an apologetic face. 'I didn't want to upset you, but the firefighter I spoke to last night said it was probably caused by a candle that had been left burning and caught something flammable.'

'Really? One candle could do all that damage?'

'Apparently. He said candles were a very common cause of house fires, especially around this time of year. They're naked flames, I suppose, so it's easy for things to catch light.'

I thought back to the beautiful display I'd arranged in the dining room. 'But I blew all the candles out,' I said stiffly. 'And I turned off the Christmas tree lights. I know I did.'

'Are you absolutely sure? I went up with Meg first, remember? You stayed downstairs to tidy up.'

'Yes, exactly, and that's when I checked nothing was still burning. I'm not stupid, Karina, I'm aware that candles are a fire hazard.'

'Of course you are, but...' She hesitated. 'You'd had quite a lot to drink.'

'Not *that* much!'

'I'm not blaming you, Rachel.'

'No? 'Cos that's what it sounds like.'

'I'm just reporting back on what the firefighter said. It was his hunch, that's all.'

'Well, he's wrong. Something else must have caused it. Faulty wiring, or a problem with the consumer unit.'

'Yeah, it was probably something like that,' she said, appeasing me in the way one might a child. 'There's no point in speculating. We need to wait for the investigator's report.'

'Yes. In the meantime, can you please stop implying that it was my fault. And don't you dare say anything to Dom.' I started to cough again. My throat instantly tightened, and I could hardly breathe. Getting upset seemed to make it worse.

We ate our Christmas beans on toast in virtual silence, both of us preoccupied by our own troubling thoughts. After we'd eaten, I gave in to my extreme tiredness and lay on the sofa with an inhaler for company, while Karina went back to the hospital to visit Meg. I felt utterly defeated. I needed to get some sleep, but I couldn't relax. My head ached and my chest felt raw.

The entryphone rang at about three. It was Dom. Just about the last person in the world I wanted to see. I let him in, bracing myself for the worst news.

'I went to the house this morning,' he said. 'It's been sealed off. They wouldn't let me in to inspect the damage, but apparently it's severe. The whole of the ground floor is destroyed and the ceiling above the sitting room has caved in.'

'Were the fire engines still there?'

'No, they'd gone, but I spoke to an investigator, asked him if he knew what had caused it.' He walked over to the window and stared out. It was a bright, sunny day, even though it was cold, and the views over the city were amazing.

'And?' I prompted.

'He was very guarded, said it was too early to tell, but he hinted that he wasn't expecting to find anything suspicious. He asked if I knew where you were staying. I gave him this address and Karina's number. I expect he'll want to interview you at some point.'

I felt the weight of his silent accusation.

'I turned everything off, Dom. *And* I blew out the candles.'

'Sure.' Somehow I felt like he didn't believe me.

'I expect it was an electrical fault. The meter's old, we should have had it replaced.'

'Yes, it was probably that.' There was a beat, then he turned abruptly. 'Right... I should go and see Meg.'

'Give her my love. I wanted to see her last night, but they wouldn't let me.'

'Of course I will. Oh, I collected the car,' he continued. 'I thought you might need it. It's parked downstairs in a visitor space.' He took a key fob out of his pocket and handed it to me. 'Here you go. I imagine yours melted.'

'Thanks,' I said dully.

He started to leave, then halted in the doorway and turned. 'Maybe... when Meg gets out of hospital, she should come and stay with me.'

'You mean with you and Charlotte?'

'Well, yes... obviously.' He blushed slightly.

'No thanks,' I replied stiffly. 'Karina has already offered to put us up here until we find somewhere else.'

'It's not ideal. You'll have to share. We've got a spare room.'

'Meg's not staying with you. I won't allow it,' I said firmly.

'It's up to her, surely. She's eighteen now.'

'You can't take her away from me, Dom, you can't! I've only just got her back.' The coughing started again. My chest burnt with pain, and I felt dizzy, as if I was going to faint. I collapsed on the sofa.

'Do you need anything?' he asked, staring down at me.

'No, I'm okay. But I'm worried about Liv. She called me last night, but we got cut off before we could speak. I lost my phone in the fire, so if she rings again today, she won't be able to get through. Have you heard from her at all?'

'No... I tried this morning, but her phone was switched off and I couldn't leave a message.'

'I don't get it. It's Christmas Day! Surely she'd want to wish us Happy Christmas at least.'

'Yeah, you'd think… I'll keep trying. As soon as I hear from her, I'll let you know.' He made to go, pausing at the door. 'I'm glad you're okay, Rachel,' he said. 'Take care of yourself.'

Karina brought Meg home with her later that day. I was very relieved that she was off the oxygen, but she looked terrible – her skin was dull, her hair lank, and there were grey circles beneath her eyes. I sent her straight to bed.

Both Meg and I were coughing, so I spent the night on the sofa. I tried to sleep, but my mind kept going over everything that had happened, trying to make sense of it all. The adrenaline had left my body and now I was an empty shell.

I was grateful to Karina for taking us in, but it was obvious that it could only be for a few days. I couldn't share the spare bed with Meg on a more permanent basis; there simply wasn't room. The sofa was comfortable enough, but Karina would soon tire of the mess. She often had Zoom meetings from home and wouldn't want me wandering around in the background. Sending Meg to stay with Dom was probably a more sensible option, but I couldn't bear the thought of her meeting Charlotte. It was way too soon for that. What if Charlotte was mean to her? What if they got on really well and Meg decided to live with them permanently? No, it would be better for us to bunk in together until the insurance company found us temporary accommodation. Or maybe just go to a hotel.

My brain was wired. I couldn't stop thinking about what had happened, particularly what had caused the fire. I was cross with Karina for implying that it had been my fault. I knew for certain that I'd blown all the candles out. As I lay in the darkness, my thoughts drifted to Jensen and the devastating fire at Briarfields. I cast my mind back to the press report I'd found online – the calm list of statistics about the number of appliances and firefighters that had been involved, and a timeline of how long it had taken to get the blaze under control. It didn't come anywhere near conveying the emotions involved, the terror and desperation, the fear of death, the feeling of hopelessness at not being able to save others. Now I had some idea of what Jensen had been through, although fortunately none of us had suffered burns and we'd all escaped with our lives. No wonder he suffered from PTSD.

How had that fire started? I wondered. I hadn't bothered to search for any further coverage of the incident, but now I wanted to know everything about it.

It was early morning; there was no way I was getting back to sleep now. I turned on the light and reached for Karina's mobile, which was plugged into its charger on the kitchen worktop. I pulled it free, punched in her access code and took it back to the sofa. I spent ages browsing for articles in the local press but couldn't find anything, drawing the conclusion that the fire had started by accident. All that came up was the original piece, which I opened and reread, simply to remind myself of the facts.

Surrey Fire and Rescue Service were called to a blaze at Briarfields, near Carlington, at 11.55 p.m. on 24 December.

I stopped in my tracks. The twenty-fourth of December – Christmas Eve. Exactly the same date as our fire.

Could it be a coincidence?

FORTY-ONE

I reminded myself that the firefighter had told Karina that fires at Christmas were sadly common. Even so, my gut was telling me that there was more to it. Jensen was the link. I *had* to talk to him and find out the full story.

After breakfast, I told Karina I needed to go to Westfield shopping centre to buy some new clothes, as the ones she'd lent me didn't fit properly.

'Are you sure you're up to it?' she asked. 'It's Boxing Day. The shops will be crammed.'

'I know, but I need something to take my mind off things,' I said.

She gave me her credit card, as my handbag had been lost in the fire. I hurried off to the Tube, but instead of getting off at Stratford, I changed lines and carried on to London Bridge. As Karina had predicted, the trains were crowded with people headed for the sales. I was still wheezing and coughing from the smoke inhalation. A few people gave me filthy looks, presumably thinking I was infectious, but I kept my head down and ignored them, stifling my coughs as best I could.

Normally London Bridge was busy with office workers and tourists, but today it was quiet. There were surprisingly few homeless people around compared to the numbers I'd seen before. I guessed there'd been a big effort to find them space in hotels and hostels for Christmas, which was good, although they'd only be chucked out again once the holiday was over. Meg and I had also lost our home, but at least we'd had family to turn to, and an insurance policy that would hopefully pay out. These people had nothing.

I'd already googled homeless shelters in the area, so I knew where I was going. I had no idea whether Jensen had been telling the truth about volunteering there, but it was the only lead I had. I found the place easily. It looked like an old factory, with flat, grilled windows. A banner hung over the entrance, saying *Sunshine and Showers – All Welcome*. The doors were open, so I stepped inside.

The main room was surprisingly empty. A few men were sitting at a table playing a board game, and another guy was lying outstretched on a sofa – one of the workers was trying to get him to sit up. I knocked on the door of the manager's office, which was off the hall, and a friendly-looking woman with braided hair came to answer.

'Hi,' I said. 'I'm looking for a friend. I think he volunteers here – or used to. He lived with my family for a few months, but he moved out recently and I don't know where he's gone. His name's Jensen Watson.'

'Jensen?' She nodded. 'Yeah, I know him.'

'Is he still working here?'

'In the kitchens.'

My heart skipped a beat. 'Oh, amazing. Can I talk to him, please?'

'He's not here today, love. He took some time off over Christmas. He's not back until January.'

'Oh... I really need to speak to him before then. It's quite urgent. I don't suppose you have his mobile number, do you? Only I've lost my phone.'

She gave me an apologetic smile. 'Sorry. I'm not allowed to give out personal information.'

'No, of course not. Sorry. Shouldn't have asked. Would you mind calling him and asking him to get in touch? My name's Rachel. Tell him I'm staying at Karina's, that's my sister. I'll give you the address.'

'Sure. Write it down and I'll see what I can do.' She handed me a piece of paper and a pen.

'He needs to come round as soon as he can,' I said, writing. 'It's really, really important.'

Her eyes narrowed. 'What's this about?' I hesitated. 'He's not in trouble, is he?'

'No, not at all,' I blustered. 'He left some stuff at our house and I need him to pick it up.'

'And that's "really, really important"?' She looked at me doubtfully.

'It's about a personal matter,' I admitted.

'Hmm... We have a duty to protect our staff and volunteers—'

'There's nothing sinister about it. Just pass on the message, please.'

'Okay, I'll give him a call,' she said.

'Thank you so much,' I said, handing her the scrap of paper. I used Karina's bank card to make a donation to the shelter, which seemed to alter her attitude towards me a little, then got straight back on the Tube.

'There you are! Where have you been? You've been gone ages,' my sister said as I walked through the door with not a carrier bag in sight. Her tone was strained and there was an anxious look on her face.

'What's up?'

'The police are here.'

'Really? I thought there were no suspicious circumstances.'

'So did I. But there's been a development, apparently.'

I went straight into the living room, where two police officers were sitting on the sofa. One was about my age and the other looked young enough to be his daughter.

'I'm Detective Sergeant Grant Baxter,' the male officer said, holding out his hand. 'And this is my colleague Police Constable Leigh Picard.'

'Sorry I was out,' I said. 'What's this about?'

DS Baxter remained cool. 'I'll explain when everyone's ready. It would be good to talk to you all together.'

Karina went to wake Meg. We made small talk about the weather and remarked on the amazing views. I offered to make them a cup of tea, which they refused. Finally Meg emerged, wearing her dressing gown and slippers, hair sticking out at angles.

'What's going on?' she asked, her eyes flitting between us. I patted the sofa next to me and nodded at her to sit.

'As you may know, when there's a fire, the police only become involved if there's serious injury or a fatality, or if there's a suspicion of arson,' Baxter began.

'Arson?' I echoed, my chest starting to tighten. 'I thought it was too early to tell.'

'Indeed it is. However, yesterday we received a call from one of your neighbours. A Mr Singh.'

'Harinder, yes, I know who you mean,' I replied. 'He lives opposite.'

'Apparently he saw somebody lurking in his front garden on the night before the fire. He talked to some other neighbours, and a couple also saw somebody the previous evening.'

'Actually, Dom, my husband, saw them too,' I said, remembering. 'He thought they were looking for Amazon parcels.'

'That may be the case.'

'But you think they might have started the fire?'

'It's definitely a line of enquiry.'

'Like, how? You mean, putting a burning rag through the letter box or something?'

'We don't know,' Baxter replied patiently. 'We haven't got that far yet. Did you see them?'

Meg and Karina shook their heads.

'I didn't see anyone on Christmas Eve,' I said, 'but we stayed in the whole time.'

'Do you have any idea who this person might be?'

We all said no.

'Did anyone manage to give a good description of them?' asked Karina.

'Not really, but it seems like it was the same person each time. They had their hood up and a mask over their face, dark jeans and a black jacket.'

'Male or female?'

'Two witnesses said male, the other said female,' said PC Picard.

I thought of the three of us huddled together on the sofa, watching movies and stuffing our faces with chocolates. Had this person been standing outside all that time, watching the house, waiting for us to go to bed? I shivered inside.

'We made some house-to-house enquiries this morning,' DS Baxter continued. 'Another neighbour who was coming home from a party on Christmas Eve saw someone answering that description standing outside the Tube station. The trains had just stopped running. The person looked like they were waiting for a taxi and seemed agitated. As the witness approached, they ran around the corner and hid.'

My heart rate started to speed up. 'I see. So the timing fits with the fire.'

'Yes. Quite precisely. If this person took an Uber, we should be able to track it down. We've got people working on that at that moment,' said PC Picard. 'We're also examining CCTV from earlier in the evening, as it's possible that they arrived by Tube. Maybe they expected to take the Tube back, not realising it had stopped for Christmas.'

'Well, that's all very... alarming,' I said.

Baxter leant forward. 'Mr Singh also told us that there'd been some graffiti sprayed on your windows a couple of weeks ago. Apparently it said "KYS".'

'That's not connected,' I replied quickly, avoiding Meg's gaze. 'It was a stupid prank. We know who did it.'

'You didn't report it.'

'No. Honestly, it's got nothing to do with the fire, I promise.'

'How do you know that?'

'I just do.'

There was a long, uncomfortable pause, then Baxter resumed. 'Have you had any fallings-out with anyone recently – apart from the person who told you to kill yourself?' I didn't like the slight tone of sarcasm in his voice.

'Um... not as such.'

'Tell him about Jensen, Mum,' piped up Meg.

The officers swung back to me simultaneously. 'Jensen who?' enquired DS Baxter.

'Jensen Watson, he's my daughter Olivia's boyfriend – ex-boyfriend. They were both living with us until very recently, but then my daughter moved out, so he had to as well.'

'And how did he feel about that?'

'He was a bit upset, but I think he understood.'

'When did he leave?'

'Just over a week ago.'

'If he was living with you, presumably he had a key to the house.'

'Yes.'

'Did he give it back when he moved out?'

'No, actually. He still had some stuff to pick up. Why do you ask?'

'Just because it's useful to know who had access to the house.'

'I see...' My brain was starting to whirr. Could it have been Jensen standing outside, watching us? Why would he have done that?

'Do you know where Jensen Watson is living now?' asked PC Picard.

'Um... no. Sorry.'

'Do you have his mobile number?'

'I *did*, but it was on my phone, which I lost in the fire. He volunteers at the Sunshine and Showers homeless shelter near London Bridge. If you ask the manager there, she'll give you his contact details.'

She wrote it down. 'Thanks. We'll speak to him.'

DS Baxter looked at us one by one. 'Is there anything else you can tell us that might be useful?'

I took a breath. 'Yes. I don't know if this is at all relevant, but Jensen was involved in another house fire, two years ago. It was at a place called Briarfields, in Surrey, his family home. His foster parents died and he was badly injured. The thing is... it also happened on Christmas Eve.' The officers raised their eyebrows simultaneously.

'Rachel!' blurted out Karina. 'Why didn't you say this before?'

I turned to her. 'Because I only realised this morning when I reread the incident report. I thought it was just a weird coincidence, but now we know there was somebody lurking outside that night...'

'Who *could* be Jensen,' said Meg. '*And* he still has a key. He could have let himself in and started it.'

'You said yourself that you'd definitely blown all the candles out,' Karina reminded me. 'Maybe this explains it.'

I shuddered. 'It doesn't look good, does it?'

'It's important not to jump to conclusions,' Baxter said carefully. 'The investigation is still at a very early stage. First we need to identify the person who was seen outside your house. They may have had a legitimate reason for being there.'

'There's something else,' I said. 'My daughter Olivia. She left home on the twenty-second of November after an argument with Jensen, and we haven't seen her since.'

He caught his breath. 'Okay... that's interesting. Did you report it to the police?'

'Yes. I filled in an online form, but you didn't consider her a missing person, so nothing was done about it.'

'She hasn't completely vanished, she's been in touch by text,' Karina explained. 'And she sent Rachel a voice note. But she won't actually talk to any of us. Or meet up.'

'She tried calling on Christmas Eve,' I added, 'but the line went dead before we had a chance to speak.'

DS Baxter put down his pen. 'You're still in contact, so I can see why it wasn't taken any further. To be honest, most people reported as missing turn out to be perfectly safe. Sometimes they just don't want to be found. But taking the fire into account, and looking at the whole picture, I can see that there's a lot to untangle here. Jensen Watson is the link. We'll look into it straight away. If you can give me your daughter's mobile number, we can apply for access to her call records and get a fix on her location. I'm sure she's fine, but there's no harm in checking.' Karina read the number off her phone, and he took it down. Then he shut his notebook and stood up. 'Anything else?'

'No,' I said.

'Try not to worry about her. We'll be in touch as soon as we have news.'

'Thanks,' I replied. Now the police were taking me seriously, it was as if a huge weight had lifted from my shoulders.

Karina saw them out. 'Oh my God,' she said as soon as she closed the door. 'Do you really think Jensen could have started the fire?'

'If you'd asked me a couple of weeks ago, I would have said no,' I replied. 'But... he lied about his background, his parents, the job... I'm starting to think anything's possible.'

'And the fact that the fire at Briarfields happened on Christmas Eve, too. That freaked me out. I mean, are you thinking what I'm thinking? That maybe that wasn't an accident either?'

Meg gasped. 'What? You mean he murdered his parents?'

'It sounds extreme, but maybe, yes,' Karina said. 'Maybe he tried to murder us too.'

'No! Don't! It's too much. Too much!' Meg stood up and ran off to the spare bedroom.

'You shouldn't have said that,' I muttered. 'She can't take it.'

'Sorry. I don't know about you, but I need a proper drink.' Karina reached for a bottle of gin. 'Do you want to join me?'

'Please. A small one.'

I went back to the sofa and lay down. My head ached; my body had twisted itself into one huge emotional knot. Karina brought our gin and tonics over and sat down next to me.

'There you go. See if it helps.'

I took a few sips. 'There's something else I need to tell you,' I said quietly.

Karina groaned. 'Now what?'

'I didn't go to Westfield this morning.'

'Ah. I was wondering why you came back empty-handed. Where *did* you go?'

'I went to the Sunshine and Showers shelter. To see Jensen.'

'Jesus, Rachel...'

'The manager wouldn't give me his number, but she said she'd pass on my message.' I paused, frightened to continue.

'And what was the message?' Karina asked suspiciously.

'I asked him to come here.'

'You did *what*?!'

'I didn't know then that he was a possible suspect! I just wanted to talk to him about the fire.'

'But the guy could be dangerous!'

'I'm sorry. Like I said, I didn't know... He probably won't turn up anyway.'

'If he does, I'm dialling 999 immediately. In fact, we should let the police know right now.' She tutted. 'Why didn't you say anything?'

'I don't know... I'm not thinking straight at the moment.'

Karina put in a call to DS Baxter. I sat in silence, sweaty with embarrassment as she confessed on my behalf. But then the conversation took a different turn.

'Are you absolutely sure?' she asked. 'I see... Yes, well it does change things... I understand... Yes, of course, I'll send you a photo... Thanks.'

The call ended and she put the phone down. Her face had paled; she looked as if she'd just been told that somebody had died.

'What is it?' I demanded. 'Karina! Tell me! What did he say? Whose photo do they want?'

She swallowed hard. 'The person seen outside your house caught an Uber from the Tube station shortly after the fire started.'

'Yes. And?'

'The police have traced the ride and know the account that paid for it.'

'Great! So who was it? Jensen?'

'No,' she said, starting to cry. 'Not Jensen. Liv.'

Karina came towards me, arms outstretched for a hug, but I didn't need consoling. 'I don't believe it,' I said, backing off.

'It's not about believing, Rachel, the facts are there. They think she probably arrived by Tube, so they're checking CCTV at the station to see if they can get a positive ID. That's why they need the photo.'

'It doesn't mean she started the fire. She came to see us. She was probably trying to work out if Jensen was still there, or to build up the courage to knock on the door.'

Karina frowned. 'I don't think so.'

'She called on me Christmas Eve, remember? She wanted to see us! She just lost her nerve.'

'She was hanging around outside for hours. She left just after the fire started. She also has a key. If that isn't suspicious behaviour, I don't know what is.'

But I wouldn't have it. 'They don't know yet that it was arson. It could easily have been me. In fact, I'm sure it was. It was late, I was tired and pissed. I left the candles burning.'

'Except you told me you didn't.'

'Well, I was wrong! It wasn't Liv. She'd never set fire to her own home. I *know* my daughter!'

'Do you?' She held my gaze. 'You've got to admit, she's been acting very strangely the last few weeks – leaving without telling you, going into hiding, refusing to talk to anyone, cutting herself off completely. I think she's mentally ill, deeply depressed, psychotic even. She needs help.'

Karina's theory struck home, but it only made me feel worse. I felt my chest tighten and I started to cough. 'Oh God, you think...' I couldn't complete my sentence.

'I don't know, I'm just trying to make sense of it. It's hard to get your head around. I'm still reeling from it. God knows how Meg's going to react.'

'Maybe we shouldn't tell her.'

'We have to, Rachel. She's a grown-up. She has a right to know the truth. Shall I speak to her?'

'Please. I'm too upset... I can't deal with it.'

Karina knocked on the door of the spare room and went in. I waited outside, my mind in such a spin that I was barely able to stand. How could Liv have done this? It was incomprehensible.

As soon as I heard the sound of Meg sobbing, I went to join them. She was lying on the bed, her face in the pillow. 'Darling, I'm here, it's okay, talk to me.' I swallowed hard, trying to suppress the coughing fit.

'She tried to kill us,' Meg mumbled into the pillow. 'Why, Mum? Why?'

I steadied my voice. 'We don't know what happened yet. Nobody knows. It's all just guesswork. We don't know for sure that it was arson. It was probably my fault.'

'It was Liv, Mum. The police know it, you know it and I know it.'

'Well I'm not going to believe it until there's more proof,' I answered. 'And nor should you. We've got to be patient and wait.'

She lifted her head. Her face was stained with tears. 'Will she go to prison?'

'Don't even think about that. But no... I don't think so. If she *did* do it, and we still don't know for sure, it'll have been because she's ill. Diminished responsibility, they call it. Liv's not an evil person, Meg. She loves her family.'

'The police are looking for her. They'll arrest her!'

'They'll want to question her, for sure. But that's okay. Once we've found her, we can help her. It'll be all right. I promise you, Meg.'

I didn't totally believe my own reassuring words, but they seemed to calm Meg a little. I left her to rest and went back to talk to Karina.

'So what happens now?'

'I've sent DS Baxter a photo of Liv so they can check it against the CCTV images. They're also tracing her bank card use.'

I sank onto the sofa, defeated. My nerve endings were frayed. I tried to speak, but my throat was too sore. I took out the inhaler and tried to soothe it.

With my phone and laptop lost to the fire, I had no photos of my own any more. I'd been meaning to back them all up on the cloud but hadn't got round to it. Too late now, I thought miserably. 'Which photo did you send?'

'The most recent I could find. I took it at Meg's eighteenth. She had her arms wrapped around Jensen, but it was a good shot of her face.'

'I guess the police aren't so interested in him now,' I said. 'Sounds like he had nothing to do with it.'

The police promised to get back to us once they'd tracked down Liv's location, but the hours went past and we heard nothing.

Meg refused to leave her room. Karina and I watched TV, but we couldn't concentrate on even the simplest of programmes. Everything on terrestrial had some festive theme, cruelly reminding me of what we'd lost. I wanted Christmas to be over and done with, struck off the calendar.

Without my own phone, I felt – almost literally – disconnected from the rest of the world. I realised how much I usually fidgeted with it, checking for texts and emails, scrolling through Instagram, playing stupid games. Time was passing at a glacial pace, and I longed for some distraction. But more importantly, I felt powerless, reliant on Karina to relay messages and news.

Eventually we crawled our way to six o'clock in the evening. Karina insisted on heating up more ready meals, even though neither Meg nor I was hungry. 'We have to keep going,' she insisted. 'Keep our strength up. We don't know what's going to hit us next.'

It couldn't get any worse, I thought. Could it?

That night, Meg and I tried sleeping in the same bed. I thought it might comfort her to have me close. But we were both still coughing, and she had a very wheezy chest. The hours wore on. I couldn't stop thinking about Liv, refusing to accept that she could have done such a terrible thing, even though the evidence against her was strong. I needed to see those CCTV images before I would believe it.

We all got up late, even Karina, who was usually an early bird. I wandered from one room to another, not knowing what to do. It felt as if I were in a hospital waiting room, preparing myself to hear bad news. I'd always found the period between Christmas and New Year strange – everyone rushed around like mad to get ready for the big day, then spent the next week with oodles of time on their hands and nothing to fill it. But this was far worse than anything I'd experienced before.

It was about 11 a.m. when the entryphone rang.

'It must be the police,' I said, rushing to answer it. I picked up the receiver.

'Hi, it's Jensen,' he said. 'Is Rachel there?'

'Yes, it's me,' I replied with a sigh. 'You'd better come up.'

A minute or so later, he emerged from the lift. His clothes were dirty, his hair was slick with grease and he looked badly in need of a shower and a hot meal.

I stood by the entrance to the flat. 'You got my message,' I said.

'Yes. Mandy said it was urgent. Is it about Liv? Is she okay?'

'Come inside and I'll explain.'

We went into the living room. Karina was in the kitchen area, tidying up. Her mouth dropped open when I walked in with Jensen.

'Oh,' she said. 'It's you.'

He looked around nervously. 'What's this about? Why am I here? Why didn't you ask me to come to your house, Rachel?'

I gestured at him to sit down. 'Because it caught fire on Christmas Eve,' I said.

'No...' He gulped. 'Christmas *Eve*? Oh my God... What happened?'

'We were fast asleep. Luckily the smoke alarm woke me. A neighbour called the fire brigade and they rescued us. Meg and I had smoke inhalation. Karina was okay, apart from the shock. It was horrendous, I thought we were going to die.'

He shook his head as if he couldn't quite believe it. 'Do you know what started it?'

'On the surface, it looks like it was an accident, but there's a possibility that it was arson.' I took a breath. 'Somebody was seen outside acting suspiciously. At the moment, the evidence suggests that it was Liv.'

'Liv?' he echoed, eyes opening wide.

'That's how it looks, but we don't know for sure. It's very early stages.'

'Doesn't make sense. Liv would never do anything like that.'

'That's what I think.'

'Was there much damage?'

I nodded sadly. 'I haven't been back, but Dom says the whole of the ground floor has been destroyed and much of the upstairs. We've lost everything.'

'Fuck... I'm really sorry to hear that, Rachel. But why did you want to talk to me?'

I took a deep breath. 'I know the fire at Briarfields also happened on Christmas Eve.'

'So... what are you saying? You think I had something to do with both of them? I was a victim,' he said bitterly. 'I was in hospital for two months. I nearly died too.'

'I know. I'm sorry. But surely you can see how it seems like more than a coincidence.'

'I suppose so, but that's all it is, there's no connection—'

At that moment, Karina ran into the room. 'The police have just sent these images through,' she cried, holding up her phone. 'They're from inside a train carriage on the Central Line, earlier in the evening of the twenty-fourth, heading east. At the beginning of the journey her hood's down and she's not wearing the mask. She only puts it on when she gets to Stratford.'

'You mean Liv?'

'No. That's the thing, it's not Liv – it's some other woman.'

'What?! Are you serious?'

'The police are asking if we recognise her. I don't, but maybe you do. Is she one of Liv's uni friends, perhaps?'

I almost snatched the phone from her. The CCTV image was of a woman about Liv's age, very pretty, with blonde hair cropped in a pixie cut.

'I've never seen her before. Maybe Meg knows her. Go and get her.'

Karina left the room. I stared at the grainy photo, my mind

racing. What was this stranger doing pretending to be Liv? And why had she tried to burn down our house?

'Can I have a look?' asked Jensen. He took the phone from me, gasping with horror as he saw the photo. 'Oh no! I don't believe it. It can't be her, it can't!' His hand started to shake, and he dropped the phone.

Liv arrived at Sofia's flat in the middle of the night, carrying only a rucksack.

Her parents had left her and Jensen alone for the weekend so they could get their relationship back on track, but instead it had taken a nosedive. They had argued non-stop for hours, screaming and shouting so much it was a wonder the neighbours hadn't called the police. She'd never seen anyone so angry. At times he'd only just managed to stop himself striking her, and she had wanted to hit out herself – if only to knock some sense into him. He'd said some wild things, made strange, incomprehensible threats.

You won't get rid of me that easily.

I've lost one set of parents – I'm not going to lose another.

You've no idea what I'm prepared to do to stay in this family!

She'd been so frightened of him she'd had to back down and say sorry. She pretended it was all her fault; told him she loved him and that together they would work things out. He bought her lies easily, which gave her time to plan her exit strategy. She encouraged him to go for a run to clear his head, and while he was gone, she packed a rucksack with essential stuff, hiding it in the cupboard under the stairs.

He returned home in a calmer mood, apologising for pushing her up against the wardrobe and shouting in her face. They had a takeout for dinner, stole another bottle from her dad's wine rack and watched a film together. Sitting next to him made her squirm, but she kept up the charade. He seemed to think everything was okay between them, and they went to bed. She drew the line at making love, saying she had the proverbial headache. It was actually true.

As soon as she'd realised that Jensen was deeply asleep, she'd crept downstairs, collected her rucksack and left the house, taking a late-night Tube along with dozens of drunk partygoers.

Now she positioned herself in front of the entryphone and pressed the buzzer several times. There was no reply.

'Shit,' she said under her breath. She had thought about calling in advance but hadn't had the chance. Also, she was worried that Sofia might try to dissuade her from leaving. On the way here, turning up unannounced had seemed like the best option, but she stupidly hadn't accounted for Sofia being out. If she'd gone clubbing, she was unlikely to turn up before 4 a.m., if at all. With nowhere else to go, Liv sat on the stone steps, leant against her rucksack and waited, the day's ugly events churning in her head.

Half an hour later, a Tesla pulled up outside the house. Sofia poured herself out and said goodbye to the driver. She was wearing a strappy blue satin dress that shimmered like water in the street light and carried a pair of heels in her hand. She staggered up the path, rummaging in her purse to find her door key. As Liv emerged from the shadows, Sofia screamed and reached for her pepper spray.

'It's okay! It's only me!' Liv cried.

'For fuck's sake! What are you doing here?'

They fell into hysterics of laughter. Sofia let them in and deactivated the alarm. Liv was ready with her story, but Sofia wasn't up to chatting. She'd obviously had a big night, and was on her way down from a cocktail of drugs and alcohol.

'Gotta crash,' she mumbled, heading towards her bedroom.

'Need any help?'

'Nah, I'm fine... You know where your room is, right?' She stumbled over the threshold and slammed the door shut behind her.

Liv went into the all-white spare room. The bed was already made up. She unpacked her rucksack and tucked herself under the duvet, but she was too excited to sleep. She'd done it. Left Jensen. Left home. For the first time in her life, she felt free.

Sofia didn't resurface until the following afternoon. She said she felt like shit and had no memory of Liv's arrival. But she was absolutely fine about her being there.

'You've needed to get out of those toxic relationships for a while,' she said, fixing herself a smoothie. 'Stay as long as you like.'

'Thanks so much,' Liv replied over the sound of the juicer.

'I'll give you some keys. You can have the run of the place – apart from my room. That's my sacred space, okay?'

'Sure.'

Sofia leant against the worktop. 'Does Jensen have any idea where you've gone?'

'No. He doesn't know about you, or where you live. Nor do Mum and Dad.'

'Good. Keep it that way. The last thing I want is an angry ex-boyfriend turning up on the doorstep. Or a hysterical mother.'

'I need to cut myself off completely,' Liv said. 'Can you help?'

'Sure. I'm the world's greatest expert at disappearing.' Sofia poured the green concoction into a glass and took a slurp, wincing as she swallowed. 'Too much lemon... Boyfriends are easy to ghost, but you have to be careful when it comes to family.'

'How do you mean?'

'If you cut off from parents, they panic. It's understandable, especially if you haven't actually fallen out with them. They assume something terrible has happened, like you've been abducted or murdered. Before you know it, half the country's police force is looking for you.'

'I don't want that,' agreed Liv. 'But if I tell Mum where I am, she might tell Jensen. They've got this special bond going, I don't trust either of them.'

'Awkward.'

'So what do I do?'

Sofia wiped her mouth and put down the glass. 'Okay. You stay in touch, but only occasionally and always on your terms. Send them the odd text saying everything's fine, you're just taking some time out, ask them to give you some space and not to call.'

'Mum won't take any notice of that. As soon as she and Dad get back from Southwold, she'll be on that phone.'

'Then don't pick up. Ever. Keep your phone turned off. She can't track your location, can she?' Liv shook her head fiercely. 'Good. Eventually you can change your contract, get a new number.'

'Won't that make them panic?'

'No, because you'll have drip-fed the idea that you want nothing more to do with them.'

Liv wasn't sure that she wanted to cut off completely from her family. Over the next few days, especially at night as she lay alone in that strange little white bedroom, she scrolled through all the pleading messages she'd received, mostly from her mother. Dad had only texted her a couple of times; either he was more respectful of her wishes or less bothered by her disappearance, she couldn't tell which.

It was Jensen's reaction that shocked her. She'd expected him to be the most difficult to shake off, but he didn't try to contact her at all. It offended her that he'd accepted her departure so quickly. Why wasn't he distraught?

Meg worried her the most. She called a lot, leaving plaintive messages on voicemail. Liv felt guilty about abandoning her, especially with that horrible bullying going on, but Sofia insisted that it was all or nothing.

'The less Meg knows, the better,' she said. 'Then neither Jensen nor your mum can put any pressure on her.'

'It just feels mean. Like I don't trust her.'

'Sorry, but it's how it is. You can stay here rent-free for as long as you like, but if you're going to start handing out this address to a load of people, I don't know—'

'No, it's fine, you're right. I need to be strong.'

Sofia snatched up Liv's phone. 'Hey, I've got an idea. Why don't I handle all the communication from now on?'

'No, it's okay.' Liv reached out for it, but Sofia backed away.

'You don't need them pestering you all the time. I'll drip-feed stuff, like I said. It'll be fine. They won't worry, and you can relax and get on with your exciting new life.'

'But I can't be without my phone.'

'Of course you can. You'll be fine. This is the only way, Liv. If you need anything, just ask me.'

Sofia locked the phone away in her room. Liv felt instantly bereft, almost panicky, but she didn't feel able to ask for it back. She was the guest here, and it was a case of do things Sofia's way or leave.

A couple of times during that first week, Sofia took her out to dinner at expensive restaurants, but mostly Liv stayed in all day and watched Netflix. They lived off takeaways. Sofia paid for everything. Liv was grateful, but also felt beholden. With little money in her bank account, no job on the horizon, no phone and no access to the internet, it made for a very boring existence. She realised that rather than creating an exciting new life for herself, she was in danger of having no life at all.

Christmas wasn't far off now. She had never spent it away from home. If she didn't go back, it would break her mother's heart. Meg would be devastated, too. But Sofia was insistent that they have Christmas together, just the two of them. It seemed to be non-negotiable, part of the deal.

'Don't you want to spend it with your parents?' Liv asked. Sofia rarely spoke about her mum and dad, and there were no photos of them on display.

'We fell out years ago,' she explained. 'I don't see them any more. It's just me and my trust fund now.' She pulled a mock-sad face.

Sofia had abandoned the idea of getting a job and was planning a round-the-world trip. She browsed travel websites, creating exotic itineraries in South America, Africa and Asia. She planned to go straight after Christmas and would be away for at least six months, possibly a whole year.

'Are you still okay for me to flat-sit?' Liv asked.

'Of course! In fact, I'll be furious with you if you don't.'

'Thanks... that's amazing.'

'Actually, you can have a practice run this weekend. I'm going to Bristol to meet up with some old uni friends. I would invite you along, but you'll be bored out of your skull. We'll only end up talking about Exeter the whole time.'

'I wouldn't mind. I might meet someone who knows Jensen,' Liv replied.

'I already asked around, but nobody remembers him. To be honest, Liv, I'm not sure he was ever there. Or if he was, he must have dropped out after a few weeks. Just forget him, okay? It's over. He's toast.'

Sofia left for Bristol on Saturday afternoon. At first Liv felt a little aggrieved to have been left alone, but as she started to relax, she realised there was an advantage to Sofia not being here. She could do what she wanted and no longer had to worry about saying the wrong thing or having her host's approval. It was liberating. She felt like a teenager who'd been left in the house by her parents for the first time.

More than anything, she wanted to call Meg and see how she was. Sofia still had her phone, and she didn't know Meg's number – or indeed anyone's number – off by heart. She really needed to look at her messages and find out how Mum and Dad had taken her departure. Had they asked Jensen to leave? It would make sense if they had. Dad would want him to go straight away, but Mum was probably holding out for a bit longer, in case Liv came back and they made up. Right now, that was unlikely to happen. Liv didn't like the idea of Jensen being there without her, sleeping in her bed by himself, eating meals with her family, taking her place.

Presumably her phone was still somewhere in Sofia's bedroom. She kept the door closed and locked it every single time she went out. It was as if she thought Liv might borrow her make-up or try on her designer clothes. Liv was disappointed not to be trusted, and it only increased her curiosity about what secrets lay hidden there. Maybe there was a safe behind the large painting she'd glimpsed hanging on the chimney breast. Or a stash of jewels under the floorboards. Or thousands of pounds in cash stuffed under the mattress.

Sofia kept the key in her bag, but there might be a spare somewhere.

Liv went into the kitchen. She emptied the drawers onto

the granite worktop, rummaged in the hall cupboard and the sideboard in the sitting room. There were no keys of any kind. She was about to give up when she remembered the utility room, which was next to the second bathroom. A biscuit tin sat on the top shelf of the cupboard housing the washer-dryer. When she picked it up, it gave a hopeful rattle. Prising the lid off, she found several keys of different types and sizes, each with their own neatly labelled plastic fob. It wasn't a level of organisation she would have normally associated with Sofia, but she didn't stop to wonder. Grabbing the key marked *Bedroom 1*, she ran back down the hallway and let herself in.

She suddenly felt anxious. What if Sofia had installed a nanny cam? She could be watching her right this minute from her laptop. Oh well, she thought, it was too late now. Anyway, she had a right to search for her own property. All she wanted was her phone, then she'd retreat.

But where had Sofia hidden it? Liv opened the bedside cupboards and ransacked the dressing-table drawers. She opened the vast fitted wardrobes that took up the whole of one wall and delved into boxes of designer handbags and shoes. Frustratingly, there was no sign of her mobile. Perhaps Sofia had taken it with her so that she could carry on pretending to be her for the entire weekend.

The bed – a super-king-size – had drawers in its base. Liv knelt on the thick-pile carpet and pulled them out one by one. The first three were full of spare bed linen, but the fourth contained designer shoeboxes labelled *Memorabilia*. Liv couldn't resist opening them. She sifted through Sofia's childhood records – photos, school report cards, gymkhana rosettes, swimming certificates, dance badges, and programmes from West End musicals. In another box were more grown-up items – the service book for her Alfa Romeo, some correspondence with an insurance company over a lost Rolex watch, the programme from Exeter's graduation ceremony, a wedding invitation...

Liv opened the cover and read the message inside.

To Sofia and Jensen, we're getting married and we'd love you to share our special day!

Sofia and Jensen?

Her world started to spin uncontrollably.

FORTY-FOUR

Karina and Meg rushed into the room. I turned to Jensen. 'You know her?'

'Oh yes. Only too well.' His face was full of pain. 'Her name's Sofia.'

'Who is she? A friend from Rutherford?'

'No.' He picked up the phone and looked at the screen again. 'How come you've got this?'

Karina explained. 'She was seen lurking outside the house on the twenty-third and twenty-fourth. She used Liv's bank card to travel there on the Tube in the evening, then used her Uber account from the station at some time after midnight. The theory is that she waited until we'd all gone to bed, let herself into the house using Liv's key and started the fire.'

Jensen kept shaking his head, as if the information had got caught somewhere uncomfortable in his brain and he was trying to dislodge it. 'It makes absolutely no sense. Liv and Sofia don't know each other.'

'Yeah, well, it seems they do,' replied Karina. 'The important thing is, we've got a positive ID. What's her full name?'

Jensen glanced at me quickly before replying. 'Sofia Ambersley.'

'Ambersley?!' I echoed. 'Sofia *Ambersley?*'

'I've heard that name somewhere recently.' Karina furrowed her brow.

'Yes, I told you,' I answered. 'It's the name of the couple that died in the fire.'

Karina turned to Jensen. 'Okay, so who is Sofia Ambersley exactly? This is serious. You've got to tell us everything you know.'

He sat down on the edge of the sofa. 'She was my girlfriend. Ex-girlfriend, to be precise. Claire and James were her parents.'

'Ah, the ex,' said Meg, as if she was very familiar with problematic previous relationships. 'Liv must have found her on social media. That's such a Liv thing to do.'

'Except I never told her about Sofia,' Jensen protested. 'When I transferred to Rutherford, I started from scratch, never mentioned her to anyone. I just wanted the whole thing out of my head. But Liv saw the burns on my back and wanted to know how I'd got them, so I kind of wrote a new version of the story, leaving Sofia out of it. I pretended I came from a rich background, but that everything had been lost to debt. I know it was wrong, and stupid, but I was messed up, still grieving. I thought Liv might not be so keen on me if she knew I'd grown up in care. And the Ambersleys truly did feel like my own parents.' His face crumpled in pain. 'They were wonderful people.'

'We don't have time for this,' Karina tutted. 'Give me Sofia's number, Jensen.'

'Sorry, but I don't have it. After the fire, she ghosted me. Changed her contact details, blocked me from her life. I haven't seen or heard from her for two years. She's twisted. I've got to talk to Liv, tell her to stay away.' He reached into his pocket.

'No, don't do that,' I said. 'I think Sofia may have control of

Liv's phone and is sending messages pretending to be from her. If she knows we're on to her, she might harm Liv.'

'She may have harmed her already,' interjected Meg.

'Stop it! We have to try and stay calm,' said Karina, picking up on our anxiety. 'Think about it logically. Why would Sofia have a thing against Liv? She dumped Jensen, not the other way round, right?' He nodded. 'So why would she care about who he went out with next?'

'Because she changed her mind and decided she was still in love with him?' I suggested.

'No, not that,' Jensen said. 'She never loved me in the first place. I was her little social experiment. All I can think is that she blamed me for her parents' death.' He huffed. 'Forget the fact that I nearly died trying to save their lives. She was so frigging ungrateful, didn't even visit me in hospital once. Just cut me off completely.'

'I need to speak to the detective,' said Karina. 'They'll want to interview you, Jensen, find out what you know about her.'

'Sure. I'll help in whatever way I can.'

'Apparently the Uber dropped her off in Notting Hill. Does that ring any bells?'

'Notting Hill? Yeah. Her parents had a flat there – it was their London pad. I suppose she must have inherited it. I only went there a few times. It was in a big Georgian house.' He screwed up his face. 'Can't remember the address. Sorry.'

'That's a big help. I'll call them now.' Karina ran out of the room.

'I can't take this,' said Meg. 'It's too horrible!'

'Don't worry, sweetie,' I said. 'I'm sure Karina's right. Sofia wouldn't have harmed Liv. She's just playing games.' Jensen opened his mouth as if to disagree, but I held up my hand to stop him. 'Why don't you go and lie down? You're still not well.'

'No, Mum. I want to know what's going on.' Her eyes were brimming with tears, but they had a fierce look in them. She turned to Jensen. 'You've told everyone a load of lies. Now you're going to tell us the truth.'

'Please tell us what happened,' I said more gently.

Jensen took a breath. 'I met Sofia at Exeter uni. In the first term. I don't know why she was attracted to me, really. We were so different. Her family was very wealthy – she was super posh, came from boarding school, got a sports car for her seventeenth, that kind of thing. While I was a "looked-after" kid.' He drew inverted commas in the air. 'I was taken away from my mum at birth and brought up in care, fostered out to various families. Growing up, I tried my best to fit in, but nobody ever wanted to adopt me. Still, I worked hard, did well at school. The head teacher supported me a lot, and got me onto this scheme that helped looked-after kids go to university. I was incredibly lucky—'

'So you arrived at Exeter, and you and Sofia got together,' I interrupted, trying to push things along.

'Yeah. Sofia liked the fact that I came from a deprived background – she thought it would shock her parents. She seemed to get off on their disapproval. She took me home for Christmas that first year. Claire and James were so welcoming. We hit it off straight away. They instantly made me feel like I was one of the family. After that, Sofia and I spent loads of time at Briarfields – weekends, holidays... I was accepted as her partner, invited to her cousin's wedding. Her mum even talked about us getting married ourselves.'

I listened uncomfortably, recognising my own behaviour. Jensen had obviously had the same enchanting effect on Sofia's mother as he'd had on me. We were nothing like as rich, but there must have been some other similarities between us. A longing for a son, perhaps?

Jensen continued. 'Her parents bought me clothes, a state-of-the-art laptop, a new phone, but most of all, they took an interest in me. Sofia didn't like it. She was jealous. As an only child, she wasn't used to sharing. By the start of the second year, the novelty of having a boyfriend from the other side of the tracks had worn off. I knew she'd had enough of me. I guessed she was seeing other guys, too, but I didn't want to lose the relationship I had with James and Claire, so I held on.'

His eyes flicked towards the door as Karina came back into the room, interrupting his flow. 'DS Baxter is on it,' she announced. 'They should be able to find an address for Sofia pretty fast.'

Meg gestured at Jensen. 'Carry on. What happened next?'

He resumed his narrative. 'We staggered on through the autumn term, and things seemed to get better just before Christmas. I really wanted to spend it at Briarfields – the last one had been so magical...' He took a deep breath. I could tell he was finding it extremely difficult.

'You're doing really well,' I said, encouragingly. 'Keep going.'

'Sofia drove us up from Exeter in her Alfa Romeo. We arrived on the twenty-third. That evening she manufactured an argument and dumped me – told me to get out, like immediately. I think she'd planned it all along.' He took a breath. 'Briarfields is in the middle of nowhere. I had no transport, no money, nowhere to go. Claire and James were really angry with her, said she was cruel. There was a huge row, it was dreadful. Sofia accused them of loving me more than her and drove off. I didn't know what to do. The Ambersleys said I could stay. I felt really awkward, but they insisted.'

He was becoming more and more emotional. I gestured at him to slow down, take his time.

'Christmas Eve was very strange,' he went on, his voice starting to break up. 'Sofia didn't come back or get in touch. The three of us had dinner together that evening, chatted, played cards for a bit, then wished each other Happy Christmas and went to bed. An hour or so later, the place went up in flames. I tried to save them, but the fire had already taken hold in that part of the house. I couldn't get to them. The fire brigade arrived, but it was too late. They died in their bedroom – of smoke inhalation.'

There were several seconds of silence as the three of us tried to take it all in. 'Wow...' said Meg under her breath. 'That's massive. Sorry, Jensen...'

'How did the fire start?' I asked.

'Claire loved candles. She put them everywhere. She left them burning when she went to bed. The investigators reckoned one of them had collapsed and fallen into the table decoration and set it alight. Earlier in the evening, James had knocked over a bottle of spirits. It was a fatal combination.'

'And nobody suspected arson?'

'No. Why would they? It was seen as a tragic accident, nothing more. Nobody questioned it.'

Karina leant in. 'Do you think Sofia could have started it?'

'It never occurred to me before, but it's possible that she came back to the house on Christmas Eve. She was really angry with Claire and James for taking my side, and she *did* have a violent streak. But would I go as far as to say she'd kill her own parents? I don't know.' He blew out his cheeks. 'To be fair, I'd still say it was an accident.'

'What happened after the fire?' Meg asked.

'I don't know much about it. I was in hospital for several weeks with burns. Missed the funeral and everything. I felt awful about James and Claire, guilty for not saving them. I'd lost the only people who'd ever made me feel I belonged. I was in a bad way for months – physically and mentally. I couldn't face going back to Exeter, so they let me finish the rest of the year remotely. Then I transferred to Rutherford for year three. Met Liv straight away... you know the rest.'

Karina looked perplexed. 'It still doesn't explain the connection between Liv and Sofia.'

'No, it doesn't,' replied Jensen. 'I can't see how either of them would have even known the other existed, let alone be able to find each other. When I left Exeter, I shut down my social media, cut myself off from all the friends I'd made there. I just wanted a fresh start.'

'Perhaps they met by chance,' I said. 'I remember Liv met some girl at that interview she went to on the day of Meg's party. They travelled back together. The girl bought food and wine on the train and Liv was quite drunk when she turned up. Could that have been Sofia?'

'I guess,' said Jensen. 'She loves throwing her money around. Liv never mentioned meeting anyone to me, but after that, I remember she kept texting someone. She was being very secretive. I thought it was some guy, but she said it was an old school friend.'

'This is all just guesswork,' said Karina. 'We have to wait for the police to track down Sofia's flat, and hopefully Liv will be there too.'

It was another hour before DS Baxter rang back. They'd found the Ambersleys' flat. Unfortunately it was empty. But one of the neighbours had seen a young woman matching Liv's description coming and going, and the lady who lived on the ground floor had heard two female voices arguing on a Sunday, about two weeks ago. Sofia had last been seen on Christmas Day, but nobody had seen Liv for a while.

'It's starting to look like a missing persons case,' said Karina.

'Starting?' I echoed. 'It's obvious, isn't it? Liv's in trouble. We have to find her before it's too late.'

Liv sat on the floor in the sea of papers. She felt as if she were drowning. Her hand shook as she read the invitation again. *Sofia and Jensen.* It couldn't be a coincidence.

She cast her mind back to the day she'd met Sofia at Birmingham New Street. Had it been a chance encounter, or had it been engineered? Perhaps Sofia hadn't been at the interviews at all – Liv hadn't noticed her there. But how had she known who she was and where to find her?

Her brain struggled to retrieve their exact conversation, but she remembered that when she'd mentioned that her boyfriend had been to Exeter, Sofia's face hadn't so much as twitched. And when the subject came up again, she'd cleverly got his name wrong, calling him Jackson instead. Exeter was a huge university, with thousands of students, so Liv hadn't questioned it at the time. Nor had she queried Sofia's suggestion that they keep their friendship a secret. She'd been in awe of her, because she'd spoken with a privileged drawl and paid for everything on the train.

She examined the invitation more closely, trying to work out a timeline. The wedding had taken place two and a half years ago, at the end of Sofia and Jensen's first year at Exeter. That was five months before the fire. When did they split up, she wondered, and why? It suddenly occurred to her that Jensen could be the boyfriend that Sofia had ghosted. If so, she'd done an excellent job.

When Liv had met Jensen, he'd been in a bad way. He'd found talking about his past very difficult. Even a small, inconsequential memory of his childhood or his time at Exeter could trigger a panic attack. He'd come to Rutherford to start afresh. They made a pact not to talk about their former boyfriends or girlfriends, which had suited Liv at the time. But now she wanted to know every detail.

She started turning the bedroom upside down. She wasn't sure what she was looking for – just anything that might give her clues about Sofia and Jensen's relationship. She went back to the wardrobe, where she'd seen a box of framed pictures when she'd been searching for her phone. Dragging it into the light, she flipped through the photos, but they were mainly of an older couple, sometimes together, sometimes in a group of three with Sofia. They had to be the parents with whom she'd fallen out so badly.

She was about to put the box away when her brain made a sudden connection. She'd seen that couple before somewhere. She picked up the largest of the frames and studied it more closely. They were younger in this photo, but they were definitely the same people. She'd seen their older faces many times, smiling out of Jensen's laptop. Her heart almost stopped beating.

What the fuck was going on?

These people weren't Jensen's parents, they were Sofia's. She couldn't think straight, none of it made sense. She had to leave, get out now.

Her heart started beating so fast she thought it was going to jump out of her throat. She felt dizzy and couldn't breathe. Her hands and feet went completely numb. She lay down on the carpet, terrified that she was going to die of a heart attack, alone in Sofia's bedroom, the victim of some horrible deception she couldn't understand.

After a few minutes, her pulse started to slow and the feeling in her limbs returned. She filled her lungs with air, then exhaled. Slowly she stood up and left the room, going back to her pristine white cell.

It didn't take long to pack the few belongings she'd brought with her into her rucksack. She had no idea where she was going to go. Home, perhaps? Although Jensen might still be there. If she burst through the door shouting accusations, things might turn nasty. She needed to absorb the information properly, order the chaos. She'd been a pawn in other people's chess games. Now she needed to take control of the situation.

She went to open the front door of the apartment, but it was locked. Sofia must have deadlocked it by mistake, forgetting that Liv was inside. She felt in the pocket of her jacket, which was hanging on the row of hooks, expecting to find the set of keys Sofia had given her when she first arrived. They weren't there. She checked the rest of the flat, but she already knew she wasn't going to find them. Sofia had deliberately locked her in and taken her key. The apartment was on the second floor and there was no other way to get out.

Before, she might have happily stayed indoors for the entire weekend, but now that she *couldn't* leave, she felt claustrophobic. There was no landline, so she couldn't call for help. She thought about shouting out of a window, but they were locked too. She tried banging on the ceiling, but there was no response from the upstairs apartment. She was trapped.

The rest of the day and the night passed slowly. She prowled around like a caged animal, her emotions rocking between anger and despair. What was going on? Why had both Jensen and Sofia lied to her? She slept fitfully, alert for the sound of Sofia's return, even though she knew she wasn't due back until Sunday afternoon.

The morning passed slowly. Liv thought she would go mad if time didn't speed up. She sat in the stylish living room, feet up on the massive velvet sofa, watching yet more rubbish on the giant screen that took up most of the wall. It was a beautiful apartment. She would have loved to live here rent-free for six months or so. Now it was clearly not to be. Had Sofia *ever* intended her to stay here once she'd gone abroad, or had it just been a ruse to bring her here? Was she still in love with Jensen, or did she hate him? And why had Jensen pretended Sofia's parents were his? It was like trying to do one of those fiendish jigsaw puzzles people brought out at Christmas – snowy land-scapes featuring fifty shades of white, or festive street scenes with too many sparkling lights. She couldn't even put two pieces together.

It was just gone three when she heard the front door opening.

'Honey, I'm home!' Sofia called out jokily.

Liv didn't reply. She stayed where she was, wondering how long it would take for Sofia to come into the room. She went to the bathroom first, then into the kitchen. Finally she entered the sitting room, holding a glass of wine.

'There you are!' she said. 'I thought maybe you were asleep.' She kicked off her shoes and flopped onto the opposite sofa. 'Remind me never to go to Bristol by train again. If only I still had the Alfa Romeo, I could have bombed it there and back in an hour or so.' She broke off, sensing Liv's coolness. 'You okay? Had a good weekend?'

'Oh yes, it was fantastic,' replied Liv sarcastically. 'I went to Portobello Market yesterday, then up to Hyde Park, then out for dinner, met some friends and went clubbing until dawn.'

Sofia looked surprised. 'Really?'

'Yeah. It was so good to get out and about.' There was a

loaded pause. 'No, of course I didn't do any of that. Because you locked me in.'

'What? No! Did I? Oh my God, how stupid of me. I'm sorry, Liv. I'm used to living on my own, you see, it's just a habit. Poor you, you've been stuck inside all weekend!'

'Yes, I have, because you also took my keys.'

'No I didn't!' she protested. 'Why would I do that? You must have lost them.'

'Please stop lying. I know what you did.' Sofia ignored the accusation and sipped her wine, but Liv wasn't going to let her get away with it. 'Why didn't you want me to leave, Sofia? Were you frightened that I'd go home to see my parents? Or my boyfriend?'

'Of course not. Why should I care about that?'

'Because then I might find out the truth.'

Sofia laughed nervously. 'Sorry?'

'You heard.'

'The truth about what?'

'You know what I mean.'

'I don't.'

'I went looking for my phone. Your bedroom door was locked, but I found the spare key and let myself in.'

'How dare you?' Sofia scowled. 'I told you before, it's strictly private.'

'And now I know why. It's where you keep all your secrets. Stuff you don't want me to see.' Liv paused for effect. 'I know you and Jensen were a couple.'

Sofia paled instantly. 'What the hell are you talking about?'

'I found an old wedding invitation.'

There was a long pause. 'Shit... I thought I'd got rid of everything.'

'And I found some pictures of your family. It was *your* parents who died in the fire, not his. Am I right?'

'Yes...' The mask suddenly fell from her face. She looked

more vulnerable than Liv had ever seen her before. 'I didn't know he was going round pretending they were his. That was a particularly sickening lie. He stole my life, basically. When you told me that, I was so angry I wanted to go straight round to your house and kill him.'

'Did you already know who I was when we met? Did you seek me out?'

'Jesus, no, it was pure chance. I don't know how I didn't shout out loud when you mentioned his name. I couldn't believe it. But I wasn't going to let on. I'd been looking for Jensen for nearly two years. You delivered him to me on a plate. No way was I going to lose him again.'

'So that's why you befriended me.'

'Afraid so.' She pulled a face. 'Sorry. I *do* like you, but...'

Liv was panicking inside, but she tried to keep her voice steady. 'Okay. So what's the plan? Because I don't understand what all this is about.'

'It's just the usual stuff. Justice. Revenge.'

'For what?'

'For Jensen killing my parents.'

I gasped. 'What? Are you serious?'

'Totally. I wasn't estranged from them, by the way. I loved them to the moon and back. We were everything to each other.'

'But I don't understand. The fire was an accident, wasn't it? Jensen nearly died himself trying to rescue them. I've seen the scars.'

'Yes... it was a risky plan, but it worked. He got them completely rat-arsed, waited until they'd gone to bed, then set the fire, making it look like a drunken Christmas accident. He had to make an attempt to save them, or people would have suspected. But as it was, the investigation team didn't even consider arson. The police saw Jensen as a hero, not the perpetrator.'

'But you have no proof—'

'I don't need proof. I *know*... Jensen wormed his way into my family, rotting it from the inside. They totally fell for it – gave him loads of expensive gifts, and a pile of cash. I don't care about the money so much. But he turned them against me and tried to take my place. That's why I wasn't there for Christmas.'

'But if he'd got them where he wanted them, why kill them?'

She bit her lip. 'That I don't know. But he did. I'm sure of it. And when you told me he was doing the same thing with your family – being the perfect guest, sucking up to your mum – I became completely convinced.'

'Oh my God, Sofia. Why didn't you tell me this before?'

'Because you were in a relationship with him! I thought maybe you still loved him.' She paused. 'To be honest, I didn't know if I could trust you.'

'Trust me in what way? What are you planning to do?'

Sofia stood up. 'Come with me to Briarfields and I'll explain everything.'

'Briarfields?'

'It's the burnt-out wreck that used to be my home. Where I grew up. Where I was happy. He took it all away from me, ruined my life. Okay, so I've got the trust fund, but money means nothing to me. Getting justice for my parents is all I care about.'

'Why do we have to go there?'

'Because you won't fully understand until you see it. Please? This is really important to me, Liv. I'm sorry I lied about everything, and I shouldn't have locked you in all weekend. It was bad of me, but I sensed you weakening and I didn't want you to go home. I wanted to keep you safe.'

'I can't, Sofia. I need to see my family. They'll be worried about me. If you can just give me my phone back...' Liv looked at her pleadingly.

'Okay, you can have the bloody phone, but only after we've

been to Briarfields. It's not too much to ask, surely? I need to show it to you. That's what juries do, they visit the scene of the crime. It helps build a picture. I promise you, Liv, once you've seen it, you'll want to help me.'

'Help you do what?'

'I'll explain when we're there. Put your coat on. I'm calling an Uber.'

It was nearly dark by the time they arrived. The taxi driver dropped them off in a lay-by and Sofia insisted they walk the rest of the way, down a long, overgrown track. There were no street lamps, and Liv had to follow the torchlight from Sofia's phone.

Why am I doing this? she kept thinking. As soon as they'd left the apartment, she should have made a dash for the Tube. But although she was angry with Sofia for deceiving her, she was just as angry with Jensen – if not more so. She wanted to side with the angels; she just wasn't sure who the angels were yet.

'Here we are,' Sofia whispered. 'This was my home.'

They stopped. Liv peered into the darkness and shuddered. The enormous house looked sinister and forbidding, like a set for a horror movie. Its walls were charred black, the roof was open to the rafters and all the windows were boarded up. Liv almost expected a gang of chainsaw-wielding zombies to burst out of the front door to greet them.

'It was so beautiful,' Sofia went on, her voice choking with tears. 'In the spring, it was covered with wisteria. And in the autumn, Virginia creeper smothered the back of the house. I grew up here. Mum and Dad restored the place, brought it back to life. We had wonderful summers here, just the three of us. I liked my boarding school, but I couldn't wait to get back to Briarfields.'

'I'm really sorry,' Liv replied. 'It must have been so shocking for you. Not just losing your parents, but losing all this... Why didn't you get it repaired?'

'I couldn't face it.'

'And you're certain Jensen started the fire deliberately?'

Sofia nodded. 'Come on. I want to show you around. There's a way in.'

'No thanks.' Liv backed off. 'This is far enough. The place must be dangerous.'

'I know a safe route. I need to show you where they died.'

'I don't need to see.'

'But you do. You absolutely do.'

Liv didn't want to go into the house, but there seemed to be no choice. Sofia was determined to show her every gory detail. And without her, she had no way of getting back to London and her own home, which would be warm and full of light, Mum and Dad and Meg waiting to welcome her back. Hopefully Jensen wouldn't still be there too, but if he was, she would deal with him. But first she had to deal with Sofia – humour her, say the right things, do as she was told.

They walked round to the back of the house. Liv could make out the shape of a swimming pool, and a stepped terrace. The views in daylight would be stunning, she thought. Sofia swung back a piece of hardboard and gestured at Liv. 'Go on,' she said. 'It's quite safe.'

Liv ducked and squeezed her way through, finding herself in what must have once been the kitchen. The devastation was terrible to see. Sofia came in behind her and waved her phone across burnt-out cabinets and the remains of an Aga.

'Horrific,' murmured Liv.

'Wait until you see the dining room. That's where it started.'

'I don't think I can do this. It's making me feel ill.'

Sofia grabbed her arm. 'Come on. Upstairs. I want to show you their room.'

'No, really, I'd rather stay—'

'Upstairs!' Sofia commanded.

The wooden banisters had been burnt to stumps, and some of the treads had caved in. Sofia virtually pushed Liv upwards, and along a narrow corridor.

'In there,' she said, pointing to an open door on the right.

They went in. Sofia passed the torchlight across the walls and the furniture. There was glass all over the carpet and the window had been boarded up. Grey streaks ran down the walls, and the ceiling was jet black. Everything was covered in a thick layer of dust. Liv felt as if she were standing in a tomb.

'Your parents died here?' she asked, although she could feel it in the atmosphere.

'Yes. Of smoke inhalation. The fire didn't get this far. They were found in bed, so it was assumed they were asleep. The tox report said there were high levels of alcohol in their blood. I think Jensen was probably to blame for that. He was always topping them up, like he was the host and they were the guests. It was a game they played.'

Liv shuddered. 'Okay, I get it. A terrible thing happened here. Maybe it was an accident, like Jensen said, or maybe he did... you know, start the fire deliberately. But there's nothing you can do about it.'

'Oh but there is,' Sofia said. 'When I realised that Jensen was doing to you and your family what he did to mine, I thought... what if the same thing happened? What if your house burnt down too? On Christmas Eve. A candle fire, exactly the same. It would be too much of a coincidence to ignore, wouldn't it? The police would have to re-examine the case. They'd discover all the lies Jensen had been telling – how he'd pretended my parents were *his* parents, how he'd turned your parents against you, just as he had done with mine. It would seem so suspicious.'

'But Jensen's not going to burn down my house, is he?' said Liv.

'No. Probably not. Which is why *I* have to do it.'

'You?' She couldn't believe what Sofia had just said. 'You're going to murder *my* parents just to point the finger at Jensen?'

'No! Don't be silly. They won't *die* – they won't even get hurt. They've got smoke alarms, haven't they? My parents were a bit lax with that kind of thing. But yours will be fine. And they're bound to be insured.'

Panic rose in Liv's throat. 'This is insane. I won't let you get anywhere near them—'

'Yes, I was worried you'd say that. It's a bit of a nuisance, really. I should never have gone to Bristol. I might have known you'd start snooping around. The timing's gone all wrong.'

'What do you mean?'

'It's not Christmas Eve yet, is it? You've messed everything up. I didn't want to hurt you, but I can't let you go running to the police. You'll have to stay here.'

'What?' Liv started to laugh. 'You can't be serious.'

'Sorry, but there's no choice.' Suddenly Sofia swung her arm back and delivered a heavy punch smack in the middle of Liv's face. Crying out, she staggered backward, hitting her temple on the edge of the cast-iron fireplace before falling to the floor. She lay there, still and silent, blood seeping from her head onto the carpet.

'Sorry,' said Sofia. She stepped away, closing the door and plunging the room into total darkness. The last thing Liv heard before she passed out was the sound of a key turning in the lock. She was trapped again. Only this time, she had no chance at all of getting out.

FORTY-SIX

'I'd better go down to the police station,' said Jensen. 'Make a statement or whatever. I'll tell them everything I know about Sofia.'

'I'll come with you,' I said.

'It's okay...'

'I want to talk to them myself anyway.' I was sick of everything being filtered through Karina, or even worse, Dom.

We got into the lift together. 'I'm so sorry,' Jensen said. 'I shouldn't have lied.'

'Liv's all that matters now... I hope to God she's all right.'

'Me too.' We reached the ground floor and walked out of the building. He stopped and turned to me. 'I don't want to worry you, Rachel, but I'm scared. I know Sofia. She's got a really violent temper. She used to throw things at my head. And once she picked up a kitchen knife and threatened to stab me.'

A shiver ran through me. 'What are you saying, Jensen?'

He looked away. 'She's a very entitled person, doesn't think normal rules apply... If she and Liv fell out, she wouldn't think twice about hurting her.'

'The flat was empty,' I reminded him. 'It looks like Liv got away.'

His expression darkened. 'Unless she killed her and dumped the body.'

'Don't say that!'

'Or kidnapped her and took her somewhere.'

'Like where?'

'Briarfields would be the obvious place, but I'm guessing she sold it ages ago.'

'No, it's derelict,' I said. 'I visited the place when I went to Carlington. Do you really think Sofia could have abducted Liv and taken her there?'

He nodded. 'This is all about what happened – the fire, her parents' death. If Liv is still alive, that's where she'll be.'

'We've got to tell the police. Now. Come on.' I took his arm and yanked him forward, but he resisted.

'No, that's not a good idea. Sofia is unpredictable. If she sees the police arriving, she'll go into panic mode. Believe me, I know how she ticks. She's capable of doing anything.'

'But the police are experts in this kind of—'

'No! I know Briarfields well, I can get inside without being seen. Let me go there and take a look around. If there's anything suspicious, I won't confront Sofia. I'll call the police immediately.'

'It's too dangerous.'

'I don't care. I owe it to Liv. I love her. She's in this mess because of me. Honestly, it's the safest way. I *have* to go, Rachel.'

It only took a few seconds for me to make up my mind. 'Okay,' I said. 'But I'm coming with you.'

'No, no – I don't want you involved.'

'The house is miles from anywhere, and you don't have any transport. You need me.'

'I don't want you to get hurt. This is about me and Sofia. I'll sort it. Promise.'

I stood my ground. 'If you won't let me drive you there, I'll tell the police where you're going.'

'Okay,' he sighed. 'But you've got to stay in the background and let me do this on my own.'

We left immediately. The roads were quieter than usual, businesses still closed for the holiday period and children off school. I tried my best to concentrate on the driving, but dark thoughts kept pulling me away. I'd sensed something was wrong from the beginning but hadn't listened to my instincts. What if Liv was already dead? I would never forgive myself for not raising the alarm earlier.

I glanced across at Jensen. He was looking out of the passenger window, one hand propping up his chin. I suspected he was blaming himself, too. If he hadn't lied about his past, Liv would have known about Sofia and wouldn't have trusted her. Now we both wanted to redeem ourselves by rescuing her. But the nearer we got to Briarfields, the more I started to question our judgement. What if Sofia was armed? We weren't trained or properly equipped.

'This is too scary,' I said, voicing my misgivings out loud. 'We should have told the police.'

He kept his eyes on the passing scenery. 'Why don't you stay in the car? Then, if there's trouble, you can dial 999.'

'No, I've come this far, I'm not chickening out now.'

'We don't know what we're going to find, Rachel.'

'I know. I'm prepared.'

'Okay.' He turned his head towards me. 'You're an amazing person. Liv's very lucky to have you as her mum.'

'I'm not sure about that...'

'*I* am.'

'What's the real story?' I asked. 'I mean, with your parents. You said you were taken away from your mum at birth. Do you know why?'

'She was a heroin addict. I was rescued as part of a raid on a crack den. They found me lying on the floor among used foils and syringes. My mum tried to get me back, but she couldn't stay clean for long enough.'

'Do you remember her at all?'

'Nah. Not really.' His gaze returned to the window. 'All I know about her is what's in my file. After I lost Claire and James, I thought maybe I should try to find her. She used to hang out in the London Bridge area.'

'Is that why you volunteered at the homeless shelter?'

'Yeah... I kept hoping that one day she'd walk in. I'd be serving breakfast and she'd be in the queue. Our eyes would meet and somehow we'd just know. Of course it never happened. I asked around, but nobody had heard of her. I expect she's dead by now.'

'I'm sorry,' I said. 'You've had a tough life.'

'Doesn't excuse it, though, does it? Trying to be somebody I'm not. Deceiving people. It's not good. Do you think Liv will forgive me?'

'I don't know, Jensen. Let's find her first.'

We spent the rest of the journey in silence. I left the motorway and followed the sat nav as it took us through Carlington, then turned onto the private lane that led to Briarfields. It was late afternoon, and the light was already beginning to fade.

'Don't park right outside,' Jensen advised. 'There's a passing place just before the road opens out. Pull up there and we'll walk the rest of the way.'

I did as he suggested. We got out of the car and made our way towards the house. I felt cold without my proper winter coat, and my borrowed shoes squelched in the mud.

'You sure you're okay with this?' he asked.

'Of course. I'm fine. But what about you? You haven't been back since the fire, have you?' He shook his head. 'How's this going to affect your PTSD?'

'I don't know. But there's no choice. I have to face it.'

The lane rounded a bend, giving way to a gravel driveway. The house loomed in front of us. We stared up at the eerie, burnt-out ruins, the rafters black against the twilight sky. Jensen gasped and held his chest.

'Jesus,' he whispered. 'I didn't think it would look this bad. It was such a beautiful house.'

'Yes, but it needs pulling down.'

'Look!' he pointed. 'Tyre tracks, there by the pond.'

'I could have made those last time I was here.'

'Or they belong to Sofia's car. She has an Alfa Romeo... at least, she used to.'

'Her car's not here. Is that a good sign or a bad one?' I looked towards the house, as if expecting it to answer.

'Good,' replied Jensen. 'If Liv is here, it means she's on her own.'

'*If.*' I grabbed his arm. 'What if we're too late?'

'Don't think like that.'

'But how will we get in? Everything's locked or boarded up.'

Jensen thought about it for a few seconds. 'James used to keep an axe in the wood store. He liked to chop his own logs. Wait there.' He ran down the side of the house and disappeared from sight, leaving me on my own.

Suddenly it all felt hopeless. If Sofia had been here at all, it had probably been to dump Liv's body. The thought of her lying in some shallow grave made my insides turn over. I retched. Perhaps Jensen was right. I wasn't up to this.

He returned a few minutes later carrying a chopper. 'It was still there,' he said. 'Come with me. I think I've found a way in.'

I followed him back down the side of the house. There was

a small door at the rear of the garage. It was locked, but the wood was thin.

'If I can get past this, there's an internal door leading straight into the kitchen,' he said. 'They never locked it.'

He lifted the axe and brought it down on the central panel. It splintered, but didn't break. It took several more swings to remove enough of the door for him to climb through. Once inside, he found a key on the windowsill, unlocked it and let me in.

'Liv!' I shouted as loudly as I could. 'Liv! Are you there?' My voice was weedy, the sound quickly dissipating.

As predicted, the internal door was unlocked, so we were able to walk straight into the main house. The damage downstairs was horrific – the ceilings and walls were black, and everything was charred. I could see the remains of a table and chairs. The appliances had turned to lumps of twisted metal, and there were piles of unidentifiable rubble all over the floor.

'Liv!' I shouted again. Jensen joined in. 'Liv! Liv! Are you here? Where are you?' Our hearts were in our mouths as we waited, but there was no reply.

We picked our way through the obstacle course of charred pieces of furniture and broken glass. I poked my head around the door of one of the reception rooms. It was completely burnt out, every bit of it utterly destroyed. Jensen held back.

'My God! What room was this?'

'The dining room,' he said, his voice strained. 'It was where the fire started... I can't go in there.'

'No, you mustn't.' I led him away. We went into what would have been the main living room, which was in almost as bad a state. 'She's not here,' I said.

Jensen gritted his teeth. 'I'm not giving up yet. Let's try upstairs.'

We went back to the hallway. The wooden staircase rising

up through the centre of the house looked close to collapse. The banister had gone and some of the steps had burnt away.

I put my hand on Jensen's arm. 'I don't think we should attempt it. It's too dangerous.'

'It's okay, I'll be careful.'

I watched with bated breath as he started to climb slowly, step by step. The stairs creaked and groaned beneath his weight. He cried out as his foot went through one of the treads, almost falling, nearly dropping the axe.

'Liv?' he called, reaching the landing. 'Are you there, Liv?'

There was a beat, then out of the silence came the faintest of sounds. I couldn't work out what it was – a bird, perhaps? Could it possibly be a human voice?

'Did you hear that?' I shouted up.

'Yes! It sounded like "help". It's coming from the other end of the house!' He disappeared down the dark corridor, calling Liv's name again, banging on doors. 'Liv! It's me! Jensen! Where are you?'

I couldn't wait a second longer. I bounded up the stairs, not caring about the danger. Somehow I made it up without doing myself an injury and ran towards Jensen. He had his ear to one of the doors, listening.

'I think she's in here,' he said. 'It was Claire and James's bedroom. It's locked.'

I stood by the door. 'Liv, darling? It's Mum. Can you hear me? Say something if you can.'

'Mum?' It was a small, weak voice but it was definitely my Liv. Relief flooded through me, a wave so huge it was overwhelming.

'Yes! It's me. Listen, darling. I'm here with Jensen. We're going to break the door down. You need to stay well back, as far away as you can. Do you understand?'

'Okay.'

I stood to one side while he attacked the wood with the axe.

The panels came away easily. He climbed through the hole, and I followed.

The room was dark, the window boarded up. My gaze shot around the room. I couldn't see her at first, then I spotted her auburn hair poking out from under a mound of blankets on the bed. I rushed to her side and knelt down.

'Oh my baby! You're here!' She opened her eyes and blinked at me slowly. 'How are you?' I gently pulled back the covers. Her eyes were hollowed out, her cheekbones sharp. She looked as if she'd lost a lot of weight. 'Did she hurt you?'

'She hit me with something. Can't remember. It's all a blur.'

'I'll call an ambulance.' Jensen took his phone out of his pocket.

'And the police,' I said, before turning back to Liv. 'Where's Sofia? Is she coming back?'

'No. She's gone. Days ago. She left me...' Tears filled her eyes. 'I've had nothing to eat for... I don't know how long. Just water from the bathroom. I thought I was going to die.'

I stroked her hair, just as I used to when she was a little girl. 'I know, but it's over now. You're safe. We're here and you're going to be okay, Livvy. I'm telling you, everything's going to be just fine.'

EPILOGUE

Jensen stared out of the window as the train sped towards York. He'd never been to this part of the country before and was surprised by how rural the landscape was – green fields, rolling hills, farms, the occasional church spire. It was good to get out of London for the weekend. His room in the flat share was poky and looked on to a brick wall. Not that he'd spent many nights there since meeting Lara five months ago.

She sat opposite him, her long legs outstretched, their shoes just touching. Her attention was focused on her phone, so she didn't look up. He contemplated her for a few moments, breathing her in, assessing her in a loving way. Feeling grateful for her. She wasn't as pretty as Liv – or Sofia, for that matter – but she had pleasant features, and shiny blonde hair that reached to her waist. She usually wore it scraped back into a ponytail, but today it was cloaking her shoulders. Apparently her mother preferred her to wear it down.

Today he would meet Lara's parents for the first time. They lived in a village not far from York, having moved there recently 'for a better quality of life'. They weren't as rich as the Ambersleys, but were probably richer than Rachel and Dom. Not that he was bothered about their comparative wealth. It was just an observation.

Although he'd proved that he was good with other people's parents, he felt anxious about the weekend. They were bound to ask him questions about his family, his childhood, where he'd grown up, his education. He wanted to make sure he had his story straight. It was important that he didn't say anything that would contradict what he'd already told Lara.

This time, he'd kept it simple, ditching the boarding school lies and giving himself a more modest background. Suburban home, state primary, a reasonably good comprehensive. Exeter and Rutherford had been replaced with a small, obscure college in the north-west that nobody had ever heard of. He'd awarded himself a 2:1, a grade up from what he'd actually achieved.

More importantly, he'd changed the screen saver on his laptop. Now it featured a photo of him and Rachel, taken in the back garden during those first few happy weeks. Before it all went wrong. According to his new legend, his father, Dominic, left the family when Jensen was only two years old, and his mother, Rachel (may she rest in peace), had brought him up single-handedly. Tragically, she'd died in a house fire on Christmas Eve, eighteen months ago. Everything had been destroyed. Jensen had tried his best to save her but had sadly failed. The burns he'd suffered were a testament to his bravery, but the emotional scars would never heal. He'd made it very clear to Lara that he couldn't bear to talk about it. Every time she tried to delve into his past, he hyperventilated.

Thank God for PTSD. Nobody dug deeper if they thought you were going to have a panic attack.

He returned his gaze to the window and tried to prepare for the weekend ahead, rehearsing his lines, thinking about how he might navigate any tripwires. But his mind forced him back to the past and the people who had once meant so much to him.

He hadn't seen Liv since she'd been taken away from

Briarfields in an ambulance. That was eighteen months ago. How time had flown. He didn't know what she was doing now, but he presumed she'd recovered and had found a job. She'd blocked him from her social media accounts, not that he blamed her. He knew more about Meg, who posted regularly on Insta. She was 'living her best life', nearing the end of her first year at Sussex University, and had a boyfriend by the unlikely name of Boz. He had no idea whether Dom was still with his new girlfriend. After a substantial refurb, the house had gone on the market and quickly sold – he'd followed its progress on Rightmove. Rachel had moved on, but he knew not where. He hoped she was happy and not feeling too lonely. He thought about her often and wished – although it was impossible – that they could have kept in touch. Everyone's life had changed, all because of him.

Nobody had thanked him for rescuing Liv and saving her life. On the contrary, he'd been closely questioned by police, though not charged. They'd seemed to think he knew where Sofia was hiding, which he didn't. The police discovered that she'd caught a flight to Nairobi on Christmas Day. Since then, the trail had gone cold. She appeared to have vanished into thin air. Jensen doubted she'd ever be brought to justice. She had the money to buy a new identity, and would probably slip back to England unnoticed at some point in the future. No doubt she would find a way to access her trust fund. Privileged people got away with murder, sometimes literally.

The last eighteen months had been very tough. He'd spent some of it on the streets, but had eventually managed to haul himself up and move into a dodgy flat share. He worked in a shop selling art supplies. That was where he'd met Lara. She'd turned up one day with a large poster she'd wanted framing as a birthday present for her father. They'd got chatting about families. When she came back to collect the finished job, he invited her for a drink.

He'd heard a lot of good things about Lara's parents. Now he was going to meet them in the flesh. That wasn't to say that he'd forgotten the Ambersleys. Despite everything that had happened, there would always be a place for them in his heart. They'd been so kind and welcoming to him, treated him like a son. That had been the problem, of course. Sofia had been jealous. She'd believed that they'd chosen Jensen over her, but that wasn't the case. And only he knew it.

He closed his eyes and allowed himself to go back in time to that terrible night, three and a half years ago now. Sofia had driven off in a temper the previous evening, leaving Jensen alone with her parents. It'd been an awkward situation for all of them. Knowing that he had nowhere else to go, James and Claire had insisted that Jensen stay and spend Christmas with them. He'd felt grateful, and a little triumphant.

On Christmas Eve, he helped Claire lay the table for dinner. She was very good with her hands and had made a beautiful table decoration using pine cones, holly and ivy picked from the garden. Candles of all shapes and sizes were added to the display. When lit, they gave the room a magical glow.

James cooked boeuf bourguignon – the meat was astonishingly tender and the vegetables done to perfection. They drank a twenty-year-old Château Margaux, followed by a Sauternes with dessert, rounding off with cheese and vintage port. Both James and Claire drank heavily throughout the meal. Afterwards he realised they'd been giving themselves Dutch courage, but at the time he thought they were simply enjoying his company and having fun. A great feeling of contentment came over him. He could get used to this! It was much better without Sofia, too. Calmer. More civilised. She was always making provocative remarks, threatening to break into a tantrum.

'Thank you so much,' he said, putting down his spoon. 'That crème brûlée was utterly delicious. I've never eaten so well. I can't believe there's more to come tomorrow!' Claire was cooking turkey and goose, bought from their local organic butcher.

'Such a shame there's only going to be three of us,' Claire said. 'I'm so sorry about you and Sofia. Such dreadful timing.'

'That's all right. I was expecting it,' Jensen admitted. 'To be honest, she's been cheating on me for a while.'

'Oh dear,' said James. 'We didn't know that.' He cut off a chunk of fine Stilton and placed it on top of a biscuit. 'Sounds like you're better off apart.'

'Probably.' Jensen paused, searching for the right words. 'I hope it doesn't change anything between us.'

There was a beat. He saw their faces twitch. They exchanged a glance, then Claire gave James a nod – so slight that it was almost imperceptible.

James leant forward. 'Well, obviously we want you to stay for Christmas,' he said. 'We're not chucking you out into the snow.' He gave a short laugh. Jensen didn't understand. It wasn't snowing. In fact the weather was unusually mild. 'But it seems pretty definitive that your relationship with Sofia is over. Which makes things difficult for us, going forward.'

'What James means,' said Claire, taking over, 'is that although we're incredibly fond of you, Jensen, it would be inappropriate for us to carry on... our friendship.'

'Inappropriate?' he echoed, a crushing sensation developing in his chest.

'Yes. I'm sure you understand. We know Sofia can be challenging, but when all's said and done, she's our daughter. We can't abandon her.'

No, but you can abandon me, he thought.

'Does that mean you don't want me to visit any more?' he asked, already sensing the answer.

'Well, we'd love it, but we don't see how it could work,' said Claire. 'It's not like you're married or have children. You're just an ex-boyfriend. We feel bad about it, and we're going to miss you terribly, but we think, on balance, and knowing Sofia, it would be easier to say goodbye now.'

'And part on good terms,' James added.

'I see,' Jensen said, still not quite believing what he was hearing. 'So when do you want me to go?'

'Oh, not tonight, silly!' Claire reached out and took his hand. 'Please stay until Boxing Day. Or the day after, if you like. Entirely up to you.' James gave her a warning look. 'Although it would be tricky if you were still here when Sofia comes back.'

'And when's that?'

'We don't know,' said James. 'Soon, we hope.'

Later, Jensen told the police that they'd chatted and played cards after the meal and had retired to bed after midnight, wishing each other Happy Christmas. In truth, he'd gone straight upstairs after the conversation, unable to hide his grief. He couldn't bear the thought of losing Claire and James. It was impossible, unthinkable. He'd put up with so much shit from Sofia in order to maintain a relationship with them, and now they were throwing him out.

He sat on the edge of the bed, seething. His anger was directed at Sofia, not Claire and James. Their actions were understandable. When it came to the crunch, people put their own family above everyone else. He didn't have any blood relatives – not that he was in touch with, anyway – so nobody felt any obligation towards him. He'd been adopted briefly as a toddler, but something had gone wrong and they'd given him back. No foster parents had ever considered keeping him. He didn't matter to anyone. Was he condemned to go through life alone?

If only there was something he could do to make Claire and James change their mind. He knew it would have to be big. Action, not words. Something that would make them realise how much they loved him and wanted him to carry on being part of their family, regardless of Sofia. Something that would put them in his debt.

A while later, he heard them coming up the stairs. They sounded drunk. Claire was giggling and James was telling her to be careful. 'You'll fall,' he said. 'I don't want you in hospital for Christmas!'

A plan started to form in Jensen's head.

He waited an hour before leaving his room and creeping along the landing. He stopped outside Claire and James's bedroom and listened. James was snoring loudly. He was certain they were both fast asleep. Retracing his steps, he tiptoed downstairs and went into the dining room.

The table was as he'd left it – strewn with dirty glasses, crumpled napkins, side plates smeared with cheese. Apart from blowing the candles out, Claire and James hadn't bothered to clear up. Usually they left it to the cleaner who came in every morning, but she'd gone back to Poland for Christmas.

Jensen surveyed the scene. He knew what was necessary to start a fire – an igniter and an accelerant. The candles were an obvious choice. A dozen were already on the table in various states of wear. Wax had spilled onto the linen runner where the decoration sat, the red berries drying out, the foliage withering in the warmth of the room. One end of the dining table was close to the window, which was hung with velvet curtains. As people would no doubt say, it was an accident waiting to happen.

As for an accelerant, he had a whole drinks cabinet to choose from – cask-strength whisky, Stroh 160, Bacardi, sambuca, cognac, vodka... James liked to bring special spirits back from his business trips, the stronger and spicier the better. They'd already enjoyed a glass of Golden Grain earlier that evening, which was 95 per cent proof. Lethal stuff. Jensen unscrewed the bottle and pushed it onto its side. The amber liquid dribbled out, pooling on the tablecloth.

All he had to do was relight the candles, then knock them over in the direction of something combustible. Once the fire had properly taken hold, he would pretend to respond to the smoke alarm and heroically put it out. It shouldn't be too difficult. There was bound to be an extinguisher somewhere in the house. A few candles wouldn't cause that much damage, would they?

'Hey, Jensen, wake up.' Lara's voice sliced through his memories.

He jolted and opened his eyes. 'I wasn't asleep,' he said.

'We're pulling into the station. Get your bag.'

'Oh. Right.' He stood up and took his holdall off the rack. They joined the queue for the door.

He felt dizzy. Visions of the burning house were still running through his head. The fire had taken hold so quickly, he hadn't been able to stop it. The smoke alarm hadn't gone off – maybe the batteries had run out, or it wasn't properly connected? There'd been no time to look for the extinguisher. Within minutes, the room had filled with flames.

The train trundled into the station, but he was still at Briarfields, trapped downstairs. He could feel the intense heat peeling the skin off his back, the black smoke filling his lungs, making him cough.

'Oh look, they're waiting for us on the platform,' Lara cried.

He hadn't meant to kill them. He'd tried to save them, he'd really tried.

'Are you okay, Jensen?'

He nodded. 'Yes, just feeling a bit hot. Need some fresh air.'

'Aww... don't be nervous. Mum and Dad are going to love you. I promise, by the end of the weekend, you'll be one of the family.'

Many thanks for reading this book. I really hope you enjoyed it. You can keep up to date with my books by signing up at the link below. Your email address will never be shared, and you can unsubscribe at any time.

www.bookouture.com/jess-ryder

When I embark on a new novel, I not only want to write a compelling story with believable characters, I want it to be 'about something'. This time, it's the modern family.

I am very concerned about the pressure social media puts on young people, online bullying and consequent mental health problems. The character of Meg enabled me to explore these themes, and I grew very fond of her. Through Rachel, I wanted to understand the 'helicopter mum', whose love for her children is so strong it can end up weakening them.

Liv also really interested me. These days, with house prices and rents being so high, it's extremely difficult for young people to live independently from their parents. Thousands of graduates with student loan debts and no job lined up have no choice but to return to the family home after their course has finished. I found this a rich source of drama and conflict. Of course, I wanted to put a thriller twist on it, and so the story of troubled Jensen was born. And with him, Sofia, the entitled rich kid who can't cope with the terrible loss of her parents.

Ultimately, however, a novel has to be an absorbing and

entertaining read. I hope I've managed to achieve that with *One of the Family*. If you'd like to write a brief constructive review and post it online in the appropriate places, I'm sure other readers would find it helpful.

You might also want to try my other Bookouture psychological thrillers – *Lie to Me*, *The Good Sister*, *The Ex-Wife* (now a TV drama on Paramount Plus and Channel 5 UK), *The Dream House*, *The Girl You Gave Away*, *The Night Away*, *The Second Marriage* and *My Husband's Lover*.

With best wishes, and thanks for your support,

Jess Ryder

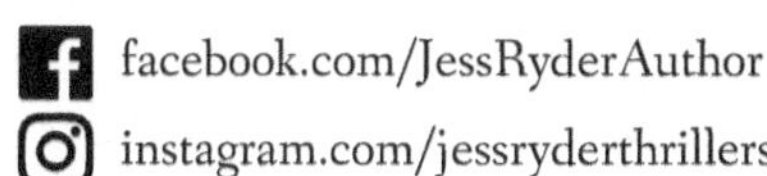

facebook.com/JessRyderAuthor

instagram.com/jessryderthrillers

ACKNOWLEDGEMENTS

As always, there are several people to thank for their help and support in the writing of this novel.

My researcher, Brenda Page, who rises to every challenge I set her with enthusiasm and ingenuity and saves me lots of precious time.

My literary agent, Rowan Lawton at The Soho Agency, who not only works extremely hard on my behalf but is also kind and understanding. Also, my media agent, Christine Glover at Casarotto Ramsey & Associates, who is always looking out for opportunities to put my stories on screen, with considerable success. I am very lucky to have such brilliant women on my side.

My editor, Lydia Vassar-Smith. Her notes and comments on the first draft were very insightful, and her positivity and encouragement helped me power through to the end. And my copyeditor, Jane Selley, and proofreader, Jenny Page, whose beady eyes spot all my mistakes.

Everyone at Bookouture. Congratulations on winning 'Imprint of the Year' in the 2025 British Book Awards – richly deserved!

And finally, deep personal thanks to my wonderful family, especially to my mother, and my husband, David. It's been a tough year, but look, we have come through.

PUBLISHING TEAM

Turning a manuscript into a book requires the efforts of many people. The publishing team at Bookouture would like to acknowledge everyone who contributed to this publication.

Audio
Alba Proko
Melissa Tran
Sinead O'Connor

Commercial
Lauren Morrissette
Hannah Richmond
Imogen Allport

Contracts
Peta Nightingale

Cover design
The Brewster Project

Data and analysis
Mark Alder
Mohamed Bussuri

Dear Reader,

We'd love your attention for one more page to tell you about the crisis in children's reading, and what we can all do.

Studies have shown that reading for fun is the **single biggest predictor of a child's future life chances** – more than family circumstance, parents' educational background or income. It improves academic results, mental health, wealth, communication skills, ambition and happiness.

The number of children reading for fun is in rapid decline. Young people have a lot of competition for their time, and a worryingly high number do not have a single book at home.

Hachette works extensively with schools, libraries and literacy charities, but here are some ways we can all raise more readers:

- Reading to children for just 10 minutes a day makes a difference
- Don't give up if children aren't regular readers – there will be books for them!

- Visit bookshops and libraries to get recommendations
- Encourage them to listen to audiobooks
- Support school libraries
- Give books as gifts

There's a lot more information about how to encourage children to read on our websites: **www.RaisingReaders.co.uk** and **www.JoinRaisingReaders.com**.

Thank you for reading.

www.ingramcontent.com/pod-product-compliance
Lightning Source LLC
Chambersburg PA
CBHW030534190726
48283CB00006B/1916